LANCELOT'S DISCIPLE

LANCELOT'S DISCIPLE

QUEST ON THE ANCIENT SILK ROAD FOR SELF-AWARENESS AND ENLIGHTENMENT

RICHARD GARTEE

Lake & Emerald Publications

A complete list of available titles by the author can be found at www.gartee.com

Published by Lake & Emerald Publications, LLC
www.lepublications.com

This is a work of fiction based on historical characters.
Any resemblance to any person born after 550 CE is coincidental and unintentional.

Library of Congress Control Number: 2017913969

ISBN: 978-0-9906768-1-2

Cover photos: Dmytro Vietrov, Ninja SS, and Blaise Thirard

Typesetting services by BOOKOW.COM

for the Masters

PROLOGUE

In 538 AD, a massive volcanic eruption blocked the light of the sun throughout the world. The people of Britain knew nothing of volcanoes in distant lands, but they witnessed the sun dim and Camelot fall. After King Arthur's death, Guinevere entered a nunnery and sent Sir Lancelot away.

A decade later, Alura and Frith, a brother and sister abandoned at the Abbey of St. Benignus during the dark years, came into adulthood desperate for a life different from the abbey. When King Arthur's former right-hand, Sir Bedivere, arrived seeking a certain hermit who lived in the woods behind the abbey, the Abbot sent Frith to show him the way.

At the hermit's cottage, Frith learned that the recluse who for years had slipped wraith-like in and out of morning Mass was the former Sir Lancelot. Although Bedivere tried to persuade Lancelot to forsake his hermitage and return to knighthood, Lancelot refused, revealing he'd finally found the Holy Grail—within himself.

After Bedivere's departure, Frith and Alura sought out Lancelot who led them on an inner quest to conquer the obstacles keeping them from attaining the Grail themselves.

Under his tutelage Alura and Frith gained spiritual awareness. But when Alura fell in love with Lancelot, rumors of an affair incited an angry mob.

Bedivere returned to urge Lancelot to flee, but Lancelot stayed, using the little time he had left to finish instructing Alura and Frith.

* * *

Frith handed Sir Bedivere the letter. "From Sir Lancelot, my lord."

"What? Could it be?" Bedivere broke the seal and unrolled the parchment. Then he twisted the page to gain a better angle in the early dawn light.

Frith watched Bedivere read. The knight's lips tightened until they were white. His eyes raced over the words a second time and then he rolled up the scroll. "I am awaiting the return of a dispatch of knights. When they've made their report, I'll meet with you and your sister. Can you bring her?"

Frith nodded and left to attend the Abbot. Mass had ended, and the Abbot would be returning any moment. Frith found him just entering his quarters, still in his vestments. "Ah, Frith. Come."

"Certainly, my lord."

He followed the Abbot to his room, helped him remove his vestments, and hung them in a cedar clothes press. Once the Abbot was back in his ordinary robe, Frith said, "You look tired, sir."

"If you'd attended me last evening, you'd know the reason."

"I'm so sorry, my lord; I thought my work finished for the day."

"Well, to be fair, I thought so too, when I dismissed you. But it proved to be a long night. The Bishop arrived unexpectedly, a feast needed to be organized, I couldn't find you or your sister, and the kitchen staff had left. Then a company of knights showed up for Sir Bedivere. He couldn't be found either."

Frith swallowed his guilt. All three of them had been with Lancelot. "What did you do, sir?"

"I sent Little Thomas to the village to fetch two of the kitchen ladies who put together a supper. Not a proper banquet, but the Bishop and knights drank enough not to object. Still, it wasn't ideal to bring village ladies in proximity to the Bishop, what with the uproar over Lancelot and your sister."

"I assure you, my lord, Alura committed no sin."

"Oh, I know, poor Alura. But where were you? With her, I hope."

"Yes. Sir Lancelot summoned us to his hermitage."

"I thought Bedivere was keeping Lancelot away from her."

Frith bit his lip. There was so much he couldn't say. Lancelot's teachings were not his to tell. And he might fail to impart them accurately. "All has changed, my lord. It was Sir Bedivere who took us there."

"To protect her and Lancelot from further calumny, I'm sure. Not that it matters anymore."

Frith cocked his head.

"It would have been courteous of Bedivere to tell me he'd sent for Sir Bors and his men." The Abbot yawned. "Last night wore me out."

"You should delay your breakfast and lie down for a rest."

"Would that I could, but the Bishop is still here."

"I didn't see him at Mass."

"His absence didn't surprise me." The Abbot chuckled. "He woke the whole abbey in the middle of the night with a fit. Claimed it was a vision. Didn't you hear the commotion?"

Frith hadn't. He'd been in his own turmoil following the visit to Lancelot's. "Shall I bring you something from the kitchen, then?"

The Abbot massaged his stomach in a circular motion. "Just mint tea and a little porridge. I'm a bit out of sorts."

Frith left the Abbot's room and headed toward a large building with a cone-shaped roof known as the Abbot's Kitchen. In its dining hall the Abbot feted the noble guests and wealthy pilgrims who filled the abbey coffers. Women, known as "kitchen ladies," worked there as cooks, bakers, and chefs. All the kitchen ladies were married villagers, except Alura, who lived in a converted abbey storeroom.

As he passed near the monk's cloister, Bedivere called to him from an alcove, "The knights returned. Please summon your sister."

Frith waved acknowledgement and quickened his step. He returned minutes later carrying the Abbot's breakfast. "She's coming. I have to deliver this, and then with the Abbot's permission, I'll join you."

Frith delivered the tray, and begged to be excused, giving Bedivere as the reason. Alura came from the kitchen, long copper hair flying, a happy smile on her face. Frith joined her on the path. A thick, gray sky started spitting a misty rain, matting their hair.

Bedivere drew them into an unoccupied alcove and looked wistfully toward the abbey gate. "I am a knight, not a man of the cloth. I fear no man, yet I'm loath to destroy the serene joy I see in your faces with dire news. Better I should have left it to the Abbot to tell. Then again, Lancelot addressed his letter to me. This is knights' business, and I know my duty."

Frith exchanged a glance with Alura.

"It's fortunate you made your farewells yesterday." Bedivere fixed his eyes on the stone floor. "Last night the Bishop woke with a vision of Lancelot's spirit being drawn upward by angels…" Bedivere faltered. "Sir Bors sent knights, hoping to prove the vision was only a bad dream, but the men found Lancelot lying in his garden." His voice choked. "Nine knights have taken his body to Joyous Gard where he wished to be buried."

"That corpse was not the essence of the Master," Alura said.

"So the Holy Church tells us." Bedivere lifted his gaze from the floor. "The knights did say when they found him, Lancelot's visage smiled with a sweet sense of peace."

Of course it did, Frith thought. How could it otherwise?

"Did the knights see his body give off a light?" Alura said.

Bedivere looked startled. "Why would you ask such a strange question?"

"Because he often quoted us the scripture, 'If thy eye be single, thy whole body shall be full of light.' And his eye was surely single."

Bedivere shrugged. "I don't know. When Bors returns from Joyous Gard, I'll ask him."

Bedivere inhaled deeply through his nostrils. "Now, what should I do about you two? Frith, you still want to ride with me in service to the knights?"

"A kind offer, sir, and I thank you. I once dreamed of it, but no more. Sir Lancelot has commanded me to remain at the abbey to watch over my sister."

"Indeed, she needs a man's protection, but only until she weds." Bedivere turned to Alura. "I will not marry again, but I'll bring you a husband if I find one along my travels."

"Thank you, my lord, but no," Alura said. "Sir Lancelot has set my feet firmly upon another path."

"Which is?"

Her voice filled with resolve firm as the stone walls, "I shall remain at the abbey and commune daily with the me who is not of this world, at a place in myself that is not in this world."

Bedivere shook his head like a man with a gnat in his ear. But Frith sensed a holiness surround Alura as if Lancelot's spiritual mantel had settled over her.

Water drizzled off the eves, and Frith envisioned Alura metamorphosed into the virginal girl holding the vessel from which pours out that which sustains life.

Bedivere let out a prolonged exhalation, like he'd reached a decision. "There is a vacant hermit's hut…"

Alura smiled. "I am sure Lancelot would like you to have it."

CHAPTER 1

Abbey of St. Benignus two years later, August, 554

The mind is a small place to live. Frith smiled. That sounded like something Lancelot would have said. Maybe he was making progress.

Frith was sitting on a shady hill with his boots off, leaning against the stone wall that enclosed the abbey grounds. Sheep nearby grazed with single-minded purpose. Monks hoed the gardens below, intent on their rows of peas. Not Frith. He'd completed his daily duties for the Abbot, and the old man was deep in his afternoon nap.

He pondered Lancelot's admonition, "Memories and dreams may seem like a boundless place to dwell, but the world unfolds outside the confines of our mind."

A fat rabbit nibbled grass at the edge of the flock. Frith remembered when the pastures weren't so rich, nor rabbits and sheep so abundant. The dark years when the sun weakened and crops wouldn't grow.

Beyond the abbey gates a small village straddled the old Roman road. Frith had no idea where the road led, for he'd only traveled it once, when he and his sister, Alura, were brought from their ancestral home. He'd been five, she six. The Abbot had taken them in as a favor to their once-wealthy father. Too bad the family didn't want them back when better times returned. Even though neither of them ever took vows, the Abbot let them stay on, more or less as children of the abbey.

A pungent odor, like wet sheep on a hot day, brought him out of his reverie. He looked up. Brother Fastidious was standing over him. They'd known each other since they were boys, when Fastidious was a novice. Truth to tell, Fastidious was a little jealous of Frith.

"You have been called to the Abbot's office," he said.

Frith scratched his back on the ancient stone wall. It had been built to keep dangers out. But it also separated him from the world as surely as a monk's cell. He'd once felt as trapped as he imagined the monks to be, forced to live lives cut off from everything that mattered. He reddened at the memory. Now he understood the inner journey was what mattered. And Lancelot, with a touch to their foreheads, had shown them that.

Lancelot gave them a single glimpse of his own inner state and endeavored to teach them to penetrate the veil of mind. The Holy Grail, he said, wasn't an object, but a portal to a higher spiritual state within them, shuttered only by their own habits of thinking. At first Lancelot's ideas seemed like nonsense. Could a man ever be so lost in thought he didn't even know he was thinking?

"Frith! Did you hear me? The Abbot wants you in his office." Fastidious spun and stalked off. "The Abbot lets you get away with everything."

Startled, the rabbit hopped a few yards in the opposite direction. Frith reached for his boots and noticed his toe protruded through his stocking. Alura would mend it. He stretched the fabric over the hole, pulled his boots on, and started across the abbey grounds.

Frith spied his sister standing at the abbey gate, surrounded by hordes of children from the village. Little ones hugged her knees and older children pressed upon one another, clamoring for her attention. A stranger witnessing the scene might have assumed she was the mother of a large brood. And she was, though not in the usual sense. Whenever she went to market, the deep pockets of her skirt bulged with leftovers from the Abbot's kitchen. Their weight caused her skirt to swish with a sound that alerted children playing outside the gate.

He watched as she blessed a child and put a morsel of food in its mouth. It made him long to be one those children huddled around her, receiving a bit of nourishment. She'd begun the ritual shortly after Lancelot's death. At first the monks reprimanded her. How dare a mere cook from the Abbot's kitchen pretend to be a saint? Eventually, her simple charity overcame their objections. Nowadays they looked the other way and counted their beads.

Two years ago Frith wouldn't have let her go into the village unaccompanied. He'd promised Lancelot he'd protect her. But, he had to admit, these days she didn't seem to require much protection. The only mob that came for her now was the mass of adoring children. He waved, and she waved back. He yearned to go to market with her, but he had better see what had disturbed the Abbot's nap.

* * *

Frith slipped into the Abbot's office without knocking. After a dozen years as the Abbot's personal aide, he had a freedom in the old man's presence none of the monks would dream of. Frith stopped short. The Abbot was talking to a man dressed in fabrics richer than any he'd seen, even on the gentry. The man's deep blue cloak and the yellow tunic beneath it seemed to shine with a luster beyond the finest wool or linen. Ornate images of flowers and feathers appeared to spring from the fabric itself—not stitched or embroidered on later. How was that possible?

"I see you have a guest, my lord," Frith said. "Shall I bring refreshments?"

The Abbot nodded.

Frith stole a backward glance as he left the room. Now he understood why he'd been called back to work. This was someone of immense importance. Might he be a foreign nobleman?

Frith ran to the cellars and returned with two goblets of cider. When he walked in, the Abbot was saying, "As much as I'd like for Frith to put on a habit, I've come to accept he doesn't feel the calling of God."

Maybe the man was a Cardinal. Frith had never met one, but he'd heard they dressed with more opulence than kings.

"Forgive me, my lord," Frith said, "but I do feel called to God."

The Abbot raised one eyebrow.

"Just not to rules and austerity."

The Abbot laughed and shook his head. "Frith, you're a man now. You can't be my lackey all your life. It's time you accept a vocation. This is Jacob ben Zion, a merchant and world traveler sent by your father."

Frith half bowed. So, neither Cardinal nor nobleman, just his father's representative. Frith felt freer to speak his mind. "You mean the father who abandoned me?"

The skin around Jacob's eyes crinkled as his face broke into a soft smile. "Your father's letter cautioned me to expect such a reaction, improper though it may be. The law handed down from Moses tells us to honor our father. It's the seventh commandment."

"But what if the son's been discarded?" Frith said. He probably should have held his tongue, but the words tumbled out of his mouth. "Isn't respect the son of trust, not the child of abandonment?"

Jacob laughed. "I see you have a clever tongue. But your father has neither abandoned nor forgotten you. He loved you very much. That is why I am here."

Frith did not respond. He knew the polite thing would be to express some gratitude, but in matters of his family he did not trust what he might say.

"Your father regretted not being able to give you the upbringing he gave your brothers. As a father myself, I understand the pain he felt when he couldn't do anything for you earlier, but now—"

"Forgive my interruption, but may I ask how you know what my father feels? You speak as if you are close to him."

"He and I were partners—a shared investment in a tin operation in Cornwall. Perhaps you heard him speak of Jacob the Jew?"

Frith shook his head. His scant memories of home didn't include mention of a Jew.

"I'm here because of your father's concern for your future."

Frith scuffed the floor and glanced at the Abbot, who was observing with his usual look of benevolence. "I thank you, sir, for your consideration. But please tell my father I was well brought up. The Abbot here was father to me." He did not add what was in his head, that the Abbot was more a father than his own father ever was."

"Perhaps you don't know…" Jacob took a breath. "Your father is dead."

Frith suddenly realized that throughout the conversation, Jacob had been speaking of his father in the past tense. So…

Lancelot had taught him to observe his thoughts as they happened. He observed now that the news left him strangely unaffected. It was his father. But it was also the man who had thrown him and his sister away, a figure too distant to be a memory.

Jacob cleared his throat. "I've been away or I would have come sooner. When I returned from my last voyage I went to settle accounts and learned he'd passed on. Your brother was holding a letter for me that your father left, asking me to give you a place in my next excursion. I've concluded my business in Britain and am readying to travel again."

"It's true," the Abbot said. "I've seen the letter. As much as I hate to lose a man I love so dearly as you, I'm releasing you into merchant Zion's care."

Frith jutted his chin toward Jacob. "What care did my father give for his daughter, Alura?"

"He left no dowry for her," Jacob said, "but if this trip is prosperous, it'll put coin in your eldest brother's purse to buy her a husband."

"No disrespect to you, sir, but neither my sister nor I have reason to trust our sibling."

"Oh, I'm sure he'll—"

"Nevertheless, since it was our father's wish, my sister and I will accompany you."

Jacob's eyes widened. "A woman on such a trip? That's impossible."

Frith tightened his jaw. "Then I'm afraid I can't go either."

"This is a long, perilous journey; too difficult for a woman."

Frith furrowed his brow. He understood Jacob was talking about traveling somewhere far, to Gaul, perhaps. But Alura wasn't some weak-stemmed flower. "How long?"

"A year there, another year back, at least six months buying and selling—about two and a half years."

"I won't leave Alura that long. I can't."

The Abbot patted Frith's arm. "She won't be alone. She'll be with the kitchen women where she's always been. And I'll watch over her."

Frith shook his head.

"You must go," Jacob said. "Your father wills it."

"My father's will does not outweigh my honor. I've given my word to Sir Lancelot."

"I confess Abbot, I'm at a loss," Jacob said. "To meet such resistance when I am just trying to do a favor for my old partner? Well… it surprises me."

The Abbot leaned toward Jacob, cutting Frith out of the conversation. "I have an idea how to persuade him."

Frith held his tongue and waited to learn how the Abbot planned to change his mind.

"Why don't you stay the night?" the Abbot said. "Share some repast in the dining hall?"

"I'm twice surprised," Jacob said. "You know I am not of your faith."

"You are, however, my guest."

"Never have I been invited to stay in a Christian monastery."

"Is it prohibited by your religion?"

"I cannot worship in your cathedral, for it has graven images. But if the sleeping quarters are without icons, my conscience is clear. However, wouldn't your people consider it improper for you to house a Jew here?"

"Was Elijah not a Jew? If the prophet appeared at my door, I'd give him a bed and a meal."

Jacob stood. "In Elijah's name, then."

The Abbot clapped Jacob on the back and guided him out the door. "Come Frith. Let's show your father's friend a fine banquet."

CHAPTER 2

Frith followed the Abbot and Jacob past the abbey gardens toward the Abbot's Kitchen. The Abbot steered Jacob around a gaggle of geese. "When we get to the dining hall, I'll introduce you to Frith's sister, our finest cook and the sweetest child of God you will ever encounter."

The Abbot's kitchen was Frith's favorite place, and not only because Alura worked there. It was always full of savory aromas—venison or boar roasting on one fireplace, a chicken or a goose on another, and a great pot of vegetables on the third. The monks had their own kitchen and ate a simpler fare. Frith had a number of reasons for never wanting to become a monk, but one of them definitely was that he was too fond of meat. Plus the monks only got one meal a day. Frith ate as many meals a day as the kitchen ladies would feed him. Even with all he ate, Frith remained beanstalk lean, unlike the poor Abbot who only ate breakfast and supper, but somehow stayed plump as a meat pie.

The Abbot stopped a monk who happened across their path. "Brother Fastidious, I have a guest. Go prepare a room for him in the pilgrims' quarters."

Fastidious eyed the merchant and muttered to Frith behind the Abbot's back, "Why didn't he have you do it?"

Frith ignored him and ran ahead to open the door for the two older men. A score of pilgrims, already at supper, turned their heads to see who had entered. As the Abbot proceeded through the room, he stopped at each table to offer a kind word or a blessing—making sure the abbey patrons felt noticed and appreciated. Frith expected to hear envious comments about Jacob's cloak, but he didn't. Perhaps to them, Jacob was just another wealthy guest. In his years as the Abbot's aide he'd come to know the nobility well. Their pilgrimage garments might be plain gray, but the wool was of the finest quality. They smeared ash on their foreheads, but heavy, bejeweled crosses of gold dangled from their necks. For all Frith knew, they all dressed like Jacob when they were at home.

When the Abbot reached a table for four, he tried to give Jacob the seat of honor, but Jacob declined. Frith went to take his customary seat near the wall, but the Abbot pulled out the heavy chair opposite his own. "This conversation is likely to be about you, Frith. You may as well join it."

Jacob took the chair between them. This arrangement left the fourth seat, the one across from Jacob, empty. Frith knew every man in the room hoped to be invited to a place at the Abbot's table.

A postulant came through the door that separated the kitchen from the dining hall carrying three goblets and a pitcher of wine. Novices typically assisted the kitchen ladies—washing and cutting vegetables, stirring cauldrons of soup, turning spits of meat, and serving food to the Abbot's guests. When the boy had filled their cups, the Abbot asked him to fetch Alura.

She responded at once, sweeping into the room with a smile that could melt the candles in their stands. Upon seeing Frith, the intensity of her smile doubled. Brushing wrinkles from her skirt, she curtsied to the Abbot. "What would be your pleasure, Holy Sir?"

"Your company, dear one."

"I don't understand."

"I wish you to join me in a meal with our guest."

Alura dipped her head and wrapped her hands in the pleats of her skirt.

"No, the offer's genuine," the Abbot said. "Permit me to introduce Jacob ben Zion, a merchant friend of your father's."

"My father?" She turned to Jacob and curtsied. "Pleased to meet you."

"Now, take this vacant seat and grow acquainted," the Abbot said.

Alura hesitated.

"Please, do as I ask."

As Alura walked toward the empty seat, Jacob and the Abbot stood. Frith jumped up and pulled out her chair. When Alura sat, the men resumed their seats. The room around them buzzed. The server dashed into the kitchen and returned with another goblet for Alura and poured her some wine.

Alura gazed at the merchant with straightforward interest. "Thank you, Lord Abbot, for introducing me to someone who knows our father."

"Oh, I know your whole family," Jacob said.

"Regrettably we don't," Alura said. "It's been too long. Except for a bottle of wine we received two years ago, we have heard nothing from them."

"That's unfortunate," Jacob said, and then he was silent.

Frith expected the merchant to forge ahead with the news about their father's death. When neither he nor the Abbot did, Frith thought, perhaps the responsibility fell to him.

Frith took Alura's hand. A sense of serenity passed up his arm and over his being at touching her. "Alura, the news this merchant is reluctant to share is that our father is dead."

"I know," Alura said. "I've sensed it for some time."

"I don't mean dead to us," Frith said. "I mean deceased."

"Yes." Alura sat still for a time, a look of deep grief on her face. No one spoke.

Frith didn't know what the Abbot or Jacob feared she would do, but if they worried she'd run out of the hall wailing, they were quite mistaken. His sister lived in a state of deep peace he'd seen only in Lancelot.

Alura took the Abbot's hand and closed her eyes. "Let us say a blessing for Father. Lord Abbot, will you lead us?"

Without thinking, Frith took Jacob's hand in his own. The only gap remaining was between Jacob and the Abbot. Jacob clasped the Abbot's free hand to complete the circle.

The Abbot commenced a long Latin prayer. To Frith's surprise Jacob joined him. As the two men chanted, Frith sensed Alura draw a sentiment from him he'd not realized he had. Although Frith swore he would never cry for his father, wet rivulets flowed down his cheeks. He heard the Abbot's voice crack and sneaked a look. Tears pooled in Jacob's eyes, as well. Through his connection with Alura, Frith felt the emotions of the other men flowing into her. By the time the Abbot said, "Kyrie eleison" the third time, Alura had taken each of them beyond their grief, into honoring her father, and finally into acceptance of his passing.

Frith, blushing, broke the circle and wiped his wet face. The others did the same.

Jacob picked up his goblet. "Is it not your custom to raise the cup in salute before taking the first sip?"

The Abbot nodded.

Jacob tipped his chalice toward Alura, "Then to the Lady." Frith and the Abbot raised their cups.

Alura shook her head. "That title of nobility doesn't apply to me."

"Then to your father," Jacob said.

"Yes," said the Abbot. "To the Baron... and all his children."

When they had all drunk, Alura said, "How do you know our father? You seem much younger than he."

"I am. I'm only a decade older than your eldest brother." Jacob ran his hand through his curls, thick and black, with only a scattering of gray hairs. "Your father and I first met buying and selling horses for his estate. Later, we became business partners. He was my mentor in my early years and later my friend. Now I hope to return the favor by mentoring his son."

"Don't worry, Alura," Frith said quickly, "I'm not—"

"Not now, Frith," the Abbot said. "Alura, tell us what the kitchen has prepared."

Alura dimpled and named a long list of delicious meats and dishes. The Abbot patted his ample stomach. "You see, Jacob, a sumptuous feast."

"Might I have a large plate of vegetables and some bread?" Jacob said.

"Oh, that's the diet of the monks," the Abbot said. "We have meat for our guests."

"It's not my intention to offend your hospitality," Jacob said. "But please, just the simple fare for me."

Alura started to get up, but the Abbot touched her arm. "No, Alura, let the kitchen boys fetch it. You dine with us tonight."

Alura glanced at the kitchen door, and back to the Abbot. Frith couldn't remember the Abbot ever treating Alura like anything more than a cook. If the pilgrims in the hall were shocked she was invited to sit with the Abbot, imagine when word got around the abbey she was being waited on by young monks.

Jacob gave Alura a sympathetic smile. "I'm a little embarrassed, too. This is my first time staying in an abbey... And I must say, everything about this evening is strange, but not unpleasantly so. I find you quite... remarkable."

Alura looked down at the table.

"You know, Alura," Jacob said, "there was little your family could do for your situation. The money just wasn't there."

Frith doubted it was true. The family was rich, always had been. They simply never wanted him and Alura back.

Alura gave Jacob a small smile. "I admit being frustrated when I was younger. But I'm contented now."

"Too bad you aren't of my faith," Jacob said. "In our culture the groom pays the bride's family."

Well, that was rude. Their family's neglect had made Alura a spinster. She had found contentment, true, but there was still no need to rub it in.

Alura shrugged. "Isn't marriage an earthly complement of our desire for unity with God? I no longer need to marry. I am whole."

Frith kept a close eye on Jacob. Alura used to conceal her intellect to hide the fact Lancelot was teaching a woman. Once their secret relationship was exposed, she felt it unnecessary to disguise her wits. But such candor might cause her to still need protection from the world at large, and Jacob had just met her.

"In my tradition, the need for love and family is paramount," Jacob said.

"We are not put here to get love," she said. "Our purpose is to share the love flowing from our higher being."

Jacob ben Zion was silent. But it was not an angry silence. More... surprised?

Alura gave him a sweet smile, "I didn't mean to disparage family."

"I'm not offended," Jacob said. "I'm impressed."

Alura blushed. "What about you? Have you a family?"

"Two sons, Micah and Levi, both in business with me. They're old enough to manage their own ventures now, so we're seldom in the same city."

A young monk brought their food, and they began eating. During dinner, Alura said, "The Abbot introduced you as a merchant. What do you sell?"

"Silk, and, well everything else. The route of the silk trade is long. I strive to make every step worthwhile."

"If you don't mind explaining to a woman..."

"If a woman is bright enough to ask, she deserves an explanation. We take tin from Cornwall to Italia by ship. Once it's sold, we purchase oil and wine to sell in Egypt, where we buy cotton to sell in Damascus. With the proceeds, we buy silk to sell to the nobility in Gaul and Britain. This time I am organizing a caravan from Damascus inland to buy silk at better prices."

"A wonderful adventure, but it must be lonesome for your wife."

"Unfortunately, I'm a widower," Jacob said. "This will be my first trip without one of my sons. Of course, it gives me an opportunity to train Frith."

"Oh?" Alura said.

"It was your father's dying wish," Jacob said, "to make a vocation for his youngest son."

Frith stopped eating and put down his knife. "Alura, I've already explained to them why I can't go."

"It will also favor you, Alura," Jacob said. "The profits from this venture will give your eldest brother money for your dowry."

"Thank you, sir. But as I said, I no longer feel a need to wed. But Frith, what good fortune for you."

Although he was aware it was impolite, Frith leaned to his sister's ear and said in a hushed undertone, "Have you forgotten Lancelot's final instruction? 'Live at the abbey as an unwed sister and her doting brother. Support and cover for each other.' I promised him I would."

Alura whispered back, "He said, stay together during your inner quest, *until* you achieve the Grail. You must agree that what happened the morning after he died fulfilled his charge to you?"

After another moment, Frith straightened and found Jacob staring at him. Alura said, "Jacob, I thank you for this kindness to our father—and my brother. I believe Frith should go, but he feels it is his duty to protect me."

"So he has told me. But I am surprised that you have a say about your brother's life. Is he not supposed to be your protector rather than the other way around?"

Frith jittered with the urgency of a boy about to break out of a church pew at the end of Mass.

"Frith," the Abbot said, "Alura's under my protection—safe within the abbey. You need not worry about her."

"Thank you, my lord," Frith said, "but this trip will take years. Something could happen to you while I'm gone. No offense sir, but you *are*... old."

The Abbot laughed. "The abbey walls will not fall when I die."

Frith shook his head. "Still, sir—"

"I have an idea," the Abbot said. "What about Bedivere? You know he'd protect Alura."

"Sir Bedivere?" Jacob said. "Is he still alive?"

The Abbot laughed. "He'll probably outlive us all. He's practicing austerities in a small hut in the woods behind the abbey."

Frith couldn't argue. Sir Bedivere had been a stalwart knight.

The Abbot slapped his hand on the table. "I propose Bedivere come in from his hermitage and dwell in the abbey. He can practice his asceticism with the monks as well as by himself. His presence will assure Alura's safety, should I meet my end before your return."

Alura touched Frith's hand. "The Abbot's plan frees you of responsibility. As do I."

Frith looked into Alura's eyes. "You really want me to leave you?"

"I will miss you. But I think you must take this journey for your sake."

"What if Sir Bedivere doesn't agree to come?"

"He will. Talk to him in the morning."

Frith turned to the Abbot, "You're certain it is the right thing to do?"

"Yes, Frith, this seems to be the providence of God. You should submit yourself to it."

Frith struggled to find another objection, but couldn't come up with one. "All right, Jacob ben Zion, I accept your offer."

CHAPTER 3

The bell to end morning meditation sounded, and the monks filed out of the chapel in silence. Frith dashed for the door, his mind already twenty steps ahead of him. Meditating while the monks chanted hadn't quelled his mind this morning. His thoughts had circled in little vortexes that tugged at his attention like whirlpools, dragging his consciousness downward.

Lancelot would have laughed. No, on second thought, Lancelot would have corrected his mental drift with gentle suggestions. Lancelot wasn't one to mock him.

A sliver of magenta sunrise backlit the cone-shaped roof of the Abbot's kitchen. First, he'd have a good breakfast, then visit Bedivere. Perhaps the old knight wouldn't want to move into the abbey, then he wouldn't have to go with Jacob.

Alura met him in the dining hall and insisted on coming with him. They left by the abbey's back gate and entered a dense forest whose thick canopy made the morning light as dark as evening. Ferns carpeting the forest floor all but obscured the faint trail. Frith remembered the way well enough, even though he hadn't been out here in the two years since Lancelot's death.

They walked until they reached the fallen tree that served as a makeshift bridge over a fast-moving river. Frith was pleased to find the log still in place. He tested it with one foot, then spied Bedivere's footprints on its moss-covered bark. If it bore Bedivere's weight, it would certainly support them.

Alura crossed ahead of him and skipped down the path toward the clearing that held Lancelot's cottage—well, Bedivere's cottage now. Frith lagged on the bridge, unexpectedly melancholy. He peered into the swirling waters below and remembered walking beside the river as Lancelot taught them that nothing they encountered in the world was seen for itself, but rather as an impression inside the mind.

"These impressions," Lancelot had said, "are like leaves caught on a snag in the river. They build up like a dam catching others. Soon, we're so imprisoned by past impressions, we can't see beyond them."

For Frith this place was rife with past impressions.

Alura paused at the fence separating Bedivere's yard from the forest. She whirled around and ran on tiptoe back to Frith, urging him onward. Apparently the memories of this place weren't affecting her the way they were him. But that was the difference between them. She'd found Lancelot's Grail. Frith had only been given a glimpse of it and was still searching. But then, Lancelot himself had searched for decades before he found it.

When they reached the gate, he opened it and let her enter first. Frith noticed Bedivere kept the fence in good repair, but the flower gardens Lancelot so carefully tended were not blooming as they once did.

Bedivere came out of his cottage and quietly greeted them. No longer the boisterous knight Frith remembered towering over the Abbot, he now seemed to be merely a holy man, bent on asceticism.

Frith found himself unable to speak. Too much about this place reminded him of the days when he was the disciple and Lancelot was master. He was glad Alura insisted on coming since she talked enough for all three of them. While Alura explained the Abbot's plan and won Bedivere over to it, Frith ran his hand over the cool, smooth, blue stone altar where Lancelot had prayed.

He watched Bedivere nod and Alura followed him to the cottage door. Frith inhaled the woodsy smell. The trees in this very bower had witnessed Lancelot teaching them. A breeze stirred the branches overhead, and the leaves whispered Lancelot's words. "I did not achieve my first experience of the Grail on merit, but because I was present as young Galahad received it.

"For me it was as if I lay my head on the feet of the divine and floated in absolute peace… The first time I knew such a state was possible." Lancelot's eyes turned toward heaven. "Galahad's ecstasy overflowed onto the rest of us like a cascading waterfall."

Well-being had permeated Lancelot's garden that day. As he told his wondrous tale, a golden light overtook them. Alura, with a beatific smile on her face, had said, "The real Grail was not what was under the veil, but the holiness Sir Galahad saw within." Oh, that had pleased Lancelot.

"Frith. Frith, take these."

Alura brought him back to the present. She was standing in front of him with an armload of Bedivere's belongings. She shoved them into Frith's hands. "Sir Bedivere has accomplished true poverty in his hermitage. We can move him to the abbey in one trip if you'll help." She went back for more.

Frith crumpled onto the bench where Lancelot had taught him to read Latin. Alura returned and pulled him upright. "If your mind's going to dwell on Lancelot, remember what he taught us, 'Only the now is real.' And right now, Bedivere is packed and we're leaving." He felt her hand in the small of his back, a gentle push toward the gate. "The past is over. The future has not happened."

No, but it was about to.

The walk back was agonizingly familiar. The three of them returning to the abbey on the very path they had trod together in silence the night Lancelot had given them their final instructions.

Why was he going along with this? When Bedivere tried to get Lancelot to leave, he'd refused. Now Bedivere joined in the scheme to send him away. Frith kicked a rotting branch from the path and it shattered into blackish-brown splinters. The sun, now higher, filtered through the boughs, yielding a cool green light. But it gave Frith no comfort, offered no illumination as to why he hadn't found the Grail like Alura. He'd been right next to her when it happened.

In the niche when Bedivere told them Lancelot was dead, he had sensed the phenomena. Bedivere noticed it, too. Not an object hovering beneath a white samite cloth, not a ray of light shining down from heaven, but light in its other meaning. As if Alura had lost physicality and could float with Christ on clouds or walk with Him on stormy seas.

And he and Bedivere had been left standing like Lancelot before Galahad, experiencing the Grail second-hand as it imbued Alura evermore.

CHAPTER 4

They reached the hedgerow of thorny bushes separating the woods from a scruffy area outside the abbey wall. Bedivere pushed through first and held the branches for Alura and Frith. Frith opened the heavy gate at the rear entrance to the grounds. They entered and Bedivere bolted it behind them.

Frith got Bedivere situated in a cell the Abbot had selected for him and then went to his own room to pack. His was no different from any monk's cell —stone floor, mud plaster walls, and a simple wooden bed with a straw mattress. The beds were built for shorter men, and he'd had to tuck a board under the end of the mattress to keep his feet from hanging off. A feather quilt folded at the foot of the bed had been a gift from the kitchen ladies one year. He'd have to leave it behind.

He sat on the bed and put his head in his hands. So much to leave behind. And for what? To learn a vocation he didn't want. But Bedivere would watch over Alura, he no longer had that excuse. All he had was a nagging fear he would miss out. Lancelot had attained enlightenment here as had Alura. If he left, he might not. He lay on his side and pulled the quilt over his head. The quilt was too hot for summer, but he welcomed the darkness.

He had no idea what to take with him. The Abbot would probably know.

The Abbot! He threw off the cover, jumped up, and ran to the Abbot's office.

Frith tapped on the Abbot's door and started to open it when it was abruptly jerked inward. He nearly stumbled. A young postulant everyone called Little Thomas was holding the door while trying to balance a tray of dirty dishes.

"Holy Father, Frith is here," Little Thomas said.

Frith blinked. It hadn't taken the Abbot long to replace him.

"Oh, come in, Frith," the Abbot said.

Little Thomas left and Frith closed the door behind him. "I'm very sorry sir, I've neglected you already."

"Don't be concerned. You've too much to do to bother about me."

"Never!" Frith said.

"The new boy will serve well enough. But I'm glad you came, I have something for you." The Abbot pointed toward a brown heap of leather on the floor near his desk.

Frith picked it up, and it formed itself into a cylindrical bag that came up to his waist. It was scuffed and looked well used, but the seams were double-sewn and sturdy. Around the opening hung narrow leather straps that could be drawn to close the top. They were creased and worn where they'd been tied.

It was the Abbot's own bag, perhaps from when he made his own pilgrimage. Moisture formed at the edges of Frith's eyes, but he didn't cry. "Thank you, sir."

"It's not a gift, it's a loan." The Abbot's eyes twinkled. "I expect you to bring it back."

Frith smiled at the Abbot—more a grimace. "I shan't fail to... But maybe I shouldn't go."

"Nonsense, this is your chance. Now, take that bag to your room and start packing."

The Abbot too? Jacob, Bedivere, even Alura, everyone seemed in a hurry to send him away.

Frith was back in his room before he realized he still didn't know what to bring and what to leave behind. He'd never gone anywhere before. He decided he needed Jacob's advice. Frith searched the abbey and learned

Jacob had gone to the Abbot's office, so he returned and found the two men sitting by the window, in deep discourse.

"You're saying after God parted the sea and Moses led the people across—"

Jacob nodded. "When the Red Sea closed behind them, it not only prevented the Egyptians from following, it also kept the Israelites from turning back."

"But back into bondage?"

"The Israelites had been under the Egyptians for twenty generations. Many didn't want to forsake their old life—it was all they'd ever known."

Frith cleared his throat. "Forgive me for interrupting."

"Frith, come in. I've been having an intriguing conversation with our new friend. He has a unique perspective on Exodus."

Frith made a quick bow. "Master Zion."

The merchant stood. "Just call me Jacob. Anything else is too formal for fellow travelers."

Is that what they were, already? Frith twisted his hands. "Sir, I've no travel experience, I don't know what to—"

"Ah. Pack light, what clothes you have and a good pair of boots. Oh, bring your winter cloak, too. Some days at sea will be cold even in summer. If you have items necessary for worship, bring those as well."

Frith didn't need icons or relics. But the length of this journey was beyond his ken. He couldn't think that far ahead. "That's all I'll need for two years?"

"Don't worry, I'll provision us. We're going to lands twice as hot as Britain on a good day, other places twice as cold as Britain on a bad day. We'll buy clothing appropriate to the regions as we get to them. Again, less is better, not more than will fit on a horse—"

"A horse?"

Jacob nodded. "Some of our journey will be by horse, some by donkey—"

"Frith never learned to ride," the Abbot said.

Frith wished the Abbot hadn't embarrassed him. Even more so, he wished they weren't going by horse. When he was a boy still at home, his brothers had made sport of him, putting him on a horse and striking its rump. The memory of his humiliation, and the rage he felt, was as fresh as when he was four.

"In a few places we may be on foot," Jacob said. "So, don't pack more than you'd like to carry."

Frith nodded.

"It's too late to start today," Jacob said. "We'll leave at dawn tomorrow."

Frith didn't go back to his room. Instead he headed for the kitchen, intending to spend as much time with his sister as possible before he left, but his thoughts were troubled. He wasn't an Israelite who didn't want to leave Egypt, but the abbey *was* his home. Jacob claimed the family wanted him to take this journey, but weren't Alura and the Abbot his real family? Of course they wanted his exodus, too.

The thought of riding horses and the upcoming journey pained his stomach. Outside the kitchen door, he doubled over and threw up. He scuffed sand over his vomit and leaned his head against the building. He retched again, but nothing more came out.

"Frith?" Alura stepped out the backdoor. "I thought I heard someone—"

"I can't go," Frith said. "I'm sick."

"That's come on all of a sudden. Better see Ethelburg."

Ethelburg was the oldest of the kitchen ladies. Her eyesight was poor and she no longer had the strength to manage a cauldron or to heft a spit of meat from the fire. But she held a repository of recipes in her head and a remembrance of things like how to make candles when tallow was in short supply, how to make a special soap to remove rust from the ironware, and how to make young monks behave in the kitchen. She knew remedies, too.

Ethelburg put her hand on Frith's forehead, felt the pulse in his neck, and examined the color of his tongue. "It's nothing serious." She put a small piece of white rock in a mortar and ground it with a pestle. When it was powdered fine as bread flour she dumped it in a goblet, added a ladle of water, and stirred it with her finger. "Here, drink this."

It made him belch, but he did feel better.

Ethelburg patted his face. "Alura, pick two mint leaves and have him chew them like a cud. He'll be good as ever."

Alura got his mint and walked him back to his room. "Do you want me to help you pack?"

"You're not allowed inside."

"On this day, I don't think anyone would object."

Frith felt tightness in his chest. "Do you really want me to go?"

"Haven't you always said you wanted adventure?"

"When I was a child. Now, my only interest is in finding what you found. You, above all, understand my quest isn't leading me away from here."

"Dear brother, don't you remember? Lancelot said to us, 'We are all arrows in God's quiver. Our lives go where the archer aims, too swiftly for us to change the course.'"

"What if I prove to be as poor at being a merchant as I have been at being Lancelot's disciple?"

She patted him on the shoulder and pushed him toward his door. "Go pack."

CHAPTER 5

Horses trampled Frith's dreams. He came awake and lay in bed thinking until he could tolerate it no longer. He went to the chapel to meditate, but his mind wouldn't cooperate. He scolded himself, but that didn't help. Yesterday's meditation was poor and today's was worse. He'd better find a way to follow Lancelot's teachings outside the abbey since he was going to be gone for two or three years… Years!

Still, letting one part of his mind berate the other part wasn't going to help. It never had. He knew better.

At the hour of prime, the monks joined him and began their rhythmic chant. When meditation ended Frith returned to his room and got his bag. It was barely half-full. He didn't own much. He debated going to Jacob's room but chose the dining hall instead.

Jacob was already at breakfast, sitting with a knight. "Frith, come join us. But eat quickly, for we've a long ride."

Frith's gut wrenched at the thought of a whole day on horseback, but he'd better eat something.

"Sir Otto," Jacob said. "This is my old partner's son, Frith."

Frith bowed to the knight.

"Let's put aside formality," Otto said. "We're to be companions on a mighty adventure, and you are our master's apprentice." He slapped the seat next to him. "Sit here. What a feast!"

The table was covered with dishes of vegetables, baskets of bread, and platters heaped with every meat and cheese a man could desire. This wasn't the typical breakfast the abbey served pilgrims. It was a banquet Alura would have prepared for a bishop. Frith took his seat and tried to decide where to start. Otto resumed his attack on the large mound of food on his plate.

Alura came from the kitchen carrying two bundles wrapped in muslin kerchiefs. "I packed you something for later in the day." She halted. "Oh, I didn't know there were three of you. Let me get another."

Jacob stood. "That's very thoughtful, but don't worry about Sir Otto. The knights have provisions."

Knights? More than one?

"Sir Otto, is it?" Alura said. "Please. Let me make up another parcel, it'll only take a moment."

"Don't be discomforted," Sir Otto said. "You couldn't have known. I only arrived in time for breakfast. I'll just take a leg or two of this bird." He drew his knife and cut off both drumsticks from a spitted chicken.

Alura offered Jacob the parcel in her right hand. "This is yours, sir. It has no meat. Frith, this other's yours. I put in all your favorites."

Frith leaped from his seat. He took the package from her and kissed her on the cheek, paying no heed if others saw.

Alura grabbed a napkin from a nearby table and spread it out for Sir Otto. "Here, good knight, take what you will."

Otto smiled at her and laid his drumsticks on the napkin. As he studied the choices on the table Alura lightly touched his hand. "Sir, you're Jacob's protector, right?"

Otto puffed himself up. "Of course."

"Promise me you'll protect my brother as well, and bring him back safe."

"You have my vow as a knight."

Jacob stood. "The men are waiting on us at the stable."

Frith opened his leather sack and put Alura's lunch parcel on top of his clothes. He started to retie the straps when she drew a second, smaller package from her skirt pocket. It smelled like lavender—her handmade soap. She pried open the top of his bag and tucked it in. "Don't forget to bathe once in a while."

Sir Otto guffawed.

Alura wrapped her arm around Frith's waist and walked out with them, holding fast to him all the way to the gate. But he stopped her there. Jacob and Otto went ahead.

Alura pressed her cheek to his and their tears mingled. "I've got you," she said. "You'll never be anywhere but in my heart."

A sob from deep in his chest escaped his throat.

She kissed his cheek and whispered in his ear, "This isn't something you want Jacob's men to see."

"No, it isn't. That's why I won't let you walk me to the livery."

"I know." She pulled off the scarf binding her hair and dried his face.

"I guess it's time," he said. It sounded hollow, even to him. Why should he leave his sister at the abbey and ride off with these men? He tightened his embrace, and she kissed him again. He didn't care if anyone saw. It'd be a long time before he saw her again. She pushed him out the gate, but his hand trailed back holding her fingertips until her arm could stretch no further.

Frith crossed the road to the stable where he found four knights and half-dozen horses milling about. Frith eyed the horses, saddled and waiting. They were... big. Several of them were pawing the ground and huffing, others moseyed about looking for the odd sprig of grass or nuzzling another horse.

Sir Otto waved him over. "Jacob's inside settling the bill." Standing next to his peers, Otto seemed the largest among them. While he wasn't as tall as Frith, his chest was twice Frith's size, and his arms were as large as Frith's thigh.

How strange it all was. His childhood dream had always been to ride with a knight, to follow some quest, facing new adventures at every turn. Now he simply wanted to remain in the abbey and follow his inner quest, just as Lancelot had. But it had come about as Lancelot predicted. "When you stop craving, you may find you get the very thing you wanted."

Otto introduced his fellow knights as Sir Baldori, Sir Euric, and Sir Nazar. All four were in chain mail, but the styles were as varied as the men, whom he surmised were not of one nation. He found himself staring at Nazar. In the Abbot's service, he'd met travelers from foreign places, but never one who looked like him. The man's face was the color of an old boot, with deep creases around his eyes, and a nose like a hawk's.

Jacob exited the livery. Gone was the fine garment he'd worn earlier. Now he dressed in leather armor and wore a short sword. The knights all had broadswords, Frith only a knife suitable for eating with. He felt naked.

"Let's get mounted," Jacob said. "Otto, show Frith how."

Just like that? Tell the entire company he hardly knew which end of a horse was which? The knights turned to look at him. Frith could have died.

Of all the beasts at hand, Otto reached for the largest, most muscle-bound specimen. Would these men be like his brothers, toss him on an unwieldy creature and then laugh?

Otto gripped the bridle under the horse's jaw and brought him uncomfortably close to Frith. "Look where my right hand is," Otto said. "Lead your horse holding here, not by the reins. Walk on his left, mount from his left. It's what he's used to. He'll behave himself as long as you don't surprise him."

Frith watched the horse's muscles ripple and quiver under its sleek coat. He took deep breaths to calm himself. "Couldn't I start with a smaller one?"

"This is our steadiest animal," Jacob said. "Because he's big, he'll be comfortable with your weight. You'll feel more secure on him, and he'll sense your confidence."

Frith didn't feel confident.

"Stroke his neck like this a couple of times so he knows you're friendly." Otto ran his hand down the horse's neck. "Then hold the saddle here, and hoist yourself up. I'll give you a hand."

Frith tentatively touched the beast's neck, watching its huge eye watching him. He slid his palm over the corded muscles. Then decided to show he wasn't the child he felt like within. He swung himself onto the saddle in one motion.

The horse stutter-stepped and Frith gripped the reins in his fist.

"Very good mount. Beginners rarely make it on the first try." Otto pried Frith's fingers apart. "Let me show you how to hold the reins." Otto threaded the reins through Frith's hand. Once he had the reins arranged, he pushed Frith's forearm down. "Don't hold them so high. Lower them so your forearm and the rein form a straight line to the horse's mouth."

Frith did as told.

"Good," Otto said. "Now, when you pull the reins to either side, the horse will turn in that direction. To stop him, give a short pull back. To go, give him a little nudge with your heels. If he doesn't start, nudge him a bit harder —you won't hurt him. While you're riding don't lean forward, sit upright."

Stay upright? He'd be glad to just stay on.

"Now, if something spooks him and he starts running, pull back on the reins with several short tugs. If he doesn't stop, turn him in a tight circle. That will usually make him halt."

"And if he doesn't?"

Otto laughed. "Then you'll either fall off or you won't." He let go of the bridle and mounted his own horse.

"That's it? That's my riding lesson?"

"You'll be fine," Otto said. "Horses are herd animals. He wants to keep with the others. It's his nature." Otto gave a kick and his horse trotted off.

Otto was right, Frith did nothing, yet his horse moved when the others did. The ride was at first jarring, but after he settled into the rhythm, it became rather... thrilling. The old desire wasn't completely dead. He was riding in a company of knights!

Frith's horse followed Jacob and his men through the village past the two-story guild hall that more or less defined the town square. The dozen or so stalls that comprised the market were still shuttered. No one was about for him to wave at. Not that he'd dare take his hands off the reins. Still, if a few of the journeymen who had teased him when they were apprentices could see him ride out with four knights, it wouldn't be a bad thing.

No, that was vanity. Even the Abbot would have frowned on it, and what would Lancelot have said?

The riders around him picked up speed, and his horse broke into a trot. Frith gripped the reins tighter. The road was rutted. Weeds grew along its margins. It dipped irregularly with rain-washed gullies. He'd heard pilgrims complain the road hadn't been well kept since the Romans left, nearly a century ago, and now he was seeing it for himself.

Frith didn't join the knight's banter. He concentrated on staying on his horse. Over the next hours they passed large tracts of farmland. Frith realized for the first time how remote the abbey was. His heart started to pound and his breathing grew rapid. There was too much sky above the empty fields, too much open land. The abbey walls might have hemmed him in, but at least he'd known where the edges of his world were.

He wasn't getting enough air. Maybe he was dying. He should tell Jacob. No, it'd be too embarrassing. He felt hot and sweaty and longed to lie down on the cool stone floor in his room.

The horses continued to canter toward... he didn't know where. Cornwall? Sir Otto had said, Euric was from Cornwall, and that was where they were headed.

Frith had nodded as if he knew where that was, but Cornwall was nothing more than a name to him.

The road entered a deep wood. Trees arching cathedral-like over the road reminded him of the woods behind the abbey. He inhaled the familiar forest scent. That was better.

No doubt, Lancelot and Bedivere had ridden this very road, but surely these four knights were different from any company Bedivere or Lancelot ever commanded. Arthur's knights traveled the world to do the king's justice and quest for the Grail. These men were in it for the money. Still, these men were all Frith had. The world he'd known was behind him.

As the morning aged, the road wandered in and out of dark woods, through more unused fields, and then into another forest. The tree cover which comforted him earlier now blackened his mood. They hadn't passed another human in the last hour. He felt unsteady on horse, and unsure in his mind. Why had he left his comfortable life for an unknown destination with strangers?

Frith wavered between accepting and questioning his decision until midday when they came to a clearing with a pond and good visibility in all directions. Jacob called a halt. The knights dismounted and led their horses to the water. Frith slid from the saddle and landed awkwardly. He didn't think anyone saw—they were already at the pond. He remembered Otto's instruction, gripped his horse's bridle near the jaw, and started to lead him. But the horse didn't wait. If God had not blessed Frith with long legs and quick feet, the horse might have dragged him to the pond.

While the horses drank, the knights fastened leather straps between their forelegs. "Come Frith, let me show you how to hobble your horse," Otto said. "This lets them graze without us having to chase them down later."

No one had yet told Frith his horse's name. If he ran off, how should he call him?

Once the horses were fettered, every man went to relieve his bladder. After Frith was done, he retrieved the kerchief Alura had packed and began eating. Otto was already gnawing on one of the drumsticks he'd saved from breakfast. The other knights took food from their packs. Everyone ate standing.

When they'd finished, Baldori passed around a jug of wine. "I'll be glad when I get to Rome where a man can buy decent wine."

"Sir Baldori's from Italia," Jacob said. "That's where we're taking the tin."

"I think the horses have rested enough," Otto said. "We'd better mount up if we're to make Jacob's before dark."

The remaining ride seemed to last forever. The saddle rubbed his inner thighs raw. A sign pointed toward Bodmin, but the company turned south, away from the settlement. The road weaved between giant moss-covered boulders, and then entered a marsh. The air smelled different here, like fish and peat-moss. The trail forked, and they proceeded down a soggy path of brown muck. His horse's hooves made a sucking sound as they slogged through the plaster sludge.

It was dark by the time they arrived at… wherever it was. Frith could only see dim silhouettes of buildings. A stable boy took their horses. Frith made a smoother dismount this time, but God, was he sore. Walking felt as if his legs had forgotten their normal function.

A servant came bearing two torches. He handed one to Jacob, and Otto took the other. Frith could now see a large house, several smaller cottages, and two enormous storehouses. Jacob started toward the main house. "Come with me, Frith. Good night, men."

The knights waved and followed Otto toward the smaller houses.

A servant in front of the main house exchanged Jacob's torch for a lit candle. Jacob led Frith through a massive oak door, down a corridor, and into a bedroom. "You can sleep here. This was my son's room." Jacob touched his candle to one on the night stand. The candle cast patches of yellow light on the wall, dimly illuminating a hanging tapestry.

"Is this whole estate yours?"

"I rent the property." Jacob yawned. "I'm too tired to eat. If you're hungry, there's food in the kitchen."

Frith wasn't about to search out a kitchen in the dark. He still had a little of the food Alura had packed. That would do. "Before you go, I wanted to ask about your knights—they all seem to be from different places."

"They are. Not every knight in Christendom wants to ride for a Jew. They must have a desire to roam far from home and a taste for adventure." He winked at Frith, "Like you, I hope."

CHAPTER 6

The cries of an unfamiliar bird woke him. Frith luxuriated in the embrace of the plush feather mattress a moment longer, then his eyes fell on the tapestry. Pale candlelight last night had concealed its majesty. The image was of a man in a robe sleeping on the ground. Behind the sleeper, columns of angels ascended and descended a broad ladder extending into the clouds. Beams of light pierced the clouds in several places.

He stretched and his muscles felt stiff—now he knew what the older monks meant when they made that complaint. He eased out of bed and found himself standing on soft carpet. The rug was crimson, with blue and white flowers woven into its design, itself worthy to hang on the wall. He was astounded such beauty should be trod upon. This was indeed a rich man's house.

The abbey didn't have tapestries, but he held a vague memory of his parents' cathedral where several hung high above the reach of small boys. Never allowed this near before, he stepped gingerly to the edge of the carpet, to look more closely. The sleeping man, the angels, every detail was formed from tiny loops of colored thread. Yet from a distance it had the perfection of a painting.

His stomach rumbled, but his meditations had been pathetic the last two days. Lancelot had warned him there could be many distractions on one's quest. Did traveling with Jacob qualify as a quest or a distraction? He didn't know, but he'd best sit and do the practices Lancelot taught him.

After meditating, he located the kitchen. No one was there, but a plate of cheese, fruit, and bread had his name on it. While he ate, he wondered if he should say something to Jacob. The merchant was bound to notice his meditation practices if they quartered together.

He wiped the last crumb from the plate, licked his finger, and went outside. Frith spotted two warehouses. Voices were coming from behind the second, so he walked in that direction. He rounded the corner and saw in the distance a wide body of water. The warehouse stood on a hill that sloped gradually toward the water's edge. The first boat Frith had ever seen sat heavy and low in the water. In its midst stood a leafless tree, sheared of all but two branches.

What had he done? Yesterday, he'd been so concerned to not look a fool on horseback that he'd been swept from his purpose like a cobweb from a corner. He'd made an enormous mistake. This wasn't his destiny; that boat wasn't going to the Grail.

It wasn't too late though. He could return to the abbey.

A voice spoke from behind him. "There she is Frith, our home for the next three months."

Frith turned around. "Oh, Sir Euric... Is this the ocean?"

"Ocean? No, the sea is two or three leagues downstream. This is the River Fawi."

"And is that the boat Jacob is taking to Rome?"

"Yes, but call her a ship, not a boat."

Frith scratched his head. "It seems to be impaled on a tree."

"The mast is part of the ship. When we cast off great sheets of cloth will be tied to those crossbeams to catch the wind and push us along."

Frith turned his face away. "I'm a novice in all aspects of travel."

"We all were, once. Let's go aboard and have a look."

Frith and Euric walked downhill. The ship sat off shore a bit, and long sturdy planks spanned the gap. Rotations of men were carrying provisions aboard. Euric waited while a man came down the planks, and then followed aboard another man shouldering two sacks of beans.

"Come, Frith."

The three men's weight caused the boards to sag and then bounce with every step. Frith felt unsteady, as if they were about to jounce him off. When they reached the top he jumped to the deck.

The ship shifted. Never had a solid floor made him feel so uncertain.

Jacob, already aboard, was in a heated argument with a man holding open a large scroll. "I've leased your ship for the whole run, there and back," Jacob said. "I have the right to determine where I want to get on and off."

"That man is the captain," Euric said in Frith's ear. "More or less Lord of the ship."

Frith was bewildered. The monks had never raised their voices. And wasn't Jacob sort of Lord, at least over the knights? Why not over the ship?

"Other ships have reported good winds all the way to the Pillars of Hercules," the Captain said. "If we diverge, it'll cost us days." The Captain stabbed his finger on the parchment he and Jacob were studying. "It makes no sense. We won't have off-loaded the tin, so you can't add cargo in Gaul, unless you want us to founder."

"I've friends among the Frankish kings," Jacob said. "It feels safer, than risking Visigoth Hispania."

As the two men continued to debate the issue, Frith wished he could get a better look at the scroll. It must be a map. The abbey had a map in the library, but he'd never been allowed to unfurl it. Too precious, the monk in charge of the library had said.

Euric tugged on Frith's sleeve. "Let's have a look about."

The open deck was not much larger than the room he'd stayed in last night. Frith wondered how the six of them plus the ship's crew were going to fit. Also, were they bringing the horses?

Frith heard the squawking bird calls that had awakened him. He whirled around and saw white and grey birds the size of large pigeons, but with longer yellow beaks and webbed feet like a goose. The birds sat on the ship's railing studying the water below.

"Gulls," Euric said. "Nuisance birds—snatch your dinner right off your plate. They'll stay with us down the river, but they won't follow us far out to sea."

Jacob, finished with the captain, said, "Are you men packed? We sail with the tide."

Frith had no idea what tide meant, but he never unpacked, so he was as ready as he was yesterday.

"Let's go to the house," Jacob said. "Euric, find your fellows. We have time for a decent meal before we cast off."

Once Euric left, Frith asked Jacob what he and the captain had been arguing about.

"I am risking a fortune on this venture," Jacob said. "I thought if I sent the shipload of tin around the Iberian Peninsula while we took the rest of my treasure across Gaul, we'd lessen the odds of total disaster."

"Treasure?"

"A portion of my wealth sufficient to mount a second endeavor, should the ship be lost to vicious attack."

Frith's eyes widened. "That won't happen, will it?"

"Well, unfavorable weather could force the Captain to make landfall among hostile people. So… it's always a risk."

Frith shivered.

"Don't worry. My knights are fierce warriors. Anyway, the Captain has convinced me not to leave a sound ship to cross Gaul on horseback."

Frith had yet to sail, but was sure he'd prefer it to horseback.

At the main house, Jacob's staff had laid a fine table around which the knights, Jacob and Frith gathered. Jacob said a blessing and then put a large portion of lamb on his plate.

"Sir, I thought you abstained from flesh, like our monks."

"What? No, I eat meat, but only when I know how it's been butchered and prepared. My religion has strict dietary laws. I don't ask my men to follow those rules, but I do."

"But surely Alura could have—"

"We've only just met, but as we travel together you'll see I keep my spiritual practices steady without offending my host."

Frith realized this turn in conversation provided an opportunity to confide his own situation. He glanced at the knights and lowered his voice. "Several years ago, I was privileged to receive the tutelage of a holy teacher, Sir Lancelot."

"Yes, you mentioned your vow to him while we were at the abbey."

"Once considered the greatest knight, he forsook knighthood to become a holy hermit. Knights spent years questing for the Holy Grail. Lancelot found it only when he ceased the outward quest and turned within."

Jacob raised his eyebrows. "Found the Grail?"

"During his hermitage. Later, he took Alura and me as his… er… students."

"Interesting. Your father never told me."

"He had no way of knowing. Lancelot swore us to secrecy."

"Yet you've shared your secret with me…"

"Because of what you said about keeping your spiritual practices. You see, Lancelot taught me certain meditations which I continue to this day. Inasmuch as you may see me perform them, I thought you should know."

Jacob touched himself on the forehead with his middle finger.

Frith looked away.

Jacob cut a bite of lamb and ate it. "I know a story of the Grail you might like."

Frith stopped eating and turned toward Jacob.

"In Roman times, a Jewish merchant named Joseph of Arimathea used to come to the Port of Fawi. Later today, on our way to the sea, we'll pass where he landed. I'll point it out to you."

What chance brought this? He knew that name from Lancelot's stories.

"It is said Joseph became a disciple of the Rabbi Yeshua and brought the Holy Grail to Britain." Jacob cocked his head. "Do you know this legend?"

Frith glanced around. The knights were engaged in their food and conversation. "Yes, Lancelot told us. But the Grail I seek is the soul."

Jacob's eyes glistened. "Well then, I will support your efforts in every way I can."

* * *

As soon as they finished eating they boarded the ship. One sailor pulled the planks aboard while the others tugged on ropes that spread the huge sheets of cloth, which bellied out in the breeze. The captain stood at the stern gripping a staff attached to an oar of some sort.

The ship moved. Slowly at first, then gaining speed with the current.

Frith had never experienced anything like it. Lush valleys streamed past him as if he was standing still and the land were moving. He walked to the railing and looked into the deep water. Long, thin, white wavelets spread from the side of the ship toward the shore until they were swallowed by the river current. Little eddies formed where the wake and current met. Thick bushes grew along the banks, but beyond them were verdant pastures.

Squawking gulls flew alongside, swooping about here and there. Occasionally, a bold one would light upon the railing, only to be shooed away by one of the crew. Bird droppings splattered the ship rails.

Two sailors at the front of the ship leaned over the right and left railings and shouted information to the captain as he threaded the ship down the river. The captain gave orders to men manning the sails to make them slack or taunt, which caused the ship to speed up or slow.

Frith went forward to observe the men on the bow. "What are you looking for?"

"Obstructions or shallow places," one of the sailors said.

"Mind the depth," the Captain said. The sailor leaned back over the edge.

"Frith," Jacob said. "Come back here. Leave those men to their work."

Frith turned crimson, scooted under the limb holding the sail, and tried to stand somewhere out of the Captain's sight.

After a time the riverbanks became less defined, widening into a marsh populated with an assortment of birds Frith had never seen. Sir Otto, who traveled this route with Jacob many times, stood next to him and named them. Ahead, at either side of the river marsh rose rocky hills sparsely covered with trees. The river emptied into a bay overlooked by a castle on the highest prominence. Numerous stone houses lined the shore and the water was crowded with small fishing boats.

And... there was the ocean.

It filled the world, an entire universe of nothing but water and sky. It was terrifying—he thought that the wide fields of yesterday made him feel small —but it was also astounding. He knew that people like the Captain made their lives there, following the unmarked paths of this great, wide expanse. And he realized again how small his life in the abbey had been.

All the sailors except the captain ran about adjusting the sails. The ship sped up. Wind lashed Frith's hair against his face and the bay receded in their wake. They followed headlands with green tops and stone faces for a while, but eventually Frith could not see land in any direction. He tried breathing deeply to calm his nerves, but his eyes darted about and sweat dotted his brow.

Sir Nazar came and stood next to him. "Your first time at sea?"

Frith nodded. "I heard visitors to the abbey talk of sea travel, but I had never grasped just how large it is. I've never seen so much water in my life. I've lost my bearings. I feel like I've lost myself."

Nazar pointed to the sky on their left. "See those clouds? We're not far from land. Except in a storm, the clouds will generally be on our land side."

The ship rose and fell, higher and harder now, and his stomach with it.

Nazar pulled him toward the railing. "You're turning green. If you're about to give up your supper, offer it to the sea. If you intend to keep it, fix your eye on the evening star and take some deep breaths."

Frith took Nazar's advice and soon felt a little better. A crescent moon and another star appeared, although daylight had not waned. Even so, Frith felt drowsy.

He carried his pack to a quiet, out of the way place on the deck, slumped down, and slept.

* * *

Something, perhaps the prayers being intoned in a foreign language, woke him. He opened his eyes a tiny slit. The horizon was faintly pale. It must be well past the time of lauds, but not yet prime.

He saw Jacob wrapped in a cloth woven with blue stripes and edged with knotted fringe. Whatever Jacob was saying wasn't Latin. Maybe it was Hebrew. He looked around. No one else was awake. It seemed like an opportunity to do his morning meditations.

Frith sat up, took a breath and focused his attention at the point between his eyebrows. He relaxed and allowed his breath to flow naturally. The breath carried his consciousness upward to a point of stillness where he felt an increased peace. If thoughts came, they flowed beneath him, as though he sat on a cloud high above them. Whenever he became engrossed in a thought, he noticed his eyes had drifted downward. He turned his eyes up again, and the thoughts passed below him. It was tranquil sitting in this way, just breathing, swaying with the ship. He enjoyed this untroubled state for as long as his mind let him.

Eventually, a particularly engrossing chain of thoughts cost him his peace, and his meditation ended. Frith leaned against his bag and went back to sleep.

In the morning, sailors who'd handled the ship all night, traded places with those who'd slept. The change of shift woke Frith. One of the men gave Frith a breakfast of cheese, dried fish, and hard flat bread. He took it to the ship's rail and ate while studying the horizon. The view was the same as the evening before—water. Frith decided to use their time at sea to become better acquainted with the knights.

Baldori was the first one awake. Frith attempted conversation, but the knight turned his head away and picked his teeth. Maybe Baldori had difficulty hearing, like old Brother Caedmon, the cook in the monk's kitchen. Baldori lay down and went back to sleep. It seemed knights preferred to sleep away their time at sea.

* * *

Life aboard ship for the next six weeks was boring, at least for the passengers. When Frith mentioned this, Jacob said, "Praise God that He gives us a boring voyage, neither hindered by storms, nor becalmed."

The part of Frith that still loved stories of knightly adventures coaxed the knights to relate their exploits. It helped the days at sea pass and Frith made friends—except with Baldori.

One morning while meditating, he heard Baldori say, "Why does Jacob favor him?"

Frith opened one eye. Euric and Baldori were leaning against the ship rail.

"Otto says he's the son of Jacob's old partner," Euric said.

"A partner we've never met. We don't owe him allegiance."

"We owe Jacob. I don't understand your problem. You got on well with Micah and Levi the years they rode with us."

"Entirely different, they're Jacob's sons." Baldori spit into the sea. "Who is this Frith to us?"

When the ship docked in Italia, Baldori said he was leaving for a few days to visit his family. Frith let out a huge sigh.

Baldori's departure caused Frith to wax nostalgic for his abbey family, especially Alura. If he wrote a letter, was there a merchant sailing for Britain who would take it? The captain might know, but he'd rather someone else ask him. Maybe Jacob.

CHAPTER 7

Abbey of St. Benignus, December, 554

Alura was in the kitchen chopping chives when his letter arrived. Until that moment, her life at the abbey had continued much as it had before Frith left. But none of the kitchen ladies had ever received a letter. They surrounded her and urged her to open it. Alura broke the seal and unfolded it like a great treasure. Everyone admired it, but none of the women could read. Women were supposed to cook, and make soap, and raise sons. In fact, this backward village forbade education of women. Part of Lancelot's undoing was teaching Alura. She'd learned many things from him, but not how to read.

Now she could see how foolish that was. She'd been present when Lancelot taught Frith Latin. Lancelot's method was to draw letters in the dirt and have Frith put pebbles in his shoes to match the patterns. The shapes the stones pressed into his soles, became imprinted in his mind, and he'd learned the entire alphabet in twelve days. She'd seen Lancelot draw the letters plainly enough. She could have put pebbles in her shoes. No one would've known. Oh, why hadn't she? Now she'd have to find someone to read the letter to her. But who?

The Abbot, of course. Alura sent one of the kitchen boys to ask the Abbot for an audience. The postulant returned promptly. "The Abbot says to bring the letter at once." Her brother, gone four months, was not forgotten. Alura flew out the kitchen door and dashed to the office.

The Abbot opened Frith's letter and picked up a wooden handle fitted with a piece of curved glass. "To aid an old man's eyesight." She looked over his shoulder, through the glass. The letters seemed to swell.

"Have a seat," he said.

Alura perched on the edge of a chair next to his desk, and leaned in to see.

He smoothed the parchment and read aloud. "'Dear Sweetest Sister...' That's nice," the Abbot said.

"I had intended to write you when we made landfall in Italia, but I didn't have an opportunity. Now I am in Egypt, land of Moses, land of the pyramids. Alas, Jacob says we cannot visit them as we are on the coast and they are several days journey inland. He says when I become a merchant I can spend my profits hiring men to take me there. He considers it a distraction, but if such fortune ever comes into my hands and I am again here, I shall not hesitate to use a portion of it to visit the pyramids. You, of course, recall the Lord and Lady we supped with at the abbey. They stuck the idea in my mind, and I carry it even now. It is frustrating to be so close to such a wonder and miss it. Still, I am grateful. I have already journeyed as far as they had, and Jacob says we are not yet half there."

The Abbot gave Alura a quizzical look. Alura remembered the Lord and Lady well. She and Frith had clandestine discussions with them about teachings which Lancelot had forbidden them to divulge. Of course the Abbot didn't know about that. "Oh, two pilgrims once stayed here who had visited Egypt," she said. "With so many noble guests, I don't expect you remember them all."

The Abbot cleared his throat and continued. "Jacob is a good man. Not only is he a worldly merchant, but a deeply spiritual man. His practices include morning prayers and a ritual where he wraps a leather strap around his left arm and ties a box to his head. I have seen him do this for some time as we share a room when we stay at inns. He has not confided its meaning, but I must confess I revealed to him our relationship with Lancelot—"

The Abbot put down the page, "There was no need for him to bring up your past to an outsider. You are a saintly person now. Your indiscretions are ancient history."

"Thank you, Father Abbot, but I don't believe that's what Frith means there. Please read on."

"Very well. 'Not of course everything, but the fact of our discipleship and the nature of Lancelot's Grail.'" The Abbot stopped again and gave her an inquiring look.

Alura wondered at Frith's foolishness. Why include all the remarks about Lancelot's secrets. He knew she couldn't read. Who did he think would read this letter to her? "Please, sir, I'm impatient to hear the rest."

The Abbot resumed, "Jacob is very accommodating and able to blend in with foreign peoples we encounter. Every day I am with him I learn more of how to deal with all manner of men. He discretely follows his own spiritual laws without giving offense to any outsider. As Lancelot would say, Jacob has learned to be in the world, but not of it." The Abbot nodded.

"Although he is sharp in his dealings, there is no sense of greed or avarice about him. He does not believe in losing money on one thing then taking excessive profit on another to make up for it. Thus, he justifies not deviating to the pyramids as no business is there.

"He is also considerate of his knights. Did I mention I am at last riding with a company of knights? You met Sir Otto, of course, but we have four men of armor with us, so hold no concern for my safety.

"An example of Jacob's character is this: any Friday we are on land, we stop before sundown and do not travel on Saturday as Jacob celebrates the Sabbath on a different day than we do. Since his knights are Christian men, he offered not to travel on Sunday so we can attend Mass. Is there any merchant in our village who would forfeit a second day's business so another man might follow his religion?

"However, these knights are not very religious, for they decline his offer and we travel on Sunday, anyway. My own intention is to quest for the Grail in the manner Lancelot showed us. As long as I am steadfast in that I feel no pressing need to hold our party back while I, alone, attend Mass. Perhaps at Christmas or some Holy day the knights will want to go, and I may partake of the sacraments." At this, the Abbot shook his head.

"Jacob treats me as our father should have, schooling me in business and teaching me how decisions are made. Often he analyzes his choice, explaining the factors he considered. He does not seem to knowingly practice the impersonal observation of thoughts Lancelot taught us, but he is aware of them."

The Abbot glanced up at Alura and cleared his throat.

"Oh, that," Alura said. "Lancelot taught Frith and me prayers and meditation. Seeking God within."

"And Frith continues to practice these? Our Frith?"

She smiled. "Lancelot made a lasting impression on both of us."

"Well, God bless him for that." The Abbot picked up the letter again. "Jacob's every kindness reminds me of how like a father the Abbot was to me and what a scamp I was to him. Now that I am separated from him, I love that old man more than ever."

A tear from the Abbot struck the parchment.

"I could return later," Alura said.

The Abbot blinked a few times. "No, no, there is no need."

The Abbot continued. "I have been long about my new master, and scant in telling the journey. I shall remedy that now. First, we rode to an estate Jacob leases. We arrived late in the evening and the next afternoon we put to sea. At first I was happy to be done with horse travel, but voyage by ship soon terrified me. The ocean is unlike anything you or I have ever seen. Cold winds pushed our little ship the way dry leaves blow across the fallow garden in autumn. Within hours we were alone in the midst of a vast watery expanse so large the mind cannot imagine it and I cannot describe it. I can tell you, the sea is a thrashing, heaving thing that jounces you up and down continually."

As the Abbot read to her, it seemed Frith was there in person, relating his adventure.

"We were at sea for many weeks and did not stop until we reached Portus, a port outside Rome. One of Jacob's knights, Sir Baldori, is from Italia and seemed happy to be in his homeland. I was glad it put him in good humor because I don't think Baldori likes me. I cannot imagine anything I said or did to provoke his attitude."

Oh, Frith, Alura thought, Don't worry about people who dislike you for no reason.

The Abbot kept going, "At Portus, Jacob delivered the tin we brought from Britain and obtained horses and a string of donkeys to transport us to vineyards and olive groves in and around Rome. We traveled for six days on horseback, and I became a better horseman for it. I had to accustom myself to my new mount, this being only the second horse I had ridden (if you don't count the cruel trick our brothers played on me as a child.)"

The Abbot smiled again. "I remember Frith telling me that story."

Alura smiled at the memory, but gestured for the Abbot to return to Frith's letter.

"This time the knights led the donkeys, and Jacob and I rode at the rear. My horse seemed to have a dislike to following donkeys, but there was nothing I could do about a horse that had preferences."

Alura recalled Lancelot's admonition against preferences and laughed.

"Twice on the ride we stayed at inns, but the other nights we slept outdoors. The knights made a fire and Sir Euric shot pheasants which he cleaned and cooked. I have learned men traveling without women must do for themselves. These men can mend a torn garment or dress a wound as easily as they can dress and cook a bird. The pheasant was delicious although Jacob did not partake. He says he does not eat game. Too bad—for all our knights proved to be excellent hunters." The Abbot licked his lips. "We've not had pheasant in a long time."

"You're right. We haven't," Alura said. "I could ask in the village."

The Abbot looked back to the page. "Rome is a great city with more people than live in all of Britain. I know it seems like an exaggeration, but everything I encounter on this journey is beyond any understanding I had of the world before I left. Jacob purchased tall amphoras of oil and wine. When the ship was filled, we set sail for Egypt. Jacob says we will be here for about two weeks." The Abbot had a wistful look. "Rome, yet he makes no mention of visiting Saint Peter's..."

"Perhaps, there wasn't time," Alura said. "But is there more?"

"Aboard ship the knights are often stoic or sleeping. Sir Otto you met, but let me name our remaining company and tell you a little about them. All the knights get on well with each other as they have been in Jacob's service for years. They say they are all from different lands, but I confess I am too ignorant of the world to understand where their countries are."

The Abbot's voice sounded scratchy. Alura spied a pitcher of water and poured a goblet for him.

The Abbot took a long drink. "Sir Euric is from Cornwall, but Jacob told me Euric's ancestors were Goths who came from Breton in northern Gaul." The Abbot looked up from the letter, "Do you know where Breton is, Alura?"

"Please, tell me after."

The Abbot nodded and continued, "I saved the most unique knight for last, Sir Nazar. His homeland is where Jacob says we are going when we leave Egypt. His features are unlike any man in Britain. His skin is the color of old shoe leather—darker than a farmer who spent every day in the sun. He is friendly, but I am told he is from the fiercest warrior tribe, and is possibly the best fighter among them. (This is not my opinion, but that of the other knights.) He and I have not conversed much, but he once said the land he came from consisted almost entirely of rocks and sand. From his description, it must resemble Egypt, dry, sandy and hot. Egypt draws the moisture right out of you, making your nostrils burn and your lips crack. If our next port is indeed like this one, I shall be a roasted goose."

Alura giggled.

"You may tell the Abbot that among the Christian monks in Egypt are two sects we do not have in Britain." The Abbot paused, and Alura perceived his pleasure that Frith included a message for him.

"The first are stylites, monks who make their hermitage atop a tall pole from which they never descend. I am told some stay up there twenty or thirty years. No one explained to me their reason. Perhaps they think themselves twenty feet closer to heaven than the rest of us. Perhaps to assure that visitors don't barge in on them as we did Sir Lancelot.

"The second group, called 'holy fools,' reject the ways of normal and act like they have lost their mind, giving no heed to what ordinary mortals think of them. It is considered a much revered state. Perhaps being a holy one frees you from care for what others say. Nevertheless, tell the Abbot not to worry, these are the exceptions. Egypt has as many ordinary monks as we do in Britain." The Abbot laughed. "Ordinary monks."

The Abbot returned to Frith's letter. "Nearly every day on land has been an adventure, but I don't get to explore much on my own as Jacob keeps me close by, teaching me his business. In Egypt we have sold the wine and oil we brought from Italia and he is purchasing cotton fabric for the next part of our journey.

"Jacob's eldest son, Levi, stopped in Egypt on his return voyage to Britain. Jacob invited me to join them at feast, but I declined for your sake. Levi has agreed to carry this letter, so I am furiously putting nib to parchment instead of supping with them."

The Abbot struggled to make out the bottom of the parchment where Frith's calligraphy seemed, even to Alura, rushed and ill-formed. "Dear one, Jacob has just returned, and Levi is sailing now so I must end my tale, but know I am ever thinking of you. I shall write you again. Your brother, Frith."

* * *

That was the first reading. In the weeks that followed, Alura asked the Abbot read it to her again and again. She also solicited the help of numerous monks and any travelers who could read Latin. Frith's letter became so fixed in her memory she instantly detected any omitted or misread word. She made it a habit to follow the shapes on the page with her eyes as the readers spoke. Eventually Alura could read Frith's letter herself. Thereafter she could revisit his travels anytime she wanted.

And she had a new skill. At times, she snuck into the chapel to look over the great altar gospel. Soon, she could read it as well—slowly, but with increasing speed. She sometimes took refreshment to the monks in the scriptorium and studied the manuscripts on the writing desks while the monks ate.

When Frith's second letter arrived, she read all but a few new words without help.

CHAPTER 8

Tyre, Lebanon, November, 554

Frith sat on an ancient stone wall looking out at the port of Tyre where Micah, Jacob's second son, had met them when they docked. At first, Frith thought Micah had come to greet them in his nightshirt. Once ashore, Frith discovered that men in this place walked about unabashedly in long flimsy gowns. Even Jacob and Nazar had donned this type of garment since they arrived. And he was going to be asked to do the same. He wasn't looking forward to it.

Frith shifted position. The wall may have been hundreds of years old, but age had not made it a soft seat. Their ship was anchored on the north side of a long peninsula where the blue Mediterranean Sea licked the vessel's waterline. Behind him was Jacob's warehouse. A steady stream of bearers made a circuit between the ship and the warehouse, carrying bolts of cotton fabric into the building and returning with hampers of dates and spices to stow aboard ship.

Frith had been assigned to keep an eye on the bearers, making sure none of the cargo disappeared. Micah and Jacob were in the warehouse going over Micah's purchases and supervising their packing. Frith marveled that Micah, who was barely older than he, had been sent on his own into this strange land, responsible for cargo worth a small fortune.

Although the dates and spices would bring a good price, Jacob said true money would be made on the ethereal fabric, silk. The markets in Tyre were full of men selling silk, but Jacob wasn't buying. He planned to seek silk farther inland at Merv where prices would be lower. Frith had no idea where that was. He supposed he'd find out.

Jacob told Frith if he wished to write Alura a second letter, Micah would take it. Frith's problem was they'd only arrived yesterday, and Micah was leaving today. Nothing newsworthy had happened in the few weeks since his previous letter. But she would want to hear from him, so he settled on describing the strange attire men wore in Tyre and his visit with Jacob to a tailor to be measured. Frith wasn't sure he'd be comfortable going out in public like that, but perhaps imagining him in a dress would give Alura a laugh.

He patted his tunic to make sure the letter was still there. He missed Alura and writing letters only made him think of her more. But if she missed him too, another letter might comfort her.

A scorpion scrabbled its way up onto the wall. Frith scooched away from it. It halted as if assessing his movement; its dangerous stinger arched, ready to strike. How could he have forgotten to tell Alura about scorpions? There certainly weren't creatures like this in Britain. He briefly considered un-sealing the letter and adding to it, but that'd take too much time. He'd definitely describe scorpions in his next letter.

When the loading was complete, and the bearers gone, Otto and Euric came out. They were sweating profusely, but at least they were still dressed as knights, not as men ready for bed. "Frith, you're relieved of your watch," Otto said. "Jacob wants you to join him and Micah."

The two knights took up positions by the ship and Frith walked toward the warehouse. He saw Baldori standing guard with one of Micah's knights. It had astounded Frith to learn Micah had four knights of his own. Frith always assumed only an older man such as Bedivere or Lancelot could lead a company of knights. True, Jacob wasn't a knight, but he had authority. In meeting Micah, Frith realized even a young man in the merchant trade —someone his age—could have knights.

Frith scooted past Baldori without making eye contact. Inside, the ware-house was like a tunnel made of stone blocks with stout doors at each end. Cool and dark as shade, it was his favorite retreat from the heat. Black soot marks streaked the stones above unlit torches affixed along the walls. When the doors were open, as they were now, enough light shone in that the torches weren't needed.

He tilted his head back and mopped his face with his sleeve. The roof tiles rising from thick beams perched on the stone walls reminded him of earthenware pots—how different from the thatched roofs back home. Most buildings here had dirt floors, same as in Britain, but the warehouse did not. It was paved with stone slabs like the abbey. They called to him to lie down and absorb their coolness.

He heard voices somewhere and followed them, winding his way through shelving racks made of Lebanon cedar. Jacob stored none of his precious goods on the floor, clean as it was. Every shelf was stacked with cotton fabric from the ship. Jacob said they'd remain in Tyre until all of it sold. Frith eyed the quantity of cloth and expected they'd be here a long time.

When he found them, Jacob held out a gown as fine and as thin as Micah's. "Here, Frith, this just arrived. Put it on, you'll be cooler."

Frith's eyes darted around the room. The doors at both ends of the warehouse stood open. Was he supposed to strip naked in front of passersby? And Baldori?

Jacob shook it at him. "Try it on."

Frith hid behind a row of shelving and removed his tunic. He pulled the new garment over his head. The simple shift was long enough to fall to his feet. It had wide sleeves and a hood. He stepped from behind the shelves, feeling like a fool. Of the knights, only Nazar dressed this way.

Nazar laughed. "Lose the breeches too, or you may as well be wearing wool."

Frith's cheeks grew hot.

Jacob came near and whispered, "It's the proper way to wear it."

Frith turned his back on the men. Wiggling a hand under the gown, he loosed the drawstring on his breeches and let them fall. He stepped out of them and hurriedly gathered them up. When he turned around, Jacob handed him a sash and matching scarf.

Frith tied the sash around his waist and held up the scarf. "What do I do with this?"

Nazar draped it around Frith's neck. "You'll want this when the sand winds come. I promise."

A breeze from the Mediterranean blowing into the warehouse entered his gown and tickled the hairs on his legs. He felt cooler than he had since they'd made landfall.

Jacob turned to the gathered men. "Micah sails with the tide, but first we feast. Frith, tell Baldori to stay here with Otto and Euric while the others go eat. As soon as Micah's knights finish, they'll come back, and our knights can join us then."

Did he have to? Baldori would surely ridicule his dress.

He approached the open doors, hesitated, and then leaned out, "Sirs, Jacob says Micah's men should come eat. When Micah's knights return, Jacob's knights can join us... err, them." He ducked back and scampered out the other end of the warehouse.

* * *

The inn Jacob had selected for Micah's farewell had a table that could seat a dozen men. As soon as Jacob finished his prayer Frith tucked in. He liked the food in Tyre. Lamb seemed to be the main meat, but it was nothing like the mutton served at the Abbot's kitchen. Rather than being boiled gray, this was cut into chunks and roasted black on the outside, pink and juicy on the inside. And the spices were... he could write Alura about them, but he didn't think he could describe them. Everywhere smelled of spice, even the dust.

Everything tasted different. The kitchen ladies would never recognize what passed for bread here—flat and thin, with a mild nutty flavor. Frith enjoyed the new flavors, especially dates—he'd never eaten a food so sweet.

Micah's knights finished eating and left to relieve the others. Once Jacob's knights arrived, he put a small stick into a candle flame, blackened it, and drew on the wood table. He drew jagged lines like a bunch of Ws linked together, and then a long curved line, with a dot on the end near him.

"Here is Tyre," he said, "and these are the mountains we'll cross on our way to Merv." He reached past Frith and made a black dot far down the table.

Frith put his fingertip on it. "How long will it take to reach Merv?"

"About six months, I hope. But we've never gone that far inland before, so I don't know what kind of hardships we might run into."

Frith had every confidence in Jacob, but for the first time he grasped the scope of their undertaking. Six months of travel? To a destination none of them had been before? He cocked his head. "Is it worth it?"

Jacob nodded at Micah. "My sons understand why we must try. There are plenty of men selling silk here in Tyre, but they all get it from someone who trades with someone who buys it from the Sogdians in Merv. By the time silk reaches Tyre, too many hands have been in the purse, and the price is quadrupled or more."

Jacob scratched a hatch pattern near the dot he'd labeled Tyre. "It won't be easy. This part is hot sand." Further down the table he drew jagged lines. "These mountains, I'm told, are cold, high, and possibly desert as well."

Jacob's knights shrugged. "It's just weather," Otto said.

Baldori stared Frith down. "You man enough for this?"

Frith swallowed and looked at Jacob. Desert and cold didn't frighten him. The only danger he foresaw in a long ride was a sore bottom, but he was afraid any answer would antagonize Baldori. "I suppose we'll find out," he said at last.

"Tide's near changing," Micah said.

The men stood. Jacob brushed the marks off the table with his sleeve, leaving only a charcoal smear.

They cut through the warehouse and Otto barred the street side doors. "To the dock, Frith, we're all going to see them off."

They exited the warehouse on the seaward side. Jacob's entire party accompanied Micah and his men to the ship. Micah's knights went aboard, but he and Jacob lingered on the quay in an embrace. Finally, Jacob kissed his son, and Micah boarded.

Sailors hoisted the anchor, and the tide drifted the ship seaward. Jacob, Frith, and the knights on shore, waved and called good wishes. The sails were unfurled, caught a strong breeze, and Micah was on his way again.

Jacob's party started back toward the warehouse. Jacob clapped Frith on the shoulder. "Come along son, we won't see that ship again for at least a year."

Frith felt stranded. Wherever they'd been in Italia or Egypt, he'd known the ship was waiting off-shore that could take him back to Britain. It'd given him a semblance of security. That sanctuary had now sailed away.

CHAPTER 9

Tyre, Lebanon, December, 554

"Careful, Frith," Jacob said. "These creatures can kick sideways as well as forward or back."

Frith's curiosity drew him in for a closer look at the strange gangly beast. He'd glimpsed camels in the distance in Egypt, but here one stood in the shade cast by a spice seller's awning. Frith heeded Jacob's advice and approached the camel with care.

The brute showed his teeth and growled like a bear. Jacob jerked Frith back.

Jacob returned to negotiating price for a purple dye produced from shellfish. Frith thought it extraordinarily expensive, but Jacob said it was rare, so he bought it whenever he could. He also bought Mediterranean coral, pearls, and amber. Each day's purchases were packed in boxes lined with straw and stored in Jacob's warehouse.

Frith had accompanied Jacob to the market daily as they sold the Egyptian cotton and bought goods Jacob expected Sogdian traders inland would prize. He supposed Jacob was teaching him the art of haggling, but the market in Tyre was vast with distractions. Why, the whole market back home would fit in a small corner of this one.

A sand-colored puppy emerged from under a table and sniffed the hem of Frith's robe. He reached down to pet it, but the pup shied away. Frith squatted, extended his hand, and made kissing sounds.

Jacob shook hands with the seller. "Come along, Frith." They walked to a stall stacked with bolts of silk. Jacob made a cursory examination and moved on.

The owner chased after them. "Wait. I'll give you a good price."

After four weeks in Tyre, Frith felt almost settled. Tyre was predominantly Christian, but it had a Synagogue, too, so Jacob was able to go to Temple, which seemed to please him. The knights guarded the warehouse in shifts, allowing those who were off duty some leisure. Frith didn't know what they did with their time, but it seemed to make them happy. Nazar had disappeared a few days ago, and if any of the men knew where he'd gone they hadn't said. Frith assumed Jacob had given him leave to visit his family as he had Baldori in Italia.

Frith was comfortable around the knights, except Baldori, whom he still avoided when possible—he still could not get that man to stop hating him. He'd tried to discover how Jacob handled men who disliked him for no reason, but so far he hadn't met anyone who didn't like Jacob. Even those he bested in negotiation seemed to feel good about dealing with him when they were finished.

Although Frith respected the knights, he realized they were not like Lancelot or Galahad or Percival who, upon hearing of the Grail, gave up everything to quest for it. These were practical men of arms, not searchers on a spiritual path, and they were more interested in earning a decent purse than looking for a Grail. Of course, Lancelot was dead. Maybe the real purpose of this trip was to bring him to another teacher. He decided to ask Christians he met in the market if they knew a man as wise as Lancelot. If such a wise man could be found, Frith would stay here and give up trying to be a merchant.

They continued making purchases until the sun reached its zenith. Then Jacob bought them bread, goat cheese, and figs. They found shade, and ate.

"Do you see how to draw the buyer up to your price?"

"Draw? I see you asking more than he will pay, and you eventually meet in the middle. I confess I don't understand why you don't start in the middle in the first place."

"The trick is to watch the buyer, to play him like he was a fish. Offer him discounts grudgingly, as if you're giving him a great gift."

"I see. I think."

"The problem is you don't see. Pay attention and learn."

"There's so much else to see."

Jacob tore a flatbread in half and crumbled some goat cheese into the pocket. "Remember, someday you'll have to be able to dicker on your own, like Levi and Micah."

* * *

In the evenings he and Jacob would return to the room they shared at an inn. Jacob had let a second room for use by whichever knights were not standing watch, but it was often unoccupied. Frith found sharing quarters with Jacob advantageous to his spiritual practices because Jacob was so steady in his own. At night, while Frith meditated, Jacob pulled his tallit over his head like a hood, said prayers, and studied scriptures.

"What is it you read at night?" Frith said at one point. He'd slipped a peek at one of Jacob's scrolls, but the letters were incomprehensible.

"The Psalms of David. I take great comfort in his words."

"Could you read me something, please?"

"It's in Hebrew, let me translate." Jacob read silently for a moment and then spoke:

> "When I consider the heavens the work of thy fingers, the moon and the stars which thou hast ordained; what is man that thou art mindful of him? And the son of man that thou visits him?
>
> "For thou hast made him a little lower than the angels, and hast crowned him with glory and honor."

"Do you think that's true?" Frith said. "That we're lower than angels, but crowned with glory?"

"I would say our body is formed from the earth, our crown is not."

"I don't understand."

"A child born into this world consumes meat and vegetables and grows. These foods are themselves grown from dirt, aren't they?"

Frith nodded.

"So in a sense, the story of Genesis is constantly renewed. Man is literally transformed from earth daily."

"But a clod of dirt isn't a man."

"Obviously not," Jacob said. "The Torah says, God breathed into us. Our true reign is from the crown—from here." Jacob pointed over his head. "Life flows into us from above."

Frith nodded. Here was something he recognized. Perhaps his teacher was with him all along. "Lancelot gave me an experience of that one time."

Jacob's eyes twinkled. "Knowledge of the crown is the state of glory David is singing about."

"But it doesn't last," Frith said. "Or it didn't in my case. One sees the truth, hears it, experiences it, but then it's so easy to forget it day to day. Why is that? Why do we fall back into our old way of thinking?"

Jacob laughed. "It's a gradual journey, our soul's ascent to the crown. But each time we ascend, we, like David, are filled with awe."

"The challenge for me is how to make it stay," Frith said. "I wish instead of teaching me to be a peddler, you'd show me how to remain as steadfast in my practices as you are."

"There's no reason I can't teach you both."

CHAPTER 10

The warehouse was finally nearly empty of cotton. Frith knew what that meant, and he wasn't eager to leave Tyre. He liked it here. He'd even gotten used to his garment, which he'd once considered ridiculous. He was picking up some of the language, and maybe learning some of Jacob's skills in the marketplace.

No reason to worry, yet. Jacob wouldn't leave without his full complement of knights. And he was still short one.

"When is Sir Nazar returning?" Frith asked one afternoon as they left the market.

"He should be back today," Jacob said.

Well, so much for that.

When they reached the warehouse, the place was in chaos—because Nazar was back. He'd brought with him ten camels and two men he identified as Bedouins. Jacob shook hands with the Bedouins and inspected the camels.

Frith had been avoiding camels since the one in the market snarled at him. Now they surrounded him. He noticed right away these animals were different. Camels he'd seen in Egypt and Tyre had one hump, these had two. "Sir Nazar, are these camels deformed?"

Nazar laughed. "No, they're Bactrian camels. Their herds originate from the regions we'll be traveling to. They can endure hotter and colder weather than camels around here."

"Because they have twice as many humps?"

"I don't think so," Nazar said. "But who knows?"

One of the Bedouins pulled his camel's head down and the animal kneeled slowly on its front legs, then the rear legs seemed to collapse forward and the rest of the creature settled to the ground. The remaining nine camels did the same, without requiring encouragement from the Bedouins.

Jacob gathered the knights. "Good Sirs, we have mere days to acquaint ourselves with our mounts for this arduous adventure. Since only Sir Nazar has ever ridden a camel, he's brought Bedouins to instruct us."

"I prefer a horse," Baldori said.

"Then you would end up walking," Nazar said. "A horse would be dead before we got to where we're going. The Bactrian can go six months without water and can forage on thorny scrub."

Jacob pointed toward the setting sun. "We'll start lessons first thing tomorrow. Whoever isn't on guard duty is to be on a camel."

The knights grumbled, but in the morning they dutifully reported for training. Jacob left Nazar in charge and headed for the market, Frith started to follow.

"No, Frith," he said, "you'll be riding with the others."

"But I can barely get along on a horse."

"That no longer matters," Jacob said. "We must master these animals and hone our riding skills quickly, for soon we'll depend on them."

Frith scuffed the ground with his boot.

"Don't mope. Join the knights in your lessons."

"But you're—"

"Don't worry. I intend to take instruction from our Bedouin brothers, too." Jacob turned and left Frith standing there.

The camels were all resting on their knees, chewing their cuds. Frith edged into the circle of knights gathered around Nazar and his camel. Nazar put his hand on its hump and climbed on. He gave a tug on the reins and the beast stood. Everyone stepped back.

"You see," Nazar said. "Camels are more accommodating, easier to mount than a horse. Now you try it. Mount up."

Frith saw the brave knights hesitate, so he held back entirely. The knights had years of horsemanship on him, so let him be last.

Baldori's camel bared his teeth and made a loud moan. Baldori, reached for his sword.

"Hold your weapon," Nazar said. "He can tell you don't like him."

"He's not making me like him any better," Baldori said.

Several of the other camels moaned in solidarity. Baldori's camel curled his lips. Frith thought it was almost a smirk. He was glad he'd waited.

"Approach them like you would an unfamiliar, cantankerous stallion," Nazar said. "As though you're in control, but without malice."

One of the Bedouin walked over to Baldori's camel, took the animal's head in his hands and whispered in its ear. He gestured for Baldori to put himself on the camel, but Baldori didn't move.

Nazar conferred with the Bedouin in a language Frith didn't understand. Then to the knights, Nazar said, "Sir Baldori, please mount the camel, the Bedouin will hold him. Sir Otto, go to that one there. The rest of you wait here. Three of us will take a brief ride and then three others will go. This will allow the Bedouins and me to help each of you with your camel."

Baldori stalled until Otto mounted smoothly and gave him a smug look. Baldori climbed on. When their camels stood, several others started to rise. The Bedouins moved among the remaining beasts making them kneel back down. With Nazar leading the way and the two Bedouins walking next to Otto and Baldori, the miniature caravan proceeded around the warehouse toward the seashore. The camels' heads bobbed, and Frith had to bite his lip to keep from laughing.

Euric, standing guard at the warehouse, shouted as they rode by, "Two finches perched on rolling carpets." Otto called over his shoulder, "You'll have your turn soon enough."

Frith waited with the other camels. Jacob returned and gave him a puzzled expression, but before he could explain, Nazar and the others rounded the warehouse. Nazar lowered his camel and dismounted. "Your turn, Jacob."

The Bedouins made Otto and Baldori's camels kneel and motioned Frith toward the waiting camels.

"Here, Frith, I've got the seat all warmed up for you," Otto said.

"No, Otto," Nazar said, "That one's yours. I want each man to get used to his own camel, just as you would know your horse."

"Makes sense," Otto said. He and Baldori took up Euric's position guarding the warehouse. "Shall we hear that jest again, Euric? I don't think we heard right, did we, Baldori?"

Euric laughed in good sport and mounted the camel Nazar indicated.

Frith timidly reached out and patted his camel's muscular neck. The hair was long and thick—more like stroking a carpet than a horse. The Bedouin nodded his approval. Frith threw his right leg over the camel's back and pulled himself on. The Bedouin handed Frith the reins and tapped the camel's shoulder.

The camel stretched his neck forward and came up on his front knees. Frith canted backwards, holding onto the reins for his life.

Then the beast raised its rear haunches, slamming Frith forward. He grabbed for the camel's neck.

The animal straightened its front legs throwing Frith rearward again. Once he recovered, Frith found himself higher than he'd ever been, able to see over the roofs of the squat houses nearby.

Nazar didn't ride this time, but walked beside Jacob's camel. The two Bedouins walked beside Frith's and Euric's. The camel's gait was nothing like a horse. Its body rocked from side to side rather than bouncing up and down. Frith felt like they might tip over—if he didn't slide off sideways first.

When they returned, Frith was glad to get off. But Jacob remained mounted. "Sir Euric, please replace the knights guarding the warehouse and send them here."

Jacob rode out again, this time with Otto and Baldori. When they returned, he suggested they eat lunch. This met with hearty approval.

While they waited for food, Jacob said, "You see, Frith, horsemanship had little to do with it."

"It was certainly different from a horse," Frith said. "You must have enjoyed the experience, you rode twice."

"I told you, we must master this quickly. I'm risking my fortune on a journey few merchants undertake. We need to understand camels every bit as well as Nazar or these Bedouins."

"But all of you have more riding experience than I have."

"It's all confidence, Frith. Approach and ride any beast of burden with confidence, and he'll respond to you."

Frith nodded, though he didn't mean it. He could never really believe that a creature that outweighed him ten to one could respect him just because he acted confident. Fortunately, lunch arrived and their conversation ended before he revealed his doubts. They moved to the shady side of the warehouse, where two servants unpacked a hamper of food. The men helped themselves, but the Bedouins hadn't joined them. Jacob went to get them.

Frith studied the Bedouins while he ate. When Nazar came over to get more bread, Frith said, "Sir, these Bedouins look more like you than any other people we've seen thus far."

Nazar's nostrils flared. "That's like saying a Dromedary and a Bactrian are related because they're both camels. There are uncountable numbers of Bedouin tribes, none of which equal my people." He threw the bread back in the basket and left.

"I was only… making an observation," Frith said. "I didn't mean to insult Sir Nazar. I should apologize."

"Leave it," Jacob said. "He's not angry at you. He's just making it clear these Bedouins aren't his relations."

When lunch finished, Jacob announced that Nazar and the Bedouins would no longer walk beside them. "We'll leave one guard; the rest of us will ride."

Everyone mounted. Jacob led them away from Tyre into the countryside. The round trip took several hours. Jacob gave them a brief rest, changed guards at the warehouse and they rode out again.

A good distance from town Frith's camel just stopped and plopped down. Frith talked to her, then yelled at her, then kicked her lightly in the sides. She turned her head and looked at him with what he could swear was contempt. It seemed likely he was going to have to walk back to Tyre.

The caravan, by then far ahead, turned around and came back. Frith looked up at the other riders towering over him. He'd never felt so small.

One of the Bedouin dismounted, walked over to Frith's camel, and cajoled her to no avail. He then turned to cursing and shouting. Frith didn't understand the words, but they weren't endearments. The man alternately coaxed and berated her until, for no apparent reason, she suddenly stood of her own accord. He had learned nothing from the Bedouin. What if this happened to him in the desert?

Nightly, the Bedouins took the camels into the countryside to feed, in the morning they returned for more riding practice. Meanwhile, Jacob stockpiled provisions. He purchased four dozen water skins, which he gave Frith to soak. "The camels can survive weeks in the desert without water, but we won't last a day."

Bearers brought large baskets of salt. "The camels need salt, as do we," Jacob said. "I've been assured they'll never run off if we reward them with salt."

While the exact date they'd be leaving hadn't been mentioned, an air of impending departure was building and Frith could sense the knights' anticipation of adventure. To his surprise, he felt some in himself as well.

CHAPTER 11

The following morning Jacob left their room early. Frith, expecting another day of riding practice, dawdled. When he finally finished his meditations, he found a note from Jacob telling him to wear his best robe. Good, obviously no camel lessons today.

By the time he arrived at the warehouse, Bedouins were loading the remaining bolts of cotton on a camel. They tied them in a bundle, covered it with a camel-hair blanket, and cinched it with rope. Had Jacob changed his mind about taking the cotton with them? Was this the end of Tyre? He wasn't packed. Frith cast his eyes about for the knights.

A hand patted his shoulder, and he turned to find Jacob at his side.

"Forgive me, master," he said, "but I thought we were going to sell the cotton here before we left."

Jacob smiled. "We are. The Bedouin is readying it for you to take to the market."

"Me?"

"It is time to see what you've learned. Replace your sash with this." Jacob handed him a length of royal-blue silk. "Sell the last of our cotton and bring me back the money."

"Alone?"

"This Bedouin will accompany you and see to the camel."

"But I can't speak his language."

"You won't need to, he'll go where you go, and he'll also ensure you're not robbed."

"Robbed?"

"By day's end you'll be carrying a lot of money. I hope."

"Where will you be?"

"Acquiring supplies for our journey."

Frith knotted his new sash and caressed the fine fabric. "This is nice."

"It's also helpful." Jacob took his old, plain sash from him. "Imagine you're a prosperous foreign merchant. This is your merchandise, your camel, your Bedouin." Jacob handed him two purses. "Keep the larger one hidden. As the small one fills transfer your profits unseen into the larger. Never let the customer see you have a fat purse. An empty purse will make it seem like you just started selling. Even when most of the cotton is gone, try to give the illusion that you've just arrived with only a small quantity to sell."

Jacob signaled, and the Bedouin led the camel to them. He held the rope in his left hand, a crop in his right, and wore a scimitar at his waist. His eyes were like obsidian and his beard black as a raven. He pointed his crop toward the market road, and Frith set off. The Bedouin and camel followed.

Frith entered the market with his chin up, his shoulders back, and his chest out. He had no need to pretend. He *was* foreign, dressed with a rich silk sash, and his Bedouin led a camel loaded with his cotton.

Over the past month the immenseness of the market had diminished in his eyes. Although different merchants came and went, the rows of stalls were now familiar. He proceeded through them, pausing frequently to show prospective purchasers the cotton and extoll the excellence of his fabric, the quality of the colors, the skill of the weavers. The men would rub the material between thumb and forefinger, hold it up to the light to peer at the thread count, and then argue price.

Frith always started at a price that was ridiculously high and tried to lead the customer the way Jacob had taught. Most of his customers, he left muttering that he had cheated them, so he knew he was doing well. He'd emptied the small purse into the larger twice and started carrying a sample bolt of the cotton on his shoulder so he didn't have to open the camel's pack unless a deal was struck.

While he bargained with one man, a silk merchant from another stall came over, admired his sash, and said, "I can tell you're a man who likes silk. I have the finest silk this side of Samarkand. I'll trade a bolt of my best for your lot of cotton."

Frith chewed his lip. Silk was expensive; this might be a good deal. No, Jacob's plan was to buy elsewhere. He shook his head. "Thank you, friend, but I have no need of silk at the moment."

The man he'd been haggling with bought two bolts. Frith lifted the camel's blanket and allowed the merchant to choose which he wanted. He took the man's money and deposited it in his purse. The cotton was selling fast. He thanked the man, shouldered his sample, and continued through the stalls.

The silk merchant ran after him. "I see from your purse you haven't much money, so I feel it my Christian duty to offer my hospitality. Come repose under my awning and we'll take some refreshment together."

Frith smiled to himself. The man wouldn't say that if he knew the weight of my other purse. Still, it was a kindness, and he deserved a rest. He turned to the Bedouin and pantomimed drinking from a cup. The Bedouin tapped his crop on the camel's knee, and the beast settled to the ground.

"Ziad is my name." The silk merchant pulled out a stool and put a cushion on it. "Here, have a seat."

"Frith. Pleased to meet you."

Ziad unsheathed a sharp dagger, and the Bedouin reached for his sword. But Ziad halved a lime and squeezed the juice into two cups. He put a dollop of honey in each, added water, and stirred them with a stick. He handed a cup to Frith and the other to the Bedouin.

"Thank you." Frith took a sip. Its tartness puckered his lips. He set the cup on the ground next to his foot. "You say you are a Christian?"

"As are most men of Tyre. Did you know Jesus himself visited Tyre during his time on earth?"

Frith ran through what he knew of the gospels, but he'd always spent the Abbot's readings waiting for them to end. "No, I hadn't."

"Yes, and Saint Paul also came here in the early days of the church—more than once."

"Could you show me where?"

"Are you questioning the truth of what I say?"

Frith held up his hands. "No, no, nothing like that. In the land I am from, it is said a saint or holy person can imbue a place with their presence. People make pilgrimages to such sites."

Ziad's tension eased. "Sorry. No one knows the exact location. It's been more than five hundred years."

Frith's shoulders slumped, and he gave a heavy sigh.

"I see you're disappointed. Don't be. We like to believe our whole city is a special place for Christians because the Lord came here."

"Yes, doubtless that's true. But an entire city is too large for what I'm seeking."

"Tell me your desires. I am only here to help."

"I'm… not really a merchant. More a spiritual seeker, a pilgrim, now far from the source of my original inspiration."

Men from two stalls across the way overheard and wandered over.

"Back home wise teachers often live near sacred places. I wished to find the place sanctified by Jesus or Paul because I hoped I'd find someone there who had touched the divinity within us."

Ziad nodded. "You cause is noble, let us help you however we can. Unpack your goods, we will pool our money and free you of your burden, so you can continue your Christian pursuit."

Frith and the Bedouin removed the camel's pack and spread out the blanket.

One of the other men said, "I don't know, Ziad, there's a glut in the market right now. Someone has been selling Egyptian cotton here for weeks. I doubt your friend will get anything for it."

"You're right," Ziad said. "But Frith is a fellow Christian with a worthy goal. We should buy the entire lot and let him get on with his quest."

Frith was no fool. He could tell they were preparing to offer him a low price. But it would be nice to get rid of the last of his cotton at once. So he did what Jacob would do and dickered until they filled his purse with silver. With the deal done, he threw the emptied blanket on the camel, and motioned for the Bedouin to follow.

"Say, that's a Bactrian, isn't it?" a man said, reaching out to examine it.

Frith's Bedouin stepped in front of the man.

"Hold on, I'll make you a good offer," said the peddler.

"Not for sale," Frith said. He, the Bedouin, and the camel sauntered away. Wouldn't Jacob be surprised? Everything sold, and a half day to spare.

Jacob wasn't back yet, so the Bedouin took the camel to join the others, and Frith returned to the inn. He proudly laid both purses, bulging with silver, on Jacob's bed and waited. And waited.

It was long past suppertime before Jacob returned, and Frith's stomach had been growling. He could have gone to eat without him, but didn't. A celebration was in order. So when he heard the latch, he flew to the door. "Jacob, come see."

Jacob smiled and nodded. Frith loosened the purses strings and poured the contents into a pile. Jacob's face fell.

"Isn't it great?"

Jacob looked away. When he turned back, he shrugged. "Well, it was your first time. Maybe, it was too soon."

Frith couldn't constrain a grin. "Look! Look, Jacob." He knocked over the pile of coins.

"Yes, I see," Jacob said. "You'll do better next time."

"Better? Isn't this enough?"

"Not by half. What I sent with you should have brought more gold than silver. The wolves have bested you."

"No, these were good Christian men. We talked about Jesus and Saint Paul. They conjoined their money, and bought the whole lot, so I could be on my way."

Jacob sighed. "Never-the-less, they took advantage of you."

Frith sat on his bed and put his head in his hands, all pride draining out of him. "I'm not cut out to be a merchant."

"It isn't a steep loss," Jacob said. "There will be other cities and opportunities to try again."

"You might be mistaken. I may never be a good merchant. I much prefer spiritual stories to wheedling a few extra scruples from men."

"I enjoy philosophical discussions too, but we have to feed those for whom we are responsible. You have to both keep your mind on high thoughts and do the practical tasks at the same time."

"Do both? I feel I can't do either one."

Jacob covered his eyes then pulled his hands down his face. "Did you have supper? Perhaps eating will improve your outlook."

"I've lost my appetite. I'm just going to do my meditation."

"It's good you meditate," Jacob sat down and wrapped his tallit around him. "It's difficult to be a sojourner in strange lands and remain true to one's traditions."

Frith realized what bothered him the most. "Sir, those men who cheated me were Christians."

"I'm sure they were. I think we've talked enough about them. I was referring to the tendency a life of travel has to lessen some men's ardor for the religion of their youth. They become inattentive to practicing their faith."

Frith wondered if Jacob was talking about the knights. Or him.

Jacob picked up one of his scrolls. "Weigh the truth hidden in this Psalm as you meditate tonight:

> Give ear to my words, O Lord, consider my meditation.
>
> Hearken unto the voice of my cry, my King, and my God: for unto thee will I pray.
>
> My voice shalt thou hear in the morning, O Lord; in the morning will I direct my prayer unto thee, and will look up."

Jacob closed the scroll and began his prayers.

Frith closed his eyes and pondered what Jacob had read. Lancelot had taught him and Alura to turn their eyes upward when they meditated. Was that what was being said, to look up? He thought about home. Today's failure still grated—he never wanted to be a merchant, anyway. That wasn't what Lancelot set him to do. He should have gone home with Micah. Tomorrow he'd tell Jacob to find him a ship bound for Britain. He'd work as a deckhand to earn passage if he had to.

With his plan firmly set, Frith's breathing slowed, and he fell into a tranquil state.

* * *

The morning didn't start as Frith planned. When he woke, Jacob was gone. During meditation he rehearsed what he'd say to Jacob until a great commotion from the direction of the warehouse disrupted his thoughts. He ran outside to find camels everywhere and two additional Bedouins. The number of camels had more than doubled, and most of them were moaning their complaints into the morning air.

Bearers unloaded the warehouse, and Bedouins tied the cargo on the new camels, all under Jacob's watchful eye.

"Good Morning, Frith," Jacob said. "You can ride dressed as you are, but put your winter cloak at the top of your pack. The desert turns cold at sundown. You'll want warm clothes within easy reach."

Frith couldn't imagine he'd need a cloak. It was only dawn, and he was already sweating. Besides, he wasn't going, anyway. But Jacob rushed off before he had a chance to tell him he wanted to quit. There'd be no time to find a ship anyhow, their departure appeared eminent. He should have thought of it sooner. He could have sailed with Micah—or even Levi.

He walked over and stood next to Sir Nazar who was overseeing the Bedouins. The loads they were putting on the camels seemed unreasonable. Packs overhung the camels' sides tripling their width. "Sir Nazar," Frith said. "Isn't it too much?"

"Not nearly. You'd be surprised at how much weight they can carry."

That didn't mean they liked it. Frith watched a Bedouin attempt to tie two large wooden boxes to either side of a camel. The sly old fellow would wait until they were almost tied and then shift his weight abruptly, making one box or the other slide off. It finally required all four Bedouins to tie his load.

The approach of clanking chain mail made the camels agitated. Three knights arrived in full armor despite the heat. One camel spit a foul smelling liquid at Baldori. The knight cursed him.

The Bedouins chattered. Nazar translated, "The Bedouins think your armor is too heavy and inappropriate for the desert."

"Tell them to mind their camels," Baldori said. "We ride prepared."

"Prepared for the oven," Nazar said. "You'll roast out there."

"You're a knight like us," Euric said. "What if our caravan's attacked?"

Nazar gripped the hilt of his sword. "Then I shall strike swiftly and surely, but I shan't need armor, only my blade."

"Let each knight dress as he deems necessary to carry out his duty," Otto said. "…At least until we see what the way threatens."

Nazar shook his head and motioned to the Bedouins to resume loading.

Water skins were filled and fastened onto the camels. Jacob locked the doors of the empty warehouse, and Frith, barred from the reprieve its cool stone walls had brought him, realized something. A merchant's life consisted of always leaving.

The men mounted, the camels rose, and the caravan, now twenty-four camels long, departed. As they followed the old Roman road out of Tyre toward Damascus, it was a sight like nothing he'd seen before. Frith felt part of a grand procession.

The road was old and well used. After a time it turned toward the desert, away from the Mediterranean. Frith noticed the sea's absence almost immediately. He'd been on or near water a long time now and had grown so accustomed to the salt air he hardly noticed it. Now, he only smelled dust and camel, and without sea breezes, the heat beat up at him from the baking ground.

Occasionally he saw sheep in the distance eating the short brown grass. The desert here was not soft sand, but brown and rocky. Within an hour his nostrils burned and his tongue tasted like dirt.

After a long, long time, they stopped and passed the water skins among the men. Frith held it above his mouth and pleasured in the cooling sensation of water trickling down his throat. Near the road grew a thorny acacia bush, and Frith's camel rubbed her side against it in a scratching motion. Frith dug his fingers into her fur and scratched her fondly, which she seemed to appreciate. He decided he ought to give her a name. The men started remounting. It looked like their brief rest stop was over. They planned to ride until nightfall. Maybe he'd think of a name for her before then.

As dusk fell, they made camp along the road, setting up a circle of two man tents. Frith and Jacob shared one, the knights and the Bedouins divided up the other four. The tents were constructed by stretching long pieces of camel hair fabric over poles held upright by taunt ropes. Bedouins made everything from camel hair, clothes and blankets from the fine wool next to the camel's skin, and rope from the coarse outer hair.

Frith gave his camel a loving pat. In a few moments, one of the Bedouins would come to take her into the desert to graze. Unlike horses, there was no need to hobble camels. The Bedouins had them trained to return in the morning. He'd decided to call her Parisa, a name he'd heard in the market. When Nazar heard it, he said not to. Parisa was a Persian fairy, and there was nothing fairy-like about a camel. Frith didn't care. She was Parisa to him. He dug his fingers into Parisa's fur and she leaned into his hand.

CHAPTER 12

Jacob predicted it would take four days to reach Damascus, and it did. In Damascus, they spent the night in an inn and Frith was glad for it. But Jacob warned him, "From here on we'll be sleeping in the tents. Even where we find a caravansary, it's likely to be merely a walled oasis with tents."

A tent was not an inn to Frith's way of thinking. In the morning he savored his bed until he could dally no longer. Jacob was already out of their room, and he hadn't even meditated yet. By the time he finished meditation he heard the others gathering outside.

He came out and found the knights had Jacob surrounded. "Now we know the road," Euric said, "we can see the Romans built it for horses."

"True," Baldori said. "There's no need for these…" He pointed toward their herd of camels.

"An ass is unruly, but less so than the camel," Otto said.

"Is that so?" Jacob said. "Has an ass never kicked a man?"

The knights laughed.

"The road we've been traveling does not continue to where we're going," Jacob said. "None of us have ever been in the type of lands where we ride next. I've studied the matter and these are the only creatures that meet our needs. Look at what they feed on."

Several of the camels were gnawing scrubby bushes nearby.

"But we are adept at managing an expedition of horses and donkeys," Otto said. "Using camels puts us at the mercy of these local tribesmen—strangers whom we know nothing about."

"I trust Nazar's choice of Bedouins," Jacob said.

"Oh, we all trust Nazar," Baldori said. "Just not his shaggy beasts."

The nearest camel kicked up sand with his back leg.

Nazar laughed. "Baldori, he heard you."

A Bedouin went to the camel and petted it, speaking in a tone that, to Frith, sounded apologetic.

Baldori scoffed.

"A camel can carry ten times more weight than an ass," Jacob said. "It'd require so many donkeys as to make the venture unprofitable. We must take the camels." He turned on his heel. "Nazar and I are going to buy provisions for the ride to Palmyra. Frith, make sure the water skins are full."

Frith was left behind with the three remaining knights, the Bedouins, and the camels. He'd rather have gone with Jacob. The camels migrated to an eastern wall and lay against it in a patch of morning shade. The knights gathered near Frith, who was filling skins at the well.

"If Jacob wants to use camels for cargo, fine," Otto said. "But the knights should ride horses."

"Otto's right," Euric said. "Horseback is a knight's natural home."

"Our success in defending Jacob may depend on it," Otto said. "The strength, agility, and bravery of a knight's horse can make the difference in battle."

"Sir Bedivere once told me almost exactly the same thing," Frith said.

"Then you see our point," Otto said.

"And who of us would ride into battle on one of these lumpy rugs?" Baldori said. "We might kill our opponents, but only because they died laughing."

Euric clapped Frith on the shoulder. "Listen son, you're not a knight, so it would seem impartial if you made our case to Jacob for us. Persuade him to give us horses."

"But he is knowledgeable," Frith said. "What if he's right about the lands ahead and we really need the camels?"

"Let him bring his camels, but there should be horses for the men," Otto said. "If he proves right and the horses cannot fare… Well, we'll have camels at hand."

Frith recalled the horse he'd ridden in Italia who hated donkeys. "Suppose there's another reason. What if camels and horses don't get along?"

"I can handle an unruly horse," Baldori said. "If camels don't like horses, that's the Bedouins' problem."

"Let's not imagine a problem that may not exist," Euric said. "Frith, I think that Bedouin over there speaks Latin. See if he knows if the two species are compatible." Euric gave Frith a nudge in the Bedouin's direction.

Frith stumbled, but caught himself. He looked back at the knights who all nodded at him with encouragement. He hesitantly made his way between the camels to the Bedouin Euric had pointed out. After a few attempted phrases he determined the man actually did speak Latin. Unfortunately Frith read Latin better than he spoke it. The Bedouin couldn't read, but was so proficient in Latin that Frith repeatedly had to ask him to slow down. Between the two of them they managed a conversation part words, part gestures and signs. From it, Frith grasped that fierce, sudden sandstorms arose in the desert.

The Bedouin was now alternately pinching his nose and using a phrase Frith didn't understand. If the man could have written it, Frith might have guessed its meaning.

Frith pinched his own nose and said in Latin, "I agree camels stink, but does the horse find the smell offensive?"

The Bedouin shook his head no. He pinched his nose again and put his finger into the camel's nose. The camel snorted. Frith laughed. He didn't mean to offend, but the Bedouin with his finger up a camel's nose struck him as so funny he couldn't help himself. The Bedouin rattled off something in his own language. They were at an impasse, but just then, Jacob and Nazar returned.

Nazar told the Bedouins to start loading the camels as bearers arrived with additional supplies. Frith's Bedouin called to Nazar who came at once. The Bedouin recapped their conversation to Nazar in his own language.

"I'm not sure what you asked him," Nazar said, "but what he's trying to tell you is that, unlike horses or any other animals, camels have muscles inside their nose to close their nostrils in a sandstorm."

Nazar patted the camel's neck and slid his hand gently up onto its head. "They also have an extra eyelid we don't. Sudden sandstorms can be deadly to both man and beast. The camels can sense when a storm's about to happen. The old camels start snarling, close their nostrils and bury their mouths in the sand. When the camels do this, men must immediately wrap their burnooses over their faces."

"And for horses?"

"There's no hope."

Frith knew it. Jacob and the Bedouins knew best—camels were the wisest choice. True, on this journey he'd learned to be a horseman, but he wouldn't say he loved horses any better than his camel. And even though they looked like ungodly plodding creatures, he estimated they were making as good time on camels as they would've on horseback. He decided not to speak to Jacob on the knights' behalf.

The supplies arrived, the caravan left Damascus for Palmyra, and the knights did not get their horses.

CHAPTER 13

Syrian Desert, January, 555

By the time the caravan reached Palmyra, they were actually becoming comfortable with their mounts. The knights no longer demanded horses and had even shed their armor after the second day. They stopped only to add additional supplies—enough to last the men a month or more. Water, too; Nazar said they would not find water until they reached an oasis.

The sandstorm struck their first day out of Palmyra. It came out of nowhere, like a thunderstorm back home. And Frith thought that's what it was. A massive thunderhead cloud suddenly formed behind them. It ran from the horizon line high into the sky and seemed as wide as the whole desert.

The camels immediately fell to their knees and began to moan. Then the dark cloud descended on them, but this was no rainstorm. It blasted Frith with sand from every direction. He instinctively covered his face with his burnoose, but the wind tore at it. He let go of his camel's reins and held the burnoose in place. Sand rasped the back of his hands.

He kept his eyes squeezed tightly shut. He couldn't see, but he heard beneath the howl of the wind shouts and cries of frightened knights. If these brave men despaired, then what hope was there for him? He'd not led a dangerous life, never faced death, but surely it was at hand. Was there a prayer one said when dying? If so, he didn't know it.

Keeping his hands to his face, he bent and embraced Parisa's neck with his elbows, and buried his face in her fur. Terror roared about him. Lancelot had said death was just another experience. Lancelot was wrong.

Abruptly the sound stopped. Was he dead? No. The storm had lifted just as quickly as it came. Frith was elated, but he finally understood Nazar's warning. A horse wouldn't have survived.

With the sandstorm past and the wind dropping, Frith uncovered his head. The Bedouins moved along the line of camels, urging them to stand, and the caravan resumed its trek. Little eddies of sand still swirled about, causing the men to hold their hands over their eyes. Frith peeked between the slits of his fingers, but saw mostly the rump of the camel in front of his. The tan horizon of dunes resembled waves on a dusty brown ocean, broken only by a black rock protruding from the nearest dune.

They'd already passed it when his intuition told him the black lump was a person. He pressed his camel ahead and raced to tell Jacob.

"Otto, ride back and check," Jacob said.

Soon Otto returned with a woman. Her face was thick with sand, only her eyes and mouth visible. Her lips were cracked and dry, but her eyes were a bright blue, a blue he had only seen before in manuscript illuminations and stained glass. Their vivid color enthralled him.

Jacob called the caravan to a halt and had water brought to her. With his own scarf he wiped the sand from her face. She drank the water carefully, like one who had been in the desert before. Jacob tried several languages, but she only croaked incomprehensible responses. However, once the water had done its work, they discovered she was fluent in all of them.

"God's mercy you found me," she said.

"Praise Him that is the ruler of the universe, that we have," Jacob said.

She drank another swallow. "I am Elsa."

"I'm Jacob. These men are Sir Otto and Frith. It was Frith who saw you."

She flashed those azure eyes at Frith and smiled.

"This is too desolate a place for a single sojourner," Jacob said, "especially a woman."

"I was with a caravan coming from Dura Europos to Palmyra. But then the storm…"

"We've not passed another caravan," Otto said.

"It was an earlier storm. I don't know what direction I've wandered from them."

"This is our first day out of Palmyra," Jacob said.

"And our first sandstorm," Frith added.

"We can't return to Palmyra," Jacob said, "but perhaps I can send one of the Bedouins to see if he can locate your caravan. Otto, ask Nazar to come here."

"No," Elsa said. "I've been lost for several days. They're no doubt already in Palmyra."

"What shameful men," Frith said. "They should have searched until they found you."

"Who's to say?" Elsa said. "They might have searched. But in this terrible country, a single moment away from people and you become the sand itself."

Elsa took the scarf from her head and shook the sand from it. Hair the color of midday sun cascaded over her shoulders and down her back. An audible wave of astonishment undulated throughout the caravan. Frith could never have imagined a woman plaited in gold. He didn't think the men with him had seen such as her, either, for they all had dark hair like his. Alura and two of his brothers had copper colored hair, but this beauty had been touched by Midas.

Jacob averted his eyes. "We're searching for the Euphrates. Once we find it, perhaps you can make your way back to Dura Europos. Your city is on the Euphrates, isn't it?"

Elsa covered her head again, the scarf hiding her beautiful tresses in its folds. "Yes, but I'm not from there. The caravan was coming from Dura Europos, but I joined them in Sergiopolis—my former home."

"Well, we won't leave you in the desert," Jacob said. "Can you ride a camel?"

"I can."

By now the camels were at rest, and the men crowded around Elsa. Jacob turned to Nazar. "Ask the Bedouins to redistribute cargo from one of the camels to the others, so Elsa may have a mount."

Nazar spoke to the Bedouins, but an argument ensued. Finally he said to Jacob, "Perhaps she can ride with one of us until we stop for the night."

"Why so?" Jacob said.

"They have concerns which you and I can discuss later. For now, we shouldn't tarry in this open space lest the storm turn back on us. Let this matter wait until we make camp."

"I see the Bedouins' wisdom," Jacob said. "Otto, can you continue with her, or should we look for a rider with a bit more room in his saddle?"

"I think we fit fine," Otto said. "What say you Elsa?"

Elsa moistened her lips with her tongue and formed a smile. "You found me, I will stay with you."

Frith didn't argue, but it was he who had found her.

The men returned to their camels, and the caravan proceeded 'til nightfall.

* * *

At sundown Jacob called a halt. While the tents were being set up Frith made a fire. Firewood was scarce in the desert so there wasn't much to it, just enough to cook on. After dinner the knights gathered around Elsa, who lounged near the tiny fire and fed it small twigs. The Bedouins sat apart.

Jacob took Frith with him to the tent they shared. They began preparing for their evening meditations when Nazar and Otto came in.

"The Bedouins want her gone," Nazar said.

Frith shook his head. Gone? Out here so far from a city—that would mean her death.

"What's their reason?" Jacob said.

"I haven't puzzled that out yet," Nazar said. "Perhaps some superstition…"

"We're not leaving her in the wilderness," Jacob said. "Make that clear to them. We'll take her with us to civilization or some safe habitat."

Frith was relieved. But he should have known. Jacob was a good man.

"Sir Otto," Jacob said, "you must have talked with her on the ride here. What did you learn about her?"

"Elsa is from a mountainous place far north of Italia. As a young girl she was the lover of an Eastern Roman soldier who brought her into Syria through Constantinople when the army stationed him at Sergiopolis. Her Roman died in a battle with the Sassanian army several years ago. When a caravan to Palmyra stopped in Sergiopolis last week, she left with them. She became separated from them in a sandstorm and wandered directionless until we found her."

"What's she been doing in Sergiopolis since his death?" Nazar said.

"I didn't ask," Otto said.

"She says she can ride," Jacob said. "Tell the Bedouins to free up a camel for her. Insist if you have to. Now, who will give up his tent?"

"She's staying with me," Otto said.

Jacob raised his eyebrows.

"It was her choice and I've no objection," Otto said.

Jacob just shook his head and shooed the men out. He turned to the east and prayed, "Blessed are you our God, King of the Universe who has sanctified us and commanded us to provide aid to the lost and desolate."

"Amen," Frith said.

* * *

The weeks that followed fell into a rhythm of striking the tents, packing the camels, riding between peaks of sand hundreds of feet high until twilight, unpacking the camels, setting up the tents, scavenging enough scrub for a fire, eating and then retiring for the night. For a while the caravan followed a dried river bed, but never found moisture in it. Twice they'd located wells, but everywhere else was desiccated.

One time, when they'd sucked the last drop from their water skins and their tongues were parched, a dark cloud roiled on the horizon. Neither Parisa, nor the other camels, forewarned a sandstorm, so Frith didn't cover his face. Then blackness fell upon them with a downpour. Unlike Britain, there'd been no warning thunder, no strike of lightning, just the abrupt crush of water on their heads as if dumped from a pail. Layers of dust that had coated men and beasts dissolved in the rain and ran off them in a milky slurry.

The Bedouins leaped from their camels and hastily threw up a tent awning between four poles. The knights rushed under for cover, but the Bedouins shouted for them to get out. Stunned by the selfish lack of hospitality, the knights refused to comply. But the reason became clear when, in seconds the center of the awning began to sag. The knights dashed to the corners to help hold the corner posts upright. One of the Bedouins pierced the sagging center with his knife while another held a water skin beneath the outpour. They filled as many skins as they could before the storm disappeared as if it had never been.

The desert sands swallowed the remnants of the rain faster than a thirsty camel drinks. And the air was so dry that it absorbed every bit of remaining moisture. Parisa's fur didn't smell wet for long, and Frith's gown dried in the time it took Jacob to raise his face to heaven and say a prayer of thanks.

* * *

Bedouins claimed camels could get water from their food, but Frith didn't see how. The shrubs were stiff and thorny; the sparse grass looked dead.

One evening as he waited for the Bedouins to take Parisa out to forage in the desert with the others, she started rolling on the ground.

Otto shouted, "Stop her! I had a horse twist his guts and die from doing that."

Frith tried to drag Parisa upright, but she wasn't having it. He ran to find Nazar.

"Don't worry," Nazar said. "It doesn't harm camels. The moist earth cools their skin and dust gets in their wool to keep insects out."

Frith squatted down and rubbed his hand in the dirt. It didn't feel moist to him. He was sick of this place—nothing but dry shades of brown. He'd practically forgotten what the color green looked like. He also missed Elsa's blue eyes—whenever he wasn't looking into them. Nightly, she sat with him and the knights around the dinner fire. He'd gaze into her pupils, where the reflected firelight shimmered like a yellow moon in irises blue as sky. If it was up to him, he'd never leave, but Jacob would pull him away as soon as they'd eaten.

He wasn't the only one affected by Elsa. She merely had to drop her head-scarf to get a man's attention, glance in his eyes to mesmerize him, or so it seemed to Frith. She stayed with Otto but flirted with other knights, too. One morning she came out of another knight's tent, and a few days later, another's. Frith was too inexperienced to understand exactly what went on, but the knights didn't seem troubled by her passing among them. He mentioned it to Jacob whose only comment was, "I'm aware of the situation."

That the knights weren't jealous puzzled Frith. But then, Lancelot said anger and jealousy were both offspring of fear. Perhaps the men weren't jealous because knights had no fear.

Frith had long ago realized that his boyhood jealousy of Alura had sprung from his fear of abandonment, but what had he to fear with Elsa? Of course, Lancelot also taught that fear was caused by wanting—the mind fearing it won't get what it wants, or will lose something it has. Frith had no doubt he wanted Elsa. He wanted to drown in those magical eyes and never take another breath.

Originally, Elsa said she'd gotten lost in the storm. But sometime later she claimed she went out one night to pee, got lost in the desert and never found her caravan. Nazar said the Bedouins didn't believe any of her stories. They thought she'd been cast out and abandoned. Frith wasn't deterred. He'd grown up with the sting of abandonment and sympathized with Elsa.

Although Frith enjoyed his conversations with Jacob, they took him away from Elsa. The scent of her perfume would dance like sweet vapors around the edges of his heart as Jacob shepherded him away. She'd linger in his mind and he would have to take slow meditative breaths before he could focus on what he and Jacob were discussing.

One night, after journeying for several days through a particularly desolate land, Jacob said, "Frith, this makes me think of Moses and the Israelites after they crossed the Red Sea."

A lit candle between them flickered as a gust shook their tent.

"Some days I feel that way, too. Lost in the desert."

"No, Frith, they only thought they were lost. Moses was leading them."

"For forty years? They were surely lost."

"Spiritual awakening is like the Israelites crossing the Red Sea. Once we've done it, our freedom's ensured, but God will not allow us to go back. We must face whatever discipline and purification is necessary to complete our journey upward, to reach our inner Mount Sinai. That's why God made his people wander the desert."

"It seems… cruel."

"There was no other way to do it. Temptations and challenges of life refine the dross from our inner self. If we're as rebellious as my ancestors, then we'll be buffed by sand and wind until we are shiny and new. But if we stay steadfast in our quest, then His countenance will shine upon us, and revelation will burst our ordinariness. That is the promised land."

Frith was quiet while he pondered what Jacob had said. Crossing the desert had not been simply following a trail as they'd done in Britain and Italia. Although the only obstructions in the vast, empty, desert were sand dunes, they hadn't proceeded on a straight and true heading. Their route had been serpentine. Their course wasn't determined by the direction they wanted to go, but by the location of the next watering hole. Had he been brought on this journey to wear away his dross as Jacob suggested? Even if his father had intended it to give him a vocation, there was no reason he couldn't use it to quest for enlightenment.

"We assume if we keep our thoughts to ourselves, no one will find us out," Jacob said.

Frith jerked with a start. Did Jacob know what he was thinking? Lancelot had shown that ability on several occasions.

"The Bedouins are essential to us, for they understand the camels and the desert," Jacob said. "But Bedouins aren't a centrally governed people like the Romans or the Sassanidae. They consist of many individual tribes who don't necessarily get along with each other."

"They don't?"

Jacob shook his head no, "I've learned the Bedouins have a saying, 'I against my brother, my brothers and I against my cousins, then my cousins and I against strangers.'" Jacob gave a heavy sigh. "Thus far they've altered our course numerous times just to avoid unfriendly clans."

"I didn't know," Frith said.

"None of the men do. It's a burden I carry—the result of my erroneous supposition that traveling with Bedouins would ensure diplomatic passage through their territories. Who knows to what extent my assumption has kept us in the desert longer than necessary."

"I certainly won't say anything," Frith said.

"My knights aren't fools. They may not know their way in this strange land, but these men are worldly travelers. They can plot direction by the stars and sun as well as I can. If we don't reach the Euphrates before Elsa ceases to amuse them, they may become as discontent as the Israelites were with Moses."

CHAPTER 14

Euphrates River, March, 555

After six weeks in the brown dusty desert they found the Euphrates. It was a great wide river with dark blue-green water. And green. Tall green grass and many green shrubs grew along its edges. It wasn't as lush as the lands of Britain or Italia, but it was green, and that was good enough for Frith.

They turned south and followed its banks. The greenery along the river's edge penetrated into the desert only a small distance on either side before giving way to brown, short grass, and then to tawny, arid, emptiness.

Occasionally they saw herds of sheep or goats grazing on their own. Once they passed a man watering a few skinny cattle at the river's edge. He waved. It made Frith happy, for they'd not come across another human since finding Elsa. Although Jacob had predicted they would encounter other caravans, they hadn't. Perhaps that was their Bedouins' doing.

Their first night by the Euphrates Jacob announced it was the time of Passover. The caravan would not travel for three days while he prepared and celebrated. Although they stopped weekly for Shabbat, the promise of three days' rest next to running water made the men cheer.

Jacob roused Frith before daybreak. "Come with me to the river."

Frith rubbed his eyes. "I thought we could rest today."

"I thought you were interested in your spiritual quest."

"Well, yes, of course… I'm coming."

As he and Jacob made their way past the other tents, no one else seemed to be awake. Even the camels, who'd returned from foraging, lay with their necks extended, their chins on the ground, and their eyes closed. Frith wondered just how early it was.

When they reached the river, Jacob undressed and entered the water, immersing himself. Frith saw his head go under and shouted, "Jacob, you'll drown!"

In a moment Jacob emerged with a look of satisfaction.

"I thought you were going to perish," Frith said.

Jacob, standing shoulder-deep in the water, motioned for him to enter. Frith eyed the little eddies swirling in the current. "I bathe in June."

"That may be your custom, but we're in a different place now. You see how precious water is, how the sand gets in every pore. I intend to bathe every day we are near a river."

"I've heard it isn't healthful."

"Perhaps not in Britain where it's cold and damp, but it's so hot here—"

"The desert's plenty cold at night."

"True, but it's warm enough this morning. And water is life. Try bathing before your morning meditations, you may find it has a good effect."

Jacob's suggestion reminded Frith of the time Lancelot had poured water over his hands. Lancelot said running water had a neutralizing effect that balanced the energia. Frith surrendered. He removed his shoes, kept his robe on, and hesitantly waded in. The current tugged at his clothing.

"Come in all the way," Jacob said. "This is something more than just taking a bath—it's Tevilah, immersion in living waters. Submerging, I become one with the waters of creation. Emerging, I remember the second day of creation when God divided the waters above from the waters below." Jacob ducked under again.

Frith wasn't about to put his head under, but he tried to imagine the water as purifying his energia. And it did feel… energizing.

After a short while, Jacob returned to the shore and dressed in silence. Frith dashed from the river, stuffed his wet feet into his shoes, and dripping a trail of water behind him, followed Jacob back to their tent. He changed into dry clothes while Jacob began morning prayers. Frith took a seat and started his own practices. Did the water have any spiritual effect? He couldn't tell.

* * *

The caravan started out again after Passover and followed the river for many days. Frith changed his mind about bathing and eventually became comfortable leaving his clothes on shore. Tevilah became part of his and Jacob's morning routine. As he left the water, Jacob would recite:

"Thou wast before the universe was created; Thou hast been since the universe hath been created; and Thou will be in the universe to come."

One day the caravan reached a section of the river where the bottom was covered with round flat stones. Jacob said, "The Bedouins are beyond their familiar territory and none of us know where we'll find a better ford. I suggest we cross here and continue south on along the eastern bank."

A Bedouin crossed it on foot and returned, declaring it provided safe footing, although the current was strong in the center.

The men dismounted to lead the camels across, but as the camels waded into the water they stopped to drink… and drink… and drink.

"Don't let them linger in the middle of the river," Nazar shouted. "It puts the cargo at risk. They can drink their fill once they reach the other shore."

The Bedouins got their camels across, but those led by Jacob's men wouldn't cooperate. Even Parisa stood with her face in the water, ignoring Frith's pleas. The Bedouins returned and coerced the remaining herd to cross. Maybe you had to speak their language.

Travel along the eastern side of the Euphrates was the easiest since they'd left Damascus. As they moved farther south, the land became even greener than what they'd been through. There was plenty of feed for the camels. They saw more people and even passed through settlements with structures more permanent than tents. One hamlet in particular had houses made of mud with cone shaped rooftops that reminded Frith of the kitchens back at the abbey.

In another village Frith saw two men with large mallets standing on either side of a wooden trough. They alternated blows, crushing grain into meal. "Jacob, should we replenish our provisions?"

Jacob agreed and called for a brief halt. While he bargained with the men, Frith watched an old woman roll out circles of dough as wide as her shoulders and thin as a pie crust. A large pan, shaped like an upside down bowl, sat over a hot fire. The woman stretched the dough over the dome and in a minute it was done. It smelled like Alura's biscuits. Frith licked his lips.

Jacob joined him. "Saj bread." He selected eleven large breads and offered the woman a coin. She looked at it and shook her head. He offered salt, and she smiled. He gave the woman a small bag of salt and handed the breads to Frith, "Here, pass these out to all our company."

Frith ran back to the caravan and gave each man a warm bread. Murmurs of appreciation followed him up and down the line. But he'd saved the very best one for Elsa. When he gave it to her, she put her hand over his and gave a little squeeze. Frith's heart surged

Travel along the Euphrates was pleasant in all aspects except one—the knights kept embarrassing Frith. Whenever Jacob wasn't around they persisted in encouraging his flirtation with Elsa. Otto had started it, "Men, don't you think it's time Frith had a woman."

"We happen to have one at hand," Euric said.

"Frith, talk to Elsa," Otto said.

"About what?" Frith said.

The knights laughed. He clenched his jaw. They were making sport of him.

"She won't be hard," Euric said.

Baldori cooed. "No, she's very soft."

But Frith didn't know how to talk to women. His only experience had been with the abbey cooks who mothered him and with Alura who'd been his playmate. At home, village girls who talked to him made him all fumble-tongued, and so he'd only admired them from afar. Although he fancied himself in love with Elsa, she was with a knight or maybe knights. Certainly out of his reach.

"Romans say a man ruled by Mercury loves to study," Baldori said. "But, under the influence of Venus, a man studies love. Do you find Venus less appealing than Mercury?"

The tips of Frith's ears burned. He sprinted to his tent.

His failure to progress with Elsa only led the knights to further prompting. They contrived for her to sit next to him at meals. Whenever the caravan paused midday, she was the one who brought him olives or dates. Jacob noticed her attentiveness to Frith and shooed her away. Frith was sorry for that.

That night in their tent Jacob read him Psalm 1:

> "Blessed is the man that walks not in the counsel of the ungodly, nor stands in the way of sinners, nor sits in the seat of the scornful.
>
> "But his delight is in the law of the Lord; and in his law does he meditate day and night.
>
> "And he shall be like a tree planted by the rivers of water, that brings forth his fruit *in his season.*"

Frith noted Jacob's emphasis on the last words.

> "The ungodly are not so," Jacob read, "but are like the chaff which the wind drives away."

* * *

As they continued south, Frith worried the situation was getting worse. If Jacob wasn't present, the knights would openly suggest Frith to Elsa, right in front of him. He felt obligated to apologize for the knight's unmannerly comments. She'd smile warmly and pat his face, making his heart flutter.

On the next Shabbat, Frith finished his morning meditations and went looking for breakfast while Jacob, who tended toward long contemplations on Shabbat, remained in their tent. Elsa was the only one up. He sat down next to her. "Where are the others?"

"Sleeping I hope."

She fed him some bread and dates. The sweet brown fruit had never tasted so good.

She put her face close to his. "I'm glad it's just us. I have a favor to ask."

Her breath on his ear was very pleasant, but it also made him anxious. He craved this intimacy yet feared she wouldn't like him. But why did he imagine that? She acted like she wanted him. Or was that just her manner?

Involuntarily he turned his face downward. Oh, why, when Lancelot taught him how to remain centered, hadn't he mentioned what nearness to a woman could do to one's awareness of self?

Elsa lifted his chin and brought his eyes level with hers. "I see you're an honorable young man. I feel I can trust you."

Her reliance on him revealed itself in the blue pools of her eyes. He nodded.

"I'm aware you bathe daily. You're a very clean young man."

What did that have to do with anything?

"We ride every day by this river, and I too would like to have a bath. But I worry the Bedouins will spy on me."

Entranced, Frith nodded his head.

"You, I trust. Let's go to the river and bathe while the others are still in their tents."

"But I've already had my bath—I bathed with Jacob before dawn."

Elsa spontaneously hugged him. "Oh I don't mean we should bathe together. I know you're too honorable for that. I merely want you to keep watch... to make sure other men do not exploit my vulnerability."

Her warm, soft, breasts pressed against him. How could he say no?

Elsa let go of him. "I so hoped you'd be my protector I've already brought a change of clothes." She took his hand and pulled him toward the river.

Frith sat on the bank as Elsa unabashedly stripped as naked as Jacob ever had. He quickly looked away, but when he heard her splash into the water he looked back. She was submerged to her chin and her golden tresses floated on the surface like reflections of sunbeams.

Elsa washed her hair and body vigorously, ducking and rising numerous times, providing brief glimpses of various bits of her. Even though he was supposed to be watching for Bedouins, Frith couldn't take his eyes from her. He made a hasty glance in both directions and was satisfied they were alone.

Elsa stood and strode swiftly out of the water toward him, and Frith stared. He couldn't help it. He'd never seen a naked woman, and the sight was not as he'd imagined. The kitchen ladies' bosoms swayed beneath their blouses when they moved, but this sight was... compelling. His eyes swept down her and he was captivated. She laughed and his eyes jerked up to meet hers. She smiled and he flung his eyes away.

"It's all right, Frith. If I minded I wouldn't have asked you to stand watch."

She began to put on her clothes, but he refused to look at her again until she had dressed. By the time they returned to camp the knights were awake, so he left her with them.

The rest of Shabbat Frith stayed in the tent while Jacob read him Psalms and discussed the difference between mercy and justice. Frith didn't add much to the conversation.

That night the desert was as cold as it'd ever been. Frith shivered in his bed while Jacob snored. Sometime after he'd fallen asleep, he felt warmer. He was dreaming of Elsa's warm breasts against him, and it felt so real, so warm.

He came awake. Elsa's hand was under his nightshirt, stroking his chest, his abdomen, his thighs. Before he was fully awake, she grabbed him, rolled up on him, and put him inside her. He started to speak, but Elsa clamped her hand over his mouth. "Let the old man sleep," she said.

Elsa took command and led him through the act. Afterward, he snuggled against her. What an experience! Surely this was love. His bed was warm at last and he slept with the angels.

* * *

A tug woke Frith with a start. Jacob dragged Elsa from the bed. "What have you done? Get out!"

"No!" Frith said.

"Be quiet!" Jacob snatched up Elsa's nightshirt and threw it at her. "Cover yourself." He pushed her out of the tent. "Go find yourself a knight."

Elsa scurried out of the tent without a backward glance.

"Get up now, Frith, we're going to the river to pray." Jacob stormed out of the tent before he could answer.

Unsure what to do, Frith stumbled out of bed and followed him.

When they returned from the river, Jacob ordered the camp struck. While the Bedouins loaded the camels, he berated the knights. "She's not alone in blame; I know this is your doing. You put her up to it."

The knights looked at one another, but none of them spoke.

"If we weren't a thousand leagues from nowhere," Jacob said, "I'd trade the lot of you for a good dog."

Otto snorted. The others broke into laughter.

"If you think this is funny... I'm not in a mood to be trifled with—you are not in my favor."

"Frith's a grown man," Otto said. "What's wrong with his acting like one?"

Jacob's face turned fiery red, but his voice cold and logical. "You've forgotten your own youth. Men his age think sex *is* love. Now he'll not think about anything else. And consider this; his heart will break when she moves on. As we all know she will. So how have you done him a favor?" He turned abruptly and climbed on his camel. "Mount up, we leave now."

* * *

Parisa followed the other camels automatically. It was a good thing, for Frith's thoughts were stuck on Elsa. He replayed last night's events, he burned to ride beside her, but Jacob obstructed his purpose and kept them at opposite ends of the caravan. What Jacob had told the knights was wrong. Elsa wouldn't break his heart. She wasn't going to leave.

At dinner, Jacob prevented Elsa from sitting next to him, but as they went to their tent Frith passed by her and straggled a moment to smell her hair.

She turned her face up and said into his ear, "In the morning, when Jacob finishes his bath, tell him you want to tarry longer in the water and that you'll catch up. I'll be hiding nearby and will come to you as soon as he's gone."

Jacob leaned out of their tent. "Frith, where are you?"

She pressed her warm mouth against his lips and sent him away to a night of anticipation with little hope for sleep.

The next morning Frith followed her plan, and as soon as Jacob was out of sight she appeared on the shore. He ran from the water as naked as Adam, and she his Eve. He spread his robe on the sand for her. As they made love on the river bank, the dawn tinted pink, and then lavender. It was an even more beautiful color than green.

CHAPTER 15

Baghdad, April, 555

Frith could not have imagined a city as large as Baghdad. It took time before he grasped its scope, for when they first approached, it seemed to be just another farm village. Only the village didn't end. Dirt roads became stone streets. The buildings grew larger, their architecture more sophisticated. It became apparent the surrounding villages—already larger than the village outside the abbey—were just the fringe of a carpet that went on forever.

Frith would have been more excited by it all, but last night, while camped on the outskirts of the city, Jacob had reminded him Elsa had to leave the caravan in Baghdad.

"We mustn't abandon her," Frith had said.

"We're not. This has always been the plan."

"No, it wasn't."

"Yes, it was. When we rescued her from certain death in the sands, I only agreed to take her to civilization. Tomorrow we'll fulfill that obligation."

"It'll break her heart." Really, it would break his. He couldn't imagine life without her.

"I... think not," Jacob said.

Why shouldn't Elsa's heart break? Hadn't he professed his love for her? No, actually he hadn't, he realized. But he would. It didn't matter if she was older, or a foreigner. This was love, he was sure of it. And it was everything people ever said it was.

"Anyway," Jacob said, "Where we're headed after Baghdad, not even Bedouins have ventured. It will be no place for a woman. Besides, we'll need her camel for cargo."

"She can ride with me," Frith said.

"No, she can't. But since you have such an affectionate rapport with her, I think you must be the one to tell her."

"Me? Why me?"

"Because it's the right thing to do. If you're man enough to have been with her, then you're man enough to tell her to her face. I shan't let you leave it to one of us."

"But it's not my decision."

"No, it's mine," Jacob said. "But Elsa's a woman of this world. She's known all along she'd be leaving."

That was last night. Today, as they rode, Frith kept staring at his hands holding the reins. Whose hands were they? These hands belonged to a man who wanted to hold on and never let go—someone he had never been before. Frith finally understood what Alura had gone through when she fell for Lancelot, and she'd been right, love hurt.

On the way into Baghdad his thoughts flitted between trying to imagine how he'd tell Elsa and how he could leave the caravan with her. He'd rather make a life with her among the Sassanians than spend another year on a camel without her. A third possibility—stay in Baghdad with her and rejoin the caravan when it returned. He had to admit it didn't seem likely Jacob would agree.

Jacob located an inn in the part of the city where caravans were quartered. The "inn" was actually a cluster of cottages whose walls were made of stones, stacked, but not mortared. The roof was constructed of wooden beams stretched between the supporting walls and layered over with flat rocks. The door was short, and once inside, the cottage felt to Frith like a cave.

Elsa appeared at their door. "You wanted to see me?"

Jacob stepped outside. "I'm going to see about our supper. Frith has something to say to you."

Elsa pulled Jacob's shoulder down to her level and said, "I owe you my life for what you've done. Thank you."

Jacobs used his quietest voice, barely a whisper, "I did only as God commanded me. But I'm not pleased with what you've done to Frith. Say goodbye, but do not make love in my house. And don't break his heart."

Jacob left and Elsa entered.

"I heard that," Frith said.

"Perhaps it's good you did."

He grabbed her and kissed her. She kissed him back, but then slid her hands up on his shoulders and pushed their bodies apart.

"We'll not go against his wishes regarding his house," she said.

"Then let's go somewhere else."

"No, it's better we part now with kisses than spend our last night in tears."

"I don't have to leave with the caravan."

"Yes you do, and I know I can't go with you."

"You do?"

"Jacob's been more chivalrous than any soldier ever was, but this was always the way it had to be. I'll make a new start here. I'll be all right."

Tears rolled down Frith's cheeks. Was it unmanly? He didn't care.

Elsa wiped them with her hands and put her mouth to his. "Treasure our time by the Euphrates," she said. "That's something our parting can never take away. Remember the pleasure of it. Don't let your joy be stolen by unhappy thoughts."

And with that, Elsa kissed him again and left.

Jacob returned and announced he'd arranged for their dinner. For the second time in his life that he could remember, Frith wasn't hungry. "Dine without me," Frith said. "I can't eat."

"That's all right," Jacob said. "Fasting will do you no harm."

CHAPTER 16

Frith's weeks in Baghdad were busy. Jacob kept him close as he bought more provisions for the trip to Merv and more goods to trade there. The first days after Elsa left, Frith was stricken by a clutching pain.

"Jacob, it's as if the talon of a sharp-clawed creature has penetrated my chest and pierced my heart. I'm not sure I can stand it."

"Perhaps if you looked at it differently," Jacob said. "Elsa's given you more than one type of experience. This sadness of separation has value."

"I'd rather do without it."

"That's the problem, you're trying to push it away," Jacob said. "You feel loss, but grief is natural. Honor that it's showing you a depth of your being you were never aware of."

"But I don't like it."

"What has like and dislike to do with it? Didn't you tell me Lancelot taught you not to set what you like against what you dislike?"

"Well, yes."

"Then stop it."

"I can't help what I feel. My heart is torn."

"I'm not saying to stop feeling. In fact, feel it more fully, but do it from the place you claim Lancelot showed you. Raise your consciousness back to where it was before Elsa, then watch as your heart goes through what it must to mend. Don't try to stop it, give it permission to let her go."

"Is that what you would do?"

"No. I would acknowledge my sin, forsake it, repent, and pray for atonement and higher ascent."

"But I don't feel sin; I feel loss."

"Then that's what you must deal with. You simply asked what I would do. Try in your own way for higher ascent."

Jacob's mention of Lancelot reminded Frith of something Lancelot had said: "Someday we will lose what we have, but we cannot lose what we are. If we have things we obtained by wanting, they too will pass from us. But when we know the essence that is our Self—that, we never lose."

While Frith busied himself with preparations and his heart and mind underwent its catharsis, he had an insight. It wasn't his mind that touched Elsa's body. After all, only a body can know a body. It was in his heart where he felt bliss, and later, so profoundly awful. So why was he caught in his mind?

The answer was he'd used thinking to hide from his feelings. In the effort, he'd forgotten his purpose was to become enlightened like his master, like his sister. He remembered Lancelot's stories of how he had vacillated between questing after the Grail and thirsting for Guinevere. No wonder his mind was troubling him over Elsa. A quest was never supposed to be easy. Frith needed to find someone who could teach him what Lancelot hadn't —what Alura couldn't. That certainly wasn't Elsa.

In the subsequent weeks, he and Jacob continued their forays into the markets of Baghdad. They bought pistachios, mustard, indigo, castor beans, storax, and many spices unknown to Frith. Jacob said Sassanian silverware was highly prized where they were going, but he was concerned it would overload their camels. He consulted Nazar as to how much weight was too much and then bought less silver than Nazar thought the camels could bear.

"Why didn't we buy more?" Frith said.

"Nazar knows the camel, but neither of us knows what hazards lie ahead. If we lose a camel or two along the way, I don't want to be forced to abandon their cargo as well. When you become a merchant someday, remember not to overtax your animals or your men. Leave a little something in reserve."

In the evenings Jacob hosted dinners for merchants coming from the east. Frith watched him tease information from his competitors about the routes ahead and the markets at the other end. Jacob was skilled at it and soon confided in Frith he had the details necessary for the next portion of their journey.

On their last day he took Frith to Ctesiphon, the capital. They rode southeast, following the Tigris River for about an hour. When they located the palace of King Khosrau, Jacob informed a high-placed official they planned to caravan eastward across the king's empire and asked if they needed any special permission. The official laughed and said there were so many merchants no one even tried to track them. However, if Jacob were willing to pass him some coin, he would prepare a document stating that Jacob traveled with the king's consent. The fee was settled and shortly they returned to Baghdad with a small scroll.

"I doubt this has authority," Jacob said. "The courtier we talked to probably has a trunk full of them in his room."

"Then why'd we pay him?"

"You never know what you don't know," Jacob said. "There may be some bandit or petty official along the way whose fear of King Khosrau is greater than his desire to extort us."

The next morning Frith kept watch as the camels were loaded. Nazar once told him if a camel was overloaded it'd refuse to stand until its burden was lessened. Apparently the silver wasn't too heavy. These camels had no problem standing, and when the caravan set off, they walked as though the cargo weight was inconsequential.

As the caravan made its way out of Baghdad, they passed a woman using a short broom about the length of her forearm. It had no handle, and she had to bend over to sweep. Frith, who had a newly awakened interest in the female form, took notice of her shapely behind. She stood, put her hands on the small of her back and stretched her shoulders back. She turned toward the sound of the passing camels and spying Frith, waved.

Elsa!

Frith's heart leapt, but she just waved again and bent back to her work. As they passed her, Frith pivoted, straining to keep her in sight, but the caravan rode on and he with them.

CHAPTER 17

Elsa! Seeing her again as they left Baghdad undid the balm of all Jacob's advice. The feeling of a raptor's talons tore the fresh wounds of his heart open, exposing all the pain he'd been ignoring since Jacob forced him to leave her. Well, Jacob might have compelled him to journey on without her, but Frith would make him regret it. He'd never speak to him again.

The rest of the day Frith rode at the back of the caravan, staying as far from Jacob as possible. That night he sat with Otto and Euric at sup instead of with Jacob. When they'd eaten, Jacob said, "Frith, time for our devotions."

Frith just stared intently into the campfire embers and said nothing. When Jacob walked over and laid his hand on Frith's shoulder, he jerked away.

"Suit yourself," Jacob said. "We ride at dawn, whether you sleep or not."

Frith stayed at the fire until the last of the men had gone to bed. Finally, he entered the tent. Jacob had finished his Psalms and was snoring. Frith made the briefest meditation, but he may as well have been darning a sock for all the good it did him.

The sound of Jacob's morning prayers woke him. He sat up in his bed and began his own meditations, but they didn't go any better than they had last night. His thoughts had the stench of rotted meat. His feelings were a beast he was riding without reins. For the few brief moments he managed to center himself, he saw his heart like a rent pomegranate, that new fruit he'd discovered in Baghdad. Pomegranates bled red juice like blood when split open. Inside were fleshy seeds that also bled when bitten. Each flowering memory of Elsa gave seed to distasteful weeds of thoughts about leaving her behind—and about Jacob, who made him do it.

Lancelot had taught him the heart and mind were chained like a drawbridge to a castle. You could not move one end of the chain without affecting the other. Frith knew this, but his will wasn't strong enough to stop the tug-of-war within him. When his stomach began to rumble, he gave up on his prayers and went to breakfast.

That day and the next Frith rode apart from Jacob and refused to speak to him in camp. On the third night, during Frith's meditations, Jacob began to translate Psalms in a voice so loud Frith couldn't ignore it:

"Blessed is he who is forgiven... When I kept silence, my bones waxed old through my roaring all day long."

Frith squeezed his eyes tightly shut, pretending he didn't hear.

On the fifth day, as Parisa swayed across a shifting sea of sand his mind returned to Elsa, as it had every day since Baghdad. Love of Elsa, could it be cured? No. But it could be endured. And through endurance, overcome. Never forgotten, but maybe overcome.

Day six Frith began to regret his behavior toward Jacob. After all, Jacob had mentored him, and provisioned him, and had done more for him than his father ever had. Then again, what had Elsa ever done to Jacob that he should've just abandoned her to the streets of Baghdad? So Frith continued his silence.

For the next few days the vista of a great mountain range loomed ahead of them. Frith shaded his eyes from the midday sun with his hand and looked at it. There had been much deliberation last night about how to find the pass that bisected it. In Frith's opinion it was wasted discussion. The tracks of thousands of caravans who preceded them were carved in the landscape. Even he could've followed the trail. He didn't say this to Jacob of course, because his pride was keeping him silent, even though his thoughts about Jacob were mellowing.

The skies over the mountains had clouds that the desert skies had not. On one day they obscured the peaks. Another day they rolled gently down the slopes to cover the foothills with a dense fog. Today a small sandstorm formed at the base of the range and began to swirl toward them.

Frith wasn't concerned. They'd been through worse. He waited to see if Jacob would halt the caravan. It would probably depend on the camels. They sensed the severity of a sandstorm better than even a Bedouin. That they hadn't already dropped down and buried their mouths in the sand was a good sign. This duster was probably nothing to worry about.

As the roiling brown cloud grew, men pulled their burnooses up over their noses and mouths. But still the camels gave no sign of distress. That was curious.

When the storm came closer, they saw at its edge a great horde of warriors racing toward them.

Their numbers were overwhelming. The caravan closed ranks and stopped. Knights drew their swords and Bedouins their scimitars. Even Jacob had his sword drawn. Frith owned only a short knife he used for eating. Still, it was better than nothing. He pulled it and held it at the ready.

They were quickly confronted by a line of men on horseback. Frith's first thought was bandits, but these men seemed more organized—like a company of knights. They brandished swords and spears, but they also carried a banner. An army, then.

Jacob dismounted. The four knights raced to his side. "No, return to your positions," Jacob said. "And remain mounted. We don't know their intentions and need to be prepared. Frith, come hold my camel."

Frith wanted to, but there was still some urge in him to disobey Jacob.

Jacob spun around and gave him a hard look. "Frith!"

Frith told Parisa to kneel, and he dismounted.

The leader jutted his chin toward Frith and said something to the man nearest him.

Before Frith knew what was happening, the soldier galloped in, leaned from the saddle, and grabbed him by his arm. The soldier's fingers dug into Frith's muscles so deeply he felt like his sinews were separating. Frith was yanked up and thrown face down over the horse's withers. As they galloped away, the horse's shoulder blades pounded Frith's stomach and sand thrown by its hoofs got in his mouth. When they reached the line of soldiers, the man threw him off the horse like a child's doll.

The leader of the group grinned. "Now we have your son, we'll talk."

Son? He wasn't Jacob's son. He wasn't any more related to Jacob than a lamb was to a goat. Frith sat up and massaged his arm. They had the wrong man. It didn't seem like the best time to tell them so, though. One of the horsemen put a spear on him and Frith stayed where he was, but he could hear everyone.

Otto reacted first, shouting commands and organizing an attack. Jacob held up his hand. "No, Otto, just give me Nazar."

"No, Jacob," Otto said. "This is what we're here for."

"I know," Jacob said. "But we don't know what they're here for."

"It's pretty obvious."

"Not necessarily." Jacob remounted his camel. "Nazar, come with me. The rest of you stay with the caravan."

The knights grumbled as Nazar rode forward, his hawk-like nose and sharp eyes looking fierce.

Jacob looked back at Otto. "I didn't mean you shouldn't arrange yourselves for battle."

The grumbling stopped and the knights and Bedouins shifted into strategic positions.

Jacob started his camel slowly toward the line of horsemen. "Do you know their tribe?"

Nazar rode beside him. "No, I don't recognize the clothing. Their only resemblance to Bedouins is that they wear burnooses."

Jacob looked over at Nazar. "Sheath your weapon, but keep a hand on its hilt. Let's not appear too threatening until we see who these men are."

As Jacob and Nazar approached, the leader rode a few lengths closer to them. He wore a silk tunic covered by a fur vest. His pants, puffy like the sleeves of a blouse, were tucked into boots made of fur.

Jacob spoke in Sogdian, slowly enough for Frith to pick it up. "You have my man."

The man answered in the same, slow Sogdian. Frith got the impression it wasn't his native tongue. "You have a small army in my liege's territory."

"No army," Jacob said. "Just a large caravan. Who is your master?"

"The Prince of Behistun."

Jacob breathed a sigh of relief. "And you are his captain?"

The captain yielded a small smile of pride, then quickly regained his stern expression. "I am."

"And who is your Prince's master?"

The captain looked offended. "No man. The Prince is his own master."

"I meant no offense. I probably misspoke. What is the name of the king to whom he owes his allegiance?"

"King Khosrau, of course, ruler of all Sassanian lands."

Jacob turned and reached inside one of the packs tied to his camel. Two of the guards charged to the captain's side, spraying Frith with dirt in their wake.

"Ease your men's minds, Captain—I have a document to show you." Moving slowly and deliberately, Jacob fished out the scroll and held it open so the captain and his men clearly saw the royal seal.

The captain leaned in closer. When he looked up he said, "On behalf of the Prince, we will be pleased to escort King Khosrau's guest to the palace of Behistun."

Jacob put the royal permit back into his pack. "Frith, you can come now."

Frith was still shaking, but he walked with as much dignity as he dared to the side of Jacob furthest away from the captain's men. "Thank you. Thank you. Jacob, I'm so sorry for the way I acted before—"

"Not now, Frith," Jacob said. "Go mount your camel."

Nazar rode back to the knights and quickly filled them in on what had happened. The captain turned his company around and the caravan followed it up into the mountains.

The rest of the way to Behistun, Frith alternated between gratitude for being saved and guilt over how he'd treated Jacob. It seemed silly now to have ever blamed him for Elsa. Jacob was right, the plan had always been to leave her somewhere safe and go on. And hadn't Jacob been brave? Imagine, facing an army without a weapon drawn—all to save him.

Behind him he could hear Otto and Nazar.

"Horses, Nazar, do you see? I told you we could've had horses."

"That's ridiculous. Look where we've been. A horse never could've lived all those months in the desert. What would he drink? Would he eat thorns?"

"These men have horses."

"They live in these mountains. There are probably ample streams and forage."

"Well, by God, if we ever make this journey again, I'm bringing a horse."

"You do that Otto. We can all share him for supper the second week out."

CHAPTER 18

Behistun, June, 555

Jacob's letter of passage proved its worth, for the Prince of Behistun showed them every courtesy. But Jacob said they couldn't tarry there for they still had Hamadan, Teheran and Rayy ahead of them. East of Behistun the caravan route was well established. Fortified caravansaries were located about a day's ride apart. There they'd spent their nights in safety and Frith was glad for it. Being taken hostage had scared him witless.

From Rayy to Meshed Frith needed his winter cloak even in daytime, for they were in mountains cold with snow. He rode close to Jacob, hoping to make up for the way he'd behaved. He'd apologized repeatedly, but each time Jacob told him to forget it, "That's the past."

Still, it seemed to Frith like he'd failed to become the man Jacob expected. The knights had suggested that being with Elsa made him a man. But Jacob said a man accepted the consequences of his decisions. Frith thought he'd done that when he told Elsa goodbye. But now he understood he'd only fooled himself. His resentment had been that of a child, not a man. Would Levi or Micah have treated their father as he had?

Lancelot once said, "Our minds are full of pettiness not because of emotional pain, but because we hold on to our petty thoughts."

Frith had faltered in the first test of his quest and worried he'd lost ground. Well, he would just have to work to make it up.

Merv, August, 555

The mountains ended east of Meshed, and the caravan descended into another desert. The rest of the way to Merv they endured strong winds that made the sky perpetually yellow with sand. When they finally reached Merv, Jacob seemed exhilarated. "Frith, we've arrived at the market of the world. The most precious commodities from east and west pass through here."

As they rode through the market, Frith understood what Jacob meant. He'd never imagined such a diversity of goods in one place. Stalls loaded with silk, satin, musk, and fragrant spices shared the market with men selling the more mundane—pots and pans, mutton, and rice. Jade and blue lapis were for sale everywhere. Why, the entire market of Tyre, which so amazed him at first, seemed tiny by comparison.

Jacob located a site near the market where they could set up a secure camp. "Men, unload the camels. The Bedouins are going to take them into the countryside to fatten up for the trip back. We'll remain here 'til we've sold everything and procured silk with the profits."

To create a more secure camp, Jacob had the tarps normally used to construct six smaller tents strung together into one large rectangular awning. It could have housed a dozen men, except it had no sides. The cargo was stacked in a long center row and covered. The men's bedrolls were then arranged around its perimeter. No one could pilfer anything without rousing the knights.

Otto and Jacob were overseeing construction. Frith walked over to them. "Aren't we going to set up a stall in the market?"

Jacob shook his head. "There's no reason to flaunt our abundance. We'll leave everything at camp and only carry samples to market. The knights will be able to guard it better here."

"But this tent has no sides."

"And no direction to approach unseen," Otto said.

In the morning, Frith, carrying a satchel with samples of the larger items, accompanied Jacob to the market. Jacob carried hidden pouches of gems, pearls, and coral on his person. Frith also had numerous small packets of precious spices secreted beneath his cloak. He smelled like a walking sachet.

"We're looking for merchants who seem well established," Jacob said. "They probably wouldn't remain long if they routinely cheated people. We'll show them our samples and if they express a sincere desire to purchase, I'll have the appropriate quantity brought from camp."

Frith tried to spot established merchants, but he was instantly distracted by the diversity of people gathered in the market. The merchants were as varied as the goods. Here he saw men with long thin faces, prominent noses, and deep-set eyes. There he saw men with skin the color of butter, flat faces, and round eyes that appeared to have hardly any eyelids. Still others had neat pointed beards, long dark hair, and rather corpulent figures. Many wore knee-length silk tunics belted at the waist over narrow trousers and high leather boots. Frith was painfully aware he and Jacob were the most plainly dressed among them.

Frith followed Jacob to an area crowded with spice sellers. The more permanent stalls had flat wooden trays as wide as a man is tall. These were divided into sections the length of Frith's forearm. Each section held a different spice. Poorer merchants simply spread out open sacks of their commodities in front of them and called out for buyers. The market was a cacophony of animal sounds and men's voices. Frith bumped against one of the spice stalls and a pungent aroma assaulted his nose.

"Frith, be careful with your bag," Jacob said. "You'll dint the silver."

* * *

Even after several days, the market didn't grow commonplace. The merchants in Merv were indeed impressed by the goods they'd brought from Tyre and Baghdad. Jacob was extremely skilled at bargaining and Frith tried to learn from him. Although merchants in Merv came from everywhere, the language in which they did business was Sogdian, and his grasp of the language had become nearly as strong as theirs since Tyre.

Frith wondered at how small his world had once been. He'd begun this journey knowing only English and Latin and hadn't even imagined other languages existed. Now, he could make himself understood, more or less, in three, and he sensed that was only the beginning, for it seemed every place he went people spoke differently. It was also evident most successful merchants, like Jacob, knew any number of languages.

After Jacob concluded a particularly heated negotiation, Frith said, "When these merchants become emotional, they talk too fast for me to follow what's being said."

"Yes, Sogdians learn to bargain passionately very young. I've heard Sogdian boys are taught how to read and conduct trade at age five. By twelve they're sent on their own to do business in a neighboring state."

Here he was a grown man, and just starting to learn what a Sogdian masters as a child. "So are all Sogdians traders?"

"Of course not. Many are skilled carpet weavers, glassmakers and wood-carvers. Others are ordinary farmers—every country needs someone to grow its food. But Sogdian commercial interests are protected by the powerful military of the ruling Ashina clan who ensure their trade routes remain open. Without that, none of us could do business."

Peppered throughout the market, musicians, jugglers, acrobats, and magicians vied for attention and tokens of appreciation. Some merchants shooed them away from their stalls, others encouraged them because their feats drew crowds.

One day Frith came upon a magus in the market. The man had a luxuriant beard and wore a cloak embroidered with stars. He was manifesting light from his fingertips. Sometimes it formed a blue flame, other times a partial rainbow.

Frith called to Jacob. "Come, see this."

"Ah, a man who can see the light," the magus said.

Jacob came over and stood next to Frith protectively. The flame disappeared.

"Do it again," Frith said.

The magus held out his palm and with the forefinger of his other hand made a stirring motion above it. An orange swirl of fire appeared. The fire went out, and the magus extended his empty hand toward Frith. Frith thought he wanted to be paid, so he dropped a coin into the man's palm, but the coin leapt into the air. The magus caught it with his other hand.

"I wasn't asking you for money. I was showing you my hand was empty," the magus said. Even so, the coin quickly disappeared under his cloak.

"How fortunate you can see the light," the magus said. "The ordinary man wants me to manifest mundane objects." He closed his fist and opened it again to reveal a blue lapis bead.

"Wonderful," Frith said. "How is this accomplished?"

The magus picked up the bead and held it between his thumb and forefinger in front of Frith's eye. It shimmered briefly and dissolved into emptiness.

"The veil between light and substance is very thin," he said. "A man who understands that the Word of creation manifested first as light is a man who recognizes matter as solidified light. You're among the very few I've met who can see the light behind matter."

"You saw it too, didn't you Jacob?" Frith said.

"I did. I also understand how it is accomplished."

"You do?"

Jacob tugged Frith's elbow and led him away from the magus. "You told me your master taught you there are higher worlds. Isn't that so?"

Frith nodded, still looking back at the magus.

"Any man who studies the higher realms and perfects his willpower can learn to apply it at the level of formation."

"You can do this?"

"I wouldn't try," Jacob said. "The risk to the practitioner is he can become so engrossed in *Yezirah* he ceases to strive for the worlds above. It will stagnate his spiritual development."

"Yezirah?"

"One of the four worlds or levels of creation." Jacob ticked them off on his fingers: "*Azilut, Beriah, Yezirah* and *Asiyyah.*"

Those words meant nothing to Frith, but he nodded as if he understood.

"Yezirah is the stage in which creation is differentiated into forms."

Frith quietly thought about Lancelot. He'd never witnessed light come off Lancelot's fingers, but he and Alura had both seen shafts of light surround Lancelot when he meditated. Surely, Lancelot had known the higher worlds. Frith didn't believe for a minute Lancelot had been stuck in Yezirah, wherever that was.

"Master, with respect, could you have been perhaps too quick to judge the magus," Frith said. "How do you know his miracles didn't have a higher purpose?"

"The Rabbinical teachings say the difference between miracles and magic is that miracles are created by the will of God, magic by the will of man. That man was clearly doing magic."

They'd reached camp. Frith stopped Jacob outside the tent. "I mean no disrespect by arguing the matter further. I merely want to finish our discussion before we join the knights."

"I'm not offended," Jacob said. "I'm always pleased by these conversations."

"Have you heard of Merlin?"

Jacob smiled. "All men, even beyond Britain, know his legend."

"Sir Lancelot told me that while he was in King Arthur's favor he saw Merlin several times. Lancelot said Merlin was more than a magician—that he used his magic to create situations that allowed men to find answers."

Jacob shook his head. "The difference is, though a miracle may change the course of events to alter an individual's life, it originates in Beriah, the spiritual world of creation. Magic, on the other hand, takes things out of their proper order, altering the balance of the worlds."

"Merlin was a magician, yet he touched the source from which all knowledge comes."

"Unlike the magus in the market."

"Why are you so certain about the magus?"

"Because he was selling his spiritual accomplishment in the marketplace. And for what purpose?" Jacob rubbed his thumb against two fingers. "Greed—madness for a bit of shiny metal."

Frith remembered Lancelot telling him King Arthur believed in living a spiritual life, not in demonstrating spiritual powers. He'd said Arthur treated every knight with equanimity, as if addressing the soul inside the man. Jacob was like that.

"Frith, are you still with me?"

"Sorry, just remembering something Lancelot said."

"Don't be dazzled by phenomena or take a fancy to learning how to create them. King Solomon knew the higher worlds. But despite his wisdom, he fell into a period of madness, lost his kingship, and the inner connection to his spirit."

"He did?"

"Yes, a fall is possible even after attaining the higher realms."

"Jacob, I know you're well-studied, but may I ask, how you know about magic and miracles?"

Jacob pursed his lips and hesitated. "That's not something I'm permitted to discuss. I probably shouldn't have revealed as much I did."

Frith understood. There were things Lancelot made him promise not to tell either.

CHAPTER 19

Bokhara, end of August, 555

Merv was a success, and by the end of three weeks most of their silver goods had been traded. But Jacob still hadn't found silk at the price he wanted. He held back the precious purple dye, certain it would be of greatest value to the men who traded in silk. In the interim, in lieu of silk, he settled for rubies and sapphires, the likes of which Frith had only seen in the rings of bishops visiting the abbey.

"Nazar, have the Bedouins bring our camels in the morning," Jacob said one evening as they ate dinner. "We'll try Bokhara, a city closer to the source of silk."

They crossed the Oxus River and traveled for a week through good pastures to Bokhara. However, the price of silk in Bokhara was not as low as Jacob had hoped. He decided they must press on to Samarkand, the capital of Sogdian trade.

"It'll be an easy journey," Jacob said to his men. "The camels have eaten well ever since we crossed the Oxus and their humps are fat. With our heavy goods sold, they carry almost no burden and it shouldn't take more than two weeks."

Samarkand, September, 555

They rode through the countryside of Sogdiana to reach Samarkand. The soil was rich and the farms productive. At that time the first harvests of summer were being gathered from the fields. Small powerful horses about fourteen hands high were bred here and Frith saw the knights look at them with envy.

The approach to Samarkand was thickly forested with poplar trees that Frith recognized for they also grew back home. Samarkand itself was a fortified city at the base of ancient mountains standing in the distance. They entered the gates and located the place caravans camped, on the city's eastern boundary where the Zarafshon River flowed. Thick vegetation, flowers and fruits were plentiful along the river. What a welcome change from the desert.

Jacob and Frith set out early the next morning, making the acquaintance of as many silk merchants as they could. The king's army was evident everywhere, but Frith found the people of Samarkand exceedingly courteous and polite. Unfortunately there wasn't much silk left. Several of the merchants suggested Jacob and Frith meet the Sultan.

The Sultan wasn't hard to locate. They found him strolling among tables of silk brocade, running his eye quickly over the lot, occasionally rubbing the fabric between thumb and forefinger. The Sultan was a portly man, dressed in a long, deep yellow silk tunic belted at the waist in the fashion Frith had seen in Merv. On his head was a bright purple, conical, soft felt Phrygian hat worn in the local style with the top bent slightly forward. He stood out, to say the least.

They introduced themselves, and the Sultan was very affable. "Let's take some refreshment together. There's a nice place nearby." He pointed toward a covered area where small carpets were spread on the dirt. The Sultan selected a spot, and they sat on the carpet. A boy brought a short table and set it between them. "Bring us something light," the Sultan said. The boy returned quickly with plates of fruit and cups of beverages.

Frith leaned over to Jacob and said in a quiet voice, "I don't want to embarrass you, but I don't know the title 'Sultan.' What's the proper protocol to address such a personage?"

Apparently nothing escaped the Sultan's ears. "Your companion has a question?"

"He merely wishes to give you the respect due your station," Jacob said. "Sultan's a royal title, isn't it?"

The Sultan smiled and nodded. "But I'm not an actual Sultan. That's just what the people of Samarkand call me because I'm related to several Sassanian Sultans."

"Doesn't using such a title make the Sogdian king feel threatened?"

"Not in my case, and here's why. My sovereign, King Khosrau, made a treaty with Istemi, the Sogdian king, to help defeat the Hephthalite peoples. After the war, he had me marry one of Istemi's nieces. The fact that one of my wives is related to the Sogdian king puts me on very good terms with him."

One of his wives? Had Frith heard right?

Jacob cocked an eyebrow. "You don't have an official role in the government?"

"No, I am Sassanian, not Sogdian—a silk merchant like you. Call me 'Sultan' if it amuses you. It can do no harm."

Jacob nodded. "I saw you examining the silks earlier. Are you taking a caravan back to your homeland?"

"This is my home now, no more caravans for me. I'll never leave Samarkand."

"Never?" Frith said. He should have kept his mouth shut, but the thought of never leaving suddenly made him homesick.

Before the Sultan could respond to his outburst, Jacob said, "So, what is your role in the silk trade? I ask as one merchant to another."

"Exactly in the middle," the Sultan said. "Samarkand is the destination from all the lands east of us. Silk is brought here, stored here, and sent west from here. I have contacts with all the best sources in China. They give me first choice. What I don't take, some lesser merchant ends up with."

"May I ask what you do with it?" Frith said. "Um... sir?"

"Why, sell it to someone like you—someone with an eye for better quality," the Sultan said. "You didn't come all this way to take home inferior fabric. You could've bought that in Damascus."

"That's exactly my plan," Jacob said. "It's most fortunate we met you. Tell me, are there others here who buy from the east and sell to those going west?"

The Sultan waved his arm at the market. "That's what all those men are doing, but I've already secured the best. What they're trying to sell you are my leavings."

Frith looked at the tables of silk around them. These were pretty nice leftovers.

"You seem very congenial," the Sultan said. "I should like to help you. Come to my home for dinner tonight and we'll talk more." The Sultan snapped his fingers, and the boy was instantly at his side. "Run to my home and tell my wives to get cooking. We have guests for dinner."

"How many shall I say?" the boy said.

The Sultan looked at Jacob.

"Ten," Frith blurted.

Jacob shook his head no, "Just Frith and I."

"Oh, bring your whole company," the Sultan said. "My wives love a crowd."

Frith caught that—*wives*—he'd said again. It wasn't just his poor understanding of the language.

"Thank you, but no, just the two of us. We only arrived last night and my men have things I need them to do."

"Of course. Shall we say sundown? Ask anyone for directions. They all know where the Sultan lives."

They stood, shook hands, and the Sultan left. Jacob and Frith perused the bounty of silks for several more hours. Frith couldn't believe such riches, and these were second-rate stock. Back home even a small silk stole was the sign of vast wealth, yet here were bolts of it at low prices.

"Sir," Frith said, "when you're ready to purchase, I'd like you to apply a portion of my wages toward a piece of this fabric for my sister."

"Certainly. Choose one she'd like and we'll mark it for her before we load the camels."

As they returned to camp Frith said, "I should think the knights would've liked to dine with the Sultan. Why'd you tell him no?"

"Everything we've earned thus far sits in a few boxes at camp. We can't leave them unguarded. The Sultan seems like a friend, but a dishonest man could use such an invitation to lure unsuspecting travelers away from their treasure."

Frith's eyes grew wide. "Do you really think he would?"

"No, actually, I don't. I like the man, but I'm explaining to you how to be prudent in your travels."

"Still, the knights will be disappointed."

"They'll be fine. They knew what the job would be when they agreed to it."

CHAPTER 20

The Sultan's home was as easy to find as he'd said. Every person they asked knew the way. The house was larger than any Frith had ever seen, larger than the main house at Jacob's estate in Britain, and certainly larger than the abbey rectory and scriptorium combined. A servant was waiting for them outside. At the servant's touch the heavy door swung open smoothly on silent hinges. He ushered them through an open courtyard lit by torches. Sculptures of male and female figures decorated the garden, their shadows dancing on the walls in the flickering orange light.

To Frith it was an eerie sight, but quickly forgotten when he glimpsed the inside of the house. A huge interior court was surrounded on three sides by archways that he could see led to other large rooms. In the center of the room a half-dozen cushions surrounded a low table full of covered serving dishes. Frith wondered if this was more than just a home. Perhaps the Sultan ran an inn. The attendant asked them to leave their footwear in the outer courtyard.

All the inns they'd stayed in thus far had dirt floors. Rugs were put down only where men sat or slept. The Sultan's court was completely covered in layers of rugs so thick one hardly knew there was a ground beneath them. Frith's feet sank into the carpet and rejoiced. It felt like soft, grassy pastures on a summer day.

The Sultan appeared and greeted them warmly. Immediately thereafter, three curious-looking men entered the court from the surrounding arches. The first was dressed only in a large orange sheet wrapped around him and draped over a shoulder. He wore a turban. The Sultan put his palms together and bent his head as if he was going to pray. "Namaste, Swami."

"Namaste," the Swami replied.

Frith tried to remember the new word, na-ma-stay.

Meanwhile, the Sultan reverently greeted the other two men and then introduced them to Jacob and Frith. "First, let me present Swami Yogeshwar," he said, indicating the man with the turban.

Frith was unsure what to say. He had no idea what a swami was. The fact that the Sultan had bowed to the man could mean he was a royal. He decided the safest course was to follow the Sultan's example. He bowed and repeated, "Namaste," although he had no idea what the word meant.

Jacob did not bow to the Swami, but merely touched his middle finger to his forehead. It was simple, a sign of respect.

Should he continue to emulate the Sultan or greet the others as Jacob did?

"And this is Budhitra," the Sultan said of the second man. "He's from Nalanda, the great Buddhist center of learning in India." Budhitra was dressed like a monk, but his robe was the color of a burgundy sunset. He had a bald head and a broad smile.

Frith had never heard names like these. He tried to fix the men in his memory by repeating to himself, Yo-gesh-whar, orange robe; Boo-deet-ra, burgundy robe.

Budhitra put his hands together as Yogeshwar had, and he also said, "Namaste."

This must be the formal greeting in Samarkand, so he responded in kind.

"Finally, let me introduce Da Shi," the Sultan said of the third man. "He is from that distant land which is the source of silk."

"Da-shee," Frith said. It didn't quite sound right.

Da Shi was dressed in a silk tunic similar to the Sultan's, except the sleeves were more voluminous. His complexion was yellow hued like the strange merchants in Merv, but his face was thin and delicate. He resembled several of the sculptures in the Sultan's courtyard and Frith wondered if he'd posed for them.

"Dao Yu," Da Shi said. "…Friends."

Frith was thrown by the change in protocol. He didn't know what to do, so he simply said, "Namaste," again.

Da Shi gave him a benevolent smile.

"Holy sirs," the Sultan said. "These are my guests, Jacob and Frith. They come to us from farther west than any merchants I've ever met. Perhaps we'll learn of their land and you'll tell them of yours."

The company took their places around the generously laid table. Servants uncovered plates of goat, lamb, and a meat Frith didn't recognize. A tureen held a soup layered thick with grease that smelled like melted butter on warm bread. Numerous dishes held fruits and vegetables. A central platter was heaped with a mountain of plov, a dish made from a long slender grain Frith hadn't seen before Bokhara. The first time he tried plov he liked it. The plov in Bokhara contained bits of mutton and fat. Here the meat was replaced with shredded carrots, raisins, and spices. Frith scooped a mound of it on his plate.

Frith noticed Yogeshwar filled his plate to brimming with every non-meat dish. Budhitra and Da Shi took smaller portions than Yogeshwar, but similarly avoided the meat. Frith heard Jacob give a sigh of relief as he copied the three holy men. Frith happily sampled meat from each of the three platters. The Sultan took from every dish and then ladled the soup over his plov. That looked like a good idea, so Frith spooned some soup over his as well.

"Jacob," the Sultan said, "are you like these monks? Do you abstain from meat?"

"I eat meat on some occasions, but I also refrain on certain days," Jacob said.

"That's a very wise practice," Da Shi said. "Diet's extremely important, not only to our physical health, but our mental and spiritual health as well."

"I saw it wouldn't cause offense to refuse meat in this company," Jacob said. "Sultan, you would do me a great favor if you could teach me a Sogdian phrase I could use in my travels to courteously communicate that I don't want meat."

"Why certainly," the Sultan said, "Man Butparast naim. That should work in every situation."

Jacob carefully repeated, "Man Butparast naim." To Frith's ear, he pronounced it exactly right.

The three foreigners laughed loudly.

Jacob smiled as well. "Did I mispronounce it?"

"No, you said it perfectly," Budhitra said.

"Then what?" Jacob said.

"The Sultan has taught you to say 'I am a Buddhist,'" Budhitra said.

The men laughed again. This was the first time Frith could ever remember seeing Jacob embarrassed.

Jacob took a drink, gathered his composure and then said calmly, "Thank you, but that would be an untruth."

Frith set about sampling bites of each thing on his plate. When he came to the mystery meat, he took a bite and savored it. It was quite good. "Sultan, may I ask, what is this delicious meat?"

"Camel."

"Camel?"

"Good, isn't it?" the Sultan said. "Camels are not only good for transportation. They're also good sources of meat, milk, wool, and leather. I admire the camel. Everything about it has a purpose."

Frith thought of Parisa. He pushed aside the camel meat and ate the lamb.

"Food is one source of our qi," Da Shi said.

"Chee?" Frith said, trying to copy Da Shi's pronunciation.

"That's correct," Da Shi said. "Qi is the active life force in any living thing. Some foods have more of it, and others can deplete our qi."

Jacob nodded. "The explanation's not quite the same in my religion, but certain foods are proscribed."

"There was a time, a golden age, when humans didn't need to eat at all," Da Shi said. "Instead they could absorb qi directly from the cosmos."

The Sultan laughed merrily, "Well I for one am glad those times are over. I see Frith agrees with me."

"I knew such a man," Frith said without thinking.

The table grew quiet and everyone looked at Frith.

When was he going to learn to keep his mouth shut? He hesitated, but there was no going back now. "My spiritual teacher lived without eating, except for Eucharist—"

"Eucharist?" the Sultan said. "You mean the Christian rite?"

Frith nodded. "A bite of bread no bigger than my thumb, and a swallow of wine was all he ever ate in a day."

"None of these men have mastered that," the Sultan said. "Did he elucidate how this was accomplished?"

"He once quoted a scripture, 'Man does not live by bread alone, but by the Word that proceeds out of the mouth of God.' He also described something I think must be similar to what Da Shi called qi. He called it *energia vitae*, the power keeping all things alive."

The Sultan leaned eagerly toward Frith. "You say he lived without eating by drawing directly from the source of life?"

Frith scratched his chin. "I don't know… apparently."

The Sultan's nostrils widened. "But did he teach *you* how to do this?"

Frith shook his head. "Oh, no. As you say, I like to eat."

The Sultan searched Frith's eyes. "Do you know from whom he learned it?"

"I don't think it was something he learned," Frith said. "It was more a Grace that came to him while he was otherwise engaged."

"Explain," Da Shi said.

"Lancelot told Alura and me—she's my sister—it was unintentional. He was practicing solitude and meditation, having no care for everyday things, when he noticed it had been weeks since he'd eaten anything except the bit at Communion. Mysteriously, he no longer required food."

The holy men nodded wisely, but the Sultan looked disappointed. "Too bad he didn't give you a better explanation. The esoteric secrets of many different religions have found their way out to the world through Samarkand."

"How so?" Jacob said.

"Samarkand has always been a place where different religions coexisted peacefully. First was Zoroastrianism, which has been here since the city was founded. Later, came Manichaeism from Persia, and Buddhism from India, followed by Christianity." The Sultan waved his arm expansively toward the men at his table. "And nowhere in Samarkand do these religions find more common ground than in my home. Here we have a Taoist, a Buddhist, a Hindu, a Christian, and a Jew. One of my wives is even a Zoroastrian."

"And which are you?" Jacob said.

"All of them—or none of them," the Sultan said. "I am a simple seeker of truth. I believe there ought to be a place where men of various spiritual beliefs can live and sup together and try to find which truths in their own religions can be found in another man's religion. To that end, I am using my time in Samarkand and my vast wealth to facilitate it."

"Forgive me, sir," Frith said. "I've noticed you keep using the plural, *wives*. Does Sogdian law permit a man to have more than one wife?"

"If he can afford them—and I can."

Frith looked at Jacob. "Have you heard of this?"

Jacob nodded yes, but held his tongue.

"A man's first wife is chosen for him by his family," the Sultan said. "Is that not the custom everywhere? But if he's prosperous, he chooses his second wife to his own liking."

"May I ask how many you have?" Frith said.

"Three," the Sultan said. "But the third wasn't my choice. Her Uncle Istemi arranged it. She's a cousin of the Khan."

Frith had more questions, a lot more, but he didn't want to risk disharmony. Jacob, who'd always shown such skill at navigating uneasy conversations, was silent. Frith wished Jacob would take over for him.

Then Da Shi made what had to be a social blunder. "In my country, Princes and Princesses are sometimes married into a rival king's family to keep the peace between various factions. They serve as hostages."

The men at the table looked from Da Shi to the Sultan. But the Sultan just waved his hand. "Fortunately all of my wives are jewels. They are my real wealth. They've given me many children. Among the men seated here, only Jacob and I know the worth of children."

Jacob raised his cup, "I honor your progeny." The men drank to that.

"Thanks to King Istemi," the Sultan said. "It was Istemi who arranged to bring my family to Samarkand—not as a hostage, but that I might marry his niece. You see gentlemen, in life, family is everything."

"To family," Jacob said.

Since amenity seemed restored, Frith leaned toward Jacob and said quietly, "Shouldn't we make an appointment to see the Sultan's silk?"

"There'll be time for that later," Jacob said. "Tonight's about getting to know each other. Let's not spoil the mood of dinner with business."

But the Sultan had overheard them. "No need to wait. Let me show you what quality silk looks like."

The Sultan called for his wives and daughters to dance. Shortly, half a dozen lovely women in colorful dresses appeared and rhythmically circled the table. They removed their shawls, swirled them about, draped them at their waist and undulated their hips. Frith was mesmerized.

When the dance ended, the Sultan had each woman show Frith and Jacob her garments. He encouraged close examination of the fabric. Jacob complimented each woman and commenced to teach Frith the merits of her silk, but Frith was too dazed by the beauty around him to study the silk as Jacob did.

When the women left, Jacob said, "Most excellent."

"The best you have ever seen," the Sultan said.

"I agree. If what's in your warehouse is like this, I'll be very pleased."

"Soon," the Sultan said.

Jacob frowned. "Um… soon?"

"You have arrived at an inauspicious time of the year. Every good brocade in Samarkand has been taken away by caravans that preceded you. Just those poor remnants you saw in the market remain."

Frith suspected Jacob now regretted not having paid the prices men were asking in Merv.

"Don't worry," the Sultan said. "I'm awaiting a new caravan from the east, the last of the season. Since good silk takes longer to produce, the best silk of the year comes with the last caravan. I'll give you first choice."

Jacob's face betrayed uncertainty. "Would you know how long?"

"Oh, who can say? Maybe a week…"

Worry lines creased Jacob's brow.

The Sultan smiled and opened his arms wide. "Please, enjoy the wait. Stay with us, tell us about Britain, learn from my company of enlightened masters."

Jacob nodded reluctantly.

"Swami Yogeshwar, for example, has powers of intuition," the Sultan said. "Swami, please reveal what you perceive."

Yogeshwar looked at Frith, but answered the Sultan, "This one is unsteady. He has moments of clarity when he's seated in the Atman, but he's easily drawn out of there."

Frith bristled, but said nothing, if only because it was true.

Yogeshwar's eyes met Frith's. "Someone taught you to observe your thoughts and feelings, but you've not yet mastered it. While you were watching the dance, I saw your attention flee the Self in feminine attraction."

Frith swallowed hard and stared at his dirty plate. Again, there was no denying it. Though he wasn't too pleased to have his innermost being displayed at the table.

"It doesn't have to be like that," Yogeshwar said. "You can stay within, even while noticing how your lower self is drawn outward. Know you are the consciousness as well as the flow of consciousness."

Yogeshwar reached over and plucked a fresh fig from the platter of fruit. He turned his focus to Jacob. "Jacob's a wise man. He has knowledge much deeper than he's revealed to his companion. Jacob, do not be concerned about the next caravan. Each of us, and the circumstances which we encounter, has an origin in the ten thousand things that have come before it. No one except God can contemplate such a large number of influences as have created the now."

Jacob nodded. "Everything that ever was, caused all that is."

Yogeshwar lifted the corners of his mouth in a small smile. "You see Sultan? He has a knowing, as I've said." Yogeshwar took a bite of the fig.

Jacob yawned. "Sultan, I thank you for the wonderful dinner and enlightened company, but I think it is time for Frith and me to go."

"Oh, no need to leave," the Sultan said. "I intend for you to be my guests."

"Thank you for the kind offer, but we must return to our caravan. I don't want my men to feel I'm luxuriating while asking them to stay at camp."

"Bring them all. I have plenty of rooms here."

"Thank you, but no." Jacob stood and gave a short formal bow to each man. While doing so he prodded Frith with his toe. Frith jumped up and imitated Jacob, adding the word "Namaste" to each bow.

"If you must leave," the Sultan said, "do come to dinner again tomorrow. In fact, I insist you join us every night until you leave. You have much to add to the conversation."

"You're most gracious," Jacob said. They returned to the outer courtyard, put their boots on and left.

On their way back to camp Jacob said, "I suspect Da Shi is right, the Sultan's a prisoner."

"A prisoner?" Frith said. "I thought he was a prince."

"His response to Da Shi's story seemed forced. I expect the Sultan's marriage holds him hostage, and despite his wealth he cannot leave Samarkand."

Frith had missed that, but it could be. All the same, the Sultan's palace looked like a pretty nice prison.

CHAPTER 21

For the next few days, Frith and Jacob dined nightly at the Sultan's. After the men had eaten, before the oriental masters' intense discussions lasting late into the night, the Sultan's wives would come in to say goodnight. Often, the women performed dances, songs, or poems for the Sultan's guests, and he would puff himself up like a gander.

Frith didn't blame him. All three wives were smart, poised, and beautiful. But the youngest wife stirred something in him, unbidden. When the hem of her veil brushed him as she whirled by, blood rushed in his ears. And elsewhere. Somehow she engendered feelings of Elsa, but why? The women were nothing alike. Elsa was tall and radiantly blonde; this woman was petite and dusky. Yet, Frith couldn't keep his eyes from following her as she moved around the room.

"Frith?"

His eyes jerked away from her to meet the Sultan's, who looked back at him without malice.

"A poem from Da Shi's homeland says, 'Soldiers kill men with swords, women slay men with their eyes.'" The Sultan laughed. "Let me buy you a wife of your own."

"Thank you," Jacob said quickly, "but Frith isn't ready for that responsibility."

"He's certainly old enough to wed," the Sultan said.

Jacob shook his head. "It'd be a sham marriage he'd have to abandon when our caravan leaves."

The Sultan gestured at the opulence around them. "I have wealth beyond measure. At least let me acquire a servant girl for him."

Jacob glared at him. "Thank you, but no."

"Just to relieve his ardor for my wives."

Frith felt himself blush. "Sultan, you can't think I would act against you."

The Sultan laughed. "Oh Frith, I'm not offended. You and I are real men. These monks don't have to deal with the force of manly urges. They don't know our struggle."

"Sultan, you're wrong," Yogeshwar said. "I experience the same passions as any man. I simply choose to remain above them."

Jacob's lips squeezed into a tight line. "This conversation has moved beyond all propriety."

The Sultan looked chagrined. "Of course, I didn't mean to impugn your virility, Jacob. You have two sons, so you must have—"

Jacob's face was scarlet. "Let me speak plainly, Frith doesn't need you to buy him a companion."

"Oh, I didn't mean to imply you couldn't afford it. I was only trying to make a gracious gesture."

"Well, thank you," Jacob said, "but can we discuss something else? While we are still friends?"

There was an awkward silence. Finally, the Sultan said, "Yes, of course. Let's begin with a passage I found in the writings of the Greek, Pythagoras."

Such a transition was not unusual. The Sultan frequently started the evening's philosophical discourse. The men at his table had a profound understanding of the universe and Frith had noticed the Sultan liked to show them off by presenting them with some challenge. His pride in them reminded Frith of his pride in his wives.

The Sultan looked around the table. "Master Da Shi, why don't you give us your interpretation of this passage: 'Seek not for a name for God, for you will not find any.'"

The master in the yellow silk tunic pulled on his pointed beard. "The Greek is correct. The Tao which can be expressed in words is not the eternal Tao. Any name which can be uttered is not its real name."

"Very profound," Jacob said.

"Those aren't my words, but the words of Lao Tzu," Da Shi said. "Tao translates as Way. That might mean the way to God, the way of God, or the eternal nature of God."

"You know what Bodhidharma said…" Budhitra gave Da Shi a broad smile. "There are many who see the Way, but fewer who practice it."

Da Shi smiled back. "That's so true."

The Sultan turned to Jacob. "What do you say about my quote from Pythagoras?"

"Your quote was incomplete," Jacob said. "Pythagoras added, 'Everything that is named, is named by letters. God, however, is not a name to God, but an indication of what we conceive of Him.'"

The Sultan looked distressed. Frith wondered if it was because Jacob corrected him in front of the others. To break the tension Frith said, "What does it mean?"

"That words are only symbols," Jacob said.

"I agree," Da Shi said. "Tao is no more the Way than the word 'water' is actually water. Drink as much of the word as you like and you'll still be thirsty."

The Sultan rinsed his fingers in a bowl. "Jacob, isn't it true certain high priests of your religion know the true name of God?"

Frith was once again amazed at the breadth of the Sultan's knowledge. "Broad, but not deep," had been Jacob's private assessment of the Sultan. At the time, he'd thought the remark judgmental, especially for Jacob.

Jacob studied his fingernails. "The question is not, 'Can He be named,' but 'Should He?'"

The Sultan fixed his gaze on Jacob. "You don't know? Or aren't you willing to say?"

"In the Torah, when Moses presses Him for a name, God says simply, 'I AM becoming that I AM becoming.'"

The Sultan flicked a bit of millet from his tunic. "That's no answer. Budhitra, what name would you use?"

"A name is only a word," Budhitra said. "A word is only a thought. A thought is not a real thing,"

Budhitra's statements shook Frith. "A thought is not real?" he said. "When I was a child, I didn't even realize I was thinking. Then Lancelot taught me thoughts *are* things. That dwelling on thoughts soon blocks our energia."

"We're way off topic," the Sultan said. "We were discussing the name of God."

Frith ducked his head.

Jacob laid a gentle hand on his arm. "Frith, I believe Budhitra meant that to name God allows the mind to conceive Him. But He exists beyond concept. There's nothing to compare God to."

Budhitra nodded.

"But isn't there a secret name of God?" the Sultan said. "I've heard that he who knows it commands the universe."

Da Shi smiled. "That which existed before heaven and earth might be regarded as the mother of the universe, but its name is not known."

"Perhaps Jews and Christians have knowledge Asian religions do not. Jacob, do you know the true name?"

Jacob touched his forehead. "That which is before creation, that which is creating, and that which is in creation are aspects of one entity." Jacob lifted his palms upward. "The name of any single aspect can't represent the totality."

Da Shi nodded. "Lao Tzu says the same. 'The Tao is eternal, nameless, and indescribable. It is at once the beginning of all things and the path of all things.'"

"I'm beginning to admire this Lao Tzu," Jacob said.

Frith gaped at him. Where was the faithful Jew who prayed morning and night to the Ruler of the Universe? "Jacob, you can't believe God is unknowable."

"I didn't say that."

The Sultan wagged his finger. "You are all avoiding the question. What say you, Frith, do Christians know God's secret name?"

Frith squirmed. Just because he grew up in an abbey didn't make him the voice of Christendom. One need only ask the Abbot to learn that. "Our priests never taught us anything like that."

"Maybe they hid that knowledge," the Sultan said.

Frith shrugged. "I may be the only Christian at this table, but I'm no scholar or authority on its precepts." In fact, he was beginning to wish he'd paid more attention. All those years in the abbey and what had he learned? To stick out his tongue for the Host and when to say Amen. That wasn't going to be much use in this company.

The Sultan scanned the men at his table. "I have exemplary representatives of five different religions; some of you claim to have personally experienced God. In your encounters didn't you learn the sacred name?"

Frith shook his head. He'd reached no such lofty state.

"'He who knows does not speak about it. He who is ever ready to speak about it doesn't know,'" Da Shi said. "I'm quoting Lao Tzu, of course."

"Too clever," the Sultan said. "Budhitra, Yogeshwar, reveal what you discovered."

Yogeshwar said, "As long as you're experiencing God you are still in duality, because you and the experience are separate."

The Sultan looked vexed. Frith felt pretty confused himself.

Budhitra shrugged. "If you experience the nothing, or if you experience the everything, both are states of experiencing oneness."

The Sultan laughed, "You are a slippery lot."

"I think my head's going to break," Frith said.

"That's not a bad thing," Budhitra said.

Frith saw concern in Jacob's eyes. "I think it's time for me to take Frith back to camp."

"No, don't. Let me keep Frith." The Sultan's eyes gleamed greedily. "I'll make you a proposition."

Jacob leaped to his feet, pulling Frith up with him. "I feared something like this."

"Don't be so quick," the Sultan said. "You haven't heard me out."

"Thank you for your hospitality. Good night." Jacob grabbed their boots and rushed Frith out the gate barefoot.

The night sand was cold on Frith's feet. He took his boots from Jacob and put them on. "Jacob, what just happened?"

"The Sultan just tried to buy you from me."

It took a moment for the words to register. Frith shook his head. "You must be mistaken."

"Frith, there are places in this world where people think they can own other human beings. Already tonight he suggested buying you a woman. Now he wants to make me an offer for you. He thinks he can purchase anything he wants."

"Obviously I'm not for sale."

"And I'm not a merchant who trades in souls. He's managed to insult us both."

"Is it possible we left in haste? Shouldn't we return and let the Sultan explain? He's been nothing but a friend to us."

Jacob didn't answer. They walked in silence the rest of the way to camp. Jacob didn't speak again until their meditations ended and he blew out the candle. "In the morning I'll meet with the Sultan. You will stay here with the knights. I'll feel safer that way."

CHAPTER 22

Frith was talking with the knights when Jacob returned and motioned for him to follow him into their tent. The knights gave Frith an inquiring look. Frith shrugged. Jacob was wearing the stoic face he showed when negotiating, so Frith couldn't guess how things had gone.

He entered the tent and sat down across from Jacob. "I assume you've been to see the Sultan. Is the discord resolved?"

Jacob nodded. "He was quite willing to overlook our abrupt exit last night, but I came very close to offending him again."

"Sir, you're the least offensive person I've ever met."

Jacob looked at the floor. "I misinterpreted his proposition—"

"I knew it! The Sultan's not like that."

"I confess, I went there so fixed in my assumptions, it required a long conversation to open my ears."

"So may I ask what it was about?"

"He wants you there to study with his gurus."

Frith gave Jacob a broad smile.

"Not forever, Frith, just until we leave."

"Of course," Frith said. "But you had already declined his invitation. Why did he bring it up again?"

"His gurus insisted. It seems they see potential for spiritual advancement in you."

"They do?"

"Certainly Frith, we all see your sincerity… Anyway, the Sultan believes you'd benefit from spending your days in his company of holy men."

"Oh, I'd like that. When will we move there?"

"Not we, Frith. You. I'll stay here with my knights. I will see you at supper, though."

Frith broke into a sunny smile.

Jacob sighed. "You don't have to be so glad to leave us."

"Oh, no, sir, it's not because I'm leaving. It's just… I envy what those holy men have achieved. All three of them exhibit a state I've only seen in Lancelot."

"Frith, in the matters of your soul, it's best not to covet other men's spiritual accomplishment. Just attend to your own."

"Err… yes. That's what I meant—to attain my own."

"I understand, Frith, but I'm torn between a duty to watch over you and a sense I should let you go through what you must." Jacob grasped Frith's arm. "These men, however holy they are, are too foreign to your religion. I saw how confused they made you last night."

Frith patted Jacob's hand. "Thank you for being so concerned. I hope I'll learn. Perhaps the Sultan's palace will be my place of spiritual awakening."

"Frith, remember the spice sellers in Merv?"

"Which one?"

"Which one doesn't matter. Tell me what would happen if a man ate all those different spices at once?"

"I'd imagine he'd get pretty sick."

"So you understand why I'm reluctant to let you live at the Sultan's."

"Mixing their religions will make me spiritually sick?"

"Exactly. Things they speak of are said from a seat of higher knowing—a different metaphysical realm." Jacob ruffled Frith's hair. "I started out to teach you my business, but found it my mandate to nurture your spiritual practices without making you change to mine." Jacob pursed his lips. "But will the Sultan show the same restraint?"

"The Sultan's a spiritual man."

"Is he?" Jacob said. "He might just be collecting holy men the way Romans collect sculptures or an abbey amasses books."

"But I don't have a fraction of their knowledge," Frith said. "What would he gain from me?"

"Perhaps he wants to learn whatever Lancelot knew."

"But I've not achieved, or even seen, Lancelot's Grail."

"I could be wrong about the Sultan's intent. But if men aren't to be sold, neither is their spiritual knowledge to be bought. Kings and wealthy men often keep saints, hoping some holiness will rub off, or their generosity will get them into heaven."

"Are you suggesting the Sultan is being deceptive about his spiritual interests?"

"No, not really. Just don't assume the Sultan has attained the same level of awakening as his holy men just because he keeps them fed."

"But these men know secret teachings I've found nowhere else."

"I, too, know many secret teachings, but I'll not reveal them to the Sultan."

Was it possible? He'd assumed Jacob's spiritual practices were like those of the monks—a regular practice of tradition that centered you in everyday life rather than a window to a higher consciousness. What secret teachings?

"If a man has a spiritual master," Jacob said, "he should remain true to his master and not jump to each new idea."

"My master didn't set any limit where I might seek the Grail. Besides, you're the one who took me away from the abbey."

"True, but I didn't try to convert you to Judaism, did I? We can honor and respect other people's religion without giving up our own."

"Yes. But aren't the Sultan's holy men concerned with Truth, rather than religion?"

"What is religion if not Truth?" Jacob said.

"From what I've seen, mostly rules and rituals."

"Frith, don't be impertinent. You know those are only the curtains that hide the knowledge inside the tabernacle. Truth is always available to those admitted behind the veil."

He thought of the monks shivering and mumbling their Latin in the predawn darkness. "No, I didn't know that."

"That's an unfortunate lack in your education. My master taught me—"

"I'm sorry. You had a master?"

Jacob hesitated. "Yes… I did… In every good religion there lies a hidden path prophets or mystics follow to the divine—a channel through which divinity coursed down into men from the higher world. But you need a teacher to find it. One who not only imparts knowledge of its existence, but who has found its source. This teacher must have inner experience of, and direct connection with, the Tree of Life. In my tradition there are two mystical schools of knowledge. One concerns ascent into the higher worlds and the other emphasizes contemplation of the divine. Fortunately, my teacher was a master of both."

Frith was stunned. "All these months together, and this is the first you've ever mentioned him."

"And let's keep it that way. I don't want you to bring this up around the Sultan or his gurus."

"As you wish, of course. But may I ask why not?"

"I've already said, I think the Sultan's a collector of spiritual men. I don't intend to be added to his collection."

"Could you be assuming his motives are bad?"

"Not bad. But not divine either."

"Well, whatever the Sultan's reasons, it's his gurus who have the knowledge. You agree they've mastered divine contemplation?"

"I suspect they have."

"Then why worry about me studying with them? Are you afraid I won't be able to keep up with their discussion?"

Jacob shook his head. "No, I'm afraid you will. Hidden teachings are hidden for a reason. The unknowable is revealed through ten emanations. These are step-by-step realizations that lead you to understand the one Divine Infinite. The Sultan's men are all several steps ahead of you. Their ideas are not for you to peruse."

"But isn't it possible the Ruler of the Universe put me before men of higher understanding for a purpose?"

Jacob became silent and seemed to be considering Frith's point.

Frith didn't give him time to have second thoughts. "Think, sir, there is nothing required of me at camp until the silk arrives. I spend each day waiting to go to the Sultan's. I may as well be there, learning."

Jacob closed his eyes and sagged. "Perhaps my reluctance is ill-founded."

"I'm sure it is, sir," Frith said. "And I feel this is something I have to try."

Jacob nodded. "Very well. I hope you're right."

"Can I go this morning, sir?"

CHAPTER 23

Frith carried his few belongings to the Sultan's palace in the Abbot's leather sack. A servant showed him to his room. Accommodations at the Sultan's were plusher than anywhere he'd ever been. Certainly better than sleeping in a tent for nine months, and he suspected the Sultan's servant's quarters were more luxurious than the Abbot's own chamber. His bedroom was beautifully carpeted with ornate rugs. On the floor was a mattress stuffed with feathers—thicker, softer, and more luxuriant than any since Jacob's house. He dropped his pack and fell onto the bed. It puffed up around him like a feather pillow. He'd like to have stayed in its mellow embrace all morning, but the Sultan's oriental masters were waiting in a great room the Sultan had set aside for them. It, too, had thick rugs plus an eastern exposure that flooded the room with light. There were cushions on the floor, but no chairs or table.

Frith had assumed the Sultan's gurus were like monks back at the abbey who held simple food and plain living as requisites for spiritual advancement. Now that he'd seen the accommodations here he wondered, why, if they disdained extravagance, were they ensconced in the Sultan's opulence?

He sat down and Budhitra smiled at him. "You wonder what spiritual purpose there could be for monks who've taken vows of poverty to live like princes."

Frith started to say something, but realized he probably didn't have to. Were they reading his face or his mind? Either way, he already felt he was in the presence of higher spiritual beings.

"We neither disdain nor desire these circumstances," Da Shi said.

"Any of us would be equally happy living in a cowshed," Yogeshwar added.

Frith looked around at the opulence. "You're not serious."

"He is," Da Shi said. "While clogged by craving, one sees nothing more than the outer form. Once freed from earthly passions, one perceives only essence."

"Your face betrays your doubt," Budhitra said.

It did? Frith tried to make his expression neutral. He should have paid more attention to how Jacob managed it.

"Samarkand is the point on the silk road where that which arrives from the east travels west," Da Shi said. "Spiritual knowledge imprisoned by high mountain ranges for millennia, now comes through vehicles such as us as surely as silk comes from heaven."

"The Sultan's sumptuous environment makes men of wealth, like Jacob, feel comfortable hearing our ideas," Yogeshwar said.

"I think you underestimate Jacob," Frith said.

Da Shi smiled. "I think we do not."

"He is the exception," Budhitra said, "spiritually deeper than most caravan merchants."

Frith felt good knowing they respected Jacob, but what did they really think about the Sultan? "What about our host? Jacob has wondered what his objective is."

The holy men looked at one another. Budhitra bit his lip. Da Shi smoothed wrinkles in his yellow blouse. Yogeshwar said nothing.

The door opened. The Sultan entered, bowed to the holy men, and took a seat.

"Good morning, Frith," the Sultan said. "Is your room to your satisfaction?"

"Oh, yes. Thank you for allowing me to stay."

"And to learn, Frith; I expect you to learn. I know from my own time with these men, they have secrets to teach you. You are the beginning of my new school."

"School?" Frith had never been to school. It was Lancelot who taught him to read and write Latin.

"Budhitra, Da Shi, and Yogeshwar know what I'm talking about," the Sultan said. "Each of them studied under a master. Here we'll replicate that, except we have three masters. You and I will be the first of many students."

Budhitra cleared his throat. "It's true I studied at the great school in Nalanda. However, dutiful study is only one step toward nirvana."

The Sultan looked at them intently. "I've set up this school because I believe exposure to the variety of your ideas will lead us to the truth. Here, the kind of discussions we've been having at dinner can be expanded into full day sessions."

"Lao Tzu says, 'Much talk—much exhaustion,'" Da Shi said.

Yogeshwar nodded. "Words or concepts, even if true, do not provide direct experience of truth. I think Budhitra and Da Shi would agree meaningful progress only occurs in samadhi."

"I'm not familiar with the word, samadhi," the Sultan said.

"Nirvana," Budhitra said. Frith didn't know that word either.

"Samadhi is a state beyond mind," Yogeshwar said. "Actual perception of truth. It does not come through discourse about it."

"Yet you all claim to know it, do you not?" the Sultan said.

"At first you know it," Yogeshwar said. "Eventually, you are able to never leave it."

Frith wondered if that's how it was for Alura. This sounded like exactly what he was seeking. He cleared his throat. "So, how does one get... samadhi?"

"In rare cases, it occurs spontaneously," Yogeshwar said. "For others it can be awakened by a master."

The Sultan spread his arms. "And you are masters."

The holy men looked at one another. Yogeshwar smiled. "Even those who have it awakened through a master are the exceptions. For most sincere seekers, it requires deep meditation to reach samadhi."

"Men don't gain higher states from listening to lectures," Budhitra said. "Words lull the self by keeping the mind thinking. A still mind is required."

Frith remembered Lancelot telling him this so frequently he'd grown bored with its repetition. And yet he continued to let his thoughts intrude on his meditation. How often had he reached the end of meditation and realized he had been planning the day's activities the whole time?

"That answer doesn't satisfy me," the Sultan said. "How can the students learn if the masters don't teach?"

Two servants entered. One set up a low table between the men and the other placed goblets on it. Refreshments already? It seemed they'd just begun. The second servant held an ornate silver pitcher containing freshly squeezed juice. He started to serve the Sultan.

Budhitra reached for the pitcher. "May I pour?"

The Sultan nodded. Budhitra took the pitcher and waved the servant away. "Let me share something from an old Buddhist story, not mine, but one that has proved useful in the past." While Budhitra spoke, he continued filling the Sultan's goblet. Soon it started to overflow.

"Budhitra! Stop!" The Sultan pressed a napkin into the pooling juice. "It's overfull. No more will go in."

"Exactly. Like this cup, if you start out full of your own conceptualizations, how do you expect us to show you nirvana? You must first empty your cup."

For a moment the Sultan looked chagrined, but then he gave a hearty laugh. "Clever."

"Instead of talking, let's meditate." Budhitra motioned for the servants. Frith watched them carry the table away. He hoped that wasn't lunch.

They meditated until midday when servants brought fruits and beverages. A long cloth was spread on the floor and the comestibles were served on silver platters. Frith ate his fill, but the holy men ate little. When lunch was finished, servants removed the dishes and took up the cloth.

Da Shi asked everyone to stand. He organized them into a single line and had them follow him around the room. "Step into the footstep vacated by the man in front of you. Be attentive to the feeling of the carpet on your soles."

"What is this?" the Sultan said.

"Don't talk, just follow." Da Shi led them around the labyrinth of intricate designs woven into the carpet. After they'd done this for a quarter hour, they took their seats and sat with their eyes closed. Frith's mind meandered. What was the purpose of stepping in the preceding man's footsteps? Where had Da Shi's walk around the room taken them? Was there a hidden meaning in the carpet pattern?

Yogeshwar spoke slowly and calmly. "As you listen to my voice, relax and watch your breath move in and out of your body."

At the sound of Yogeshwar's voice, Frith opened his eyes. Lancelot had taught him to meditate like this, using almost these exact words. Discovering he was the only one whose eyes were open, he quickly closed them again.

"Keep your attention on the physical movement of the breath... in... out ..." Yogeshwar said.

Frith had no trouble. He'd been doing this type of meditation since the days of Lancelot. In fact it was the only thing he knew to do in meditation. That and watch the mind. Lancelot had said, "Observe the mind like you are watching the breath. Witness the rising and falling thoughts. Don't hold a thought any more than you would hold your breath. Don't try to stop your mind, just don't become involved in it."

Frith sensed movement as the Sultan extended his legs and then repositioned them. He heard the Sultan give a heavy sigh. Frith returned his attention to his breath.

"Watch the breath," Yogeshwar said. "If the mind drifts away to other things, gently guide it back to the movement of air in and out of your body."

The Sultan coughed and cleared his throat. Frith concentrated on his breathing.

After what seemed like only a minute or two Yogeshwar chanted a drawn out vowel sound, "Aaaa-uuu-mmmmm." Budhitra joined him. When their chant ended, stillness hung in the room like dust motes in a sunbeam.

"In this morning's meditation it became apparent no one has provided our dear Sultan with any specific instruction for meditating," Yogeshwar said. "So, this afternoon I chose to teach you a technique."

"Breathing?" the Sultan said.

"It's the thread that ties you to life, is it not?"

The Sultan nodded. Frith already knew this but he nodded too.

"If you are the watcher of your breath, who is doing the breathing?" Yogeshwar said.

"The energia," Frith said.

"Explain," Yogeshwar said.

He felt pride, as if he had given a clever answer to a teacher. At the same time, he could see how ridiculous that feeling was. But Yogeshwar didn't seem to be mocking. "My master taught that movement of the energia causes breathing."

Yogeshwar smiled. "Prana, Frith. What your master called energia we call prana. Prana is the spiritual energy, the life force, in our body, in all living things."

Budhitra cleared his throat. "Frith's master might have been referring to Shakti."

Yogeshwar nodded to Budhitra. "That could be, however our access to Lancelot's teachings are limited to what Frith understood at the time."

"Why conjecture?" the Sultan said. "Is there any real difference?"

Frith realized Jacob was right, the Sultan pretended to know more than he did.

"Prana is the life force," Yogeshwar said. "In various forms it's the power that causes us to breathe, digest, excrete, circulate our blood, and more. Shakti is energy too, but more subtle than prana. She is the primordial cosmic energy or primordial force of all creation. As such, Shakti can be said to move within us. But to perceive Her, you must first learn to feel prana."

"So, we are being breathed by the prana," Frith said.

Yogeshwar nodded. "Well put. Now, when you watch the breath, try to sense breathing as one continuous cycle with two phases."

This interested Frith—he'd never heard that before. But the Sultan was looking out the window.

"Dear Sultan," Yogeshwar said.

The Sultan turned his head toward the swami.

"Lord Shiva taught there is a point where the breath turns from down to up and another where breath turns from up to down. There, for a split second, it seems to pause. The breath does not actually stop, but appears suspended. At these points the in-breath and out-breath fuse into one. The sages call it 'offering the incoming breath to the outgoing breath.' When performed correctly, the yogi can touch the source of life in those moments."

"I've meditated for three years by watching my breath, but I've never noticed that." Frith had often wondered if there was some flaw in his practices that kept him from realizing the Grail, sure it was his own failure. Now, he realized there was more to it. This was why he needed teachers.

"However, that's not meditation," Budhitra said.

Frith frowned. "It's not?" Lancelot had said it was.

"It's a technique for concentration," Budhitra said. "Once you are able to perfect and hold your concentration, then you can achieve true meditation."

The doors flew open and Frith heard giggles as the Sultan's youngest son burst in and raced to the Sultan. The boy's older sister and two of the wives quickly followed, apologizing profusely, but only adding to the turmoil. The child tugged on the Sultan's hand even as his mother scooped her arm around the boy's waist and pulled him away.

The Sultan rose. "Holy sirs, sadly it seems family duties require my attention. Please continue without me. I shall see you all at dinner." He bowed, and allowed himself to be led away.

Frith suspected the Sultan, tired of sitting for long meditations, welcomed the excuse to leave. He himself felt an urgent need to pee, but he didn't want to seem as flighty as the Sultan. If he could find a graceful way to make a brief exit, it would free his mind from bodily concerns.

"Let's take our meditations to our individual rooms for the remainder of the day," Da Shi said. The others nodded, and Frith was grateful.

After relieving his bladder, Frith went to his room, intending to practice offering the in-breath to the out-breath, but a servant came to tell him Jacob had arrived early and was waiting for him in the outdoor courtyard. He assumed Jacob, nervous about allowing him to live at the Sultan's, had come to check on him. Frith joined Jacob and asked one of the servants to bring them drinks.

"Are you their new master?" Jacob said.

Frith felt himself blush. "No, it's just they… they want to be helpful… so I—"

"Don't let it go to your head," Jacob said. "Your ability to command does not make them lesser or you better."

"I know that."

"It's difficult to remember though. Treat everyone with the deepest respect, or you will learn nothing here."

"Did I speak to the manservant improperly?"

"No, I was merely cautioning you. It's your first day here."

"Thank you," Frith said. "Your advice is always appreciated."

"So, how go your lessons?"

"Excellent. I have learned so much already. Jacob, do you think we could have more than one spiritual master?"

"I told you be respectful of other teachings, but remain loyal to your own."

Frith bit his lip.

"Have you learned what the Sultan intends?" Jacob said.

"He's given the gurus a great room in his palace to set up a school of philosophy."

"Are you its only student?"

"No, the Sultan is too."

Jacob laughed. "Of course, he would be."

Frith lowered his voice. "I see now, the Sultan hasn't exactly mastered the things he talks about at supper."

Jacob looked like he was about to respond when the Sultan strode into the courtyard. Jacob touched his finger to his forehead in greeting.

"You see Jacob, Frith is thriving here, as I promised. We made remarkable progress in just one day."

"Did you?" Jacob said.

"Oh, yes," the Sultan said. "Wouldn't you agree, Frith?"

"Absolutely, sir. I've told Jacob as much already."

The Sultan beamed. "My humble palace will become a great school—better than Nalanda, even. Students from both east and west will seek esoteric secrets in Samarkand."

"Is that so?" Jacob said.

"Yes. Starting tomorrow I'm sending my eldest son, too. Jacob, you're welcome to join us. These gurus know things few other men do."

"I know, I've perceived that from dining with them every night."

"Of course you have. But our evening discussions debate the merits of each man's theology. I admit I thought the school would be a deeper exploration of the same, but today's lessons provided more practical techniques."

Frith's stomach rumbled, he looked wistfully toward the door.

The Sultan heard Frith's stomach growl and laughed. "Speaking of practicalities, I think we can go to dinner early. It will be interesting to see if today's undertaking alters tonight's conversations."

CHAPTER 24

At dinner, the holy men informed the Sultan that in the future they would divide up the day. Each of them would hold a meditation and give a discourse. "There's no need for all three of us to be there," Budhitra said. "I'll conduct the first class tomorrow."

In the morning the Sultan brought his son to class. Budhitra led a rigorous meditation during which he did not allow their concentration to waver. "Perfect concentration leads to true meditation," he said. Repeatedly.

Two hours later, Yogeshwar arrived to begin his session, and the Sultan used the interruption as an opportunity to excuse himself. The Sultan's son followed his father's example and slipped out with him. That left just Frith, Budhitra and Yogeshwar. Budhitra decided to stay.

"The work we're undertaking involves a monumental restructuring of the mind, heart, and soul," Yogeshwar said.

"The challenge," Budhitra said, "is to not turn your back on the world in your quest for spiritual enlightenment, but to dedicate yourself to its divine transformation." He gave a heavy sigh. "In my country, too many monks do the former, not enough the latter."

Frith's brow furrowed. "The changes you describe sound formidable. Will there be enough time before I have to leave Samarkand?"

"Don't worry about time," Budhitra said. "The merit of spiritual effort accrues."

Frith turned to Yogeshwar. "Was that true for you as well?"

Yogeshwar looked toward the ceiling and spoke as if far away. "A change occurred where I no longer sat in meditation to do my practice, but to immerse myself in ecstasy. Instead of wanting to get up and get on with my day, I tried to remain in that state as I moved throughout the day."

That sounded like Alura.

"We can teach you practical techniques for transcendence," Yogeshwar said, "but ultimately you must not merely transcend form, you must transform it."

"What does that mean?" Frith said.

"Accept responsibility for more than just your own spiritual life," Budhitra said. "Extend love to those you encounter."

Did that mean 'Love your neighbor as yourself?' Or was he expected to become like Lancelot? "My master specifically told me to never assume I was ready to teach what he did."

Yogeshwar laughed. "Don't worry, you're not ready. What we're saying is the actual purpose of witness consciousness is the transformation of being."

"Transformation of *all* beings," Budhitra added. "A man on his quest is seeking his own enlightenment. A Bodhisattva seeks enlightenment for all."

This felt too grandiose for Frith.

"Developing your compassion for all sentient beings transforms you, and universal love is thereby attained," Budhitra said.

"So, how is enlightenment connected to compassion?" Frith said.

"There are different levels of compassion," Budhitra said. "Compassion that comes from acceptance takes oneself and others at face value. Then there is compassion from a place of absolute Truth that seems austere because it knows human problems are the result of illusion, delusion, and error. But the supreme compassion is objectless compassion."

Yogeshwar added, "This highest form of compassion is an expression of the joyous, ecstatic state. It originates from an inexpressible mystical and spiritual essence. A being who's Shakti feeds all, I call that person enlightened."

Frith screwed up his face and looked at Yogeshwar. He felt Yogeshwar's penetrating gaze. "Spirituality is not about getting more for yourself. It's about holding on to less. Whatever degree you diminish the suffering within yourself you will diminish the suffering of those around you."

Frith shook his head. The words were beginning to blur together and lose their meaning.

Budhitra answered as if he knew Frith's thought—and well he might. "He who sees with empty mind doesn't see other people as objects of his compassion. Compassion is just an expression of his nature."

* * *

Several days passed with Frith pressing the gurus for a technique for attaining true compassion. But Budhitra always said something like, "True emptiness is true compassion."

Frith was sitting alone waiting for class to begin. He still wasn't sure what Budhitra was talking about, but apparently it was something you had to do to comprehend. So he'd tried mightily to become empty. He closed his eyes and thought of Alura for whom compassion seemed effortless. Perhaps she was like the compassionate one Yogeshwar had described who didn't need to give anything because it poured out of her. Yet, Alura wasn't empty headed. She was one of the most intelligent people he knew. So why had Budhitra said an empty mind was the key to compassion?

Frith opened his eyes to discover Budhitra and Da Shi sitting across from him. He hadn't heard them enter. Either he'd been lost in thought or they moved without sound.

Budhitra raised one finger. "Empty mind doesn't mean 'without understanding.' It means a mind of perfect clarity, free of judgments, opinions, beliefs, wants, likes, dislikes. Empty mind means emptying the mind of me-ness."

Frith wondered how these men always knew exactly what was worrying him. "Doesn't empty mind require stopping our thoughts?"

"Not at all," Budhitra said. "All you need to stop is the mind's habit of creating preferences."

"Get rid of preferences," Da Shi echoed.

Frith swallowed hard.

"When I say to get rid of preferences you shudder because you think satisfying them is what makes you happy," Da Shi said. "You think if you have no preferences you'll never know happiness."

Frith shook his head. "No, that wasn't my reaction. I was thinking how many times Lancelot lectured Alura and me against preferences."

Budhitra raised his eyebrows. "Go on."

"He said likes and dislikes prevent us from seeing truly. That when we see a person or a thing, we don't see it for itself, but whether we like it or dislike it."

Budhitra broke into a broad grin. "He who understands that is very near enlightenment."

Frith bristled. "Oh, have no doubt, Lancelot was enlightened. He had direct experience of the Holy Grail four times."

"Only four?" Budhitra said.

"The fourth experience was permanent," Frith said.

Budhitra's grin softened into a kind smile. "It is right to have faith in your teacher. Did you understand he was talking about empty mind?"

"I didn't know what you meant by empty mind before, but now I think I do. You mean unclouded. Lancelot said preferences cloud our view of the Grail as though looking through a gauze curtain. He told us that when we become capable of observing the opposing forces in our mind, we'll transcend them."

"That's true," Budhitra said. "The natural state of mind is still—like the surface of a pond. If you drop a pebble in a pond, it *does* create ripples. If you leave the ripples alone, they'll naturally settle. That is empty mind. It's not that you don't encounter disturbances. It's that you recognize them to be temporary events."

"You're certain empty mind will lead to compassion?" Frith said.

"Absolutely," Budhitra said. "How could it not?"

CHAPTER 25

Throughout the week Frith struggled to develop empty mind, to develop compassion. He decided he needed to do something besides think about it. To transform the world, he needed to perform compassionate acts. One evening, as Jacob was leaving after dinner, Frith followed him into the outer courtyard.

"Coming back to camp with me tonight?" Jacob said.

"No sir, I wanted to ask you a favor. Would you accompany me into the city tomorrow?"

"Certainly."

"Also, I would like to have a few pieces of silver—an advance on my wages." Frith looked down at his feet. "I realize I haven't even been in camp and don't deserve any wages."

"Nonsense, of course you're owed a share of our profits. What do you need to buy?"

"Nothing. I want to help the poor. It's part of my spiritual work—to give compassionately to others."

Jacob broke into a huge grin. "A very worthy purpose. I'll come for you right after breakfast."

* * *

The morning air smelled of flowers as Jacob and Frith left the Sultan's. It was early and the heat was still sleeping. Frith found Samarkand surprisingly warm for a city so close to the mountains. Jacob turned on the road toward the market, but Frith pulled on his sleeve. "Not that direction, sir."

"We're not going into the market?"

"No sir, we won't find any poor there."

Frith had asked the Sultan where to find the hungry, the indigent. At first the Sultan denied Samarkand had any. He'd waved his silk-draped arm at the surrounding affluence. "Everyone here is prosperous."

Frith didn't believe him. Either the Sultan was too ensconced in his palace to know better, or he didn't want to admit any flaw in his adopted home. But thanks to Jacob, Frith had traveled more extensively than the Sultan. He'd been to Rome, Cairo, Tyre, Damascus, Baghdad, and Merv. Wherever he'd seen extreme wealth, he saw dire poverty dwelt in its midst. So he gently pressed the Sultan for answers. "What became of the lame? Where were the children without mothers?"

Reluctantly, the Sultan admitted there were pockets of unfortunates. "But you'll never find beggars in the central market. The militia ensures that... I suppose if you wished to deliberately seek them out, you might find a few out near the southern wall."

Frith and Jacob followed the sand road until its edges blended into a rocky dirt plane. There it disintegrated into tracks of bare footprints that wound around crude huts and lean-tos. Premium real-estate was under the scraggly trees that provided minimal shade. Onto these were tied as many awnings as could fit. Under the nearest a man with a missing leg was sleeping on his side.

Scores of naked children with distended stomachs squatted along the path and pointed to their open mouths. Frith clutched a knotted cloth containing the bits of silver Jacob had given him. He looked at it and realized he should have brought food instead. Against a tree sat an emaciated woman with her blouse open. In her lap lay two babies sucking desperately at breasts so thin and flat they surely contained no milk.

Frith went to her and bent down. She turned her face upward.

Her eyes were milky white.

He'd seen eyes like these before on an elderly monk who'd gone blind. But this woman wasn't old. From a distance, her gauntness had made her seem aged, but up close he could see she was probably younger than Alura.

He crouched down in front of her and worried the knots of his money cloth open. He looked at the shiny bits of metal and didn't know how to decide. What do you give a starving girl-child with two babies? How much to a man with one leg? Should he give extra for the blindness? He looked up at Jacob for advice and saw the naked, hungry children toddling toward them. It wasn't going to be enough. He looked around the camp. There would never be enough.

One of the babies in the woman's lap made a gurgling sound, and the nipple popped out of its mouth. She tenderly felt for the child's face with her fingers and turned its head back to her breast. When the baby latched on again Frith took her hand and pressed his whole purse into it. "Money," he said. "Feed as many of these children as you can."

Her cracked lips broke into a grateful smile. Several of her teeth were missing and he could see where her gums had bled. Frith stood up and walked away. He realized after a few steps that he was weeping.

He felt Jacob's hand on his shoulder. "No individual's charity can save the world, but every act of loving-kindness works to repair it."

A memory of one of the Abbot's sermons came to mind. The Abbot had started by reading a scripture, "If I bestow all my goods to feed the poor, but have not love, it profits me nothing." The pews squeaked as the monks, who had all taken vows of poverty, squirmed. "Jesus praised the widow who had only the smallest coin, yet gave it willingly. Do not think it was her poverty He praised, but the loving-kindness in her act. We, who have committed our lives to scripture and worship and charitable actions, must act with love or, as the scripture says, it is nothing."

In the abbey were pious men devoted to their worship, and a scriptorium full of scribes who clutched quills in tight fists and gave their days to copying the scriptures. Many of them did not care for the Abbot's sermon that day and were as anxious to leave as Frith.

The Abbot returned to scripture, "'Charity suffers long, and is kind.' It was not the poor woman's coin that earned Christ's admiration; it was what was in her heart. There is among kings and barons a great deal of charity without love. We strive to do better than them. Love is greater than charity because the gift is only a part of the greater whole. It is the loving compassion behind our actions that heal the world."

Frith blinked. "Jacob, what did you say about healing the world?"

"Repair of the world," Jacob said. "In Hebrew, 'Tikkun Olam.' In the Talmud, Simon the Righteous says the world's continued existence is due to three things: study of the Torah, worship, and performing acts of kindness. For me, Tikkun Olam means each of us does our part."

Frith looked at his hand, now empty. Only moments ago it held silver. Perhaps his charity was not meritorious. The money hadn't even been his. How had what he'd done been a compassionate act?

Jacob's hand pressed on the small of Frith's back. "Let's go. You've done what you came for."

Frith looked at the ragged horde. "But did I do anything?"

"You did what good you could. What did you feel?"

"Like my heart was ripped open."

"Did you give her the money to relieve your horror?"

"No, I felt it was the least I could do."

"You weren't reacting to the spectacle of misery?"

He thought back on it. "Um... no. I just saw them as the people they were. It was futile—it was arrogant—to judge who should get what, so I gave it to the mother. Something in me trusted she'd provide for as many other children as she could."

Jacob smiled like a proud father. "Maybe studying at the Sultan's school is doing more than I expected."

CHAPTER 26

Frith had been a student in the Sultan's school for nearly a month. Da Shi was the teacher this morning, but Frith was his only pupil. The Sultan had yet to arrive and might not. He had been showing up less and less often.

"Tao in the form of existence sprang from Tao in the form of non-existence." Da Shi's eyes flicked to the doorway.

Frith swiveled around, expecting to see the Sultan, and instead found Jacob, looking dour.

Jacob scanned the room. "So this is the Sultan's school."

Da Shi snorted. "Well, he thinks so."

Frith was surprised. The holy men were never disrespectful.

"I'd like to take Frith to market with me this morning," Jacob said.

"That's your privilege," Da Shi said. "Frith, go with Jacob. We'll finish your lesson later."

Frith knew enough by now not to argue. One look at Jacob and he'd seen something wasn't right.

They left the Sultan's and walked through tree-lined streets littered with yellow leaves. Jacob kicked a pile of leaves. "We should never have come to Samarkand."

Frith had seen Jacob angry and disappointed. But he'd never seen this... petulance before. "Surely not because I chose to live at the Sultan's?"

"I still worry for you, but it's more than that. Haven't you noticed? We are the only caravan left."

Frith hadn't noticed, but he tried to sound cheerful. "That's good, isn't it? We won't have any competition when the silk arrives."

"If it arrives." Jacob pointed toward the mountain range east of the city. "I've learned summers in the Pamirs are very short, and once winter comes it'll be at least eight months before any silk crosses them."

"Be patient, Jacob. The Sultan says it may only be another week."

"That's what he said two weeks ago. What if it doesn't arrive before the mountain passes close?"

"I'm confident the Sultan would invite us to winter with him."

"I'm sure he'd like that." Jacob ran his fingers through his hair. "I confess I let greed get the better of me. If we're trapped by winter, I will have made a costly mistake."

"How so?"

"I'll have to provide for my knights and the Bedouins. The extra expense of a whole season with no profit will undermine whatever we might have gained over just paying the higher prices in Merv."

"Can't we just buy and resell goods in the market until spring? You did well in Rome, and Egypt, and Tyre."

"I doubt there's any business we can do," Jacob rubbed his beard. "The Sogdians control all of it. No, we must leave very soon, or winter will bring financial disaster."

Their stroll had taken them past a foundry where Indian men were smelting steel. Frith pointed toward a furnace of fiery metal. "Sir, several years ago I had business with an iron monger visiting our village. According to him, the best iron in the world comes from India. It was highly prized in Britain. Perhaps if the silk doesn't arrive, you should consider iron."

"It's true. Indians produce the best. But it's heavy. What little we could transport by camel wouldn't bring the price of the same weight in silk. That's why everyone wants silk."

"What if we weren't hauling blocks of metal, but already formed goods—knives, swords, daggers?"

"I like your thinking, Frith… You'll make a good merchant yet."

"Thank you. But I'd rather be a yogi."

"You've been at the Sultan's too long. Let's go inside and see what these men are making."

The foundry had walls but no roof. The smoke burned Frith's eyes as the Indians poured the liquid metal into forms. Others were pounding hot iron rods into shape and plunging them into troughs of water, creating billows of steam. Boys on grinding wheels sharpened and polished the finished products.

Jacob located the headman and soon they were looking at an array of knives and swords of excellent quality. Jacob hefted a sword and tried it for balance. "I like it." Frith watched as Jacob negotiated a good price for four swords and gave directions to his camp. "Meet me there and I'll pay you upon delivery."

Frith and Jacob walked back through the market toward camp. "Sir, you didn't buy as much as I expected."

"I'm not a merchant of war. If I took a caravan of nothing but weapons, I'd have nothing but weapons to sell."

"Then why purchase any at all?"

"Gifts," Jacob said. "I've inconvenienced my knights with my Samarkand blunder, but I'll reward their patience with new swords. I think they'll be well pleased. These are beyond the quality of any they've ever seen—beyond any I've ever seen."

Frith was always amazed how Jacob seemed to find a diplomatic solution to every difficulty. But he did a quick count in his head and knew Jacob hadn't bought one for him. Still, doing a little business had lifted Jacob's mood.

"The new swords will occupy the knights for a time. If the silk ever comes, I hope it's as good as the Sultan says."

"Aren't you satisfied with what he's shown us?"

"Oh, the silk his wives wear is excellent, but that's what came before, not what's coming in the future." Jacob sighed. "Whatever its quality, we'll leave as soon as it arrives. But I dislike being in the position of having to take whatever's offered."

"The Sultan is not a spiritual adept, but I think he's an honorable man," Frith said. "He'll do right by us. You don't still mistrust him?"

"I have no choice but to trust him. It does me no good to assume he's kept us waiting for nothing, so I give him the benefit of doubt and hope all will be as he promised."

Jacob paused at a merchant's stall and began examining a large shoulder bag woven of fine camel hair and silk. "Frith, look at this. The workmanship is first quality."

Frith's fingers traced the intricate designs in the weaving. "It is. I've never seen anything like it."

Jacob tested the seams. "Sturdy too."

A strap as wide as a woman's hand and as long as Jacob's arm was sewn into the seams. Jacob looped it over Frith's head so it hung diagonally across his chest. But Frith's height made the bag ride too high on him.

"Can you make the strap longer?" Jacob said. The merchant took that as an excuse to haggle.

Frith couldn't imagine what Jacob was thinking. He took the bag off and admired it. Jacob snatched it from him, handed it to the merchant, and craned his neck peering into the neighboring stalls—a tactic Frith recognized. The man grabbed a length of string and raced over to measure Frith.

The cost and delivery date were set. They left the bag and proceeded toward camp.

"You felt bad I didn't buy you a sword," Jacob said. "This will serve you better. When you barter with other merchants, they'll believe merchandise carried in such a beautiful bag has higher value."

It seemed that everyone could read his thoughts. "But doesn't that beg protection?"

"That's what the knights are for."

"But even you have a sword."

"I do and I know how to use it, too. Had you stayed in our camp you might have learned from the knights, honed your skills. Instead you've studied strange things from strange men."

"That's unfair."

He ruffled Frith's hair. "It was only a jest. You know I support your spiritual studies. But Frith, you're no warrior. That's neither what you've chosen nor what's been chosen for you."

Frith frowned.

Jacob tapped his temple with his forefinger. "Think. Do the Sultan's holy men wear swords? Do the monks back at the abbey?"

"No."

"Wearing a weapon means you're willing to use it. I'm not sure you are, and that's no bad thing. Better to carry your wits and let those trained for battle carry out your protection."

* * *

Happy cries of greeting broke the air upon their arrival at camp. Frith hadn't been back since he'd moved to the Sultan's palace, and the knights seemed pleased to see him. They peppered him with questions about the Sultan's opulence, but his responses were stoic. He'd stopped noticing the comforts after his first few days there. Besides, how could he explain to these men who had rarely seen a feather bed that luxury wasn't the reason he was there? Jacob? Sure, he was spiritual himself, but the knights? What could he have said that they wanted to hear?

It didn't matter, his popularity only lasted until the sword bearers arrived.

Jacob paid the sword smith and distributed his gifts. The knights, excited with their new weaponry, hefted them, swung them about, and parried with each other. Frith left them to their play and returned to the Sultan's. Jacob was right. War wasn't a vocation for him. He spent his days in a state of peace in which the knights expressed no interest.

CHAPTER 27

Samarkand, November, 555

The late afternoon was unseasonably warm, so Da Shi had suggested they move out into the courtyard. Frith was sitting next to Da Shi listening to Budhitra discuss Buddhist ideas. "Mindfulness is not learning to watch your thoughts. It's learning to not become absorbed in your thoughts."

"But Yogeshwar has us watch our thoughts. Isn't that what all of you teach?"

"The technique helps you realize that you, the observer, are separate from your thoughts," Budhitra said. "Some teachers claim watching the mind will bring cessation of thought. But too often it simply makes students forsake learning to concentrate. That's a great mistake."

"It is?"

"Once you learn perfect concentration, you'll be able to direct your awareness where you want it instead of having it stolen by every passing fancy."

Frith glanced at Da Shi who nodded and said, "In thinking, let the past be dead."

"I'm afraid I don't understand what you mean."

"If we never let our mind become attached at any time to anything, we gain emancipation," Da Shi said.

"On that, Buddhists and Taoists agree," Budhitra said. "Non-attachment is a fundamental requirement."

Frith put his finger to his lips pensively. Did that mean they weren't going to help him reach samadhi?

Once again, Da Shi seemed to read his mind. "Rest assured, even though the path may be obstructed for many lifetimes by attachments, realization is ultimately attainable by all."

"Lifetimes?" Frith shook his head. "We don't have lifetimes. We must prevent attachments by breaking the habit of forming preferences."

Da Shi plucked one of the Sultan's flowers and handed it to Frith. "Very good understanding, you've not far to go."

Frith, bewildered, glanced at Budhitra who said, "How would you apply this to your own life?"

"My Master said whatever thought I put my attention on draws energia to it—I guess Yogeshwar would call it Shakti."

Budhitra waved his hand dismissively. "Either word is fine."

"Anyway, he said that when we take our attention from deciding what we want and don't want, the attachment caused by our involvement will diminish because we're not contributing to it."

Budhitra's eyes sparked. "And how did he say you could accomplish that?"

Frith spoke with confidence, now. He found his studies here were helping him understand Lancelot better as well. "We don't have to change the object or people or situation outside of us. We don't even have to change the feelings they create inside us. All we have to do is change the place within us from where we're observing them."

"Interesting," Budhitra said. "What do you mean by change the *place* within?"

Frith hesitated. He knew, but wasn't sure how to articulate it. Maybe that's what was meant by 'words aren't enough.' "Remember the connection between breath and movement of prana Yogeshwar taught the first day?"

Sunlight shimmered off Budhitra's bald head as he nodded. "We know it. Go on."

"Lancelot showed us the places in our body where we experience fear, love, wisdom, joy, bliss. He taught me, if I used breath to raise the energia from one location to another, it changed how I perceived the present moment."

"Very powerful," Budhitra said. "There are many ways to achieve nirvana, and that's certainly one of them. You should tell Yogeshwar what you can do. I know he'll be very interested."

"I agree," Da Shi said. "Swami will be highly intrigued."

The door from the palace opened, and the Sultan came outside. "Namaste … Jacob has arrived. Shall we move your discussion to the dining room?"

At dinner, Frith decided not to mention his ability in front of the Sultan. He knew Jacob would have advised against it. Let Budhitra or Da Shi tell the swami.

Chapter 28

Yogeshwar taught the first morning class, but Frith held his tongue until, as usual, the Sultan left. His son had stopped coming altogether. Not that Frith was judging—Lancelot had said not to.

Yogeshwar sat still as a mountain. He could do that for a remarkably long time. Frith considered how to broach the subject. "Have Da Shi or Budhitra spoken to you?"

"Last night, at dinner."

"Oh." He knew it hadn't been brought up then. Why hadn't one of them told Yogeshwar in private? Budhitra acted like it was important... Wait, what if asking if they had spoken was too specific? Maybe these gurus read each other's minds. "I was wondering if you knew what I told Budhitra and Da Shi yesterday afternoon."

"How would I?"

"I guess I thought—"

Yogeshwar's eyes pierced him. "Why don't you just tell me?"

Frith spoke to the floor. "Can breath flow in and out through our chest or forehead?"

"What a question! If we pinch our nostrils and close our mouth, can we still breathe? No. Obviously not." Yogeshwar's eyes twinkled. "Unless... Have you experienced that?"

Frith realized after yesterday's lessons that he'd divulged secrets he'd been warned to keep. Lancelot had said, "What we discuss must not be spoken of elsewhere. If you tell of it at the abbey, you'll be excommunicated or treated severely."

He'd struggled with this a bit that morning. But he wasn't at the abbey; and these monks certainly weren't about to excommunicate him. Perhaps Lancelot wouldn't have minded.

Frith swallowed hard. "If I have, can you explain it to me?"

"Describe your experience in more detail," Yogeshwar said.

"While she was making soap once, my sister's dress caught fire. Luckily she wasn't burned, but Lancelot said the fear caused by her ordeal needed to be removed. He taught me to move her energy by moving my own, using breath."

"Ah, I see. You're describing an effect of pranayama. Go on with your story."

"He told me to imagine an opening in my chest, to breathe in through my heart and upward until it reached the point between my eyebrows. Then I should exhale, and it would flow out of me."

"Did something move with the breath?"

Frith squirmed. "It certainly felt like it. Also it seemed to affect Alura in a manner that satisfied Lancelot."

"Have you practiced this on anyone else?"

"No, just myself. I use it to change the place in me from where I observe my thoughts and feelings. Budhitra told me to tell you about it."

"It's good you did. You understand, breath is not actually entering and exiting those places? It's Shakti you feel moving, not air."

"But can my Shakti move someone else's?"

"Wasn't that your experience when healing your sister?"

"Yes, but..." He decided to tell Yogeshwar the rest of it. "Later, Alura and I were initiated by Lancelot. He held his hands near our spines and caused sensations without touching us."

"Oh, yes. Shakti can be transmitted by a guru. We call it Shaktipat. But we also can rouse the Shakti ourselves using pranayama. I'm interested in seeing to what extent you can move your own energy. Please…"

Frith blushed. "I'm not Lancelot. Alura's the enlightened one."

"Don't be modest. Simply do as you just described. I want to observe what happens."

Frith knitted his eyebrows and concentrated on his breathing.

"Don't try," Yogeshwar said. "To try, we must think about what we're doing. The less you try, the more the Shakti is free to flow the way she wants. Prana, Shakti, are conscious-intelligence. The energy knows what to do. Trust it."

Yes. Lancelot had told him exactly the same thing. He was beginning to wonder if Jacob was wrong about having to give up his own traditions to accept the Eastern teachings. It was starting to seem as if they weren't so different.

Frith let go of trying. After practicing the breath sequence a few times, the energy began to flow as it had with Alura, in through his heart and out at the point between his eyebrows.

Frith felt Alura—their strongest connection since he'd left the abbey. It wasn't a vision of her, more a sense of her, as if she were sitting next to him. He felt Yogeshwar's presence, too. The swami's was overwhelming, like midday sun is to candlelight. Frith opened his eyes, surprised they were still in the Sultan's school.

Yogeshwar caught his eye, and then…

The swami's gaze fixed on a place deep inside him. It penetrated the layers of pretense to expose the point where mind and conscious-energy met. Yogeshwar's voice emanated from all sides of the room, from above and below, "Listen to me without conceptualizing or analyzing my words."

Frith experienced a sensation in the middle of his brain—an inch or so behind the point between his eyebrows. Not rhythmic, like a heartbeat, but rather the first half of a pulse that extended and sustained.

"There are centers in our body, called chakras," Yogeshwar said, if he was speaking at all. "These are points where subtle energy channels align along the spine. There are seven of them. The first is at the base of the spine, and the seventh is at the top of the head. What you are feeling right now is the sixth center."

Frith blinked. Yes! He remembered this, too. When Lancelot initiated them, he sent energy into each of these centers. Surely what Yogeshwar was talking about was what Lancelot had shown them.

Yogeshwar closed his eyes and shook his head. "Why did you go away?"

Frith's face got hot. "I was remembering. I experienced these centers when Lancelot initiated me."

"It's advantageous you already know what I'm talking about, but there's work to do. You turned away from the present, to talk inside your head about the past."

"I didn't *turn* away, it just happened."

"That's your next challenge. Learn to observe without leaving your seat."

"I'm sorry."

"Oh, don't regret. Just make it better each day and one day it will be completed." Yogeshwar paused for a moment and Frith took the opportunity to adjust his cushion.

"There are many ways to work with Shakti," Yogeshwar said, "Pranayama is one."

"You used that word earlier. I don't know its meaning."

"Prana, you already know. It's the life energy causing our bodily functions such as breathing. Ayama means to extend the breath. Just as prana causes the breath to move, we can use breathing to cause prana, and thereby Shakti, to move."

Frith tried again, breathing in and upward, and then exhaling.

"The real goal of pranayama is to move the Shakti the whole length of the spine, from the root to the crown." Yogeshwar drew a line in the carpet, his finger leaving an indentation in the silk tufts. "At the base of the spine, here, is a hidden reservoir of Shakti called Kundalini." He slid his finger to the top of the line. "When Kundalini is released, she moves up the spine carrying the aspirant's consciousness into the chakra at the crown of the head."

Frith lifted his eyes from where Yogeshwar's finger had stopped on the carpet. True, when Lancelot initiated him, he'd felt energia rise through his spinal centers.

"Kundalini can bring on samadhi, bypassing years of arduous spiritual practices."

Frith nodded. That sounded good to him.

"Awakening the Kundalini is just a beginning, not an end. Meditation and yogic practices are necessary to purify and strengthen the adept after samadhi. Otherwise, he will appear stupefied or insane."

"That didn't happen to my sister. She never became paralyzed or crazed."

"I've never met your sister, so I can't speak to her situation."

"Our master died, and something came upon Alura of its own accord, intangible as a rainbow. It has surrounded her ever since. Yet, we were standing together. Why did it not transform both of us?"

"I see you've carried this concern a long time. What would you have me do?"

Frith was willing to risk it all. This was why he was here. Jacob would leave as soon as the silk arrived, and he might not have another chance. "Will you give me this experience?"

Yogeshwar remained quiet for such a long while that Frith wondered if he'd gone too far. His eyes danced nervously around the room. When he looked back, Yogeshwar held his gaze. It was as if the swami was looking inside his soul.

"It's not that we go to enlightenment. It's that we don't leave it." Yogeshwar was again still.

Well, you had to get there before you could stay there. Hadn't Yogeshwar just said there was a yogic method of transmitting Shakti?

After a time, Yogeshwar sighed. "Try meditating again."

Frith closed his eyes and concentrated on his breathing. He tried to imagine following the line Yogeshwar had drawn in the carpet, breathing his energy up from the base of his spine to the top of his head.

"Frith, stop trying. Some things are moving. The breath is moving. The mind is moving. Let them settle. Instead of striving to become enlightened, cease thinking that you're not."

Stillness settled around them like an evening mist. Frith was unsure how long they sat, but it seemed a long time. Although his eyes were closed and turned upward, he knew when Yogeshwar stood and soundlessly came toward him. It wasn't a function of his senses, but perception of energy that made him aware the swami was standing over him.

An emanation from the swami engulfed him. He knew the precise moment Yogeshwar's hand hovered over his head, for at that second a lightning bolt leaped from the base of his spine up to Yogeshwar's palm.

Frith saw stars. It was like looking at the Milky Way on a moonless night. A river of stars poured upward, through him, and out into the galaxy. Coursing energy shook him so violently the universe around him trembled. Throngs of bees, sounds of church bells, gongs, and the roar of waterfalls filled his ears. The beehive split open and sweet honey oozed into his throat. Cool and warm breezes blew over his palms and soles. He entered a state of ecstasy so compelling he'd never dream of leaving it.

Later, he became peripherally aware of people coming and going. He didn't care. Yogeshwar, Da Shi, Budhitra, even Jacob, were like phantoms in fog. He sat there the rest of the night, never opening his eyes as men came and left.

It was glorious. No, it was glory itself.

* * *

Jacob rushed into the room like a ram challenging a usurper. Budhitra and Yogeshwar trailed behind him. Frith was sitting on a blue cushion, alone.

Jacob went over to Frith and studied him. He waved his hand in Frith's face and poked his shoulder. Frith didn't respond. "What have you done to him?"

"No, more than he asked," Yogeshwar said. "He's in a supremely ecstatic state."

"He's shiny with sweat," Jacob said.

Yogeshwar shrugged. "It was hot today."

"But the evening's cooled. He's burning up. We should apply a cold compress."

Budhitra took Jacob's arm. "Leave him be. You've no idea what he's experiencing."

"Don't I?"

"Forgive me," Budhitra said. "I didn't mean to imply you lacked understanding."

Da Shi entered the room. "The Sultan says come to dinner."

Jacob turned to Yogeshwar, "Bring him out of it."

"He wouldn't appreciate that," Yogeshwar said. "This is his quest. It's why he's here."

"Frith never misses supper," Jacob said.

"He's dining as we speak," Budhitra said.

Jacob looked at the Buddhist as though he had two heads.

"He's imbibing the liberating, miraculous, sound of creation, which stops worldly thought," Budhitra said. "By sustained attention on that pleasing sound, Frith entered an ocean of infinity. He's immersed in a field of pure ecstasy. His mind has expanded into a great sea of joyful intelligence where he's becoming illumined with the mystic knowledge of enlightening beings. You wouldn't interrupt that, would you? Even for a Sultan's banquet."

Jacob stood staring at Frith. Da Shi and Budhitra came over, took his arms, and guided him from the room.

CHAPTER 29

Yogeshwar roused Frith from his ecstatic state at first light. "Some physical movement will balance the flow of Shakti."

Initially, Frith hesitated to perform the strange contortions Yogeshwar prescribed. Not out of disobedience, but because when the Shakti took over, he lost all control. His consciousness would race toward a white orb that appeared above him like a full moon, and he'd lose interest in his body.

The fact Yogeshwar could cause energy to flow in him as Lancelot once had was a welcome discovery. He remembered how, after Lancelot initiated them, both he and Alura craved to re-experience the energia. He felt the same way now. The difference was Yogeshwar could turn a trickle into a torrent. Lancelot's touch had been gentler, but only Alura was taken to the infinite.

Frith's first attempts to imitate Yogeshwar's postures felt clumsy. He was doing better now. He formed his body into an arch, keeping his hands and feet flat on the floor while raising his hips. Frith brought his right foot forward, next to his right hand, straightened his left leg and swung his torso into an upright position, shifting his weight and raising his head to look forward.

Jacob stood in the doorway.

To Frith, Jacob looked like a man trying to disguise worry with a tight smile. What was it, another delay with the silk? The last time Jacob arrived unexpectedly in the middle of the day was when they'd bought swords for the knights. Frith inhaled and stood upright, clasping his hands as if in prayer.

Jacob stepped into the room. "Good morning Swami, I'm relieved to find Frith up and around."

What did that mean? He had a vague memory of Jacob being there last night, but it seemed long ago and unimportant.

Yogeshwar walked over to greet Jacob. "I've shown Frith a number of yoga postures he is to practice every morning. Loss of control isn't a desirable result of samadhi. He needs to learn to be in both worlds simultaneously."

"I agree. Listen, I'm sorry to interrupt your lessons, but I need Frith to work for me today."

"That's good," Yogeshwar said. "Practical tasks are the best thing for him right now."

"Frith, get your boots," Jacob said. "The Sultan's waiting for us at his warehouse."

Frith looked down at his bare feet. Where had his boots gone?

Yogeshwar handed Frith a bowl of fruit and gave him a gentle push toward the door. "I'm sure the Sultan will serve food, but eat this for now."

Frith nodded obediently. "Namaste," he said and followed Jacob outside. They put their boots on and walked down a side road littered with camel dung.

"Warehouse?" Frith said with his mouth full of grapes.

"The silk's here at last. The Sultan sent word this morning."

"Oh," Frith said.

Jacob put a hand on Frith's arm and stopped walking. "Are you really all right?"

Frith smiled. "I am right with everything." Walking cleared his head, and he felt very capable of being in the mystical and physical worlds concurrently.

"You had me worried last night," Jacob said. "Budhitra kept telling me you were fine, but you clearly weren't. I warned you about mixing spiritual practices. Some things are not meant for Christians and Jews."

"No disrespect sir, but I've experienced a higher region, where there's no Christian or Jew or Buddhist or Taoist, just a presence of those who've arrived at thus-ness."

Jacob arched an eyebrow. "Tell me about this realm."

Once again he faced the way that words were just not enough. "Well, it's pure and always tranquil. Its light radiates through all worlds, inexhaustible, formless, pervading unhindered in all directions. All of its manifestations are like that magus's conjuring back in Merv." Frith gave a heavy sigh. "Unfortunately, I find myself right back here."

"Well, I'm happy you've had your mystical experience, but I'm also glad you're not stuck in the great beyond. What would I have told your family —Frith was locked in some Hindu's spell and died in Samarkand?"

Frith laughed. "No, the gurus all say I've much to learn, and a lot of work left, before I reach there."

"It's good to hear you laugh. You seem like yourself."

Frith laughed again, remembering who he'd been. "Oh, I hope not."

Jacob pointed to a brick building with a pair of double doors standing open. "That's the Sultan's warehouse over there."

They entered and said good morning to the Sultan. As his eyes adjusted to the light, Frith saw the warehouse stacked haphazardly with bundles of silk apparently unloaded in haste. The hides that protected the silk during transport had been untied and laid open. The contents of one bundle covered a table in the middle of the room. Jacob's face beamed with relief. He looked ten years younger.

They walked to the table and Jacob ran his fingers through the heap of silk. Frith saw Jacob's eyes well up as he turned his back on the Sultan and whispered, "It's more wonderful than I imagined."

"Isn't it everything I promised?" The Sultan said from across the room. "Tell me, was it worth the wait?"

Jacob nodded. Frith could tell emotions had gotten the best of him. Sensing Jacob didn't want the Sultan to see his reaction, Frith intervened. "I'm not the expert Jacob is, but I've never seen anything like it."

"Of course you haven't." The Sultan folded his arms in a smug stance. "I promise you, this is the richest fabric either of you have ever seen."

While Jacob surreptitiously blotted his eyes with his sleeve, Frith took a bolt of expensive-looking brocade over to the Sultan. "Do you think this would do for my sister?"

"Is she a queen, or a goddess?" the Sultan said.

"No." Frith looked down at what he held. The material had a rich garnet background into which flowers and leaves were woven with golden thread. Unlike lighter, airier silks, this one was almost as thick as a tapestry.

Jacob turned from the table and came to join them. He looked more composed. "Is this the one you want for Alura?"

Frith looked from Jacob to the Sultan and then back down at the fabric in his hands. "I guess." He hadn't really chosen. It had just leapt into his hands in his desperation to save Jacob's dignity.

"Don't worry," Jacob said. "If you find something you like better later, I'll let you change your mind."

The Sultan smiled broadly. "I doubt he will. I think Frith has reached into a trove of jewels and plucked out the diamond."

"Speaking of which." Jacob retrieved a pouch from inside his tunic and spilled a handful of jewels into his palm.

The Sultan's smile disappeared. "Is that all?" His eyes swept the warehouse full of silk and back to Jacob.

"Not all," Jacob said. "But let's see how much this buys."

The Sultan sighed. "Jacob, you've proved to be a patient man. I promised you first selection. Take what you can afford and leave what you don't want for others. I'm not worried about what to do with it. As you can see, it's all first quality."

Jacob poured the gems back in the pouch and began examining the silk in earnest. Jacob had Frith hold one end while he fully unfurled each bolt. Then with great care they would refold the material as it had been. As the morning wore on, they added the bolts from the bundles on the floor. Virtually every one they examined met with Jacob's approval. The stack of acceptable items grew until nothing more would fit on the table. Jacob said he was ready to begin negotiations.

The Sultan suggested they have something to drink first. His servants laid down a thick carpet, its length and width about a man's height. Next, they brought in a low table and set silver glasses of pomegranate juice on it. The Sultan invited Frith and Jacob to sit. The rug was a little crowded with the three of them on it, but the situation didn't last long. As soon as he'd drunk his juice, Frith was asked to fetch one of the bolts of silk.

Over the next hours, he'd carry a bolt of silk to the men. They'd run their hands over it, rub the fabric between their fingers, hold it up to the light, and haggle. When the price was settled, Frith would carry it away and bring another. To prevent confusion, a large camel hide was laid out, and Frith stacked the purchased goods on it. The Sultan would warehouse everything until they were ready to depart. Frith thought that showed remarkable trust on Jacob's part.

Frith watched them negotiate and realized the two of them were very similar. The Sultan also exhibited Jacob's knack for making the other man feel he'd gotten the better end of the deal. So piece by piece, every bolt was analyzed, discussed, and bartered for individually. The Sultan had an abacus on which he was keeping tally. Jacob kept an eye on it.

To Frith, it seemed to take forever. They stopped for lunch and then resumed. Jacob claimed he was in a hurry to leave Samarkand before winter, but this was going to take days. Frith knew he was supposed to learn from watching Jacob, but he'd never wanted to be a merchant in the first place. And now… He'd missed afternoon meditation. He recalled Da Shi's walking meditation technique and tried to practice while carrying the silk. It made time pass.

The table was nearly empty when they came to the garnet and gold brocade Frith had selected earlier. Once the price was settled and added to the tally,

Jacob wrote 'For Alura, from Frith' on a scrap of parchment and tied it to the silk. He gave it to Frith to put with the others. As Frith carried it to the purchased pile, the addition of the tiny parchment note seemed to make it weigh more. Was this the right choice for her? He wanted her to have something truly wonderful. But what if he wasn't there to give it to her? That was something he needed to discuss with Jacob.

When the light through the warehouse doors began to wane, Jacob said, "It's getting late. Let's settle up now and start fresh tomorrow." He looked at the abacus and nodded. Frith knew Jacob had kept his own running total in his head. Jacob counted out the gems and deposited them on the table.

The Sultan swept them out of sight with an almost offhand gesture and said, "I'm famished. Let's eat."

"I agree," Jacob said. "Enough business talk today."

Jacob put the remaining jewels back in his pouch, and the Sultan counted them with his eyes. "We'll finish up in the morning."

"We'll try." Jacob slapped Frith on the back. "A good day, Frith."

* * *

The next morning Frith walked to the warehouse with the Sultan. Jacob arrived, accompanied by Sir Otto, who was bearing a large chest. Otto put the chest on the carpet next to Jacob and left. It was the Sultan's turn to be surprised. When Jacob opened the chest, it was filled with pearls. If the Sultan had expected to exhaust Jacob's remaining wealth that morning he was mistaken. Frith compared the number of bolts they'd purchased yesterday with the quantity of silk remaining and thought it was going to be a long day. He might not get to see the gurus until suppertime.

Midmorning refreshments were brought, then lunch, and then afternoon beverages, all while Jacob and the Sultan meticulously examined each piece of silk, argued its merits and set a value. Frith continued to port the fabric to and from the two men.

When the table of Jacob's choices was empty, Frith said, "That was the last bolt." But he saw numerous piles of silk remained.

Jacob held out his hand. "Help me up. My knees are stiff from sitting."

Frith pulled Jacob up and reached out a hand to the Sultan, but he was already up. The Sultan gathered the pearls he'd been paid into a goatskin bag. "My men will lock up when you're finished. I'll see you at dinner."

Jacob had maintained a stoic countenance during negotiations, but perhaps because he was now more spiritually aware, he could tell Jacob was elated. By mutual agreement, business wasn't discussed at dinner, where Jacob was happy and affable. The Sultan was too. His coffers were full. Frith was grateful for the evening hours with the holy men.

Two of the Sultan's servants entered the warehouse and began dividing the purchased silk into smaller piles. These were then wrapped in skins and tied into secure bundles, sized perfectly for a camel's back. It was obvious these men had done this many times. Jacob was in a hurry to leave Samarkand, and the Sultan's men were happy to help him go. Which meant Frith would be leaving the gurus far sooner than he wanted.

CHAPTER 30

On the third day, Jacob brought his cache of the purple dye they'd carried from Tyre. As soon as Jacob revealed it, Frith saw the Sultan's eyes glisten. Frith remembered Jacob telling him it would be invaluable to someone who traded directly with India and China, where they prized the color but had no way to make it. Frith hadn't been as interested watching two master merchants negotiate as he should've, but he learned something in that moment. The Sultan's eyes showed he had surrendered any advantage he'd had. Frith realized the Sultan would gladly trade away the rest of his silk for that dye. He knew Jacob saw it too.

They continued to work their way through the silk until the table was, again, empty. The Sultan peeked into the chest at the remaining ampules of purple dye. "I'm going to leave you two to make your next selections while I attend to some other business. Have Frith come find me when you're ready to resume."

Although Jacob professed an urgency to get started home, his actions belied his words. He was as meticulous as ever, insisting they open and examine every bolt to the end. It was a time-consuming process, but Jacob disabused any suggestion of short-cuts. Frith couldn't see any reason for it. The Sultan had not exaggerated. Every bolt had been excellent quality, better than they'd seen in any market, and this was the last batch.

Frith walked backwards unrolling the fabric. Jacob, holding the other end said, "Frith, you should see your camel. Her wool's grown long and dark in many places."

Frith smiled. He hadn't thought of Parisa in weeks. He'd forgotten how much he loved that camel.

"In the mornings, when it's cold, she stands sideways to put her darker fur toward the sun." Jacob walked toward Frith, refolding the material. "The Bedouins tell me it's a sure sign winter is coming."

"I'm sure it is. The tree limbs are bare; leaves litter the streets."

"It's time for you to come back to camp. Reacquaint yourself with her. We'll ride out in a day or two."

"No…"

"Yes. We've delayed too long as it is. Every day adds risk that we won't make it across the mountains."

"The Sultan has—"

"What?"

He was going to save this until after dinner, but perhaps now was as good a time as any. "He's invited me to winter in his school. To continue my study with his masters."

Jacob rolled his eyes. "I'm sure he has, but it's out of the question."

"Why? You don't need me to protect the silk. I don't even have a sword."

"Is that what this is about, because I didn't buy you a sword?"

Frith found himself surprised and annoyed. He had thought Jacob was a spiritual seeker himself. "You know that's not it. Ideas are being taught here I can learn nowhere else. The experiences I'm having—even Lancelot didn't give me."

Jacob pressed his lips together and was silent.

Frith thought maybe he was considering letting him stay. "Jacob, you've tried your best, but I'm never going to be like your sons. I'm grateful you brought me out of the abbey to this palace of spiritual secrets, but Lancelot's Grail is within my reach and I can't just leave it."

"Frith, you've spent your entire life with people who let you do whatever you wanted. But you're a man now. I brought you here because of my promise to your father. I'm not going to leave you here. You *are* going to come back with us. I will *not* abandon you in some Sultan's den out in the middle of Central Asia."

"The Sultan promises he'll send me back with the first caravan in the spring." Frith pointed to the bundles of silk stacked around them. "You certainly trust the Sultan. You're letting him warehouse silk you've already paid for. Surely his promise to send me to Britain is just as trustworthy."

"Yes, I trust the Sultan would keep his promise. But the people on the next caravan might sell you for a slave, or you might be captured along the way. Caravans are attacked all the time. With us, you have the knights to protect you. As you say, you can't use a sword."

"But—"

"No buts, I have a commitment to your family to return you safely to Britain."

"But the gurus say two months of study aren't sufficient to become enlightened."

"I agree. But neither are six or eight. Ask them tonight at dinner how long it took each of them. They'll admit it's a lifetime work."

Frith just shrugged. He wasn't persuaded.

"When I came to take you from the abbey you initially refused me. But now you're here, aren't you glad you did as you were told?"

"Yes, of course."

"Then believe me now. You think you don't want to go back home, but once you're there, you'll be happy you did."

Frith's body tensed with resentment. "I can't imagine—"

"Stop it. You're leaving with us. No further argument."

Frith saw Jacob's determination and knew it'd be futile to resist a man who employed a company of knights. He slumped.

Jacob's expression softened. "Tomorrow I'll be busy provisioning the caravan. If you want, I'll let you spend your last day with the holy men."

Frith nodded and gave him a weak smile.

Jacob finished folding the silk and laid it on the table. "That's the last one." He patted Frith's shoulder. "Cheer up. Today we'll conclude our business, tomorrow I'll buy our provisions, and tomorrow night we'll have a farewell celebration with the Sultan." Jacob leaned toward him. "I'm going to surprise him by giving each of his wives a jewel."

"Why?"

"Goodwill, gratitude."

"Very expensive gratitude."

Jacob couldn't repress a smile. "This silk is going to tickle the avarice of the highest nobility—the ones who buy without counting the cost. The house of Zion is going to do very well. And now that I know such a journey is possible and profitable, I intend to send Levi and Micah here next year. Maybe you'll come with them."

Perhaps. But he thought of how much he was learning, and how quickly, and how much he had yet to learn. And he'd rather not leave Samarkand in the first place.

* * *

As Jacob predicted, they concluded their business after lunch. Jacob sent Frith with the Sultan, saying he'd meet them at dinner—he needed to stop by camp first.

Everyone was in the dining hall by the time Jacob arrived. "It's a good thing we're leaving," he said. "I just discovered my knights entertaining a great crowd with their swordplay."

"There's nothing wrong with a good display of mettle," the Sultan said.

"In general, no, but it draws unwanted attention to our caravan as we're about to leave."

The Sultan waved his hand dismissively. "I've told you not to worry. Samarkand is free of thieves."

"But what if among the audience is a spy for bandits beyond the city gates?"

"Then, it's good your men are sharpening their skills," the Sultan said. "They may have grown rusty."

"Hardly. My knights are always at their peak. The only things they need to keep sharp are their blades."

"You worry too much, Jacob. If such a spy existed, he might send warning your knights' prowess is too great to tangle with."

"May God's ears attend your words," Jacob said.

The Sultan took his seat. "Shall we eat?"

Jacob turned to the holy men. "Tomorrow will be our last day here. I promised Frith he could spend it with you, but tomorrow night he must return to my camp."

"But Jacob, you are coming to dinner aren't you?" the Sultan said. "I've planned a special feast."

"Certainly," Jacob said. "I'm simply making it clear to everyone that Frith comes with me when I leave."

CHAPTER 31

Frith awoke, dressed, and packed his bag before going into the great room for his last day there. When meditation ended, Frith faced all three of his masters.

"Thank you so much for all you've taught me," he said. "But… I must leave this evening. Please teach me as much as you can before nightfall. Or better, would Yogeshwar give me Shaktipat again?"

"Don't let wanting distract you," Da Shi said. "There is much you need to understand, and we have only today."

Frith thought Shaktipat still seemed like the easiest way. He didn't say so, but then he didn't have to.

"A single experience is sufficient to convey realization," Yogeshwar said. "Now, bring that awareness into the present moment."

"That is the Tao," Da Shi said.

"That is empty mind," Budhitra said.

Yogeshwar touched himself on the forehead. "Shakti is conscious-energy. She knows what to do. Just stay out of her way."

Frith imitated the swami, touching the point between his eyebrows with his middle finger. A galaxy of golden lights appeared. They superimposed everything he saw around him.

"What are you seeing?" Yogeshwar said.

"Sparkling lights."

"Good," Budhitra said. "Allow them to infuse all five of your bodies, to operate simultaneously at all levels of your being."

Frith shook his head in wonder. "Five bodies?"

"In Sanskrit we call them koshas, perhaps you would say... sheaths." Yogeshwar nodded to the others. "This will be our subject this morning."

Frith rearranged his cushion into a more comfortable position, and the gold stars disappeared. He touched his forehead again, but they didn't reappear.

The Sultan arrived late, took his seat, and said, "Shall we have midmorning refreshments?"

"Not now," Da Shi said. "Yogeshwar has just begun."

Yogeshwar patted himself on the leg. "First, is the physical body." He pointed to his heart. "Second, is the astral kosha. The chakras we discussed the other day are located in our astral body."

Frith screwed up his face. "So there's a body inside my body?"

"Your astral body isn't made of skin and bones," Budhitra said. "It's a sheath of subtle energy surrounding us. Think of seeing a man standing against a desert sunset—how the sunlight outlines his shape."

"Good example," the Sultan said.

"Thank you, Sultan," said Budhitra. "Please, Yogeshwar, continue."

"The next kosha is the mental body or mind," Yogeshwar said. "It too, is not a physical body, but a sheath of even subtler energy."

"It's a realm that perceives personal thoughts," Budhitra said.

"I'm confused," Frith said. "You've switched from talking about bodies and started calling them realms."

"Kosha does mean sheath," Yogeshwar said. "But this is why words are so difficult. At our center is Atman—what I believe you Christians call Soul.

It is supreme, beyond all koshas. Yet, the koshas are the vessels by which the Atman knows and interacts with the lesser states."

Frith scratched his head. This wasn't a time to feign understanding. It might be his last chance to ask. Certainly he'd never meet anyone else who knew this. "Exchanging the word state for realm didn't clear anything up for me. I'm having trouble imagining this."

"All right," Budhitra said, "think of how a man dresses in winter. A sweater over his shift, then a tunic, finally a cloak. Wherever he goes, all these layers move with him."

Frith smiled. "That helps."

"Beyond the physical realm, each subsequent level of creation is made up of increasingly subtler energy," Budhitra said. "Each kosha is able to sense energies of a certain level because the kosha itself is composed of energy of that realm."

"For example," Yogeshwar said. "Our eyes and ears see and hear things in the material world because they are part of our physical body. They can't see emotions or hear astral sounds, because those are not physical energies. But, the sheath of astral energy does sense emotions—both our own and others."

Budhitra nodded. "Enter a room where two people recently had a heated argument and you sense it. Feelings hanging in the room are disturbances in the realm that the astral kosha perceives."

The Sultan's stomach rumbled like a thunderstorm. "Shall we stop for lunch?" he said.

Frith wasn't as interested in his next meal as he was in what was being revealed. "Not yet, please," he said.

Yogeshwar nodded. "You have another question, Frith?"

"Lancelot taught me my body, feelings, and mind were separate from the real me, so I understand three sheaths. But I can't imagine what the other two koshas could be."

Yogeshwar smiled. "The fourth is the knowledge or intuitive wisdom sheath, and fifth is the bliss-perceiving sheath."

"The wisdom kosha is a purer intellect," Budhitra said. "Focused beyond me-ness, it provides unclouded reasoning and perception of knowledge far above the personal mind. I call it Buddhi."

The Sultan cleared his throat. "Doesn't the Hindu god Krishna say it is, 'When thought has passed from thinking?'"

Yogeshwar nodded. "Very good, Sultan."

The Sultan looked like a child given a treat.

"But it's a state above ordinary thinking," Budhitra said. "In fact, personal thoughts drop you out of the fourth realm, back into the mental body."

The Sultan's smile vanished.

"The fifth realm is a state of peace and bliss," Yogeshwar said.

"Lancelot told us of finding a place where peace passes all understanding."

"That certainly sounds like the fifth kosha," Yogeshwar said. "However, always remember, the Atman, your soul, is higher than even this state, for it is the perceiver of this state."

"*Who* is always higher than *what*," Da Shi said.

The Sultan swatted away a fly. "What does that mean?"

"The consciousness who is experiencing is always higher than what it experiences," Budhitra said.

"Oh, of course," the Sultan said. "That's it? We're done? That's the fifth kosha. Can we have lunch now?"

"You go ahead, please, sir," Frith said. "I've only a few more hours to learn what I can."

"But you have to eat," the Sultan said.

"Not today I don't."

"I'm surprised. That's very unlike you."

Frith laughed. "It surprises me, too. But you'll have the whole winter with these men. I won't."

"What about their lunch? Aren't you depriving them, too?"

"We're happy to forego lunch," Yogeshwar said.

Da Shi nodded and Budhitra said, "Yes, Sultan, please go have your lunch. We'll keep working with Frith."

The Sultan stood and bowed to each of them. "I'll just get a small repast and come back shortly." He walked to the door and paused. "I'll send a tray of fruit, in case you change your mind."

Yogeshwar flicked him away with the back of his hand. "That'll be fine."

The Sultan left and Da Shi exhaled a heavy sigh. "The work to be done cannot be accomplished in one day, or in one month, or in one year. Your practices must continue long after you leave Samarkand."

"But the three of you will tell me what I should do?"

"Of course," Da Shi said. "Thinning out the mind will make it more permeable; make it easier to pass between higher realms. There are many ordinary things you can do as well."

"Such as?"

"Seek equilibrium. Eat, but not too much. Sleep, but not too much. Don't lose your energy unnecessarily. Seek to maintain tranquility. Don't talk much. Don't wrestle with your thoughts. Maintain a balance between the inner spiritual state and the material world."

Budhitra added, "Practice seeing all beings as expressions of the one consciousness."

Da Shi nodded. "Although Yogeshwar has shown you techniques for raising the qi up, that isn't the only way."

"It isn't?" Frith said.

"There is a great secret only the highest yogis and Bodhisattvas know," Budhitra said.

Frith sat up on the edge of his cushion, spine straight, eyes alert.

Yogeshwar looked at Budhitra, pursed his lips, then said. "In addition to raising Shakti up, the divine can be drawn down."

"Can you tell me that secret before I leave?"

Da Shi stood and the other gurus followed.

Frith looked up. Had he overstepped? Were they done trying to teach him?

Da Shi motioned for Frith to rise. "Shall we engage our qi in a standing meditation?"

Frith rose.

"Maintain a relaxed stance, knees unlocked, feet shoulder-width apart. Feel your feet sink into the carpet, experience qi rooted in Mother Earth."

He copied Da Shi's posture.

"Frith, slowly float the palm of your hand over the crown of your head until you sense a point that tingles. That is the connection where qi lifts toward heaven. Once you know it, relax and allow both arms to hang at your sides. Feel the qi at the crown gently elongating your spine. Breathe slow regular breaths. As the qi lifts toward heaven, you will feel heavenly qi descend into your body."

They meditated in this manner through lunch time. Frith had his eyes closed, but he sensed the servant enter and exit. He was able to simply let the disturbance go and concentrate on offering his incoming breath to his outgoing breath, the uplifting qi to the descending qi.

Frith hovered in a state of peace, watching his thoughts float by, but he noticed the most frequent thought was the wish that Yogeshwar would do it again.

When meditation ended, Frith opened his eyes and saw the Sultan had not returned. He hadn't really expected him to. Da Shi indicated they should sit, and Frith settled onto his cushion.

"There you have it," Da Shi said.

"But that was not Shaktipat."

"Nor as dangerous."

Yogeshwar glanced at Da Shi. "When Da Shi said earlier, there was work to be done, he meant that, before you draw cosmic consciousness into you, you must prepare your body, your mind, your whole self. If even a fraction of the divine force enters an unprepared person, it will stun him like a lightning strike."

"Yes," Budhitra said, "Many sadhus in India who seek these experiences wind up useless. It's no good to attain higher realms if nothing flows out of you to anybody else. Remember the aim of a Bodhisattva."

"Samadhi is a step," Yogeshwar said. "Its purpose is permanent awakening —enlightenment."

"That's just what I'm seeking," Frith said.

"The way to seek is to be patient," Da Shi said. "All things rise and return, seeking tranquility, moving toward eternity. Knowing eternity *is* enlightenment."

Frith gave all three of them a suspicious look. "Shaktipat isn't dangerous with Yogeshwar to help me. Wouldn't I attain something now?"

"Yes, but would it stay with you when you leave?" Da Shi said.

Frith couldn't see why not. Alura had held onto whatever state she'd obtained from Lancelot. Why wouldn't he be able to hold onto this?

"If we tell you, there's nothing to be attained," Budhitra said. "It's not an abstract concept. It's truth. Being is not the result of learning to be, it just is."

Frith felt Yogeshwar's eyes penetrate him. "Given time, the techniques will deepen awareness within you. Meanwhile, learn how to handle waves of ecstasy while functioning in this world."

Lavender light through the windows cast long shadows across the carpet. The dinner hour—his final dinner with his teachers—had come. The holy men rose and Frith stared at their feet. He guessed this was it, school was over. He stood up, but he wasn't ready to give up. "I'll do everything you suggested. But permit me one last question…"

"You're not leaving us yet," Da Shi said. "We're only going to the dining room. Plenty of time for questions."

Frith twisted the carpet with his toe. "I know but… you may not want others to hear the answer. If your vow is to bring all sentient beings to enlightenment, how can you send me away without another samadhi?"

Yogeshwar looked questioningly at Da Shi and Budhitra. The two men shrugged. He held his palm over Frith's head and with his other hand struck him on the chest.

Frith settled back onto the cushion and entered a state of ecstasy.

* * *

Jacob was waiting in the dining room when Da Shi and Budhitra entered without Yogeshwar or Frith.

Jacob rose immediately. "Where is he?"

Budhitra jerked his head toward the great room.

Jacob stormed out, running into Yogeshwar in the hall. "Where's Frith?"

"He's chosen to fast tonight."

Jacob pushed past him into the Sultan's school. Frith was sitting cross-legged on a cushion. The room was dark. Jacob returned to the hallway and grabbed a candle. Shadows from the flickering flame followed him back into the room.

Frith was awake, but in the candlelight he looked glassy-eyed, like he was stunned or drunk. Jacob squatted down and shook him. "Frith, it's our last night. Come to dinner."

Frith slowly parted his lips, "No. Fasting."

"Fasting?" Jacob said. "Are you really going to forgo the Sultan's farewell feast?"

Frith sighed softly. "I'd rather spend my last few hours in the stillness of this room."

Jacob felt Yogeshwar touch his sleeve. "Jacob, aren't there certain occasions when you find it helpful to fast?"

It was true. He stood. "If that's what you wish, Frith, but you're definitely coming back to camp with me tonight. Are you packed?"

Frith absently nodded his head.

"All right, then. I'll be at dinner. Coming Swami?"

"Of course," Yogeshwar said.

CHAPTER 32

Something jabbed his ribs. Frith turned over. Euric's boot nudged him again. "Better get up, they're about to drop this tent on your head."

Frith rose and rolled up his blanket. He didn't see why he couldn't have slept one more night at the Sultan's. Here they'd all slept in a jumble among the stacks of provisions Jacob purchased for the trip back. Now Jacob had roused them, and it wasn't even daylight.

Everything except the main awning had been disassembled and packed up yesterday. Euric pushed him outside and called for the men to loosen the awning ropes. The Bedouins arrived with the camels, and the camp was instantly crowded. While the tent they'd shared last night was folded, the Bedouins loaded everything else. East of the city there was only a sliver of silver light. Frith couldn't see where he was going to meditate or when.

"There's some meat and bread over here," Otto said. "Better eat."

Loading didn't take long, and Jacob had the caravan at the Sultan's warehouse before the sky pinked. Four of the Sultan's servants met them and began carrying the bundles of silk out to the Bedouins. Frith asked a servant if the Sultan was coming. He really should say good bye.

"He's not up yet," the man said.

While the loading progressed Jacob called for the knights to gather. Frith, still dazed from yesterday's otherworldly experiences, was looking for a quiet corner of the warehouse where he could meditate.

"Frith, you come, too," Jacob said.

Glassy-eyed, Frith joined Jacob and the four knights.

"You'll notice I've instructed the Bedouins to distribute the cargo differently for our return trip," Jacob said.

Frith glanced absent-mindedly at the Bedouins, who were tying packages of silk to each of the twenty-four camels.

"The parcels of silk are softer and weigh less than the hard goods we brought to Merv. Our camels' burden will be lighter, and we should be able to outrun any bandits. But my entire fortune now rests on the backs of these creatures."

His whole fortune? Not quite. Jacob had confided to Frith he'd been able to buy the Sultan's entire lot of silk for less than he'd planned and still had a quarter of his jewels and gold left. Of course, those were on one of the camels as well, so Jacob wasn't wrong to say his fortune was at risk.

Jacob's hand fell on his shoulder. "Are you listening, Frith? Each of us, including you, will be responsible for two camels, both carrying silk."

Frith, nodded blankly.

"When we unload at night, the bundles of silk will be used as pallets for the knights to sleep on."

Otto smiled. "I've always wanted to lie down on a fortune."

"It won't be as soft as you imagine," Jacob said.

"Better than bare ground," Otto said.

"I'll leave it to you men to decide who sleeps and who stands watch." Jacob took Frith by the elbow and guided him to his camel. "You worry me, you don't seem right."

"I've never felt better."

Frith climbed on Parisa and patted her neck. She made a snuffling sound, which he took to be an affectionate response. The camel next to him answered her back. Jacob handed Frith the lead rope for the second camel.

"You can do this Frith. Just think of your sister. When we sell this, your elder brother's share will be more than enough to give Alura a nice dowry."

Jacob's words meant nothing to him. He had no desire for material wealth. And he knew Alura didn't care about it, either.

The camels rose more or less in unison and the caravan set off. The sun wasn't fully up as they exited the western gate. Frith turned and looked behind them. The sky over Samarkand was striped in fuchsia. By now, he thought, the holy men would be at their prayers and meditations.

Frith still hadn't done his morning meditation—the first time he'd missed a day since Lancelot had taught him. As they rode into the countryside, Frith looped the second camel's rope around his waist and trusted Parisa to follow the others. He closed his eyes and observed his breath. Although her gait jostled his body, his mind quickly became still.

In his interiorized state he didn't see the leaves shed by the trees carpeting the trail. The smell of the forest didn't remind him of home. The sounds of birds, camels, and the voices of men were no louder than a hummingbird's wings. With eyes ever looking inward, he was oblivious to the fact they left the forest and entered pasture lands. Comfortably ensconced on his camel's back, he felt a unity with Parisa, as though they were one being. She knew to follow the others. It didn't require his attention, and he loved her for it. In fact, he loved all creatures, be they beasts or men.

When his meditation ended he realized he could do his spiritual work wherever he was. Soon, he made-up a little song, which he sang inside his mind:

> *I can meditate on a camel,*
> *or walking on the ground.*
> *I can do it standing up.*
> *I can do it sitting down—*

"Frith, are you asleep?"

Frith opened his eyes and saw Sir Otto had ridden up on his left. He shook his head in silent response.

"It looked like it to me. Your eyes were closed."

Frith shook his head again.

"Did you see the yaks?"

Yaks? No. Frith shook his head a third time.

"You must've been asleep. We just passed half a dozen a few minutes ago."

Frith had seen the shaggy-haired oxen before, when they were on their way to Samarkand from Bokhara. Yaks had curved horns, sleepy eyes, and a large hump behind their shoulders. The farmers here kept small herds. Frith had once seen someone in the distance riding a yak on a saddle of colorful blankets, but the caravan hadn't gotten close enough to ask questions.

Otto furrowed his brow. "Are you all right?"

Frith just nodded. He had no interest in small talk. Truth be told, he was afraid idle chatter would pull him further from the gurus' teachings. How could he explain that to the knights?

"Well, say something."

"I'm practicing silence."

Otto laughed. "Not very well, you just spoke. Didn't you?"

Frith blushed and nodded.

"So, you're not talking to us?"

Frith nodded again.

"Aren't we good enough for you, anymore?"

Oh, no. He'd insulted him. That wasn't his intention. "I'm sorry, Sir Otto. I meant no offense. It's just that I'm having difficulty making conversation, and I thought the safest course would be to practice silence."

"Have it your way," Otto said. "But keep your eyes open from now on." Otto urged his camel onward and rode toward Jacob, at the front of the column.

* * *

The knights slept with the silk in one great tent, like the one they'd constructed in Merv, but Frith shared a tent with Jacob as they had on the journey east. After dinner, Jacob came in and sat down across from him. "Otto informs me you're not talking to anyone."

Frith nodded.

"You know, in my culture, when a boy becomes a man, he reads the Torah aloud in the temple."

Frith waited, interested in what Jacob would say next.

"Before my birthday, I practiced and practiced until I could recite it from memory so there'd be no flaw in my reading. But I was no better than a myna bird wearing a tallit. Although I knew the words in my mind, I didn't know the Torah. Do you understand what I mean?"

Frith shook his head.

"When you eat a meal, you put it into your body, but it takes a while to digest what you've eaten."

Frith nodded.

"I'd put the Torah into my mind, but it hadn't yet become part of my essence. That took a lifetime."

Frith looked at Jacob, expectantly.

"The Torah contains great wisdom, but in the end a man has to sort out his own life. You've just consumed a banquet of spiritual concepts. It's going to take a while to digest them. You have to understand that."

Frith understood. But he thought that's what he was doing. He wasn't sure how that related to making small talk.

"Do what you need to do. Just don't make it hard on those around you." Jacob opened his Psalms and began to read to himself.

Frith closed his eyes and wished he knew if practicing silence was the right choice.

CHAPTER 33

West of the Oxus River, December, 555

Frith decided Jacob was right. It was wrong to make things difficult for others. He respected the knights too much to hurt them. The monks back home understood the virtue of silence, but the knights didn't. Besides, Da Shi had only said, "Don't talk too much." That didn't mean not at all. So over the last few weeks, he tried to find his way to using words again while still being aware of his spiritual state. He still only answered when asked, and he could tell from the knights' expressions that his responses weren't appreciated. But nothing to be done about that. He could only speak from his current state of mind.

They'd crossed the Oxus River earlier today and were in the desert again. From atop Parisa, Frith saw a world where butter-colored sand extended to the horizon, and cerulean sky stretched from the horizon line to heaven. A change in Parisa's gait caught his attention. She alternately listed to the left, then seemed to skip a step.

Something wasn't right.

Frith pulled the reins. When she halted, he signaled her to kneel, but she wouldn't. He jumped to the ground, regained his balance, and examined her. Parisa's foreleg was swollen twice normal size and oozing. It hadn't been that way this morning. Something happened since. He stroked her nose and begged her to kneel. She tried. She bent her back legs and started to settle, but when she put pressure on the injured leg she fell on her side, raising a cloud of dust, and lay looking at him.

The caravan ahead continued unaware, but the riders behind him stopped. One of the Bedouins came over and probed her leg with his fingers. Euric handed Frith the rope to his pack camel and raced ahead to tell Jacob. The caravan reversed course and the remaining Bedouins gathered around Parisa. One of them began untying her packs, but it wasn't easy with her weight pressing on the knots. Frith went to help him.

As Frith and the Bedouin unloaded the fallen camel, Jacob surveyed the situation. "That's it for today. Start setting up camp."

While the tents were being set up, Jacob and Nazar conferred. When they finished Jacob said, "Frith, while the Bedouins take care of your camel, let's find some firewood."

They were on a treeless plain. Frith couldn't imagine where they'd find any wood. He also hated leaving Parisa, but the four Bedouins had crowded around her and pushed him aside. No doubt they knew camels better than he.

"The Bedouins suspect something bit your camel," Jacob said. "A snake or a scorpion, perhaps. It wasn't your fault."

Well, he still felt he should have noticed it sooner. "They'll know what to do, won't they?"

"They always do what's best. If we're to find wood, we should probably move further from the heavily trafficked trail."

They walked deeper into the desert. Frith looked back to make sure they wouldn't get lost. In the distance a pale orange campfire shimmered against daylight. "One of the others must have found wood," Frith said, and they turned back.

As they approached camp, the delicious smell of dinner permeated the air. The cook fire was larger than it had seemed in the distance. Flames danced over the large carcass on the spit and flared when drops of fat fell. Two knights turned the spit, and nearby dozens of strips of meat hung in the smoke to cure. The Bedouins were scraping a large skin. Where had they found game?

No!

Frith raced into his tent, trying to escape the sight. He swore he would never eat meat again.

Frith didn't sleep well. At first, he wept for Parisa, then later, despaired that he'd failed Jacob, who'd entrusted her to him. Parisa was dead and the remaining camels were needed by the others. He'd have to walk the rest of the way to Tyre. But there was no way he could keep up with the camels during the day. He'd have to start before dawn and cover some distance. They'd catch up and pass him soon enough.

He stepped out of the tent and saw Baldori on guard duty. The Italian knight wouldn't understand how he felt about Parisa—he'd call him a fool. Frith waited until Baldori walked to the other side of the camp, then took some cooked grain from last night's meal and wrapped it in a piece of cloth. He dropped it into the fancy bag Jacob had bought him. He also took a chunk of the cheese they'd bought from friendly goat herders before they'd crossed the Oxus River. He slung the bag strap over his shoulder and looked up.

The night sky was bright with an ocean of stars. Perhaps these were the same stars that dotted the sky on their journey to Samarkand, but they didn't seem so. They were brighter, more beautiful. Dazzling. They would light the trail for him. It would be like walking in stardust.

* * *

Something woke Jacob, a vague sense of wrongness. He saw Frith wasn't in bed.

Oh dear.

He lifted the tent flap and noted it was still deep in the night. Jacob scanned the camp for signs of robbers. Baldori, standing sentry, nodded to him and he waved back.

On the starlit horizon, a tall twig stuck upright in the dirt—a trail marker or perhaps a barren tree. It hadn't been there when they'd set up camp…

Frith.

Jacob started after him, able to pick him out clearly in the starlight. Frith was moving at a slow, steady pace, the kind someone could keep up all day. A midnight breeze swirled dust finer than millet around them. As Jacob drew closer, he could see Frith was walking, staring at the stars with the same glassy-eyed, perpetually amazed look he'd worn so often since they left the Sultan's. He caught up and tugged his sleeve.

Frith turned with a start. "Jacob."

"What are you doing out here?"

"I didn't want to hold everyone back. I knew I'd be slower on foot, so I thought I'd start ahead."

Jacob held his temper in check. He had to remember Frith was seeing the world differently. But still… he had to stop this sort of madness before it started. "Hold everyone back? Had you slipped away in the night, we'd have squandered a day searching for you."

"Oh… I… I'm sorry. I see now, I should have told you to go ahead without me."

Jacob's anger melted into laughter. "What are you saying? Do you think I'd abandon you?"

"I won't get lost. The road is well trodden."

"And you expect to walk all the way to Tyre?"

"Well, my camel's dead."

"We'll give you one of the others."

"But the silk… You won't have enough camels if I take another."

Jacob turned Frith around and led him back to camp.

Nazar came out of the knights' tent. "I heard voices… Are we in danger?"

"Only from lunacy," Jacob said.

"Oh, Frith. What's he done now?"

"Tell Frith you don't have the sort of attachment to your camel he did."

Nazar laughed. "I rode a hundred different camels before I was ten. To me a camel's a camel."

"Good. Tomorrow we'll redistribute the silk, and Nazar will ride one of the camels we've been using for cargo. Frith, you can have Nazar's camel."

"I don't mind," Nazar said.

"I knew you wouldn't. Now Frith, go back to bed. We've a long journey ahead, and we're barely west of Bokhara."

CHAPTER 34

January–April, 556

They were a day east of Merv and what Frith wanted to do was drift away into higher realms, the appeal of which was so strong it took a herculean effort of willpower to keep his mind on his animal. Parisa would simply follow the caravan while he attended to weightier matters. He daren't do that with his new camel. He was still adjusting to the rhythm and sway of its gait. He supposed all camels gave the rider a similar sensation—like sitting on a pile of rocks about to tumble. One thing though, he definitely wasn't going to name this camel. That only led to attachment.

When they reached Merv, the caravan stayed only long enough to restock provisions. They pressed on toward Meshed through wintery mountains that made his teeth chatter. By then, he and his new mount—he simply called it "camel"—were getting on well enough, although he still missed Parisa.

On the western outskirts of Meshed they came upon a man beating his son with a leather strap. The father was stout, with a round belly and a strong arm. The boy was no more than five or six. With each blow Frith's heart wrenched as if it were his own backside being blistered. He wished someone on the caravan would intervene, tell the man to stop, but his fellow travelers paid no mind.

He recalled young postulants and even older monks in the abbey telling how their fathers had beaten them. From their stories, he gathered it was the sort of thing fathers did. Perhaps his household was unique; he didn't remember Father ever beating him. Of course, he couldn't really remember Father.

The abbot had once told Lancelot, "Frith grew up surrounded by women who thought he could do no wrong." That wasn't correct—his mother and sisters knew many of his mischievous acts and had their opinions of them. It was more accurate to say he grew up surrounded by women who protected him. Although his older brothers teased him and father ignored him, none of them ever laid a strap to him.

What they did was abandon him.

In a moment of clarity, he realized he'd carried his bitterness halfway around the world. His father was dead. His abandonment was history, a burden he no longer needed to carry. He spat his resentment on the passing ground and forgave his father.

The caravan moved beyond the abusive man and his son. Frith tried to extend his energies in waves of blessing toward the boy, as he imagined Alura would have done, but the child continued to wail, and Frith knew he'd failed.

Between Meshed and Behistun, Frith's trust in Parisa's replacement solidified, and he resumed exploration of meditative states while he rode. Frith required little sleep now. At night he worked to integrate the energia from higher realms into his being, but during the day Jacob kept sending one knight or another to check on him, disturbing his endeavor.

At one point, Sir Nazar rode up beside him. He knew who it was, even with his eyes closed, because Nazar always smelled of spices. Frith ignored Nazar's presence and continued contemplation of a kosha above intellect.

"Not getting enough sleep?" Nazar said.

Frith opened his eyes. "I wasn't sleeping."

"Don't let the camel's cadence lull you. We're in the mountains now. Anything could happen."

As if to emphasize the point, Nazar's pack camel tried to nose up between them. Nazar tapped it with his riding crop. "Get back there."

Frith's camel surged ahead a few strides, but the line of camels in front of them forced it to slow. Frith turned back to Nazar. "We can perceive creation from a realm above ordinary thinking. That's where I'm going with my eyes closed."

"Yes, I'm sure that's well and good, but save it for nighttime. Ride with your eyes open at least until we get out of these mountains."

Frith's fingers were cold. He pulled his sleeves down and wrapped the ends over his hands. And he kept his eyes open.

CHAPTER 35

West of Behistun, May, 556

Jacob was glad when his caravan reached the western side of the mountain range. He no longer had to worry about snow. They'd traveled quickly and should be able to cross the Tigris and Euphrates in a fortnight. Familiar with the trail from their outbound journey, they'd found protected caravansaries most nights. Jacob recalled from experience those would become scarce once they were west of the Euphrates.

They'd stayed with the Prince of Behistun last night, but Jacob decided not to try to sell the Prince any of his silk. Since the Prince's palace was on the silk route, he wouldn't get the price European nobility would pay. How long before he'd see any profit depended on whether Micah had a ship waiting for them when they reached Tyre. They'd tarried too long with the Sultan, and he'd had no way to send Micah a message.

Jacob was a camel down and a man short—more than one man, really. Frith was so unstable it took a second man to watch him lest, in his dazed state, he veered off the trail and away into the desert. The cargo formerly assigned to Frith's camel had been redistributed amongst the others, just in case.

Fulfilling his old partner's dying wish had become a greater burden than he'd thought. He prayed daily for a solution.

Nights were not a problem. Frith usually went to their tent as soon as he ate, so it was easy to keep an eye on him. But his constant state of withdrawal concerned Jacob. He tried reading Psalms or the Torah aloud, but soon decided Frith had enough of a stew stirring in his mind. There was no reason to add to it.

Jacob's failure to draw him out left only the knights. Frith had always admired knights, so Jacob instructed them to keep him engaged. It was a practical solution since he had to keep a knight riding near Frith, anyway.

The plan was failing. Jacob was running out of knights willing to endure Frith's lectures about concepts they found incomprehensible and boring. The men told Jacob they'd just as soon let Frith ride in silence with his brains scattered in the clouds. "As long as he keeps his eyes open," Nazar added.

Last night Baldori had complained, "You know what he said to me? 'Making up how we want it to be in the face of what is, is a scourge upon reality.' I was talking about buying a horse, for mercy sake."

Jacob heard hoof beats and looked back. Euric rode up. "Jacob, I can't do it anymore. Those mountains we've just left?" Euric pointed to the white capped peaks behind them. "Frith tells me, 'A man born there looks on them and feels such love, it opens his heart to see the sun rise over them.' I think, all right, he's reciting a poem—which is fine if you like that sort of thing. But no, he says to me, 'A man who suffered frostbite crossing them, looks at the same mountains and sees only dread.' Then he says, 'Euric, mountains are neither love nor fear. The two men see the mountain through the veil of their memories.' What? Do I look like his student?"

"He doesn't mean it that way," Jacob said. "He's simply sharing ideas he finds interesting."

"Well, he's got a funny notion of what interests a body. I don't envy you putting up with it all night. I'll take my turn watching him while we ride, but I won't be starting anymore conversations. I don't want to hear what crazed thing he's thinking."

Jacob merely nodded. He'd pray again for a solution.

* * *

Sir Otto was sitting by the fire, poking the embers with a stick. Nazar sat down next him. "You seem worried."

Sir Otto shrugged. "Frith."

"Oh. Say no more. But isn't he Jacob's problem?"

"I gave a knight's oath to his sister to take care of him. I can't return him to her in his condition. He's... broken."

"No. Actually, he may be holy. I've seen it a few times, but do any of us except Jacob understand what's going on inside him? We have to follow his lead."

"Whatever Jacob's plan, it obviously isn't working."

Nazar scratched his beard. "My people have a saying, 'Women weep for many reasons, but when young men cry, the cause is always a girl.'"

Otto laughed. "That might be true, and not just for young men. But what good does your proverb do us? Frith isn't crying."

"He grieved for a woman before, didn't he?"

"I'm not following you."

"Look, we're only a week or two out of Baghdad. And who lives in Baghdad?"

Otto shook his head. "Not a bad idea. But Jacob told me we're not going into Baghdad this time. He's planning to cross the Tigris and Euphrates north of the city. Skirt the edge."

Nazar dismissed the problem with a wave of his hand. "So we take a quick side trip and find Elsa. She might lure him back to normal."

"I don't doubt a woman like her could do it, but do you really imagine Jacob would agree? You remember how furious he got last time?"

"Desperation changes a man's point of view. We could at least suggest it. She may succeed where he hasn't."

"You're the one to bring it up then. It's too long a trip back to Britain for me to make him angry now."

A few minutes later, Jacob walked over and sat by them.

"Otto's worried about Frith's mind," Nazar said.

"So am I," Jacob said. "Nothing I've tried seems to bring him back to the way he was before."

Nazar cleared his throat. "Maybe it's time to appeal to his more… human instincts."

"What do you mean?"

"Nazar thinks seeing Elsa again might turn him back normal," Otto said.

Jacob's jaw dropped. Then his eyes hardened.

Nazar put his hands up. "Now, now, it's worth a try. She affected him like no one else."

"You knights think sex is the answer to everything."

"I know you were upset we paired them together," Otto said. "But you must admit, Frith thought he was genuinely in love. Better mooning over a girl than walking around with his head in the clouds, spouting nonsense."

Jacob's shoulders sagged. "You're probably right."

"There's a strong nostalgia a man feels for his first love," Nazar said.

Jacob stroked his beard. "That's true."

"And we're not saying you have to let her bed him," Otto said. "Just meeting her again is bound to tug at his heart. It might make him right again."

Jacob closed his eyes. "It's a big city. How would you ever find her?"

"Could there be more than one woman in all Baghdad with hair the color of sunlight?" Nazar said.

"True enough." Jacob opened his eyes. "We know this part of the trail is safe. We can spare one man. Otto, send a knight ahead to Baghdad. If he finds her, they can meet us where we forded the Tigris last time."

"I'll go in the morning," Otto said.

* * *

The following week Otto was waiting for them when the caravan forded the river. He was alone. "She'd moved on," he said.

Jacob shrugged. He hadn't explained the purpose of Otto's absence to Frith, and Frith hadn't noticed. So when Otto returned, Jacob saw no reason to mention the failed result. Better Elsa should stay forgotten. He'd find another way. There were things Jacob knew about realms his master called supernal palaces, mysteries he never would have told the Sultan. But if Frith's bedazzled state continued, he might be forced to describe the secret chariot that carries divine creative life force and reveals the unknowable.

His thoughts were interrupted when, for no apparent reason, Frith said, "There's nothing to know. Knowing is just thoughts off-setting the fears of not knowing. There are some things we don't know and we can be all right with that."

Jacob realized that Frith had answered his unspoken thought. *Just what did Frith really know?*

CHAPTER 36

Arabian Desert, July, 556

Months after they crossed the Euphrates, they were still a long way out of Damascus. They'd taken a different route from the way they'd come. Jacob had learned that the truce between the Roman, Justinian, and King Khosrau had been discarded, and full war had broken out in the lands to the north. "There's no telling when battles or skirmishes might shift south," Jacob had said. So they'd taken a longer, more southerly route, one with fewer watering holes.

Finally, they found a well. It wasn't set in a beautiful oasis but was merely a stone-lined hole at the edge of a rocky prominence that stretched the length of the caravan. From a distance, the elongated butte reminded Frith of the spine of a giant horse skeleton. Rocks twenty feet tall jutted out of the ground like vertebrae.

The well had a long stick hinged to a tripod by cracked leather thongs. A rope could be attached to lower a water skin and fill it, but a traveler would have to provide the water skin and rope. Even so, water was water, and the men on the caravan were glad for it. Nazar organized a queue to carry filled water skins from the well to the camels.

While the men were occupied watering their camels, a menacing-looking tribesman, brandishing a scimitar, jumped from behind the rocks.

The four knights immediately dropped their water skins, drew their swords, and rushed him. But before they reached him, a swarm of his tribesmen appeared on the rocks above, like maggots on a dead horse.

The Bedouins pulled their weapons and rushed to join the knights. Frith had only a knife, so he stayed with his camel and observed. Fortunately, the threatening tribesmen were still high up in the rocks.

"Fan out men. Cover the caravan," Jacob said. "Nazar and I will deal with this one."

The knights fell back, keeping their eye on the scimitar-armed man. He approached and stopped a scant few yards away. The others stayed in the rocks. Apparently this was their leader.

Nazar and Jacob stepped forward. The leader spoke and Nazar interpreted, "He demands we pay for stealing his water."

"Let's see if this can be settled peacefully," Jacob said. "Find out how much he wants for his water."

Despite the uneven odds, Frith wasn't worried. Jacob was in charge. Using Nazar to translate, he would negotiate an equitable settlement, and Frith was sure they'd be on their way with a plentiful supply of water.

Nazar and the man exchanged words Frith didn't understand, but emotions were clearly heated. The Bedouins, too, were growing agitated.

"He claims sovereignty over this territory," Nazar said.

"Let him," Jacob said. "We've no quarrel over who rules which sand dune. Frith, bring me that pass from the court of King Khosrau."

Frith rummaged through the pack where Jacob kept his personal things, found the scroll, and brought it to Jacob. As he got closer to the tribesman, the stink of sweat and dung fires wafted from his filthy clothes and greasy beard. Frith tried to accept that the stench was part of the universe as much as the stars and the sky, but it wasn't easy. He handed Jacob the scroll and stepped back to breathe untainted air.

Jacob unfurled the scroll and faced it outward to display the royal decree.

The man swiped at it with his scimitar, knocking it to the ground.

The knights bristled, but Jacob extended both arms and held them back.

"I suspect he can't read," Nazar said.

"But surely he recognizes the royal seal," Jacob said.

Nazar relayed Jacob's words. The man pursed his lips, made a farting sound, and shouted some invective. The men in the rocks above him laughed.

"He says he shits on any king but his own."

"And who's that?"

"Himself."

"It's not going to be an easy negotiation, is it?" Jacob said.

"He's not really a tribal ruler," Nazar said. "He's just a bandit. So it's not as if he needs to be honest with us."

"I think you're right. We're outnumbered, and he could take us if he wanted. But we wouldn't go without a fight, and he knows it. Find out what he wants to let us use the well."

A rapid exchange occurred between Nazar and the bandit without pause for translation. After a flurry of arguments Jacob grabbed Nazar's shoulder and spun him around. "What's going on?"

"He demands we give him half our camels as tribute."

"That's not going to happen," Jacob said. "But let me do the negotiating. You just translate."

Nazar agreed, but clenched his jaws.

The bandit leader waved his scimitar at the line of camels, loudly repeating his demand. The nearest Bedouin jumped in front of Jacob.

A silver flash of sun glinted off the Bedouin's razor edged blade as he slit the bandit's throat.

Frith watched in horror as a bloody gusher erupted over the Bedouin's hands and down the thief's robe. The self-styled king crumpled to the rocky ground. His blood painted the thirsty soil crimson.

For a timeless moment Frith stood frozen in stunned silence. The knights reacted around him, taking up strategic positions, but Frith couldn't move. The corpse exuded a stench of diarrhea and the dirt smelled like a slaughter house.

"Looks like negotiations are over," shouted Otto. "Nazar, tell those men in the rocks we are fierce knights, and that this is what we do to thieves. Tell them their leader is dead, and they should flee if they value their lives."

Nazar translated, and in a blink the rocks were devoid of bandits. Whether they were gone or hiding Frith couldn't tell. He still couldn't look away from what had been a man moments before. And the smell. It was—

He vomited.

This was the first man he'd seen killed, and he never wanted to see it again. And to think he had once wanted to become a knight.

Around him was chaos. Jacob shouted at Nazar, who was shouting at the Bedouin, who ignored Nazar and was waving his sword and raging at the empty crags above. Jacob pushed the Bedouin aside and snatched up the scroll. It was spattered with the bandit's blood. He wiped it off and rolled it up.

"Nazar, why did he do that? I'd have gotten us water without killing."

"Their camels are everything. Bedouins will die to defend their camels."

"And kill as well, I see. Assure the Bedouins, I would never have given up a single camel. We can't have this happen again."

Nazar tried, but failed, because the Bedouin was still screaming at the rocks.

"I thought I knew their language," Jacob said. "But I can't figure out what he's saying."

"He's reciting a list of unspeakable things his tribe will do to them and their offspring for generations to come. They're not words you hear in the marketplace."

"I suspect they've run off, and he's shouting at no one," Jacob said, "but we'd best get away from here just in case."

"And post a good guard for at least the next week," Otto said.

The men hurried to fill the remaining the water skins, dodging the dead man's body. Jacob wanted to bury it, but the others opposed the idea, "Let the bandits bury their own dead."

Jacob gave a worried glance at the rocky outcropping and acquiesced. The caravan mounted up and rode from that place with a sense of urgency that stayed with them until nightfall.

The desert in this part of the journey was replete with rocky protrusions, and they camped that night up against another hill formed by eroded stones. Fortunately these hills had no resemblance to the bones of any animal. Frith feared his mind would forever bind the look of bleached horse's bones with killing and death.

While supper was being prepared, the knights scoured the rocky hills to make sure no one was hiding there. When they returned to eat, Frith didn't join them. He just couldn't, not yet. By now they were used to his strangeness, and no one paid it any mind.

While they were at dinner, Frith slipped past the knights and went up into the rocks to reflect on what had transpired. Walking wasn't easy. The moon was new and the only light came from the stars. The desert sky had countless stars, but even so, their light didn't rival a good moon. Still, he needed to get away. There was too much disturbance in camp, too many thoughts and feelings clouding around him. The others might not admit the killing affected them, but he knew it had, could sense it in their emotional koshas.

In solitude, he could ponder what happened. He'd seen a man die…

Or had he?

Certainly, he'd seen the body bleed, but had he seen the man's spirit depart at the moment of death? When Lancelot left his body, the Bishop claimed to have seen angels "heave him up unto heaven." Frith hadn't seen anything like that. Of course, this man was a thief, so maybe there weren't any angels who cared to come for him.

Yet clearly, the man was dead. You didn't have to be a bishop to know the difference. You see a man sleeping; you know he's not dead. You see a dead man; you know he's not asleep. Once when he was younger, he and Alura had found Lancelot so still they thought he was dead—argued about it even. Never more. Now he'd seen real death, he'd know for sure next time.

That was the problem though. Something had been seared into him, something he knew he'd never lose. The image of a blade swiftly penetrating the space between beard and robe. A thick, bulging vein abruptly sliced open. The man standing there yelling at Nazar, and then suddenly no man at all.

Where did he go? If everyone alive was, as the holy men said, just consciousness watching their thoughts, feelings, and senses, where did they go when those become severed by an angry Bedouin's blade? What if there were no angels to heave us up?

He felt queasy again, like he was about to lose his dinner, except he hadn't eaten any. Still, he was about to throw up again. Not just from the horrific memories of the man's death, but from the uncertainty about what it meant. It felt like his first day aboard ship, all over again. The solid wooden deck had kept shifting as now did his roiling thoughts. The sense of aloneness he felt the first time he couldn't see land was not unlike what he was experiencing now, trying to puzzle out the answers of after-death. He hadn't seen anything leave the man's body. It had happened too quickly —if it happened at all. But the man was definitely gone.

What would happen if he threw himself off this cliff? He'd die surely, but then what? Had Lancelot felt hands pulling him up? What had the bandit felt? His toe loosed a small stone which tumbled into the chasm. He peered off the edge, and an updraft tousled his hair.

"Hello, Frith."

The voice out of nowhere should have frightened him. It didn't. He was too preoccupied to be scared. Frith saw a figure sitting cross-legged on a small ledge across the gorge. He knew no one had been there a moment before.

"Who are you?" he said. "Are you an angel?"

Starlight from the Milky Way silhouetted the figure, giving his skin a bluish tone. "No. I'm a yogi."

His presence made no sense. The knights had swept these hills thoroughly before setting up camp. "How did you get here?"

"What makes you believe I'm here?"

"Um… I can see you."

"That's a good point. Unless, of course, you're seeing me somewhere else."

"Where?"

"In Samarkand, for instance."

"Do you know Swami Yogeshwar?"

"Fairly well, I think. I am he."

"How is that possible?"

"A siddhi, a yogic power. Don't be concerned with phenomenon. And don't ask me to explain it right now."

"Lancelot told me the same thing."

"Yes, I'm aware. You told me."

The man was sitting perfectly still, with his legs folded under him—the way Yogeshwar sat. But how could this be? "Is it really you?"

"Yes."

"Why are you here?"

"Finally, a sensible question. So you won't mistakenly leap from a ledge to find out what happens after death."

"How else can I find out?"

"You don't need to know."

"Isn't that the greatest question of mankind?" Frith said. "Isn't that the promise of my religion, Jacob's religion, your religion?"

"No. It's not important in the slightest."

"How can you say that?"

"Because you're alive right now; in a heartbeat it will be the next now. It will always be now, even when you die. If religion is right, your soul will still exist, but if all the religions were wrong and you ceased to exist, then you wouldn't know you weren't there, anyway. Why waste a single heartbeat worrying about it? You'll know when you know."

"Are you saying there's no heaven?"

"I'm not. I'm saying it's foolish to waste a life trying to find out."

"Lancelot told me he was able to come and go from his body at will. Saint Paul claimed he died daily. These men must have known what was beyond death's threshold."

"They didn't learn it by jumping off a cliff."

Frith bowed his head. "Yogeshwar, today a man died at my feet. I was present, immersed in the experience as you masters taught me. But I never saw what became of his essence. Only that he was, then he was no more."

"That's the way it is sometimes with violent death. At least you were able to remain centered while witnessing a dreadful event."

"I didn't like it." Frith shuddered. "It was truly foul. Not just the reek of it, but something struck me as surely as the Bedouin smote the bandit."

Yogeshwar nodded. "It did. When a man is killed, whether he's a good man or bad man, the shock of sudden death alarms the koshas."

"The feelings from it continue to burden me."

"Anytime you're in vicinity of a death, the energy released touches you with good or bad feelings."

"Do I feel horrible because I was exposed to his bad karma?"

"Not at all. Yours is a compassionate person's response to death. We are all one being. The dissolution of the bonds of incarnation of any one of us has some effect on the whole."

"But the stench of his blood clouds my mind; the sight of his gashed neck cuts me off from higher thoughts. I can't push them away and I can't live with them. The only way I can think of getting beyond this is to understand death. To go there and come back as Lancelot did."

"But you aren't your master. You will cease as Frith, and your soul will have to start over."

"Oh." It was true. Frith wasn't nearly as spiritually evolved as Lancelot. He certainly wasn't Saint Paul. He'd been foolish to think he could do as they had.

"Suicide is not the way a saint dies. Great yogis who can do what you're talking about have discovered through meditation the path by which life flows into the body. Some of them are then able to move along it like a bead sliding up and down a thread."

"Will you teach me how?"

"It can only be attained, not taught. This exceedingly rare knowledge requires advanced states of samadhi."

Frith's face fell. "So, I'm stuck with these feelings? I'd hoped if I experienced what was beyond death I'd be able let them go."

"There is another way. Grieve."

"But the man was a thief."

"Yes, and he did many other bad things as well. But grieving, properly done, neither wallows in the feelings nor resists them. It acknowledges them and lets them pass."

"Why grieve for an evil man? I didn't even know him."

"Because the chance for him to work through his karma in this lifetime has been lost, and he will have to take on a new incarnation to evolve. Therefore it is an act of compassion to grieve for even the most evil man."

Yogeswar's words reminded Frith how Alura had brought forth his grief for their father. If only she were here now, to remove the stain of this killing.

"If you cannot weep for the man," Yogeshwar said, "then weep for his lost opportunity to make up for his bad deeds in this lifetime."

Below them, men were shouting his name. In the pale starlight he could see the orange glow of torches moving in the rocks. Oh, no, he'd made trouble for them again.

When he looked back Yogeshwar was gone. With no hope of finding him, Frith stood up and made his way back down.

Otto saw him first. "Here!"

Jacob ran to Frith and embraced him. The other knights came quickly and the circle of yellow light expanded. The heat from the torches was palpable. As they made their way back to camp, some knights questioned him and others scolded him, but Frith remained deep in thought.

Once they were alone in their tent, he said to Jacob, "Do you think we come back after we die?"

"Do you mean as ghosts?"

"No, I mean… are we born again to start another life? Are thieves doomed to reincarnate to work off their sins?"

Jacob hesitated, as if considering. "Whether it's true or not, I suspect that pondering it in your current state will only add to your confusion."

"What confuses me is how to reconcile my feelings about the man's death. Is there a way to grieve for a dead man we never knew?"

Jacob sat down on the rug next to him. "Once there was a Rabbi, Akiva ben Joseph, who encountered the soul of a dead sinner compelled by his sins to build his own funeral pyre. The sinner said the only chance for his release was if he had a pious child who would recite the Kaddish prayer. But, he told Akiva, he'd died while his wife was pregnant, so his son was a stranger to him."

Frith leaned forward, paying more attention to Jacob than he had in weeks.

"Rabbi Akiva undertook to locate the family, educate the boy, and teach him the Kaddish."

Frith waited expectantly.

"When the son went to synagogue and recited Kaddish, his father, the sinner, was saved."

Frith fell back, dejected. "But I don't know the Kaddish, and I wouldn't know how to find this bandit's family."

Jacob patted him on the shoulder. "You're taking the story a little too literally. My story was to answer to your question as to whether a stranger's prayer can help a soul. But Kaddish isn't about the dead. Its words praise the perfection of creation and our creator."

Frith pursed his lips. "I was told by... someone... if I let myself feel grief for the murdered man, I could rid myself of the pain I have from watching him die."

"A wise strategy," Jacob said. "Unusual, but wise. You know, mourning is not for the dead, but to help ourselves heal. Today's event makes us realize life is not as we plan it, but proceeding according to a divine law."

"Are you saying his murder was part of a divine plan?"

"I wouldn't presume to answer that question," Jacob said. "But being willing to look at the mysteries of life and death without becoming attached to fear leads to spiritual realization. So do what you must to balance compassion with dispassionate acceptance of what you saw."

Frith wasn't sure if he could, but he'd try. He closed his eyes. Sleep came quickly.

Later in the night, Frith entered an unusual dream state. He was in the dream, yet simultaneously aware he was dreaming.

He was in a burned-out forest on a mountain. Branchless, charred trunks leaned precariously against the few blackened trees still upright. Yogeshwar came toward him, walking amidst scruffy new growth emerging from the ashes.

"A fire two summers ago," Yogeshwar swept his arm around, "burned the entire area. It was caused by an act of nature, a lightning strike."

Frith watched his dream-self nod.

Yogeshwar rubbed his hand over a burned log and showed Frith his black fingers. "The fire was no omen, it was a reality. There was nothing anyone could do to change its coming or stop it. But that's no reason to stand immobile and let it sweep over you, or to throw yourself onto the flames.

"When a fire comes down the mountain, a man packs what little he can carry and leaves, for life is more precious than any possession he could save. We are the vessel, the channel through which the divine light is observing the objects of its creation. It is our obligation to protect and preserve that channel."

"The question is," Frith said, "how to be strong enough on the inside to endure, yet impart compassion and gentleness outwardly."

"It does require a balance of power and grace," Yogeshwar said. "Envision an iron rod in your spine, rigid and strong. Say, 'The power of God is firm within me.' Next, imagine a soft light of love encircling you, and say, 'The grace of God surrounds and protects me.'"

Frith began to chant in his sleep. "The power of God is within me. The grace of God surrounds me." He was still chanting it when he awoke. And he discovered that death, though not forgotten, had no further hold on him.

CHAPTER 37

Shabbat started the following sundown. The camp was set up, the meal prepared, and Jacob gave praise. When he and Frith retired to their tent, Jacob made a decision. He was too old to go without sleep—that was a young man's folly. But after Frith's misadventure last night, it was apparent he had to get Frith sorted. He could sleep tomorrow; it was a day of rest.

"The knights worry about you, Frith," he said. "I'm worried, too."

Frith cocked his head and raised one eyebrow.

"It's been eight months since we left Samarkand, and you're still in this kind of detached... well, deranged state."

"I shouldn't have to apologize for that, not to you. Believe me, I'm doing the inner work I was given, with all the concentration I can muster."

"It seems like you're lost in some nether world and can't get back."

Frith shook his head. "That's... not it."

"I think we should discuss what it *is* then."

Frith hesitated.

"Is it something secret?" Jacob said. "Have the Sultan's men made you promise not to reveal their teachings?"

"No. It's just I'm not... I don't know their scripture well enough to convey it the way they did."

"Then use your own words. Where are you most days? And what are you trying to accomplish?"

"Well, I'm not in a nether world. There are… higher realms. They're always there, available to us, but most people aren't aware of them. I am, or at least I'm becoming. It's not that I go away. I'm more… there than most people. It's like…" Frith said nothing more.

So far he'd resisted the urge to add anything to the stew in Frith's mind, but perhaps that hadn't been wise. He suspected Frith's growing isolation was because he thought the only men who understood heavenly realms were back in Samarkand. He should have talked to Frith about this sooner.

But could he talk about them now? Should he? The Merkabah and the Hekalot were secret doctrines—he'd not even revealed them to his sons. "All rabbis study the Torah and Talmud. They *do* find answers there." Jacob hesitated. Desert sounds filled the gap. "A few discover knowledge of the higher worlds."

"The five realms?"

"Seven."

"Seven?"

"All right, tell me about the five you know."

Frith was silent, apparently collecting his thoughts. Finally, he said, "The lowest level is the physical—our bodies, our world… every substance. Next is a level at which we perceive and express feelings—I forget the word they used for it." He ticked the levels off on his fingers. "Third, is the realm of personal mind where we observe and create thoughts about our self—our wants, desires, hopes, beliefs, opinions. Fourth, is a place of wisdom where we understand without thinking. Fifth, is a realm comprised of conscious-energy where everything emanates bliss. That's kind of where I've stopped."

"And above that?"

"What Yogeshwar called the Atman, our soul."

"And above that?"

"I… didn't know there was an 'above that.'"

"God, Frith."

"Oh, of course, why didn't I say God?"

"You've never learned the connections. The Sultan's men taught you creation from the physical realm upward, perhaps because Adam was formed from the earth, or perhaps to match the direction of ascent—I don't know their reasoning. I describe the Tree of Life from the crown downward, in the order which non-existence becomes existence."

Jacob paused. There were injunctions against discussing these mystical teachings with even one pupil unless he was wise and intelligent. 'Wise' wasn't a term he'd use to describe Frith, but he was certainly intelligent and sincere. But there was also the old rule; the secrets could be entrusted only to one who possessed five qualities enumerated in Isaiah. Frith failed those criteria.

He'd start with something known and see where it led. "Surely your priests told you about the Prophet Jacob's vision of a ladder by which souls descend into bodies and by which spiritual men ascend to meet the Creator."

Frith shook his head. "I… didn't pay much attention back then."

"Unfortunate." Not a good start. But Frith had matured since the abbey and was in desperate need of help. *Holy, Holy, Holy, King of the Universe, guide my words and forgive me if I reveal anything I should not.*

The tent made a flapping noise. Frith didn't seem to notice it. Jacob did. Was God warning him off, or could it be Elijah urging him onward? He took a deep breath and began: "Rabbi Ishmael said the ladder in the Prophet Jacob's vision traversed seven realms, seven stages of mystical ascent. To the enlightened man it's like having a ladder in the midst of his house by which he can ascend and descend without anyone preventing him."

Jacob knew this journey through the celestial realms was fraught with great risk. It required not only purification, but knowledge of the secret names of God and their powers hidden in the Hekalot Zutarti. Likely that's what the Sultan had been after in treating him so generously. He hadn't given those to the Sultan, and he wasn't going to tell Frith either. He recalled the cautionary tale of four rabbis.

"Jacob?"

"Sorry, Frith. I was remembering a story from my own training. There were four rabbis who had the knowledge and will to ascend into the spirit world. The first died, the second went mad, and the third became a disbeliever. Only the fourth, Rabbi Akiva, returned safely, because he had made a durable spiritual chariot of his lesser self."

"Chariot?"

"My teacher referred to deep interiorization into our self as 'going down in the chariot.'"

"Down, not up?"

"'Deep' might be better. Like those last few nights you spent at the Sultan's —you must have experienced some of what I'm talking about."

Frith nodded.

"In meditation or contemplation, we withdraw from the physical world and rise through the seven lower or lesser halls first. This prepares us for entry into the seven palaces, or heavens, above that."

Frith started getting a remote look in his eyes, again.

"Stay here with me, Frith. A ladder isn't stable unless its rails are firmly planted in a solid place. That's the reason Rabbi Akiva succeeded while other three men didn't. He had created that solid place within himself."

Frith shuddered.

"Traversing the ladder is not for the unbalanced, undisciplined, or the selfishly motivated," Jacob said. "Any instability in the physical, emotional, or mental bodies creates a worse and worse imbalance as we reach higher rungs."

Jacob saw Frith's eyes turn upward as though he were looking inside his head. He did that too often lately.

"Although it's appropriate to withdraw during our spiritual practices, we shouldn't isolate our self from daily life. Those everyday events and ordinary situations anchor us during our experiences of the upper worlds. Every person, every moment has a purpose, even if it's not a grandiose purpose. A palace is not carved out of a single rock; it's built stone by stone. You don't work on the whole palace. You work on the stone you have in hand. If every stone is set true, then the whole palace will be in alignment."

Frith's eyes were still rolled up. "Frith, are you with me? Say something."

"Yes, Jacob," Frith said, though he sounded distant. "I wish I'd met your rabbi."

"This knowledge isn't limited to Jews. Two hundred years ago, the Archbishop of Constantinople wrote about ascending Jacob's Ladder by following successive steps of an ascetic path." He patted Frith's hand. "It's enough you've experienced realms beyond this physical world. Now recognize you also have a role to play in the physical world. Visits to higher worlds cannot be all there is to our spiritual journey. As we strive to raise our lower self, our purpose must also be to aid in the unification of worlds—to join that which is above with that which is below."

"That's what I'm trying to do."

"You may be going about it wrong. The Sultan's gurus taught you it was important to work on yourself, and that's good. Now I'm telling you it's equally important when you climb Jacob's ladder into heavenly worlds, to also bring back with you those heavenly qualities that uplift this earthly realm. That is how to accomplish Tikkun Olam."

"Da Shi said the same, to draw the divine down into the lower worlds. That's the inner work I've been doing when I appear to be… elsewhere."

"Why don't you first work on getting yourself firmly rooted before worrying how to draw the cosmic consciousness with your will? Start observing the divine in the world around you."

"That can't be more important, can it?"

"It's a mistake to think this world inhibits the soul. The physical world is not evil. It exists by divine will, a part of the whole."

Frith slapped his fist against his palm. "But it traps us. I have to fight to get away from it and remain in a higher state."

Jacob felt a small hope. It was the most passion Frith had shown in months. "Remember, after reaching the uppermost worlds, we must descend if we're to be of any use."

"Da Shi said we reach a state from which we can draw the qi down through our purified self on to the earth." Frith's eyes turned upward again, his eyelids half closed. Jacob saw only a thin line of white eyeball.

"Frith, how can you act as a conduit into this realm if you don't fully engage in this realm?"

Frith was unresponsive.

"To the spiritual, everything becomes a divine practice, even building a fire or unloading a camel."

This was pointless. Frith wasn't even making eye contact. He may as well have gone to bed. Jacob rummaged through his pack and found a parcel of dates. They were Frith's favorite.

"Frith, open your eyes."

Frith's eyes fluttered momentarily.

"Do you know where you are?"

"In our tent, a few days out from Damascus."

"Good, eat these." Jacob fed a date to Frith, who smiled at the taste. When Frith swallowed, Jacob said, "Here," and put the dates in Frith's hand. Frith picked one up and ate it with delight.

"You've been using spiritual techniques to transcend your personal nature, and that's admirable. I can see your experience with higher realms is transforming you. But if you want to become enlightened, you have to consciously participate in the work of creation. That means engaging fully in all worlds."

"How?"

Jacob looked into Frith's eyes and saw such raw humility he was taken aback. There was no falseness there, no opposition out of wounded pride. Frith really didn't know how and desperately wanted to. He'd been right to talk to him.

"Develop an acute awareness of what you're doing and what needs to be done," he said. "Be skillful in practical life, mentally sound, and spiritually clear. Act from a center of wisdom, applying your knowledge to any task— even eating dates. That raises any encounter or occurrence by filling it with greater light and bringing to it the qualities of the higher worlds."

"Is that what you do?"

"I, myself, find it in small acts. Never forgetting to ask a blessing before I start any endeavor, never forgetting to give thanks and praise before bed. During the day I'm completely focused on doing the work put before me with all of my attention."

"I've been with you two years. It seemed to me you separated your business and spiritual life."

"I don't. In my mind I'm continuously giving thanks, even for the difficulties and crises we encounter because they are lessons, in their own form, to help me do better. Nothing is insignificant. Everything is a gift. Even dealing with the dishonest man is a blessing because it's an opportunity for me to exercise the power of my own ethical actions."

Jacob couldn't repress a yawn. It was very late, and they had been on the road a long time. "A true spiritual life is more than the ability to ascend and descend at will. When we can work simultaneously in all worlds, then we're able to aid the divine intention. In offering our will to the divine will, we become a channel for energies from the higher realms to flow downward into this world."

Frith shook his head. "I'm trying mightily. I'm practicing the gurus' meditation techniques. Do you know something better?"

"Allow light to spread through you as if sitting in its midst, drawing it not just for your own soul, but for the Earth as well. Offer the light to the one God and perform actions from a seat in the higher worlds, wholly hidden from its beneficiaries. This becomes the highest service because the personal self takes no credit for it. Service to mankind is the realized man's worship."

He saw Frith inhale deeply, turn his eyes heavenward, and his attention went away again. Time to give up. "It's late," Jacob said, "and I'm going to sleep now." Wrapping himself in his blanket, he blew out the candle, and lay down.

After Shabbat, the caravan continued toward Damascus, but Frith seemed as withdrawn as ever. All his revelations had been for nothing.

How was he ever going to face Frith's family? Instead of making him a merchant, he'd made him a madman. What good would a fortune do Frith's brother, what use a dowry for his sister, if Frith had been sacrificed in the bargain?

CHAPTER 38

Fawi River, Britain, September 556

Frith sat on deck, arms wrapped around his legs, pressing his knees to his chest. The ship moved up the Fawi River, the very river he'd sailed to the sea two years ago. The captain had picked them up in Tyre, then steady winds brought them across the Mediterranean, through the Pillars of Hercules, past Iberia, around Brittany, and into the Port of Fawi.

Frith studied the grain in the deck planks. These had once been veins in a majestic black oak whose leaves licked the rain, whose branches swayed in the wind. Its great trunk had been sawn, hewn, hammered and nailed to form the floor on which he sat.

The deck moved, side to side, up and down, but mostly forward. In his peripheral vision the vegetation crowding the river banks was tan or brown and what leaves still clung to the shrubs were yellow as an old sailor's teeth. The effect was that he seemed to stay in one place while the banks moved past him. The illusion was almost perfect, except the rocking of the ship gave it away.

Frith realized that for over two years he'd been in motion, swayed by a camel's gait or heaved by waves. Undulation was normal now.

The eager emotions of the knights encircled him. Their excitement flew off them like dandelion seeds in a breeze. The men leaned on the ship rails, stared lovingly at the weedy marshes, and talked of warm pudding and cold cider. Frith didn't mind either, but he didn't melt into their palpable anticipation. He floated just above it. Britain was a place like any other.

Whenever they got to Jacob's, he'd be fine, but he was equally content sitting on the forecastle, feeling his kinship with the oak tree that the planks had once been.

He knew the knights saw him as disengaged, in another world, but he was sharply aware of everything that had happened. And not just the big things, like crossing the desert or the death of the bandit. He saw things the others missed—the funny way camels ate, sliding their jaws left to right instead of chewing like a horse. How fine dust blown into the sky above a dune resembles wispy clouds when seen from the leeward side.

He recalled the first time he'd heard music different from the hymns and chants of the abbey. Everywhere he'd been, people had songs and dances that gave melody and rhythm to ordinary life. Music was a wonderful discovery. Notes hung in the air like rain drops and touched one's emotions like a rainbow. Music made it especially easy to be in the *now*, for when a note was played, it faded and was forever gone. Although the melodic structure yielded a delicious promise of what the next note might be, sometimes the instrument or singer would deliver an unexpected change that delighted the mind's ear.

He remembered Jacob's joy when they found Levi waiting for them in Tyre and learned they'd only missed Micah by two days. Micah had delayed leaving until Levi's arrival. He'd told Levi he had no idea when their father was coming, but to wait until either Jacob arrived or he returned.

Jacob didn't even bother putting the silk in the warehouse. Instead he had it loaded directly on Levi's ship. It was just as well. The warehouse was full of the goods Levi brought. They stayed in Tyre only until the tide turned, barely enough time to change clothes and eat with Levi, who'd stay in Tyre. Jacob paid off the Bedouins, but suggested Levi hire them to teach him to ride a camel so he and Micah could caravan to Samarkand next time.

The return voyage had been swift. Silk didn't weigh the ship down the way tin did, so she rode higher in the water and her sails pushed them home faster. That suited the knights. In another hour they'd reach Jacob's estate where workers would be waiting.

"There's still ample daylight," Jacob said. "Hopefully they'll unload the ship tonight."

Frith looked down at the ship plank. He saw it without judgment, without regretting the oak that had died. Da Shi's words came to mind, "The uncreated is able to create life, but it would be a mistake to think of the creative principle as any one quality." Frith rubbed his fingers along the grain pattern. He understood. The wood's inevitable disintegration was as much one of its qualities as its appearance, substance, or strength.

He heard cries of joy, and the splash of anchors. Sturdy boards were extended to the riverbank, and the knights bounded ashore. They'd arrived home. *But had he?*

CHAPTER 39

Abbey of St. Benignus, September, 556

Sir Otto dismounted and tied his horse to a tree near the abbey. He didn't see any reason to stable his horse at the livery; he wasn't going to be here that long. He unfastened Frith's leather pack from his saddle and threw it over his shoulder. He walked toward the abbey gate, slowly, delaying the inevitable. Damn Jacob for choosing him to be the message bearer.

Three days ago he'd been at breakfast with his fellow knights. Jacob and Frith were not up yet—probably sleeping in. All of them were glad to be back at Jacob's. The silk had been unloaded, and the captain had taken the ship downstream to Fawi where the crew would have a few days shore leave. The knights were still working, but at least they were off the ship with their feet on the good soil of Britain.

Otto had just sopped the last bit of egg off his plate with a piece of bread when Jacob came in. He looked ashen. Perhaps this continuous life of travel was getting to him. Or maybe it was just the aftereffect of the sea voyage. With only silk in the hold, the ship tossed around more in choppy seas. They'd had a rough go yesterday in the straits between Brittany and Fawi.

Jacob fell into his chair and let a folded letter spill from his fingers. "Frith's gone."

The knights looked at each other. "Not again," Baldori said.

"What do you mean?" Otto said. "Gone where?"

"I have no idea. He doesn't say."

"Probably just anxious to get home," Euric said.

Jacob shook his head. "I wish it was so, but apparently not his intention."

Otto pointed to the letter. "That from him?"

Jacob nodded. "For his sister. Frith wants one of us to take it to her."

"Why didn't he take it himself?" Otto said.

"Because he doesn't intend to go back to the abbey," Nazar said.

Jacob rubbed his face. "I'm afraid so."

"Where's he going then?" Euric said.

Jacob shrugged. "Unknown."

"He's not been right in the head since Samarkand," Baldori said.

Jacob nodded. "I know, but he had experiences with the Sultan's holy men you're not aware of. Those things can take years to settle in a man."

Baldori stood. "You should never have left him with them."

"Perhaps, but there's no point debating decisions made a year ago. We have to find him now."

"He's a grown man," Euric said.

"He's a lunatic," Baldori said.

"No," Jacob said. "But he *is* mad with confusion."

"Exactly!" Otto said. "And out wandering the moor."

Baldori looked out the window. "Has he taken a horse?"

"No, he's on foot," Jacob said. "I fear he'll stray into the marshes and drown."

"Why presume he won't just stay on the trail to Bodmin?" Otto said. "From there he can just follow the road back to the abbey."

Jacob shook his head. "You're assuming he can find the trail to Lanlivery."

Nazar gestured toward heaven. "They say God protects the mad and the holy."

"His family will say I promised to keep him from harm," Jacob said. "And they'll be right."

"Well, it's hardly your fault he decided to quit your service," Baldori said.

Jacob snorted. "In Christian minds, a Jew's always at fault."

Otto struck the table with his fist. "You know *we* don't feel that way."

"I do," Jacob said. "And as good knights you share my worry for Frith, no matter how strange he's become. This is why you will saddle your horses at once and search the countryside for him."

"All of us?" Euric said.

"Yes, every man."

"Shouldn't some of us stay to guard the warehouse?" Euric said.

"I'll be here, and I have the servants. Go now and find him."

The first day they followed roads in every direction, further than a man on foot could walk. The second day they searched the side trails, combed the marshes, and even checked the ponds for floating bodies. No Frith.

This morning Jacob wrapped Frith's letter and a truly fine piece of silk in leather. He tucked it in the top of Frith's pack, which he sent to Alura in Otto's care. Two years had passed since Otto had been to the Abbey of St. Benignus, but he'd remembered the way—too well. It was a full day's ride from Jacob's estate to the abbey and Otto had cursed most of the way. Damn Jacob for choosing him. Damn Frith for wandering off. Damn the Sultan for ruining the boy's mind. Damn Alura for being so sweet the first time he'd met her. Damn the sun for setting as soon as he got here.

Unfortunately the abbey gates were still open. A young monk stood guard. He was more a greeter than a sentry, just a pup, probably no older than twelve. "God be with you, good knight."

Otto hesitated, looked at the pip of remaining sun, and finally crossed the abbey threshold.

"Alura—" Otto cleared his throat. "I have something for Miss Alura."

The monk pointed toward the large building with the conical shaped roof. "The Abbot's kitchen, sire. You'll find her there. It's suppertime, if you haven't eaten yet."

He hadn't, but he'd hoped to just hand her the package and leave. Strictly speaking, Frith had been Jacob's responsibility, but she'd elicited his vow the morning they left. Only humiliation awaited him when she learned he'd failed.

The heavy door to the dining hall scraped on the floor, then gave way unexpectedly when he leaned on it, slamming against the wall. The heads of pilgrims and nobles jerked up from their plates. Otto eased the door closed behind him and scanned the room, but didn't find Alura.

A postulant monk scurried over. "Please be seated, noble knight. I'll be right back with a plate and a goblet of wine—or cider if you prefer."

Otto looked at the tables abundant with platters of meat and vegetables. He remembered the quality of the Abbot's fare. Bad news could wait 'til he ate. "Cider will be grand."

He took a seat at a table with three pilgrims and put Frith's pack on the floor next to his chair. Their plates were loaded with meat with the juices running, and their cheeks glowed from too many cups of wine. He could eat his fill. He had no reason to act modest in front of this lot.

Otto looked around the room again. The old Abbot wasn't there. Neither was Frith's sister among the servers. In fact, all the servers were young monks. One of them brought him a plate and a goblet, poured the cider, and left. Otto pulled out his knife, wiped it on his breeches and began slicing meats and cheeses, which he piled on his plate. One of the pilgrims handed him a warm loaf of bread and he tore off a piece.

Otto had more appetite than he expected. He ate vigorously, but since he had arrived late, the pilgrims finished before he did and drifted away.

Soon he became the lone guest at the banquet. Young postulants cleared the tables. He couldn't delay any longer. He motioned to a boy whose arms were full of dishes.

"Sire?"

"Do you know the cook named Alura?"

"Of course, sire."

"Is she about?"

"In the kitchen, sire."

"Would you send her out here?"

Moving as quickly as feasible without dropping his armload of dishes, the boy dashed away. A moment later Alura appeared in the doorway with a bevy of kitchen ladies behind her.

"Sir Otto!" Alura turned to her entourage, "It's all right, I know this knight." She came straight to his table, but the ladies kept watch from the door.

Otto's appetite disappeared when he saw her. He pushed his plate away. One of the boys took it for a sign, rushed over, and began clearing the table. The boy cocked an ear toward them, but Alura flicked her hand at him, and he scampered off.

Otto stood, walked around the table and pulled out a chair for her. "Please."

When she was seated Otto returned to his chair. He worried the straps on Frith's pack open and then waited, twisting his hands in his lap. Finally, he pulled out the parcel from Jacob and set it on the table. "From your brother."

Her eyes brightened and her cheeks glistened like morning strawberries. Her fingers pried at the leather cords binding the package. He could have helped her, but didn't. There'd be tears soon enough.

"Jacob sends his regrets," Otto said. "He'd have come himself, but he's too busy. We're only just back." Let her think Frith's still with Jacob a moment longer.

The knots gave way, and she unrolled the hide, revealing yards of magnificent silk brocade. Otto saw at once it was the finest of what they'd brought back. Jacob was certainly buttering the bread. But he knew, too, tucked in those silken folds was Frith's final letter.

A scrap of parchment lay on top, written in Jacob's hand. Alura fingered it.

"It reads, 'To Alura from Frith,'" Otto said.

"This material is beyond beautiful."

"It would make the most elegant gown."

"Better a cloak for a Bishop, even a Pope." She put it down. "But it is too lavish for me."

"You can sell it. I tell you, it's an actual fortune you are holding."

"Oh, I'd never sell it. It's from Frith."

Alura ran her hands over the opulent fabric, felt the lump, unfolded another layer of the material, and found the letter. She broke into a smile that made her dimples deepen.

Otto stared at the floor. When he looked up again, she had it open and her eyes were tracking the lines as if she were reading. She carried on the pretense for a long time, and when her eyes reached the bottom of the page, she laid it on the table and gazed at him serenely. Why not? She didn't know yet.

Otto swallowed hard. "It's a letter… Would you like me to read it to you?"

Alura glanced at the kitchen ladies hovering in the doorway and the serving boys dallying about the room. She looked at the letter again. "How kind of you to offer."

Otto hesitated. "Perhaps another time—when there's less of a crowd. I'm sure you can get a monk to read it later… in private… after I leave."

"It's all right. Frith grew up with these ladies. They're dying to hear his letter." Alura made a gesture like a queen signaling her court, and the ladies rushed his table. The boys gathered around, too. A frail old cook pushed through them and leaned over Alura's shoulder to hear.

Damn. He'd almost escaped. He hadn't read the letter himself, but he had a good idea from Jacob what it was likely to say. He handed his goblet to one of the boys. "My throat's a little too dry to read."

The pitchers had all been cleared from the tables, so they waited for the boy to fetch more cider. Frith's letter lay unfolded on the table before him, like a scorpion's arched stinger.

The boy returned and filled his cup. Otto drank deeply and held it out for a refill. The boy took it from him, put it on the table, and filled it to the brim. Otto looked at the letter. He could delay no longer. He picked it up, and skimmed it.

The Latin script was plain enough, but the characters were like those of a first year student. Frith was no scholar. Fortunately it wasn't long. Not really a proper letter, more a list of random thoughts—clear evidence of Frith's confused state. He cleared his throat and read aloud:

"Dear Alura,

"Where I am when you receive this I cannot say, but the news I have to tell you is, I am not with Jacob and not returning to the abbey yet. Fear not. Someday I will make my way back and rejoin you in our little abbey. I say little because my world is now so big it would never fit in those stone walls."

Otto gave the large banquet hall a once-over and shook his head. Any more statements like that and Alura would see Frith's weakened state of mind.

"So much has happened I could write forever and never explain it. I will tell you all the details when I return, but that will not be for some time. I still have inner worlds to explore before I can be of use in this one. I have made two kinds of journey. On one, Jacob purchased fine silks, a piece of which I have bought with my wages and sent with this letter. The other was through seven halls leading to seven palaces."

That was met with a chorus of "o-o-o-o," from the kitchen ladies. But it wasn't true. "I'm not sure what he's talking about. I only remember two palaces, the Prince of Behistun's and a Sultan's in Samarkand."

"Keep reading," the old cook said.

"Traveling with Jacob I learned how little I really knew. Growing up in the abbey I thought the only religions were Christians, Jews, and pagans. In Samarkand I met three marvelous wise men, each of different religions unknown in Britain. These masters were as wise as Lancelot. For if Lancelot told us great secrets, these men have secrets beyond secrets. Knowledge I hope to understand if I can."

Lancelot? Otto had heard tales of the old knights who'd quested for the Holy Grail, but no one said Lancelot knew any secrets. Anyway, here was the nut of the problem, plainly stated. Frith had messed about with some foreign religions and gone mad.

"Sir Otto?" Alura said.

"Sorry…" Otto returned to the letter.

"Lately, I have been experiencing bliss. When a spiritual awareness or a deep love comes, the mind stops. You know what I mean when I say I am not in my mind."

Well, there it was. The monks and kitchen ladies around him shuffled their feet. Otto took a sip of his cider and read on:

"I have noticed when I have too much mind, what it is busy doing is trying to return to a state of no mind—empty mind."

How much more of this nonsense could Alura endure? He should never have agreed to read this in public.

"Once I understood God is the state of pure ecstasy, joy, bliss, I realized the mind is trying to find those experiences of joy and bliss. It wants to avoid pain, hurt, a broken heart. It is looking for a sense of well-being."

Otto glanced up.

Alura was smiling.

"I feel as if awareness is just sitting on my skin and I need time on my own to bring it down into my bones. So I must continue my quest a bit longer to seek what all men are supposed to be seeking. The scripture the Abbot so often read, 'Thou shall love the lord thy God with all thy heart, all thy soul, all thy mind.' I understand now, it's not a commandment. It's a prophecy."

What an odd interpretation, but at least he was quoting Christ instead of some foreigner.

"I have seen that it requires something beyond the mind to see the Way. If I am lost in Britain, it is because I am lost in other realms and I cannot return to the abbey until I find my way through them. I hope Sir Bedivere will continue to protect you in my absence.

—Your loving brother, Frith."

Otto laid the letter on the table and looked up. The men and women around him appeared to be as disappointed and confused as he was. But Alura…

She looked beatific.

She picked up the letter and gently refolded it. She placed it back with the silk in its leather wrapping and retied the thongs. Didn't she get it? Frith was lost in his mind, which was just another way of saying he'd lost his mind.

He should say something. "Sometimes travelers contract… an ailment which is common in a strange land, but unknown in our own."

The old cook's voice trembled. "Is Frith sick?"

"Not in body, but in his head. Frith was exposed to strange ideas that infected his mind. You heard for yourself in his letter. He's not rightly able to be on his own. It took four good knights to keep watch over him on the journey home, and the day after we got back, he wandered off in the marshes. Jacob had us search diligently, but we don't know where he is." He met Alura's eyes. "I am truly sorry."

Her chair made a scraping sound. Otto jumped to his feet, but he was too late to assist. Perhaps he'd said more than she could bear.

Alura stepped around the table and came close to him. "I've known several knights," she said. "Is it true if a knight takes an oath, makes a pledge, he's obligated to fulfill it?"

"Yes."

"And if I ask your assistance and you agree, is that a knight's vow?"

Where was this going? "You know very well, it is."

Alura placed her hand on his chest. He heard a sharp gasp from those crowded around them. The impropriety that she would be so familiar in public took him by surprise.

But then he forgot about proprieties. His heart, beating beneath his armor, began to melt, oozing like warm wax through his chain mail. He could feel her palm through his hauberk. Armor which neither sword nor spear could breach dissolved at her touch. His breath left him and he fell back into his seat.

Before her, he felt slain. He could see, but as if through dawn mist. Voices around him were no more than distant murmurs. Perhaps this was how a ghost saw the world. But it didn't matter. Nothing mattered but her. A white shimmer outlined her form. Light radiated from her in concentric rings of gold, pink, blue, green, and then violet. It reached the far corners of the hall and colored the monks and women standing about him. It was … ecstasy like he'd never known.

"Sir Otto," her voice said, crisp and clear in his ears. "Will you search all of Britain until you find him? Will you promise to bring our Frith back to us?"

His answer came out a squeak, "Yes." It flooded him with joy to say it. He wanted to stay where he was forever, but he heard people rushing to him.

And then, he was back.

"Sir Otto's had a long ride," Alura said. "He'll stay the night. You two, take him to a guest room."

He felt men's hands under his arms. He regained his feet and stumbled out with them, stunned at what had happened. He could hear the people talking as he left. Someone attributed his fall to fatigue from the long ride. Another said it was too much hard cider. He made no effort to correct them. Apparently only he'd seen what she'd done to him.

In the background, he heard Alura send a boy to stable his horse. How wonderful she remembered to take care of his mount.

CHAPTER 40

Bodmin Moor, 3 days earlier

The morning Frith left Jacob's estate, the weather was a thin gruel, not thick enough to be a drizzle, too wet for a fog. The diffused sunlight gave no more light than a full moon. He followed a trail of hoof-prints in the loam. He had no idea where the trail led; only away from the river. It seemed a good direction to go.

Da Shi had said, "The Way is not a funeral procession. It's all right to laugh."

Frith tried to think of something funny. Why be so serious?

A bird called, and another answered. He couldn't see the birds through the mist, but it didn't matter. He didn't know which birds made which songs, and they were all beautiful.

The fancy bag Jacob had given him banged against his hip as he walked. He didn't know why he'd brought it instead of the Abbot's leather sack. Perhaps because it hung on his shoulder, freeing his hands, or maybe its ornate embellishments reminded him of Samarkand. It didn't hold much, just a change of clothes and some cheese and hard rolls. There hadn't been room for Alura's silk brocade, but he wasn't going back to the abbey, anyway. Frith was dressed as he always had in Britain, no exotic garb now. When he got up this morning he'd bathed, then put on breeches and a tunic, grabbed his cloak, and set out.

Russet-colored reeds brushed his ears as he walked. He longed to drift up into the seven palaces, but it required all his concentration to pierce the mist-laden air, to follow the ragged path. Soon the trace branched, and he took the right fork for no real reason except it seemed the way to go. When it forked again he did the same, but the third time, he went left so he wouldn't walk in a circle.

He wasn't much in this world, but knew he needed to re-acclimate to Britain —to its people. He'd been too sheltered in the abbey life, knowing only monks, pilgrims, and the local villagers who in retrospect seemed quite backward. Not that he was judging. He just felt the call to explore Britain. Somewhere out there, something would bring him back. He needed to keep walking until he found it.

It was near noon by the time the fog lifted. By then, he'd reached a forest strewn with mossy boulders. No path here, but that was all right. He sat down on a lichen-covered rock and searched his bag for one of the round loaves he'd thought to bring. He felt good about his decision. Already this morning he'd learned two ways to be fully present. The first was to withdraw awareness from the personal mind and center his consciousness in the place Yogeshwar called the seat of Self. The second was to penetrate the mind's noise by focusing on the present. It was like peering through a fog—you could see through it if you concentrated.

He realized enlightenment or non-enlightenment was mostly a matter of how distracted you were. Observing and acting while remaining in the seat of Self *was* enlightenment.

He burst into laughter at his own folly. It hadn't been a question of drawing the divine into the lower planes. It was only a matter of his not leaving a higher realm to argue with his mind about something in this realm.

He looked about him and realized a tree was just a tree, the rock was just a rock, and moss was spongy and wet. What he preferred didn't matter a bit to any of them. Once he got his personal thoughts out of the way, Shakti could flow freely between the planes.

Raindrops began to fall around him. He stood up, brushed the damp moss from his backside and ran for the cover of a large oak. As he ran he noticed he instinctively hunched his shoulders against the rain. He laughed at himself again. Why did people do that?

The tree's boughs sheltered him like a man holding his cloak overhead. It reminded him of a rainy day in Lancelot's garden following his and Alura's initiation, when Lancelot had first raised their energia. They'd braved the rain to beseech him for another experience of it. Not unlike how he'd badgered Yogeshwar for Shaktipat. He laughed once again. He could be a pest, sometimes.

"The flow of ascending energia is already within you," Lancelot had said. "You don't need me; you can control and move it yourself."

Yes, he could, but he didn't have to. The rain fell harder, vertical lines surrounding him like threads in a loom.

"The Grail comes by Grace," Lancelot had said. "It's not a reward for good deeds." Kind of like the rain, which falls on the just and the unjust. He stuck out his tongue and leaned away from the tree to catch a few drops. He got his face wet.

"But a man living in Grace will continue to do good deeds, anyway," Lancelot had said.

Frith wiped his face with his sleeve. He understood now. Lancelot was right. Enlightenment isn't the end of the journey. It is, day by day, remaining consciously aware that energia is what was performing the action. As Yogeshwar had said, "The prana is breathing us." As Jacob said, "Observe the divine in the world around you." Frith looked around and saw it everywhere.

Words from the masters poured inside him like rain. "Tao is beyond the perception of Tao," Da Shi said. "Yet it guides the expression of compassion."

"Become the channel through which above is joined with below," Jacob said.

Frith thought of the mother nursing her babies in Samarkand and saw the scene with Budhitra's empty mind. His compassion reached across oceans and desert to comfort her.

CHAPTER 41

Frith woke the next morning filled with laughter. He scratched his back on the bark of the tree he'd slept against. He looked in his bag and saw there was only a small crust of bread left, but what difference did that make? He ate it and didn't worry when there'd be more. He stood, and after he stretched he wandered among the mossy boulders until he was out of the woods.

He didn't know where he was, but that didn't matter. He needed to walk until he reached a clarity and understanding of what to do. When he was a student, Lancelot had taught him with stories of his fellow knights' experiences with the Grail. The Grail played a different role every time it appeared in a story, but in most stories the knight had not understood what to do—even Lancelot—at the time. That knowledge only came later. Frith felt the same way those knights had. He needed to do something worthy of being in its presence, but he didn't know what.

When he stumbled on a minor road, he followed it east into the morning sun. His damp clothes dried quickly. The pungent aroma of onions led him to turn around to see an oncoming ox cart, piled with them. The cart and its wheels were translucent and appeared made of stars as thick as the Milky Way.

When the cart reached him, the farmer gave him a friendly greeting, but the man was a ball of light too bright to bear, and Frith couldn't answer. An ephemeral hand tugged on his sleeve. "I said, hello."

Frith was beyond speech. He just shook his head.

"Deaf? Mute?" the farmer said.

Frith noticed that the ox was as infused with light as the farmer. He reached out and stroked the ox's head, feeling its gentleness and power.

The farmer knocked his hand away. "Don't do that, he'll bolt."

The man tapped the ox with a stick and the ox's yoke made a creaking sound as the cart lurched forward. Frith watched them in wonder until they disappeared around a bend.

Frith walked on. The day continued to warm and the sun drank the dew from the land. When the soil had no more moisture to give, his footsteps began to raise dust. He watched his feet as each footfall threw minute particles into the air. They hovered for a brief second, a small cloud in the shape of his foot, and fell back to the road.

He kicked a clod of dirt. It tumbled down the road and broke apart revealing a smooth, dark stone the size of a walnut. He continued walking, kicking the stone ahead of him. How was this pebble different from the gems Jacob traded for silk? Why were some rocks prized and others kicked aside? Did one have more light than the other? No. In the night, both stones were equally dark. Ah, but in daylight, jewels let more light pass through them.

He was struck by a memory of Lancelot in his garden, how the clouds one day parted and a ray of sun illuminated his aura. Such men were rare as gemstones.

He paused when he came upon an old woman sitting at the edge of a field weaving straw mats. "They harvested in August," she said. "Took all but this lot." A mound of straw was behind her. "They'll be back next week to plant the winter wheat." She was balding, like an old priest. What was left of her gray hair hung limp as wilted weeds over shoulders skeletal as a tree in winter.

Light surrounding her streamed toward him and intermingled with his own.

The woman had neither frame nor loom. She'd made a simple arrangement of closely aligned rows of straw into which she was weaving cross-pieces over and under until she reached the top row. Picking up another piece she did the same. When she'd interlaced three of them, she pushed them tight to remove any gaps and squared up the mat. Light rays coursed through her hands. Her quick finger movements were swirls of light that dazzled his eyes.

She swiftly completed one mat and started laying out rows of straw for another. "Go along now. Don't you have someplace to be?"

He didn't. But he left her to her work and continued on until nightfall, when he came to a harvested barley field. The heads of grain had been removed, and the straw heaped in a pile. It looked comfortable. He fell onto the mound and sighed. A pang of hunger struck—he'd forgotten to eat. He'd be happy to have just one of that farmer's onions. But he didn't, so he went to sleep.

A movement woke him in the night. He discovered a rat nibbling the bottom corner of his shoulder bag. Why? There wasn't any more food in it. The thought of food made his stomach rumble, and the rat scurried away. He examined the damage in the moonlight—not too bad. This bag was too ornate for Britain anyway—the rat's gnawing gave it a more worn appearance. But he had a good pair of boots, and he didn't want the rat eating those. He tucked them under his head like a pillow and fell back asleep.

CHAPTER 42

On the third day Frith was still in the light. It emanated not only from the sun, and moon, and stars, but from hills, and rocks and clouds. The light he could now perceive within all things was in reality the energia Lancelot had taught him about, the qi Da Shi spoke of, and the Shakti of Yogeshwar.

Soft grass along the road's margins emitted a lovely green radiance. He sat down in the road and removed his boots and stockings, then walked along the shoulder barefoot, relishing the cool sensation of sweet, tender blades of grass on his soles and between his toes. He stayed on the grassy edge most of the morning, until he came to where both sides of the road were hedged with prickly, furze shrub. Forced back onto the road, he stopped and put on his footwear.

The furze had dark-green spines and yellow flowers—also made of light, as was the tawny colored doe in the distance, sheep grazing nearby, and the venomous adder in the road ahead. Frith stopped out of respect. He'd never been one of those boys who played with snakes, and had no urge to handle this one, but from a distance he admired it. Its pale grayish-tan coloring blended into the sunny spot on the road where it was warming itself. Except for the distinctive dark zigzag marks down the length of its back, it was nearly invisible. The inverted 'V' mark on its neck moved as it raised its head and looked at Frith.

"How about this?" Frith said. "You'll not harm me, I'll not harm you."

The adder slipped into the hedge so quick he couldn't see where it disappeared. When he passed the spot where it had been, he sent it a blessing.

Frith came to the outskirts of a small village enclosed by a stone wall. Near the wall lay a fallen tree, well-rotted. Large white fungi growing on it seemed to him as beautiful as lilies. A swarm of thin-bodied insects with gossamer wings were devouring the fungus. He leaned over for a closer look, his shadow fell over them, and they flew away.

Struck by the wonder of it he slid to the ground and leaned against the village wall. God, he'd just witnessed a tree take flight, its energia transformed by fungus, eaten by the insects, and then carried aloft.

Yogeshwar had said, "You must not merely transcend form, you must transform it." If ordinary toadstools transmuted dead wood and fed sentient beings, then how much greater was his responsibility to bring light into this realm? Had Lancelot recognized this continuity of life as he tended his flower gardens? If so, he'd never mentioned it. Could a disciple's realization ever exceed his master's?

Frith wasn't sure how long he rested against the wall, watching the winged creatures flit around the decomposed trunk like hummingbirds would a sweeter flower. A small boy, about two or three years old, came out of the village. He was wearing a baggy diaper and beating the road with a long twig. He noticed the log and began striking the fungus which broke off in purple-veined fragments. He giggled. Suddenly, he saw Frith and stopped.

The boy was enveloped in a pool of light, as when clouds on an overcast day part and sunbeams form a ray. Frith glanced up in the sky, looking for clouds, but the sky was cloudless, and the day bright enough on its own. The sun hurt his eyes, he quickly looked back down.

The boy poked Frith with his stick. When Frith didn't react, the boy did it again.

A short plump woman, wearing a dirty apron and a frazzled expression, came around the wall and saw the boy abusing Frith.

"There you are." She snatched the switch from the boy's hand and struck him smartly on his calves.

The child wailed, and Frith jumped up. "Don't strike the child."

"You've no idea the trouble this one causes me." Her aura now had a smear of red light. She pulled the screaming child by one arm and disappeared into the village.

Moments later, she returned. The red in her aura had paled. "I'm sorry about him. His sisters were supposed to be watching him." She tucked loose strands of hair behind her ears and brushed flour off her blouse. "We live just the other side of the wall. Come to the yard and I'll give you something to eat."

Frith followed her like a puppy. He waited in the yard while two young girls and the little boy ran circle eights between a stone well and a crab apple tree. He crossed to the well, lifted the bucket and drank by cupping water with his hands. The water was cool and sweet. When he was quenched, he wiped his face on his sleeve.

The woman returned with a loaf of bread, still warm from the oven, and a bowl of cooked beans. He sat in the dirt and looked up at her.

"No, no, sit here on the bench," she said.

Two stumps supported an oak plank. It wasn't any different from the ground, as far as he could see, but it would please her. Frith took a seat, and she handed him his food. "Thank you, Mother."

"Mother?"

"Aren't you the mother?"

She laughed. "Yes, I guess I am."

Frith inhaled the fragrant scent of the bread and said a silent blessing. He tore off the heel and dipped it in the bowl. He bit into it and smiled with gratitude.

The children ran to their mother and stood watching Frith eat. The little boy hugged her leg, but her daughters were taller. They leaned their heads on her hips and fooled with her apron. One girl still had her baby teeth, but the other had lost her two front teeth and flicked her tongue in and out of the gap.

Frith wolfed down the meal and realized he'd not been taking proper care of his body. He touched his stomach, and the mother said, "More?" Frith nodded and she pushed the gap-toothed girl forward. "Get him some more and be careful you don't burn yourself."

The child ran over and showed him her smile, with the two slivers of white where the new teeth were coming in. He handed her his bowl, and she dashed into the house. The other girl left her mother and raced after her sister. The boy stayed where he was.

Soon the girls returned. The older one walked carefully, holding the hot bowl in her tiny hands. The younger skipped ahead, tossing and catching the bread loaf in the air. "Careful you don't drop it in the dirt," her mother said.

The girl tossed it up again, and Frith caught it midair. She pulled her skirt up to hide her face and giggled. Her sister arrived with the soup and set it on the bench. She blew on her fingers, and Frith took her hands in his and blew on them, too. He found his words.

"Ooo, I'll bet that's hot for a little girl."

"I'm a big girl."

"Of course you are."

"I like you."

"I like you, too." Frith tore the bread in half and picked up the steaming bowl.

"When my daddy gets home tonight," she said, "I'm going to tell him we want to keep you."

Frith glanced at the mother, whose light was now tinged with lavender.

"Well, it wouldn't be Christian to send you on without a night's rest. We'll see what their father says. He'll be home 'bout dark."

* * *

Frith stayed several days in the village. Not only the mother, but also other wives tried to fatten him up. It was autumn, and the harvest had been good, so the villagers had no qualms about sharing. The men left for work in the morning and the women and children spent their days with Frith, drawn to him like a lazy cat to a puddle of sunlight.

As he came to know them, their auras grew clearer. No longer were they mere balls of light. He could recognize their pleasures and upsets in subtle shades and hues. Love and anger were very different shades of red, but when tinged with selfishness either emotion would turn a hard brownish-gray. Jealousy was greenish-brown with flashes of red or scarlet. Pride made orange streaks, like a sunset.

He learned to see the person and the light at the same time. A young wife, whose husband was apprenticed to the shoemaker, had eyes like emeralds and cheeks red as ripe apples. She was pregnant with her first child—a pale blue light within her light. She walked with her forearms wrapped around her protruding belly as if she was carrying a large pumpkin and grew so enamored of Frith she offered to have her husband make him a new pair of boots. Frith declined. "The pair I'm wearing is still good."

A matronly wife, as old as the kitchen ladies at the abbey, hooked Frith's head in the crook of her elbow and crushed his face into her bosom. "All my children are grown. I'd be more than happy to take care of Frith." Her hens were good layers, and she had a yard full of chickens. She let go of Frith's head and grabbed a plump rooster. "Come sup with us, and I'll roast you this fine bird."

"No, please, don't kill him on my account," Frith said. "I swore off meat a year ago."

So, they began to feed him fruit pies and bread with honey. "You're so thin, it worries us," the mother said.

"Never worry," Frith said. "Dwelling on something troubling only makes it worse." He saw her brow furrow and knew he'd only worried her more.

When a wife complained her husband didn't earn enough, Frith said, "Material desires are like sand, they seep in everywhere. Can a crock be sealed so tight dust cannot enter? No potter ever fired such an urn. Instead, keep your vessel in a place above craving."

* * *

On the fourth night of his stay, Frith was curled up under a warm blanket in the children's bed. The children were sleeping on the floor near the fireplace, with its banked embers giving off a faint orange light. Rough hands grabbed him and the abrupt transition into wakefulness startled him, but he resumed almost immediately the peaceful bliss that had become his normal waking state. The light before him was a dense gray-brown streaked with green and flashes of red. The husband.

"Yes?"

"Put your boots on. There's something outdoors I want you to see."

Outside the fog, layered in strata, was made to glow by a bright, full moon. The family dog, lying by the porch, raised his head, recognized his master, and went back to sleep. Frith looked up at the moon, mesmerized.

"You've taken our food and bed, but I still know nothing about you," the husband said. "Where were you coming from when my wife found you?"

"The light."

The man spat on the ground. "So, where's your destination?"

"The heavenly palaces."

"Never heard of such a place."

Frith looked at the sky. "You brought me out to show me this beautiful moon?"

"I wanted to show you the road."

Frith looked at it. The moonlight and shadows gave it a dappled appearance. It was lovely.

"What is it you do?" the man said.

"I wake up in the morning without anything from the day before hanging over me. I wake up without making demands for how today should unfold."

"Easy enough if someone else is feeding and caring for you, but I wake up with plenty hanging over me. Winter crops to plant, family to feed—I know exactly how my day's going to go, and there's never enough of it." The man spat. "You knew I meant, what is your work."

Frith understood. The man was asking his purpose. "I'm waiting for a path to unfold."

"Well, it's right there in front of you." The man handed Frith his bag. "You appeared out of nowhere, and you're going to disappear before they wake up."

Frith once thought a merchant's life consisted of always leaving, but now realized that all life consisted of leaving the preceding moment in favor of the moment that is becoming. He shook the man's hand and struck out on the road. Hadn't Buddha said, "Whatever is subject to origination is also subject to cessation?"

CHAPTER 43

Frith walked a week without leaving his bliss. Blue sky filled his eyes if the day was clear or gray sky when it rained. Realization came the day he'd asked himself if he couldn't find it where he was, where did he expect to wander in search of it?

Budhitra's words had bubbled up from memory: "There's no reason to wait; there's nothing you have to do first to become enlightened."

What else had Budhitra said? "Even if you go through all the stages of samadhi one by one, when at last you attain self-realization, you will only be realizing what has always been with you." The truth of those words felt to Frith as solid as the bones beneath his skin, for wherever he walked, all of his sheaths went, too.

One thing was becoming clearer. It wasn't necessary to draw the upper realms down into this one. They descended on their own. Several times in the last few days, he'd experienced all realms simultaneously. The state of awareness for which he had quested came to him of its own accord. Like Alura's?

Even the persistent presence of Lancelot in his thoughts had receded to the back of his mind. Had he outgrown his teacher? Before he found the answer, he was interrupted by hoofbeats behind him. It sounded like two riders. The smooth, easy pace of their canter slowed to a leisurely walk. For a while they trailed him. He didn't turn to look back, they'd catch up to him soon enough. Frith's visions had become manageable, but he still had to concentrate on the road to keep his consciousness from withdrawing and his feet leading him into the ditch.

As the hoofbeats approached, the animal smell brought a recollection of his travel through Italia, when he'd first gotten to know horses. The first rider drew even, and the clopping hooves raised billows of dust like storm clouds about his ankles. He remembered the attack of Prince of Behistun's army. Frith looked up and saw, instead of two riders, a man on a mare with a donkey tethered behind him. Large wicker baskets were roped to the donkey's back the way Bedouins tied cargo on the camels. Without conscious intention he took longer strides so his pace matched the rider.

"Are you a pilgrim?" the man said.

"Might be. Perhaps I'm only a man having a vision."

"A vision?"

"Of celestial worlds crossing into this world, like Prophet Jacob seeing angels ascending and descending as he slept."

The man bit his lip and looked around as though someone might overhear, but there was only Frith. "Are you Jewish?"

"No, but I accompanied a Jew for two years." Frith eyed the baskets on the donkey. "Are you a merchant?"

"I am. Name's David. There's a cider press at the next crossroads, bit of a farmer's market around it. Thought I'd set out my wares and do a crumb of business. Come with me, if you want, but let's not bring up the Jewish matter. Not all Christians are as tolerant as you seem to be."

Frith tried to talk with David about the Tree of Life. But apparently not all Jews were like Jacob because David just eyed him suspiciously, so Frith became quiet.

The donkey got too close to the mare's rump. She kicked up her rear legs, causing David to lurch forward. He petted her neck. "Settle down, girl."

"I once had to ride behind a donkey for seven days," Frith said. "My horse didn't like it at all, but nothing I could do about it. We had to get to where we were going."

"Normally, these two get along all right."

A good size crowd had gathered at the cider press. A tangle of horse carts, donkey carts, and hand carts loaded with apples waited their turn. Farmers with other produce to sell had set up under a tree. There was also a tinker banging pots and a shoemaker tapping at shoes. David and Frith joined the men under the tree, and Frith helped David untie his wicker baskets.

While David unpacked his baskets, Frith wandered over to the cider press. It was a cylinder formed of precisely fitted slats held by iron bands and set into a large circular stone with a grooved lip. As the apples were crushed from above, sweet brown juice rushed out the lip into waiting buckets. The buckets were emptied into barrels set on the cart that brought the apples. Frith drank from a proffered ladle. The cider was sweet, with just a hint of tartness.

"Won't be properly fermented for a couple of weeks," said the plump, round-faced woman. She had red-rimmed eyes like a rabbit, teeth like a horse, and a loud laugh like a donkey. "Scrummies—apples that fall to the ground before we can pick them. Can't store 'em, they won't keep." She brayed again. "But they make a potent cider."

Frith handed her back the ladle. "May I have an apple?"

She selected one from her cart. "This one looks fair, might be bruised under the skin though."

"I'll eat it soon." He dropped it into his bag.

"Best you do. My, what a fancy sack you got there, never seen one like it."

"It's from Samarkand."

"Never heard of it."

"The other side of the world."

"You mean London?"

"Um... further."

"Rome?"

"Further still."

"I can't imagine it."

"Nor could I. I had to go there to know it."

"Hey everybody," she called out. "A traveler who's been to some far place. Let's hear his stories."

The men and women turned toward him and began to gather. A man whose wagon had been emptied said, "Up here young fellow," and pulled Frith onto the wagon bed.

Frith hadn't intended to teach. But the people pressed around him and waited expectantly. What had Lancelot told Alura? "The universe brings us exactly where we need to be." Well, here was where he was. Where should he start?

"In Samarkand are men worthy to be called masters—"

"Like Barons?" someone called out from the crowd.

"No, spiritual masters—subtle, profound, wise."

"You mean saints?" a woman said.

"Yes. Or at least they would be called saints in Britain. But you know, saints aren't easily understood. Their ideas are slippery as ice at the point of melting. They're obscure as a lake bottom in a storm. But when the wind settles down, troubled waters will clarify. We too, have to become calm before we can appreciate how these quiet beings move through our world —the way cautious men cross a river in winter."

"What are you talking about?" said the man on whose wagon Frith was standing.

"I'm talking about beings aware of the deeper meaning of things. To be in the presence of such a person is like being in a valley between high mountains. Its waterfalls irrigate the valley, yet the mountain has no desire to be elevated. More is not better than less."

"You with your fancy purse are telling us not to want more?"

Frith searched the crowd with his eyes and found the man who had spoken. "Why does the richest person in the world want to get richer? Because no matter how much wealth you have, it isn't enough."

"Be enough for me," someone said.

The crowd roared with laughter and Frith realized many of them were drunk.

"This isn't any kind of story," a woman said.

"Right!" said the man beside her. "This is our harvest celebration. Get this fellow off the stage, and play music."

"Off!" One of the vendors in the back threw a cabbage at Frith.

Frith bent down and picked it up. "Thank you, good sir, I haven't eaten yet today."

Laughter and a hail of vegetables followed. Frith took what he could carry and got down off the wagon. He'd eat well tonight.

CHAPTER 44

Frith followed a northern road for two days until it met a crossroad at the center of a town. A towering grandfather tree stood in the middle of the junction so one could not go straight across. It was as if the tree said to travelers, "I've been here a hundred years, you'll just have to go around." Generations of cart wheels had complied, carving a circular track that spun off roads in four directions.

Beneath its enormous boughs was a wide circle of shady grass quilted with fallen leaves of orange and yellow. Since Frith didn't know which direction to go, he sat down, leaned against the tree and admired the village. Pretty little purple flowers grew in the people's yards, and it had a market crowded with merchants. He didn't know the name of this place, but it was larger than other villages he'd encountered in Britain.

Soon he drew attention. Villagers went out of their way to stroll by him. Studying the stranger, he supposed, although a village centered at a crossroads should have seen travelers enough. He pawed through his bag looking for an apple he thought was there, but found only dirty stockings, his spare tunic, and a bit of soap.

A woman stopped to admire his bag. Her husband sauntered over and stood next to her.

"That's very beautiful," she said.

Frith gathered a handful of leaves and let them fall from his fingers. "No more colorful than these, which this tree supplies in abundance."

"Well, I think I'd rather have the bag," she said.

"The spiritual eye sees what our ordinary eyes ignore."

The woman turned to her husband. "Ask where he's from."

"Does it really matter?" Frith said.

"Why not tell us?" the husband said.

A crowd began to collect.

"Please take a seat, all of you, and I'll tell you a story."

As the people sat down, others came to join them, but not everyone chose to sit. Three men Frith's age remained on the edge of the crowd, resting their elbows on a hitching rail.

Frith set his bag aside. "Did anyone buy apples in the market?"

"I did," a woman said.

"May I have one?"

She handed Frith an apple. He polished it on his tunic and held it up in silent offering. The people stared at it. He took a bite, and the crowd made a disappointed groan.

What had they expected, magic? He wasn't the magus from Merv, and he wasn't going to waste perfectly good food turning it into a flame. Not that he could. But people in Britain might like to hear Lancelot's story of old Camelot. He'd been growing more comfortable with words—or rather, more comfortable with the light emanating all around him, so that he wasn't dazzled speechless any more. Perhaps it was time to try them out.

"You've heard of King Arthur and his knights' quest for the Holy Grail," he said. "Shall I tell you how it first appeared to Galahad and the Knights of the Round Table?"

There were enthusiastic nods all around. "Were you there?" a boy said.

Frith laughed. "How old do you think I am? I wasn't even born then."

The crowd laughed with him.

He sat up straight and swept the crowd with his eyes. "Veiled is the answer. When Arthur's men saw the Grail, it was hidden under a silk veil."

"That's the shortest story ever," the boy said.

"I'm sure it's not the end," his mother said.

The woman who had first stopped to admire Frith's bag said, "Tell us where you got that fancy bag you carry."

Frith shook his head. "We're talking about the Grail now."

"Well, get on with it," the boy said.

"I was just like you once," Frith said. "Impatient."

The people laughed. The boy cast his eyes down and scooped a pile of leaves over his legs.

"Anyway," Frith said, "it was Pentecost and the Knights of the Round Table gathered at Camelot to celebrate it with King Arthur. Galahad, newly made a knight, was presented to Arthur by an elderly knight who led Galahad to a seat at the Round Table. But as Galahad sat, all the candles blew out, and the thunder rumbled."

The boy hid his eyes. The adults held their breath.

"In the darkness, a ray of light appeared. The Holy Grail hovered under a cloth of white silk, like an apparition. It has been said none among them could see it, for it was veiled. But Galahad could, for well-known are stories how the Grail transformed him."

Several in the audience nodded.

"Even without seeing it, the king, queen, and every knight and damsel in the room felt its wonder. Without even touching it, each person was elevated by its presence, according to their own nature. For the gourmet, it was as if they were having the best food and wine they'd ever tasted. Those who craved beauty saw the beauty in each other. For the more enlightened, it was as if their souls levitated, lighter than their bodies, as if the heavenly worlds opened to them."

He noted a collective feeling arise in the crowd as if they were sensing the Grail from his telling.

"When the Grail left, the experience faded. Sir Gawain suggested they should quest until they saw it fully, for what they had seen, however holy, was obscured."

"By the silk cloth?" the boy said.

Frith smiled, remembering how he'd asked almost the same thing when Lancelot told him the story. "No, by their own desires."

"Desires?" said the woman who admired his bag.

"Each person's experience of the Grail was only as deep as their wants allowed. The veil was the fabric of their preferences. Only those who wanted nothing could see it as it truly was."

"I'm confused," her husband said. "How can a man's preferences hide a holy relic?"

"Ah, that confused me at first, as well. But you've got to understand, the Grail is not a relic."

"Of course it is."

"No more than a doorway is a door. The first knights who quested for the Grail looked for the wrong thing, in the wrong place, for years. The Grail is not an object. It's a portal leading to your soul. The quest for the Holy Grail is the quest to find your own Self."

"Did you find it?" the boy said.

"Yes," Frith said.

The men leaning on the horse rail straightened.

"Do you have it?" the woman said.

"We all have it. It's merely veiled. To see it, you have to want to take down the veil more than you want to get things you desire."

"It can't be that easy, or the knights wouldn't have had to quest for years," a man said.

"As I say, they were all looking in the wrong place." Frith held up his bag. "A woman here asked where I got this fine bag. It came from a far land where men buy and sell silk, the lightest of all fabrics—so transparent it can be worn as a veil. Yet, a shipload of silk is not light. Whatever a veil is made of, if you have enough of it, it will be so heavy a donkey could not carry it."

The crowd's collective aura was tinged with a little green. A voice in the back said, "He must be rich."

"The question is not, What is the veil hiding the Grail made of? The question is, How much veil is there? For that's the amount of weight you are carrying… Should we have the good fortune to see a holy light, it will be like looking through a gauze curtain. If you don't want the curtain there, stop holding it up. Just let it fall."

"We can't all go on quests," the woman's husband said. "Most of us have families to support."

"Of course you do. But you don't have to travel anywhere to take down the veil. It's inside each of you. And I'll tell you something else. Caring for your family is good, but the real purpose of life is not to get married or get rich or even to help others. The goal is to take down the veil."

No one asked anything further and people began to drift away. Before the boy and his mother left, Frith said, "Is there a lake or stream nearby where I can take a bath?"

"A bath?" the boy said.

"It's too late in the year for a bath," the mother said.

Frith hadn't had a bath since he left Jacob's. "Not for me."

The mother and her son stood. "You'll get the croup."

"Thank you for your care. Nevertheless, if you'd give me directions—"

"I'll show you," the boy said.

She grabbed her son's arm. "No, you won't." She pointed down one of the roads. "If you're determined to risk it, walk about half-hour in that direction. You'll come to a trail on your right. It leads to a good pond." She led her son away, shaking her head.

* * *

Frith stripped naked, took soap from his bag and stepped into the pond. The cold water raised goose bumps on his flesh. The gradual torture of slow immersion was unbearable, so when he was knee deep, he dove. Once the initial shock passed, the cold water on his skin felt crisp and fresh. He didn't perform any of Jacob's rituals. He just soaped himself and dunked under to rinse.

When he tossed the bar of soap onto the shore, he spied the men who'd been leaning on the horse rail pawing through his belongings. Frith rushed out of the pond. "What are you doing?"

The nearest man tripped him and sat on him. The other two men held his arms. "Where is it?"

"What?"

"The cup. The jewel-encrusted cup."

"I don't have any such thing."

"Liar! We heard you brag you have the Grail."

"Then you didn't hear well. The Holy Grail isn't a relic. It's a spiritual state."

"Bah, that can't be true. Search his bag again."

"Don't bother," said one of the men holding his arms. "Just take it with us."

In an instant they let him go and ran off with his bag, clothes, and boots.

Frith stood there for a minute, then decided to accept the loss, and not chase them. He glanced at his naked body. This was the way he was born. Well, minus the mud.

He rinsed off in the pond and walked away dripping, teeth chattering. Part way back to the road the trail forked. He didn't remember it branching when he came. Unsure which path led the main road, he made a choice.

After a long time, he realized he'd walked too far for this to be the correct path. The trail split again and he noticed the tip of a roof jutting above the tree line in the distance, so he walked toward it. He came to an isolated chapel with a small graveyard. An old monk sat next to a body wrapped in muslin.

"Excuse me," Frith said.

The old man looked up. "You're naked."

"As the day God made me."

"Why?"

"Robbers took my clothes."

"How cruel." The old man handed him a tattered monk's robe. "Here, he doesn't need it any more."

Frith stared at it.

"Take it. It's not diseased. It belonged to a holy man."

"Him?"

"Yes. He was my friend."

Frith accepted the garment and put it on. He remembered when Lancelot told him of receiving a holy man's shirt from an ancient hermit sitting wake for his friend. Curious, how memories float up from the tiniest events. "You're sitting wake?"

"Just a few prayers, until the angels take him or dawn comes."

Jacob could have said Kaddish, but he wasn't here. The dead man was Christian, anyway. At least he had an old friend to pray for him. Maybe that was as good as Kaddish.

"In the morning the gravedigger will come," the old monk said. "I'm going to keep him company until then, but I expect his soul is already gone. You can sleep here tonight if you want."

Frith no longer feared the dead, but he couldn't find any appeal in sleeping with a corpse. "Thank you, but no. I'm going to see if I can find my way to a village before dark."

"What village is that?"

"I don't know its name, but it has a colossal tree where four roads meet. I was there before I was robbed. The people seemed friendly."

"Oh, yes, I know where you mean. Continue on this trail for a bit and you'll come to a road. Turn right and you'll not be far from town."

"Thank you for the directions and for this robe."

"May it bring you the peace it brought him."

The old monk's directions brought Frith out on a different road than he had taken earlier, but after he turned right, it was only minutes before he was on the outskirts of town. Indeed this route was shorter than backtracking would have been.

The concussive sounds of hammer on iron rang down the street. The boy who had listened so attentively under the tree spied him and ran over. He took Frith's hand and led him to the iron works.

The ironmonger smiled when he saw Frith. He put down his hammer and went to a table where Frith's clothes were piled on his bag. He handed them to Frith. "Took these from three ruffians trying to sell them in the market. We all knew there was only one bag like that in Britain."

Frith felt no attachment to material goods, but his shoes would be nice. He wiped the soles of his feet on his calves and put on his stockings and boots.

The man pointed to the back of his shop. "You can change back there."

Frith looked down at the holy man's robe. "No, I think I'll wear this. But thank you for recovering my things. It was kind."

"Glad to. We don't tolerate thievery around here."

"Do you know where I might sleep tonight? I'll leave in the morning."

The boy tugged on his hand. "Come to my house."

CHAPTER 45

"Close up the shop," the poulterer said to his wife. "Saint Petroc's going to teach in the town square." He wiped his hands on his apron, took it off, and accompanied Frith down the street, leaving his wife to come after.

Frith was glad he'd stopped to ask the poulterer for directions. He knew of Saint Petroc from his days as the Abbot's aide. Petroc was well respected in Cornwall and had two monasteries, one on the River Camel and the other in Bodmin. Frith had yet to meet a saint in Britain and was eager to learn what Petroc had to say. Like Frith, Petroc had also been to Rome.

Word spread and more people joined them. When they reached the square Frith looked for the saint, but didn't see him. Perhaps he wasn't there yet. Frith found a weathered tree stump and sat down.

People milled about, waiting. Those behind him shouted for folks in front to sit down. Good. He couldn't see either. If Petroc had arrived, he couldn't tell.

The crowd began to sit, and a man in front of him turned. "Aren't you going to stand?"

"For what? As a sign of respect?" Had he missed the saint's arrival?

"No. So those in back can hear you."

"Why me?"

"Aren't you here to give a sermon?"

"Me? No, I'm here to meet Saint Petroc like the rest of you."

"You mean you're not—"

"Petroc? No."

"But your robe…"

Frith glanced down. He was still wearing the hermit's robe. But the dead man hadn't been Petroc. Saint Petroc was alive in Dewnans, ministering to Britons, as far as he knew.

"Do I look like I'm fifty?" Frith said. "Petroc's an old man."

"Well, give us *some* wisdom," the man said. "We've left our businesses because of you."

Frith stood and realized the crowd had grown. He stepped onto the tree stump and cleared his throat. "Like you, I came looking for a saint. But what do we mean by saint?" Frith saw blank looks. "Isn't it an enlightened being?"

"How would we recognize such a man if not by his robes?" the poulterer said.

"Thing is, it wouldn't matter to him if you didn't."

"But he'd be a hermit like you?"

"My clothes may be a hermit's, but I'm not a monk."

"You're not a renunciant?"

"Well… renunciation isn't about giving up life. It's about dropping the veil that hides the source of life. Enlightened men see the world clearly, not through a veil."

"What veil?"

He'd told the veil story yesterday. He didn't want to repeat it today. There had been a visiting bishop at the abbey once who had used the same homily three masses in a row. By the third time, no one was listening. "What I mean is, we are of two minds, a higher mind—the saint's mind—and a personal mind that sees this world only in relation to itself. A saint's mind doesn't cling to wants or desires. Such a being just watches life unfold, seeing in it the nature of God."

"Who are you to speak of the nature of God?" The local priest pushed his way to the front. "When they told me Saint Petroc had come, I thought it couldn't be true. You're an imposter."

"That was a false rumor. I've said plainly that I'm not him."

"Then what are you doing with these people?"

"Whatever I can. If you are a conscious person who feels the awe of *spiritus,* then that's what you do."

"Spiritus? So you speak Latin. At what abbeys have you studied scripture?"

"I didn't learn what I did from an abbey library."

"What kind of holy man doesn't study scripture? Perhaps one who can't read?"

"I can read, Holy Father. I just find the scriptures are… like a guidepost at a crossroad that points the way to different cities. Once you've read it, follow its directions and journey on."

"Is that what you believe?"

"I'm not concerned with beliefs. Beliefs and opinions are always changing. Concentrate on absolute truth, for it is the only constant."

The priest wore a gold crucifix the size of his fist. He gripped it tightly. "Are you trying to challenge my parishioners' beliefs?"

"Oh, no. I'm just telling a story to show how our personal views thwart us from seeing behind the veil."

"Humph. Let's hear it."

"Certainly. Imagine sitting in the shade watching a little brown bunny nibble lush pasture on a pleasant afternoon." The people smiled. "Suddenly a snake slithers out of the bushes and swallows the rabbit."

His audience reacted, as he had expected, with a chorus of complaints. "That's not a nice story."

"Why?" Frith said.

"The snake is evil."

"Why is the snake evil?"

"Thou shall not kill."

"Yet who among you has not snared a hare for supper? Let me tell another story. A rat scurries through the granary. A cat kills it."

"Good riddance."

Frith looked over the crowd. "You think?"

They nodded in agreement.

"So bunny, good; snake, bad. Cat, good; rat, bad. Is that it?"

They nodded again.

"What if the snake ate the rat? Is it a good snake or bad snake?"

Again the confusion set in.

"Ah," he said. "Notice how your opinions changed? Yet weren't all four creatures in this story made by the same creator? God is behind them all and in them all, but we're too busy deciding who's good and who's bad to see Him there."

"No man can see the creator," the priest said.

"What I'm saying is, God is all around. But the opinions and judgments we hold onto act like a veil that stops us from seeing Him."

The priest narrowed his eyes and puffed out his cheeks. "God is unknowable."

Frith shook his head. "Are you saying the church doesn't know God, or the Pope doesn't know God, or that you don't know God?"

"That's not what I meant. Ordinary people can't know God."

Surprisingly, some of the Abbot's lessons he'd never really listened to were coming back to him. "The Prophet Jacob was an ordinary man who had a vision of a ladder to heaven. Saul was an ordinary man who had a vision that turned him into Saint Paul. The experience of the Holy Grail that Galahad and Lancelot had is available to any man who will pull aside the veil created by wants, beliefs, and opinions."

"Those were not ordinary men, and these concepts are beyond the ordinary man." Some in the audience closed ranks behind the priest, while others leaned closer to Frith.

"Would you prefer a different word for it? Call it experiencing light, or spirit rather than God, but it is the state of bliss we are seeking."

"That's not true. What people are seeking is to find heaven and avoid hell."

"Christ came to alleviate suffering, not to inspire fear. Didn't Christ tell us the kingdom of heaven was within us? Didn't he say the greatest commandments were to love God and love one another?"

"Oh, *now* you want to quote scripture. A man must be purged of sin and become devout to receive Christ."

"Devotion comes from the heart, not the mind. Fear can't create it. You cannot make a man devoted by threatening him with hell."

The priest turned an unhealthy shade of crimson. "The apostle Paul says, 'In Christ our sins are forgiven.' That is the truth of the church."

"And Paul is right. When we are centered in Christ, forgiveness emanates to us and from us."

"I'm glad you condescend to agree with Saint Paul."

"It is effortless to forgive when we realize there is nothing to forgive."

"Nothing to forgive? Blasphemer! Who are you to presume to lecture us on forgiveness and sin?"

"Non-truth will not lead people to truth," Frith said.

The arteries in the priest's neck swelled until Frith feared they might burst.

"Leave or I'll have you burned as a heretic."

Frith shrugged and stepped off the stump. Rough hands grabbed him. "Shall we, Father?"

Frith began mentally chanting the phrase he'd learned from Yogeshwar, *The power of God is within me. The grace of God surrounds me.*

The priest stared into Frith's eyes. After a moment he shook his head. "No. Let him leave and never return." He grabbed Frith's arm and started to push him.

Frith felt his energia rush into the priest.

The priest jumped away. "Go, far from here. Never return. Do you understand?"

The crowd parted and Frith went from their village without looking back.

CHAPTER 46

Frith walked all night. The gibbous moon, yellow as an egg yolk, paled to white as dawn came, but it refused to yield to the sun and hung in the daylight sky like a ghost. The sight triggered a childhood memory of the seasons of long darkness when he was a toddler, when the sunlight was a frail old woman, hardly brighter than a full moon on winter snow. A time when Lancelot had left the superstitious and scornful to seek isolation in a remote woods.

Frith knew he'd made a mistake in believing he'd outgrown his master. Hadn't Lancelot warned him? "Don't listen to your own counsel and decide you're ready to teach others." But that's exactly what he'd done. Hadn't Yogeshwar echoed the same sentiment when he laughed at Frith and told him he wasn't ready? What had it gotten him? Run out of town.

Frith decided to avoid cities and seek solitude in woods as Lancelot had done. Throughout the day whenever he spotted a village or even smoke from a distant chimney he'd leave the road in favor of a side trail around the outskirts.

Late in the afternoon, he passed a pasture populated by a herd of milk cows behind a wattle fence, their round eyes upon him, their udders full. The herd moved toward him, making a crying plea to be milked.

"Don't come to me, I'm not your keeper," Frith said.

Or was he? Was he really responsible for all sentient beings as Budhitra said? That's not how Lancelot had been; a hermit slipping wraith-like in and out of morning Mass, isolated in the woods, hiding from his once adoring public.

Wandering Britain in a dead hermit's robe wasn't the role Lancelot would have chosen. In fact, before Frith and Alura met Lancelot, he'd kept the Holy Grail to himself. Not what Budhitra or Yogeshwar or Da Shi said Frith should do.

So whose example should he follow? Each of them in their own way had enabled Frith to see higher realms. Lancelot with his initiation of energia, Yogeshwar with his Shaktipat, even the ladder Rabbi Ishmael said was in the center of a man's house.

Since his samadhi on the Bodmin moor he'd tried living in the light, then tried telling others what he'd learned. Neither approach seemed to work. He understood why Lancelot preferred talking to flowers in his garden. But was indulging preferences ever the right choice? The holy men he'd met in Samarkand didn't think so.

Frith wasn't finding a solution to his dilemma on the earthly plane. He needed to withdraw. True destiny and purpose might be easier to see from a higher plane.

Darkness was coming. Frith had walked last night instead of sleeping. Now, he felt fatigue rise like an evening fog. He looked around and noticed he was in a wood much like the one Lancelot had chosen. Tree branches grew more naked by the hour, and their leaves carpeted the forest floor. They looked deliciously soft. He'd make his hermitage here.

Frith scooped the leaves into a great pile and fell into their umber softness. The sweet scent of autumn surrounded him as he settled in.

He thought about the two strange sects of monks he'd seen in Egypt. The stylites, who lived atop high poles, kept themselves even more isolated than Lancelot. Yet how were they fed? By the labor of those they literally towered over. Stylites lowered buckets from their lofty perches to be filled with food and water by the men whose company they'd renounced. What good were they to the men below?

Then there were the holy fools, men who hid their enlightenment in plain sight, passing easily among the masses, speaking freely, but never taken seriously because, after all, they were only fools. Men never took offense at their words, but no one understood their meaning either. How did they help anyone? At least no one threatened to burn them as heretics.

The tapestry at Jacob's house came to mind, and Frith imagined himself sleeping on the ground, ascending a ladder to higher palaces like the prophets. He knew he was now capable of ascending and descending at will, at least to certain levels. He decided he'd withdraw into the higher planes permanently. He would live in these woods, stay in the ethereal realms, and just stop troubling his fellow man.

He entered the flow of Shakti and was carried upward. The veil of heaven fell away, and the Grail hovered like a giant blue eye. At its center was a blazing five-pointed star, through which he passed into a state of pure light. He knew this realm well. Then he transcended it, to a level where spirit and nature were no longer separate from conscious-energy. In its presence he was beyond words. Concepts could not encompass it. He was no longer a separate observer who could describe what he saw. It was a wholeness where all worlds met and merged. Or did they originate and dissolve? Whichever it was, he couldn't say.

Time stopped mattering. Time was merely the measure of relative distance and movement of celestial objects. What defined a day? The sun came up, the sun went down. In a realm of undifferentiated, pure Shakti he had no way of saying how long it had been before he began to descend.

He transitioned back into his ordinary world, where time was a function of memory, where change, growth and decay were gauged by compared recollections of an object's previous position or state. Frith had seen the universe as a seamless garment. A whole cloth wasn't simply woven strands. The space and light between its fibers made it what it was as much as its threads. He trembled at the comprehension of it.

The night was cold. He gathered the nearby leaves, covering his legs and torso. He snuggled into them like they were a warm comforter, and he dreamed.

CHAPTER 47

Frith shivered. In his dream, he was kneeling in the snow before a Bishop. He couldn't see the Bishop's face, but he recognized the man's office by his rich robe and ornate ring on the hand reaching out to him. The Bishop clasped Frith's hand and pulled him upright. Frith's knees wobbled, and he nearly collapsed.

"Steady there," the Bishop said. "Bring him a shawl." Someone handed the Bishop a long woolen stole in which he wrapped Frith. He vigorously rubbed Frith's arms. "Aren't you cold?"

Frith's teeth chattered. "N-n-no."

The Bishop's face broke into a broad grin. He was as bald as Budhitra—no, he was Budhitra. Frith looked around. This was definitely Britain. He was standing in front of a Christian cathedral. What a strange dream.

"Let me tell you the story of a monk who came to Bodhidharma's hermitage one winter," the Bishop said.

Oh, this was a dream about Budhitra, like his dream of Yogeshwar in the burned-out forest. After all, what bishop would even know who Bodhidharma was?

Flakes of snow settled on the Bishop's bald head, and he brushed them off. "This monk, let's call him Shen, knocked on Bodhidharma's door and said he'd come for enlightenment. Bodhidharma, took him to be a curiosity seeker, shrugged and closed the door in his face."

The snow began to fall harder and pile around their feet. The Bishop didn't seem to notice. "Shen's journey to find a teacher capable of enlightening beings had been difficult. How could he leave as soon as he'd arrived? He resolved to wait outside Bodhidharma's door until the master accepted him."

Frith could identify with Shen. He'd shown a similar obstinacy persuading Lancelot to teach him.

The Bishop held out his palm and watched it fill with snowflakes. "It was snowing there, too, and as the night progressed, snow piled up." The Bishop brushed the snow from his hands and tucked them inside his robe. "In the morning, Bodhidharma opened his door and found Shen standing in snow up to his waist. 'Why are you seeking enlightenment?' Bodhidharma asked. Shen replied, 'I want to learn the great compassion of Buddha so I can help the suffering people in the world.'"

The Bishop smiled. "Shen wasn't the first seeker Bodhidharma had met, so he decided to test him further. 'That's a lofty vow.' Shen answered, 'What good is attaining buddhahood without Buddha's compassion?'"

Frith looked into the Bishop's eyes—Budhitra's eyes—and swallowed hard. What good indeed?

"Bodhidharma replied, 'Prince Siddhartha did not become Buddha by merely asking for it. He endured all manner of suffering which his fellow monks were unwilling to do. How do I know you have the commitment?'"

"Shen pulled a hatchet from his bag." The Bishop pantomimed swinging a hatchet. "Shen severed his own hand and laid it on the snow bank before Bodhidharma."

Frith gasped.

"Bodhidharma looked at the bloody hand. 'Your willingness to cut off your own hand proves your sincerity and determination... and foolishness.' He then tore strips from his own robe and bandaged Shen's wrist. He brought Shen in out of the snow, gave him hot beverages, and treated his wound with herbs. Bodhidharma accepted Shen as his disciple and brought him to the true meaning of no-mind."

What a strange story for a Bishop to tell. Frith was still trying to make sense of it when an angel with hair as red as Alura's descended from one of Jacob's palaces and took the Bishop's place. Her wings fluttered as if blown by a breeze, but the winter air was still as ice. She spread her arms apart as if to embrace the world. A pink jeweled sun in the center of her chest sent faceted rays toward Frith, causing his knees to collapse. He settled gently, coming to rest on the cathedral steps.

She waved her hand over his eyes, and they closed. He sensed her hand move above him as the hairs on his head leaped for her fingertips. A rush of Shakti coursed through his spine, exactly as it had with Yogeshwar. He'd never felt so joyous. She walked behind him and pressed the toe of her shoe into his sacrum. An explosion of laughter tore from his lips as energia raced up through him, out into the sky, further onward, traversing the seven realms. There was nothing funny about it, but he was so filled with delight, he couldn't help but laugh in his sleep.

"Wake up, Frith. Get up!"

Another kick to his sacrum, but this one didn't bring ecstasy. Frith opened his eyes and discovered Sir Otto kicking him in the butt.

It was just so ridiculous, so delightful, that Frith burst into laughter awake.

Otto shook his head and gathered twigs for kindling.

Frith looked around. Of course, it was too early in the season for snow, the ground had only a dusting of frost, but Frith was shivering hard.

"Help me get a fire going," Otto said. "We need to get you warmed up."

Frith's teeth chattered, but he only laughed harder. "Oh, why did you wake me? I was never so merry in my life."

Otto's flint sparked, and he coaxed a flame from some dried moss. He added tinder and got a small blaze going. He took a branch and cleared the surrounding area of leaves so he wouldn't ignite the whole forest, then added larger sticks, building up the bonfire. "Frith, move near the fire."

Frith merely smiled.

Otto grabbed him by the arm and dragged him along the ground like a child's toy. Frith giggled with childlike delight.

Frith lay on his side and stared into the flames. He watched black, dry logs transform into glowing embers. Dross into light.

"You've been missing a good while," Otto said. "Your sister is worried—we're all worried."

"No, Alura's not worried. She was just with me as an angel in my dream. Why did you interrupt my sleep?"

"Are you joking? I've been to the ends of Britain looking for you, and I found you freezing to death. I promised Alura I'd find you and I have."

Frith roared with laughter. "Yes, you have."

"Where are your clothes?"

"Am I naked? These are my clothes."

"I mean your regular clothes. Why are you wearing a hermit's robe? Have you joined an order? If that's the case, the Abbot will be very disappointed you didn't choose his."

Frith's eyes twinkled. "Ah, the Abbot. Tell the dear old man I haven't joined any other abbey. Tell him I've decide to stay in these woods as Lancelot did."

Otto jumped up. "No! I gave your sister my knight's oath I'd bring you to the abbey, and that's where you're going if I have to bind you and throw you over my horse."

Frith laughed. "I'm sorry to disappoint you. I'm staying right here until I understand what my dream meant. I believe the red-haired angel will come again, maybe the Bishop, too. Mighty forces will appear to show me how to live."

"Well, those mighty forces can find you as easily at the abbey, and you won't be a block of ice when they do. Let's mount up. We can share my horse and be there for breakfast."

"Go on without me."

"You're not listening. I can't."

"You can. Alura asked you to find me. You have. Go tell her I am all right."

"I won't do it. I promised Alura I'd bring you back, and by God, you're going to go."

Frith stood up and faced Otto. "We were fellow travelers for a long time. Let's not have enmity between us. I know you're a great knight, faithful to your duty, as surely as I feel my destiny will become clearer if I stay exactly where I am."

Otto looked to the east where the faintest edge of dawn was silhouetting the forest trees. "What about love?"

"Love?"

"Think of how much your sister loves you. How badly she wants to see you."

The laughter bubbled up again. "If anyone at the abbey would understand what I'm doing out here, it'll be Alura."

"And yet, she's the one who asked me to bring you back." Otto stepped over to Frith and embraced him. "You don't know what she did to me. I don't know what she'll do to me if I fail her."

Frith felt Otto trying to lift him off his feet. He rooted his qi to Mother Earth. Otto grunted. Frith knew Otto was the stronger man, easily able to wield a heavy broadsword. He'd once seen Otto pick up an anvil in a contest of strength at a caravansary. But Frith deepened his connection, and willed his body to become heavier. Otto strained until his face was purple. Finally, Otto let go and stared with disbelief.

"I'm sorry old friend," Frith said. "I didn't mean to disparage your strength. Don't hold it against me. I'll never tell a soul. Qi simply can't be displaced by brute force." Otto's horse pawed the ground. Frith gave Otto's shoulder a friendly squeeze. "Your mount is ready. Daylight is at hand. Go with God and tell them at the abbey not to worry. I am only a little out of my mind. But I hope to be further out soon."

CHAPTER 48

Abbey of St. Benignus, October, 556

Alura was stirring porridge when Ethelburg hobbled into the kitchen, flushed and out of breath. "Alura! There's a knight at the gate."

Alura felt her heart quicken. "Is Frith with him?"

Ethelburg shook her head. "I think he's alone."

"Is it the same knight who brought Frith's letter?"

"I don't know. With my eyesight, they all look big and shiny." Ethelburg wrung her hands. "You don't think it's bad news do you?"

"Why expect the worst? Let's first see if this knight is Sir Otto."

The two women left the Abbot's kitchen and crossed the grounds toward the abbey gates. Alura would have run, but Ethelburg could only manage a hobble. In the distance, she saw it was indeed Sir Otto, and someone was with him! Could Ethelburg's failing eyes have missed seeing Frith?

The man Otto was talking with turned. It was only old Brother Caedmon, the cook at the monk's kitchen. He wouldn't be on gate duty. Probably he'd just returned from the market and stopped to chat with Sir Otto.

When they reached the gate, Alura curtsied. "Good day, Sir Otto."

Ethelburg attempted a feeble curtsy; her old knees didn't bend well.

Otto gave a quick bow. "Ladies."

"Have you found Frith?"

"I have."

"Alive?" Ethelburg said.

"Certainly."

"Well, tell," Ethelburg said. "I haven't the years left to wait."

Alura touched Ethelburg's arm. "Patience, madam."

"He's a mere two hours ride from here," Otto said. "but I couldn't convince him. I mean I could have manhandled him, I suppose, heaved him across my horse, but what good would that do? He might wander from here quick as he did from Jacob's."

"You need me to persuade him?" Alura said.

"That's why I'm here. He dreamed he saw you. I figure he'll come along if you ask him in person. We can leave straight away if the liveryman has a horse for hire."

"Oh, no!" Ethelburg said. "Alura can't leave the abbey without a chaperone."

"All right, two extra mounts then," Otto said.

"Wait, Sir Otto. I don't know how to ride," Alura said.

Otto scratched his beard. "Oh well, it's not so far. We can walk there in half a day." He looked at the sun. "We should go now, though. Frith's not in his right mind, and if he takes it into head to stray, the search must begin anew."

"What about her chaperone?" Ethelburg said. "I'm not able to walk far. Neither is Brother Caedmon. We'd best see the Abbot."

The Abbot? He was as old as either of them. She wanted to start now.

Nevertheless, she went with Ethelburg and Brother Caedmon to the Abbot. As Alura expected, the Abbot wasn't up to the journey either. He suggested they ask Bedivere, who was visiting that week.

"But he's a Bishop now," Alura said. "He hasn't time for trivial things."

"He *is* your and Frith's protector," the Abbot said. "Besides, I suspect he'd enjoy a break from the administrative work of the church to stroll the countryside with another knight."

The Abbot was right. Bedivere was delighted to accompany her and quickly joined Otto at the gate. In the meantime, Alura rushed to the kitchen and packed food for four. Who knew when Frith had eaten last?

Otto carried the food basket for her and had eaten half of it before they were two hours out. She didn't blame him—in her rush to meet Frith, she hadn't given Otto breakfast. As soon as Bedivere agreed to go, she'd pressed them to leave. She should have packed twice as much food.

It took four hours on foot. During their journey, Otto encouraged Bedivere to talk about his days with Arthur and his knights. She'd heard the stories before and only half listened while trying to sense if Frith was near.

They spotted a body in the woods, sprawled at an odd angle next to a fallen tree. Alura's heart leapt, and she dashed into the forest, hoping Frith wasn't too badly injured. Bedivere and Otto pounded behind her.

Relief and disappointment mingled in her when the man turned out to be a woodcutter stealing a midday nap.

"I knew this wasn't the right forest," Otto said. "We're near, though."

They let the woodcutter return to his rest and walked on. Otto had a traveler's sense of direction, and soon he said, "Here's the place."

Alura spied Frith and gave a squeal of delight. He was sitting with his back pressed against a misshapen, primeval tree. His head lazed in a hollow in its trunk. She caught his eye, and he gave her a goofy smile but didn't run to greet them. She didn't care. She ran to him.

She looked deep into his eyes and understood the transformation he was undergoing. Oh, the idiot. When Lancelot's Grail first overtook her, she'd had Frith and Bedivere and even Brother Caedmon to support her. Here he was, trying to go through it alone.

Otto and Bedivere caught up to her.

"Frith, my boy, how are you?" Bedivere's thunderous voice boomed.

Frith gave him a benevolent smile.

"What'd I tell you?" Otto said. "He's not really here."

Alura leaned down and kissed Frith on the forehead, between his eyebrows. His eyelids fluttered and his eyes rolled up into his head.

"Oh God, he's worse than before," Otto said.

But he wasn't. He was better. And she would help him get better still, to grow into the world he was experiencing. Frith had been found.

"I know something of these states," Bedivere said. "Not that I've ever been in one. But I was at Arthur's court the night the Grail transformed Galahad. Then, of course, Lancelot... and this one, too." Bedivere cocked his head toward Alura.

She smiled and nodded, then turned back to Frith. He was still resting in bliss.

"Let's take him to the abbey," Bedivere said. "Frith, if you want to live in the woods, you can have my old hut."

Frith gave no sign of hearing him, although Alura knew he was aware of everything around him, more so than the knights.

Alura squatted in front of Frith and took his hands in hers. She blew gently on his face and his eyes fluttered open. Alura stood slowly, and Frith rose with her.

"Oh, hello, Sir Bedivere," Frith said.

"Bishop, now," Alura said.

Frith laughed as though it was the funniest thing he'd ever heard.

"Don't take offense, Bishop," Otto said. "That's what he was like when I found him."

Bedivere chuckled as well. "Don't worry, Sir Otto. I've known Frith since he was a pup." He slapped Frith on the back.

Alura took Frith's hand and started walking. He fell in step with her. Once they left the woods, Otto said, "Frith, we didn't think you'd eaten. Alura's made us a basket of food. Are you hungry?"

Frith shook his head.

"What about you Bishop?" Otto said. "It's midday. Shall we stop for lunch?"

"I'll wait to have dinner at the abbey," Bedivere said.

Otto shrugged, fished inside the basket, pulled out a loaf of bread, and tore off the end with his teeth.

Alura held Frith's hand all the way to the abbey. When they arrived, the Abbot and all the monks gathered around Frith, but he didn't seem to recognize them. He was friendly, but no more so than he would have been to strangers.

So he still wasn't fully there. Well, that would come with time. "Frith can speak with you more tomorrow. Right now, he needs food and a proper bed."

"That's true enough," Otto said to the gathered monks. "When I found him, he was sleeping on a pile of leaves."

Alura led Frith to his old room. "This is your place, where you stay. Get settled, and I'll send a kitchen boy over with a plate."

Frith grabbed her hand. "Alura, how could you leave here?"

"Well, Sir Otto said he'd found you, but I couldn't ride a horse—"

Frith shook his head frantically. "No, no, I mean how could you ever leave this state to come back to ordinary reality?"

"You don't. It becomes your everyday reality." She leaned over and kissed his cheek. "Have a rest, and when you wake tomorrow, come find me in the kitchen. You remember the big building over there?"

Frith nodded.

She gave him an enormous hug, pushed him toward his room, and danced away like a firefly.

CHAPTER 49

Alura watched Frith slicing carrots, holding them with his fingers folded under as she had taught him. The same way the kitchen ladies had taught her when she was six or seven. Frith's blade flew up and down, making even and precise slices, his knife moving with a speed that almost blurred the eye. Somewhere on his journey, he'd gained great powers of concentration, and when he applied them nothing could distract him.

In the weeks since he'd returned, Alura had found practical tasks for Frith that would draw him back into everyday life. "Frith," she said, "I understand what you're feeling—the way the bliss pulls you inward. Save it for your meditations. In other times work in the world. The now is not here for you. You are here to serve the now."

He'd nodded happily. "Show me what to do."

Her first idea was to start simple—have Frith sweep and mop the cathedral floors. Brother Fastidious objected, claiming she was taking work from new postulants, part of their training. "Exactly what Frith needs," she said.

"But he's not a postulant. He's never wanted to join our order."

It was still true. Frith remained adamant about not taking vows, even though he was living in a monk's habit. She could see where the vow of obedience might be a problem, anyway. Alura could have gone over Fastidious' head to the Abbot, but she'd only set more monks against her brother. Frith attended morning meditations, which pacified most of the monks, but he persisted in wearing the ragged old robe she'd found him in. Fastidious called him an imposter and told him to put on the robe of their order or return to the ordinary clothes he'd worn when he was the Abbot's aide. Frith ignored him. Yes, obedience might be a problem.

Alura's solution was to give Frith work in the Abbot's kitchen, her kitchen, where the monks had no say. His first chores were simple—chop wood, carry water, bring in vegetables and wash them. Tasks she had done as a girl when she'd first come to the abbey.

The kitchen ladies, who'd always loved Frith, weren't a problem. Frith seemed willing to work at whatever they asked of him. They welcomed him and gave him responsibility for stirring the porridge. He was at first not completely in this world, and they worried over him, one cook or another constantly making sure he didn't let the pot burn or set himself on fire.

It shocked them to learn Frith no longer ate meat, for as a boy he'd always snatch pieces from their carving table. The revelation came the first time he was trusted to cut vegetables.

"The knives are too sharp," said one of the cooks. "What if he cuts off his finger?"

"Then you can put it in your soup," Frith said.

The cook recoiled. "Do not even joke about such things."

"I wasn't," Frith said. "Who knows, I might taste good."

"How revolting."

"Meat is flesh, isn't it? Aren't we just meat on bones?"

The cook blanched. "Frith! Tell me you haven't—do those pagans in the East eat humans?"

"Not those men, they know better. The problem with eating meat is your diet consists primarily of souls."

The women's mouths dropped open.

"That's enough, I think." Alura took Frith by the elbow and pulled him out the kitchen door like a big sister dragging her wayward little brother, even though Frith was a good foot taller than she was.

"Frith, we share the experience of Lancelot's Grail, don't we?"

Frith nodded merrily.

"Yet, I eat meat, although you do not. The Abbot eats meat, but the monks abstain. Meat has no bearing on it."

"Yes, I know."

"Then why pretend it does?"

"I'm not."

"But your remarks distress the cooks. They don't see it the way we do."

"A haunch of a hart on the spit was no lesser creature than Parisa, my beloved camel. After the Bedouins cooked her, I vowed to never eat meat again."

Alura frowned. "Is working around meat in the Abbot's kitchen going to be a problem for you?"

"Oh, no," Frith said. "I was just having a bit of fun with the kitchen ladies."

"Well, they didn't share the fun. Go back in, apologize, and explain why you don't eat meat anymore."

Alura knew soon they'd start preparations for the Fall harvest festival, and a sudden influx of monks would crowd her kitchen. For many years, the abbey had celebrated a holy day in the autumn when the Abbot held a special Mass praising God for the harvest. Extra pilgrims, the entire village, and sometimes even a Bishop attended. In lieu of an expensive feast, it was the frugal Abbot's custom to have the kitchen prepare hundreds of loaves of bread from newly harvested grain. During the service, parishioners offered a tithe to the church, and monks gave them a loaf and a small scroll writ with a scripture passage. In the coming days, the Abbot would assign postulants to scrub the abbey and rake the grounds, scribes to make tiny scrolls, and send the rest of the brothers to assist with the baking. Alura worried. Frith had better be more sensible by then. The monks were already calling him a fool.

* * *

Frith settled into kitchen life. Alura taught him many of her recipes, especially those without meat. The abbey had an extensive herb garden, and Alura showed him how a garnish of chervil would give soup a subtle anise flavor. How coriander seeds, used to season many dishes, could be replaced by boiling the coriander root to flavor a stew. Similarly, juniper berries could often be substituted for costly peppercorns.

The kitchen ladies helped teach him, too. Within brief weeks, he was the happiest of cooks, always laughing and rejoicing over the simplest act, even shelling beans or scrubbing pots. During preparations for the harvest festival, the kitchen ladies were well pleased with him, but many of the monks who came to help said Frith was too merry. They thought life in a monastery should be dour. That wasn't Frith's nature now. Then again, it never had been.

Alura saw no reason for the monks to hold anything against her brother. Frith was well behaved. He held his tongue around them and didn't say to them the sorts of things he said to her in private. Like, "All forms are forms of Buddha. All sounds are the voice of Buddha."

"I don't know who Buddha is," she'd said. "But be careful not to say such things to the monks."

"I won't. It'd only start an argument. As Lao Tzu said, 'Why argue, for what purpose?'"

She didn't know who Lao Tzu was either, but as the weeks passed, he privately shared strange, wonderful things he'd learned. She loved the stories of his travels. Her only difficulty was his assumption that enlightenment gave the two of them a shared vocabulary. For instance, one day they were standing alone outside the kitchen in the afternoon sun when he said, "To argue about samadhi with someone who hasn't had samadhi is to be in the same position as those still under delusion."

"Frith, I don't know what samadhi is.

Without a word, he took her hands in his, and the two of them became fused in the moment. Grass moved in the breeze, sunlight warmed their faces, light streamed from every creature around them.

When he released her, she said, "Oh, is that the name for it?"

"Only what men in a far land call it," Frith said. "I call it, touching the no-thing."

Alura smiled at him. "Words don't matter, do they? It is nameless."

"That's what Da Shi said, too."

"Was he one of the masters you met?"

"Yes."

"Then, heed him. There's no point speaking about this in front of others. Even Lancelot wasn't able to bring about transcendence with words."

"You're right of course." He laughed. "I told you of my adventures as a teacher during my walk through Britain. Words about it dissipate like milk-weed fluff in a spring breeze."

Alura bit her lip. "I often felt I should try, especially with you. I saw how badly you wanted it, but I never found any words to bring it about. Lancelot never taught us to teach."

"No, he didn't. Don't think you were lacking, though. I learned from the masters I met, but you were my shining example."

"What do you mean?"

"You found your relationship to the world. When you meet somebody, you're not offended, or judging, never craving, just being. As the Grail is the portal to the soul, you are a portal of energia for everyone you encounter."

Alura laughed it off. "You're trying to make me blush."

Frith laughed with her. "You know I'm not. But isn't bliss a happy thing?"

Alura smiled. "What about you? Is this going to be the way you are with the world?"

"In a land where people have no ears, the tongue cannot offend," Frith said.

Alura's eyes grew wide. "You've seen men without ears?"

Frith laughed. "What do you think?"

"Don't tease me. I've never been anywhere, and you've told me about so many strange places."

"Ah, never take a fool seriously."

"You're no fool."

"If I am though, then no matter what I say, no one will set a torch to me."

"Frith, no mob will come for you here."

"Have you forgotten? Five years ago… the village wives?"

Alura admitted to herself that in her girlish years, desperate for a husband, she'd been a terrible flirt and had nearly caused a riot. It was only after she attained the Grail she'd ceased to act like a temptress. "They don't have anything against me, anymore."

"You're no longer a threat to them. But I could be. Remember? Lancelot warned us, 'Men will burn you as quickly for speaking beyond their beliefs as they will for speaking against their beliefs.' Far better if they laugh at me."

"Frith, are you sure that's the right course? You've traversed other realms. It'd be a shame not to share what you've learned."

"What did Christ say? 'Let those who have ears, hear.' If people find me amusing, well, so do I. We can all share a good laugh."

CHAPTER 50

Alura stepped out of the Abbot's kitchen and scanned the abbey grounds for her brother. The summer gardens had been harvested and replanted. The winter crops were already large and verdant, but monks who normally would have been tending their rows were absent. Old Brother Caedmon had passed on, and today was his funeral.

Frith appeared at the far end of the gardens. He was playfully following the path of a sunbeam that capered in rhythm to the sway of tall trees. Alura waved both arms over her head. When he saw her, he veered from the pathway around the garden and ran toward her, performing graceful leaps over rows of winter vegetables without harming a plant. He did look like a holy fool—jolly, somewhat silly. It made her heart smile.

When he reached her, she gave him a brief hug and pushed the hair from his forehead. "It's good you're here. We've much to prepare. A bishop is coming to conduct Brother Caedmon's funeral."

Frith followed her into the kitchen and merrily set to work shelling a basket of peas, the last to be harvested. The kitchen ladies each gave him an affectionate pat or a kind word as they passed him. They were like his mothers. It was fortuitous Frith, who couldn't remember their own mother, ended up with so many.

Alura, Frith, the ladies, and the young monks who helped them, worked diligently throughout the morning. The funeral was set for an hour past midday, and a supper would follow the burial. Because a bishop was visiting and a large number of mourners were expected, the wake would be held in the Abbot's banquet hall instead of the smaller monk's kitchen.

Brother Caedmon had been the wise and beloved cook in the monk's kitchen since before Alura had been born. Monks had sought him not only for their daily meals, but also for a friendly ear into which to pour their frustrations with monastery life. Wisdom flowed from his craggy, wrinkled face while he went humbly about his kitchen. He was the sole monk who'd listened to Alura when she was a young girl.

Generations of postulants had confessed their perceived failings while Brother Caedmon quietly chopped leeks. Complaints they would not dare voice to the Abbot were aired while he kneaded bread, and minor transgressions were dusted away like leftover flour when he finished. Each day he and his helpers made the monks bread, soup, two cooked dishes of beans or eggs, cheese, and plenty of vegetables.

Brother Caedmon once told Alura being a monk was no easier a life than hers. The difficulty was not rising for prayers before dawn, or long hours of toil, but the hard work on one's self that monastic vows required. He assured her every interaction with a pilgrim or monk was a reflection of one's own flaws. Even the solitude of the monk's cell brought awareness of one's inadequacy.

After Lancelot's death, she began to notice Caedmon's eyes twinkled when hers did. She felt he shared her perception of the bliss behind every facet of creation. It might not be something the humble ascetic would acknowledge to the rest of the abbey, but she'd seen he knew.

When all the dishes for Caedmon's wake were prepared, Alura sent the boys back to the Abbot, and she and Frith went out back where racks of herbs were drying for winter. The fragrance of freshly cut mint was particularly strong. She broke a leaf and held it under Frith's nose. He inhaled deeply and gave her an appreciative smile. She knew, of course, the abbey's pitiful collection of spices would never compare to what he'd experienced traveling with Jacob.

She heard Little Thomas' voice in the kitchen. "They're out in back, your holiness."

Little Thomas' presence must mean the Abbot was looking for her. But why wasn't the Abbot in his quarters putting on his vestments for Mass? Yes, the

Bishop was coming to conduct the funeral rite, but surely the Abbot would participate in the service, too. He'd loved Brother Caedmon as dearly as any monk there.

A strong gust blew, and the door at the opposite end of the building slammed open. Then more voices, these coming from alongside the banquet hall. She left the herb garden and stepped around the corner. Frith tagged along.

"Sir Bedivere!" Frith sang out.

"His Grace, Bishop Bedivere," Alura said out of the corner of her mouth.

Frith's eyes widened. "Bedivere's a Bishop?"

Bedivere reached them in two strides and clasped Frith in a tremendous bear hug. "Don't tell me you've forgotten. It's been no more than a month since I found you in the shires."

"Frith wasn't himself that day," Alura said. "We haven't seen you since, and I'm sure he never received the news of your elevation while he was away."

Bedivere let Frith go and turned to her. "Alura, my dear."

She curtsied and reached to kiss his ring, but he pulled his hand back. "That's not necessary among us three."

Alura nodded and rose.

"Now, how is he, truly?" Bedivere said.

"Good, really good. He's as cognizant as you or I."

There were disgruntled clearing of throats among the group of monks who trailed Bedivere.

Bedivere spun on them. "Thank you for your assistance, brothers, you can go now."

"Bishop, it's nearly time," Little Thomas said.

"Yes, Thomas, thank you," Bedivere said. "You should go help the Abbot —and take these other monks with you. I'll be there shortly."

Little Thomas gave a doubtful look and then led the brothers away. Bedivere turned back to Alura and Frith. "I should like to see for myself. Frith, the abbey has been your and Alura's home for most of your young lives. God willing, it should always remain so. But you trouble some of the brothers unnecessarily."

"How do you mean?" Alura said.

"He dons a monk's habit, yet refuses to join their order." Bedivere turned to Frith, "Your hermit's robe offends them."

Frith laughed. "What man, holy or otherwise, is offended by a rag?"

"It's what the rag means. They see it as an insult. There have long been monks among us who resented your living at the abbey without becoming a renunciant."

"It'd be better if those who take pride in their renunciation concentrated on going toward something rather than away from everything."

Bedivere frowned. "That doesn't explain why you're dressed like this."

"Lancelot was once given the shirt of a holy man. Did he tell you the story?"

"He did."

"Well, I was naked, and the universe clothed me in a holy man's garment. How can I refuse to honor it?"

"Then why not join the order instead of seeming to these men like an imposter?"

"Lancelot told Alura and me not to join religious orders. He said theirs was an obsession with rules."

Bedivere grimaced. "Taking off my sword and putting on a cowl enriched my life."

"And I am glad for you, truly," Frith said. "But can we purchase spirit by impoverishing our human self? The problem is, if a man must withdraw to an abbey to find God, then he loses the fullness of life. If he leaves the abbey to make an outward life, then he risks losing God. It's rather like having a hot coal in your mouth that you can neither swallow nor spit out."

"What a distasteful image."

"That's our dilemma until we realize we are caused to live by the will of the universe. Then we become humbly and deeply grateful."

"Very profound. But are you humble before the Brothers of St. Benignus?"

"Even when faced with quarrelsome people, I never let my mind entertain any thought of retaliation."

"Turning the other cheek?"

"An ancient verse I learned from a holy man in Samarkand says, 'The man who sees God sees God everywhere.'"

Bedivere beamed. "Several of the brothers said you were a fool. But you know, you don't sound foolish at all."

"If people can hear my meaning, good. If they can't understand me and think I'm a fool, then it's just as well."

"Is it ever the right choice to let people think you're a fool?" Bedivere said.

"Among Egyptian Christians it's a much revered state."

"This isn't Egypt. I thought you were going to take up residence in my old cottage in the woods where Lancelot and I had our hermitage."

"What worked for Lancelot wouldn't help me. When I came back, I found it difficult to participate in ordinary life, but Alura and the ladies of the kitchen have helped me find my way there. Withdrawing from the companionship of the abbey would have only left me in the state you found me last month."

"So you intend to stay at the abbey?"

"As Lancelot wished."

Alura gave Frith's arm an affectionate squeeze. He looked at her and smiled.

"So all will be as it was before?" Bedivere said.

"It can never be that. But I will try to deal with whatever is brought before me, in a way that doesn't put Alura or the abbey at risk."

"The Abbot will be comforted to know that, but doesn't your... Doesn't the Grail obligate you to share what you've learned with mankind?"

Frith laughed. "You forget I was present when you posed the same question to Lancelot. And my response to you is the same as his was, I've no desire to become a public figure. During the weeks I walked about Britain, I quickly learned men cannot hear the answer to a question they haven't asked. So it's better they think me a fool than a heretic."

"It isn't necessary for him to teach," Alura said. "Frith's joviality lightens the hearts around him, allowing Grace to manifest its presence in them."

"Something similar could be said about you," Bedivere said. A bell from the chapel tolled. "Come, it's time for Brother Caedmon's funeral. I'll talk to the Abbot after."

* * *

Brother Caedmon was buried, and the community of monks gathered for the wake in the dining hall. When the meal ended the Abbot stood and cleared his throat. "I have considered who should replace Brother Caedmon in the monk's kitchen and decided to assign his position to Frith."

Rebellious murmurs rolled around the dining hall like the rumble of a millstone. "Frith's a grinning nitwit," someone said. "Passing off nonsense as wisdom," said another.

The Abbot held up his hands. "Hear me out. Although Frith has not joined our order, he has, for a considerable time, abstained from meat. His sister, our finest cook, has taught him well. While we all endeavor to a calling higher than mere gratification of our stomachs, I believe our monks will find satisfaction in Frith's cooking."

The whispers resumed until the Bishop stood. His eyes swept the assemblage. Many looked down at their plates. Bedivere, who towered over the

Abbot, put his arm around the old man's shoulders. "While the Abbot carefully considered how Frith might serve the abbey, I have contemplated our inevitable mortality."

The monks looked at Bedivere expectantly.

"None among us knows the hour of his death," Bedivere said. "But it is certain someday we shall each follow Brother Caedmon to heaven."

The monks nodded.

"Whether we've chosen this abbey or it has been chosen for us, we have a home herein and a purpose in our service." Bedivere patted the Abbot's shoulder. "I have this day entered a proviso into the abbey records bearing the full authority of the Bishop's office. Frith and Alura shall unconditionally be allowed to dwell here for so long as they desire."

Fastidious threw down his napkin and slapped the table.

Bedivere, every inch the former knight, fixed his eyes on Fastidious. "Furthermore, this edict remains in effect after my passing and is binding upon all future abbots of Saint Benignus."

Fastidious glanced around the table, but the other brothers avoided his eyes. He fished his napkin out of his plate, and busied himself brushing food off it.

Alura slipped from the dining hall into the kitchen. She looked around the room. This was her world, which she'd shared with Frith since his return. But now he'd have his own kitchen on the other side of the abbey.

The kitchen fires had died down, and the fireplaces were banked. Cooking was finished for the night and the ladies had left for home. Piles of dirty pots waited to be scrubbed, but the kitchen boys were in the dining room listening to the Abbot and Bishop. They'd be back to clean later. The only person in the room was Frith, standing, quietly swaying.

Alura heard a snuffling sound and realized Frith wasn't alone. Ethelburg, so petite, like a frail bird hidden behind Frith's body, was blubbering into his ratty old robe. He was holding her, gently rocking her back and forth. It reminded Alura of the way a father might console his daughter, except the age roles were reversed. Frith patted Ethelburg on the back and smiled over her shoulder at Alura.

Ethelburg lifted her face an inch or so off Frith's chest. "Brother Caedmon was such a good man. I've known him since he was a boy, since he first came here. I was newly married then, cooking for an abbot now long dead …" A new flood of tears came. "Oh, we'll all be dead soon enough… But why take Brother Caedmon? He gave nothing but help and wisdom to the new postulants, nothing but hearty food to the monks in his kitchen."

Frith closed his eyes and pulled her tightly to him with his left arm. He began to move his right hand up and down her spine like Lancelot had done for them. Alura saw streams of light surround Ethelburg and begin to move in a vertical ellipse. The old woman's sobs became a whimper. Frith's energy grew stronger and emanated in concentric waves across the room. Alura could not only see the light but also feel it from further away than ever. She could sense Frith drawing grief from Ethelburg, as Alura herself had drawn it from him when Jacob told them of their father's death.

Ethelburg's weeping subsided, and Frith let her go. He stepped back and wiped the tears from her face. "Your real self is the one that doesn't change. Life changes around you, but you are always the one who sees. Be that great observer."

Ethelburg got the hiccups. He led her to a chair and gave her a cup of water. Frith turned to the pile of dirty pots, poured water into a cauldron, and started scrubbing it.

"You don't have to do those," Alura said. "Haven't you been told? You've been appointed cook of the monk's kitchen."

Frith smiled his contented, mirthful smile, and kept scouring. "Whatever work is before us is what we are meant to do."

The Brothers of St. Benignus might think Frith a holy fool, but Alura knew what he'd become. If only Lancelot could see her brother now. She was sure he'd be pleased.

AUTHOR'S NOTES

If you enjoyed this book, please take a moment to leave a short review on Amazon and/or other booksellers. Reviews help to sell books and sales help an author keep writing. You can readily find links to online booksellers' websites by visiting www.leublications.com and clicking on the book cover image. You can also sign up there to receive updates on new publications by the author.

This book is a sequel to Lancelot's Grail. If you have not read the first book, rest assured, you will find Lancelot's Grail an enjoyable read and learn more about Lancelot's explanations of higher consciousness. Available from the same bookseller where you purchased this book.

About the Author

Richard Gartee is an award-winning novelist, the author of seven college textbooks and five collections of poetry. He has studied eastern philosophy and meditation for 45 years. A complete list of his available titles, upcoming events, and forthcoming books can be found at www.gartee.com

Acknowledgments

The extent to which this book (and my life) has been informed by my friendship with Mickey Singer is almost incalculable. Mickey not only introduced me to my guru but also to the many wise beings who visited the Temple of The Universe where he has lectured for over 40 years.

Historical research included a visit to every site in Britain associated with King Arthur. Sir Thomas Mallory was my principal resource for information about Lancelot, Galahad and Bedivere. Sources influencing the spiritual discourses by the Sultan's holy men, Lancelot, and Frith include Paramahansa Yogananda, Jesus, Buddha, Pythagoras, Jianzhi Sengcan (Sengstau), Swami Muktananda, the ancient Taoist masters, Lao Tzu and Lieh Tzu, the writings of Thomas Clerry on both Taoist and Buddhist teachings, and *Bodhidharma* by Lin Sen-shou. The story of Budhitra overflowing the cup was paraphrased from "A Cup of Tea," in *Zen Flesh, Zen Bones*, by Paul Reps. Jacobs stories of Rabbi Ishmael are adapted from *Pirke Hekalot*. The Abbot's sermon on charity was adapted from *The Greatest Thing in the World and Other Addresses* by Henry Drummond. The line Frith quotes about seeing God everywhere is from the *Sri Atman Gita*.

The African proverb, "It takes a village to raise a child," can also be said of the beta readers and members of my critique groups who helped bring Frith's journey to maturity. Many thanks to Mike Allard, Jim Allen, Linda and Steve Bean, Daniel Blumberg, Rick Buncher, Pat Caren, Penny Church, Gene Cowell, Art Crummer, Justin Diamond, Robin Ecker, Tammy Euliano, Dick Gartee, Skipper Hammond, Ron Hasse, Steve Lodel, Kimberley Mullins, Catherine Pucket, Dennis Shuman, Fran Sweeney, and Wendy Thornton. Each of their comments helped me refine this work. Special thanks to Tojiddin Rahimov for transliteration of the Yaghnobi language, to Dave King—copy editor extraordinaire, and to proofreaders Pat Caren, Cindy Elder, Judy Gold, and Joyce Pearson.

LANCELOT'S GRAIL

by Richard Gartee

Alura and Frith, abandoned at an abbey as children, have grown up in social isolation and are desperate for a new life. **Sir Bedivere**, desolate over the knights' abandonment of the Round Table after the fall of Camelot, has come up with a plan. **Sir Lancelot**, abandoned by his once-adoring public, has found enlightenment while living as a hermit.

Their lives converge when Frith leads Sir Bedivere to Lancelot's hermitage. There, they learn that Lancelot has found the Holy Grail – within himself. Bedivere tries, without success, to persuade Lancelot to come help him rebuild the Knights of The Round Table. After Bedivere departs, Frith begs Lancelot to teach him, hoping to become a knight. Soon Alura joins them, hoping to snare herself a husband.

Lancelot, torn between a desire to be left alone and an obligation to pass his knowledge on, agrees to teach them, but soon realizes that everyone simply wants to use him. Yet, seeing the spark of awareness growing in Alura and Frith, he persists and leads them on a quest to penetrate the barriers in themselves that keep them from attaining the Grail.

Then Alura falls in love with Lancelot and incites an angry mob. Bedivere urges Lancelot to flee, but Lancelot stays, struggling to finish his work with Alura and Frith in the little time he has left.

Available in paperback and ebook from Amazon and other booksellers.

Learn more at www.lancelotsgrail.com

www.ingramcontent.com/pod-product-compliance
Lightning Source LLC
Chambersburg PA
CBHW031214120726

47905CB00002B/335